He reached for the doorknob. Jennifer said, 'Vandalized and burgled, all in one week.' He turned slowly
to smile at her, a glutinous movement like a man
wading through syrup.

And then the door was racketed open as if an
express train were hurtling through it, and John was
ripped across the chest by something that felt like
red-hot wires, and was slammed against the bureau,
hitting his head and falling to the floor.

Jennifer was screaming, too, high and piercing. And
the huge black monstrosity raked her open from
shoulders to thighs, blood bursting everywhere.

The huge black thing rushed away again. All John
could do was lie on his side on the blood-sprayed
carpet, whimpering with pain. When he opened his
eyes, he saw his son's bare feet, close to his face.

'Lenny,' he whispered. 'For God's sake, Lenny, save
me.'

DEATH DREAM

Graham Masterton

SPHERE BOOKS

A *Sphere* Book

First published in the U.S.A. by
Tom Doherty Associates, Inc 1988

First published in Great Britain by
Sphere Books Ltd 1990
This edition first published by Sphere Books 1996

Photoset in North Wales by
Derek Doyle & Associates, Mold, Clwyd
Printed in England by Clays Ltd, St Ives plc

ISBN 0 7515 0539 0

Sphere Books
A Division of
Macdonald & Co (Publishers)
Brettenham House
Lancaster Place
London WC2E 7EN

One

John discovered the scratches soon after Lenny had gone to sleep that night. Six deep parallel gouges in the corridor wall, a little above head-height, straight through the new floral wallpaper and right into the plaster, V-shaped and narrow, like marks made by a lino-cutter or a thin-bladed chisel.

'Goddamn it,' he swore, touching the torn wallpaper with his fingertips. The decorating had been finished only last Wednesday, and he had lectured Lenny for five minutes about treating the walls and the fresh white paintwork with respect. This house was their new beginning, the opening of a fresh and happy chapter in their lives. For Lenny to have defaced it so soon was just as upsetting as if he had said that he hated Jennifer, and that he hated their new life together.

This wasn't childish carelessness. This wasn't wear and tear. This was a gesture of hostility and rejection, and John felt more annoyed with Lenny than at any time in the past three years.

'God*damn* it,' he repeated. The scratches were too forceful to have been done by accident. Lenny hadn't just run a toy car too enthusiastically along a flower-patterned racetrack; or smashed a Transformer robot too violently into a make-believe cliff. This was deliberate. Premeditated, tongue-between-teeth, and deliberate.

5

John took three deep breaths. Then he walked the length of the corridor to Lenny's bedroom at the end. It was hot in there, and dark, and smelled of rubbery new carpet. Lenny's bed stood against the far wall. Lenny himself was lying on his back with his mouth open, his cheeks flushed, one hand still holding the Gobot he had been playing with when he fell asleep.

John stood over the bed for a while, letting his eyes grow accustomed to the darkness. Lenny was nine – which meant that he was still young enough to do some really ridiculous things, but old enough to inflict some serious damage when he did them. He was curly-headed and blond and almost pretty, except for that wide, impish grin. He looked so much like his mother that John sometimes found the tears pricking the corners of his eyes even though he hadn't been thinking about Virginia at all.

'Lelly,' Virginia had called him, because of the way he had tried to pronounce his own name when he was very small.

John had allowed Lenny to grieve openly for his mother, the same way that he had allowed himself to grieve openly for her. Some people (especially his own mother) had thought that he'd allowed Lenny to grieve too much. There had been a bad eighteen months of tantrums, wildness, uncontrollable violence. Once, after Lenny had thrown paint around at school, John had almost believed that he had lost his son altogether, that Lenny would spend the rest of his life screaming and kicking and refusing to understand that people die whether you want them to or not, and that can sometimes include your own mother.

However, he had tried to be patient with Lenny, and he had persuaded Lenny's teachers and his friends to be patient, too. Gradually, Lenny's behavior had improved; and John would never forget the day that

6

Lenny had come home from school and put his arms around him and said nothing at all, and John had *known* that at last Lenny had come to terms with losing his mother.

These days, John didn't allow Lenny to throw tantrums. He expected cooperation, and friendship, and trust. The memory would always be there, but the grieving had to be put behind them; life had to go on. Last May, John had found a new job as production manager for the *Philadelphia News* and had sold their old house in Newark; and late in October he had met Jennifer and soon asked her to marry him.

John wondered if Lenny might have resented all of this upheaval, without outwardly admitting it. Maybe Lenny felt that, by selling the house in which they had lived together, by changing his job, and by falling in love with Jennifer, John had somehow betrayed Virginia and tried to erase her memory. After all, they couldn't visit the grave anymore, not regularly, not like they used to when they still lived in Newark.

Maybe that was what the scratches in the wall were all about: a dumb protest against his new life. A mark to show that even if John didn't care about Virginia anymore. *Lenny* did.

Lenny began to snore a little. John was still angry with him, but he didn't really want to wake him. Lenny's eyes were shifting under his eyelids in REM sleep. He was dreaming, about something. Baseball? *Star Trek*? His mother? John didn't want to wake him in the middle of a dream.

All right, young man, he thought. *This can wait until morning. But don't expect me to feel any better about it then*.

A shadow fell across the doorway. It was Jennifer, looking for him.

'Is he all right?' she whispered. 'I wondered where you were.'

'He's okay.' John tiptoed back out of the bedroom and closed the door. He kissed Jennifer on the forehead; he still loved the freshness of their marriage, the excitement of loving somebody new. 'The little tyke just scratched the wallpaper. Did you see it? I'm going to flay him alive tomorrow. Forty-five dollars a roll, and he's torn it.'

He led her back along the corridor and showed her the scratches.

Jennifer frowned at them. 'Did Lenny do those?'

Jennifer reached up and touched them. 'They look awfully high up for Lenny to have done them. And he must have used a terrific amount of strength, to dig in that deep.'

'Who do you think you are – Sherlocka Holmes?'

Jennifer smiled, and gave him a quick kiss. 'Don't be angry with him, John. I'm sure he didn't mean to do it.'

'He didn't mean to dig half a dozen darn great grooves in the wall? It probably took him most of the evening!'

They went down the curving, white-banistered staircase. The corridor and the stairs were carpeted in pale apricot, and the walls were covered in green-and-apricot flowers.

'It couldn't have taken him any time at all,' Jennifer remarked. 'He was playing Trivial Pursuit with me for most of the evening. Then he had his bath, came down for his milk and cookies, and went straight to bed.'

'Well, maybe he did it yesterday evening and I just didn't notice it before,' John grumbled. 'Do you want a drink?'

Jennifer went through to the sitting room and sat down. 'I'll have a martini if you're having one.'

John went across to the drinks table. A chilled glass jug was waiting on the tray. That was the only domestic service that Jennifer ever did for him: mix him a jug of martinis so that it would be ready when he came home from the office.

'You have a spare roll of that wallpaper, don't you?' Jennifer asked. 'I could get Mr Kahn to come around to fix it tomorrow.'

John poured drinks. 'Ah … I don't know. It's not the actual damage so much. It's the fact that Lenny felt like doing it.'

'Maybe he *didn't* do it.'

'It sure as hell wasn't you, and it sure as hell wasn't me. So who else is there?'

'Come on, don't get upset,' Jennifer said. 'He's only a boy, after all.'

John swallowed ice-cold gin and shrugged, then sat on the sofa beside her and kissed her. 'Did I tell you that Arnie Walters is thinking of buying himself a Jeep?' he told her. 'He says he wants to drive around the country, answering the call of the wild.'

'Arnie? In a Jeep? I can't imagine it.'

'Bill Chapman said Arnie can't even answer a straight-forward question, let alone the call of the wild.' He reached behind him and picked up the paper from the table in back of the couch. 'It looks like they're going to go ahead with that rebuilding at the Annenberg Center.'

Jennifer smiled and watched him as he took his half-glasses out of his shirt pocket. She didn't mind the small rituals of his arrival home from work; in fact, she found them reassuring. He wasn't the kind of man who allowed himself to live in a rut. He frequently took her out for unexpected dinners-for-two, or drove them out to the Brandywine Valley or the Poconos on the spur of the moment, so she quite happily allowed him the nightly procedure of pouring a martini, opening the paper that he spent all day producing but never had the time to look at, taking out his glasses, and sitting silently

9

for a quarter of an hour, reading.

Although they had met only nine months ago, John and Jennifer were as comfortable and at peace with each other as if they had been rubbing along together for years. This was partly because they were both accustomed to living with somebody else: Jennifer had been divorced four years ago from her alcoholic husband, Pete. But they were well matched, too. Both were forty, both young-looking for their age, both interested in music and theater and food and art. When they were first going out together, they had practically lived in the Philadelphia Museum of Art.

John was dark-haired and stockily built, with a largish nose and deeply cleft chin. He looked more like a carpenter or a tobacco farmer than a newspaper executive. There was a photograph on the bureau of him wearing a plaid shirt and a denim cap, and anybody could have been forgiven for mistaking him for the narrow-eyed man in the Camel advertisement who lights his cigarette with a burning twig.

Jennifer was ash-blond, very lean, with wide gray-green eyes and a mouth that – in John's words – always looked as if it were kissing or gasping, or both. She had been working as a secretary at the *Philadelphia News* when John had first arrived there; now she ran a small perfumery store next to the Head House Inn on Society Hill.

She was smart in appearance, smart in behavior. It was she who had decorated the house in whites and peaches, filled it with antique furniture in figured walnut and palest oak. It always mystified John that she had stayed married for so long to a ranting, blustering loser like Pete Marcowicz. Well – not so much mystified him as made him jealous, although he wouldn't have cared to admit it.

But they lived together now in this freshly

remodeled three-storey colonial house on Third Street, feeling at last as if life had rewarded them with what they deserved. All that John admitted pining for now was a BMW 5-Series and a Corum wristwatch.

As the wall-clock in hall chimed eight, Jennifer finished her martini and said, 'How about some dinner? It's tuna salad, that's all.'

'Are you watching my waistline again?'

'I'm thinking about your alimentary canal.'

'If I eat any more tuna, my alimentary canal is going to start looking like a rerun of *Flipper*.'

Jennifer lifted his reading glasses off his nose. 'Flipper was a dolphin, not a tuna.'

They sat down to supper in the Dutch-tiled kitchen. John opened a bottle of Chablis, and poured out two generous glassfuls.

Jennifer said, 'I'm going to be selling products for men starting next month. It's a new range, natural skin-care for the gentleman in your life.'

'You're looking at me as if you think *I* need natural skin-care,' John protested.

'Every man does,' Jennifer said, smiling. 'You wax your car, you polish your shoes, you creosote your fence – why don't you lavish even a tenth of that kind of attention on your face?'

'I just think I'd look kind of stupid with a creosoted face, that's all.'

'I'll bring you some samples,' Jennifer persisted. 'There's cucumber wrinkle cream; partridge-pea moisturizer; and some really fabulous preshave lotion made from evening lychnis.'

John was reaching across the table for the chopped onions when the ceiling was shaken by a thunderous banging, followed by the sound of smashing glass. The banging was so loud that he thought for one terrifying moment that the whole house was going to collapse on top of them.

'What the *hell* was that?' he shouted.

'My God,' said Jennifer, white-faced. 'It sounds like the roof's fallen in.'

John ran across the hallway and bounded up the stairs. When they'd remodeled the house, they had taken out three upstairs walls in order to create a home gym and an en-suite bathroom. He was convinced that he was going to find that the steel joists had given way, and that their bedroom complex was filled with rubble and open to the sky.

He pushed open the bedroom door, with Jennifer close behind him, then stopped and stared at the bedroom in total shock and bewilderment. He couldn't even think of anything to say. He stepped over broken lamps and torn cushions and tipped-out drawers, and he found it almost impossible to believe what he was looking at.

The ceiling hadn't collapsed. There was no structural damage. But this recently pristine, freshly decorated bedroom now looked as if it had been attacked by a gang of berserk hooligans. The white duck-down bedcover had been slashed open, again and again; the pillows had been ripped apart; every mirror had been smashed. Every picture had been torn out of its frame and crumpled up. The wallpaper had been torn down in long strips; the plaster was gouged.

Inside the closets, every single article of clothing – every dress, every shirt, every coat, every shoe – had been slashed or wrenched to pieces. John picked up a handkerchief. Even that had been ripped. He let it drop to the floor, and looked numbly around the rest of the room. In the broken mirror behind the bed, his reflection looked pale and peculiarly distorted, as if he were a hunchback.

'I just don't understand it,' Jennifer whispered.

'They must have been tearing this whole place apart while you and I were – downstairs, just drinking.'

Mechanically, John said, 'I don't know how they could have done it. How the hell did they get in, without us even noticing? And what the hell have they done it for?'

'You don't think they're still here?' said Jennifer, shaking. 'You don't think – Lenny!' she shouted. 'Lenny!'

John said, 'Stay here!' He went to the bedside table, and fumbingly unlocked it with fingers that refused to do what he wanted them to do. Thank God the vandals hadn't broken into this one drawer. He lifted up the copies of Reader's Digest and took out his .38 revolver, the one that he'd bought after they had been burgled in Jersey, three days after Virginia's death, and all her jewelry had been taken.

'John, for goodness' sake,' Jennifer begged.

But John, trying to be firm, trying to stay in control, said, 'It's okay; I'm not going to do anything stupid. Call the cops. Go on, call the cops! I'll go check on Lenny.'

The telephones in the bedroom had been smashed, so Jennifer hurried back downstairs while John ventured along the corridor toward Lenny's room, his revolver clasped in both hands. 'Lenny?' he shouted. 'Lenny?' He had a terrible vision of Lenny sitting up in bed with some crazy burglar holding a knife to his throat and keeping his hand clamped over the boy's mouth.

'Lenny, do you hear me? It's Daddy!'

There was no reply. The house was silent, except for the faint sound of traffic outside, and Jennifer's voice as she talked in a quick, frantic tone to the Philadelphia Police Department.

As he approached Lenny's room, John saw to his

consternation that there were more deep scratches along the wall, similar to the first scratches he'd seen when he had come home. That could only mean that the burglars had been here *before* he got home – and that all the time he and Jennifer had been laughing and reading and drinking martinis and eating supper, those maniacs had been tearing their precious bedroom to shreds.

He reached Lenny's door and eased it open, keeping the revolver pointed at the ceiling. He didn't want any accidents, not with Lenny, his last living connection with Virginia.

'Lenny?' he whispered.

He remembered what somebody in *Miami Vice* had said about making yourself a target, so he stepped quickly into the room and dodged to one side to avoid being silhouetted against the light in the corridor. He paused, feeling chilled and frightened, breathing in the greasy smell of the revolver.

To his relief, Lenny lay where he had left him, still fast asleep, his mouth still open. John leaned forward to make doubly certain that he was breathing; then he crouched and moved away from the bed making a quick inspection of the rest of the room. He checked behind the door, and almost fired when Lenny's white bathrobe came swinging out at him. He eased open the closet. He crouched down on his hands and knees so that he could look underneath the bed. He cautiously parted the curtains with the barrel of his gun.

There was nobody there. It looked as if the intruders had ventured partway down the corridor, tearing at the walls, but they seem to have stopped short of Lenny's room.

John tested Lenny's window. Only the small top window was open; the main window was still closed and locked. He looked down into the brick-paved yard. There was a small patio with a fountain and white garden furniture, and an arrangement of seven well-cultivated bay trees in earthenware pots. No sign that anybody was hiding down there.

He eased down the hammer of the .38 and went back along the corridor, checking the guestroom, the second bathroom, the linen closet, the closet where Jennifer kept the Hoover. He tried the attic door: it was locked, and the key was still hanging on the hook beside it.

John called out, 'It's okay, Jen! Lenny's still asleep – and they're gone, whoever they were!'

Jennifer was coming back upstairs. She ran a trembling hand through her hair, and tried to smile. 'I talked to the police. They're sending somebody around.'

'We'd better see what's been stolen,' John told her, putting his arm around her shoulders.

'Oh God,' she said, shaking her head. 'Why should anybody want to *do* anything so meaningless?'

'I don't know, honey. I can't even guess.'

They went back into the ravaged bedroom. John began to gather up pieces of broken china and picture frames, while Jennifer sorted through the jewelry and the perfume bottles and cosmetics. Half a dozen bottles of nail varnish had been smashed open, and the white shag carpet was sticky with glutinous scarlets and sticky pinks.

John was so dispirited that he gave up collecting the smashed pieces, and dropped them back onto the floor. But Jennifer slowly stood up, her hands full of rings and necklaces and brooches, and she was frowning in surprise.

'Do you know something? They haven't taken a single thing – not one.'

John leaned over and picked through a heap of

15

jewelry. 'Are you sure? How about that ring I gave you after the Philly Pops concert?'

'Here it is. It's got nail polish on it, but that'll clean off.'

'And that watch from your father?'

'There, on the floor.'

John found his own drawer, upturned on the floor. Underneath it he discovered his gold cuff links, his gold bracelet, and the gold Julius Caesar medallion that Virginia had given him in 1973, when medallions for men had still been fashionable.

'This doesn't make any kind of sense at all,' said John, picking up the medallion and staring at it as it spun around on the end of its chain. 'Anybody could pawn this for two, three hundred dollars, and three hundred dollars buys a whole lot of crack.'

'You think drug addicts did this?' asked Jennifer. Her eyes glistened with tears.

'Sure – that was my first reaction. But if it was drug addicts, why didn't they take anything?'

'Maybe we surprised them, rushing upstairs like that. Maybe they frightened themselves with their own noise.'

'Jennifer,' said John, 'they've taken this room apart. They've broken everything – absolutely everything. How long do you think it took them to do that? Look at it – every dress, every coat, every picture, everything. And those nail-varnish bottles! Six of them, all broken. You know how damned hard it is to break one of those. If they had time to do that, they had time to steal anything they wanted.'

They heard the scribbling sound of police sirens growing louder. John went to the window and saw a patrol car and an unmarked car with a flashing red beacon on the roof draw up outside. 'The cavalry,' he said, and went downstairs to open the door for them.

Jennifer went out to the landing. She heard John open the front door; heard deep men's voices; heard somebody cough. As she stood there, Lenny came shuffling along the corridor, hot-cheeked and dandelion-headed, in his Gobot pajamas.

'Jenny?' he said blurrily. 'What's wrong? I heard police cars.'

Jennifer held him tight. 'We've had burglars,' she told him. 'Don't worry, they haven't stolen anything. Your Daddy and I frightened them away. They've just made a mess, that's all.'

Leeny peered toward the main bedroom. 'Did they mess up your whole room?'

'I'm afraid so. But we have insurance. We'll just have to go out and buy ourselves a couple of new pillows and a new comforter.'

Lenny said, 'I'm going to get a drink of water. My mouth feels awful dry.' He disappeared into the second bathroom.

John came up the stairs, followed by two detectives and two uniformed police officers. The detectives were both pale-skinned blacks, remarkably alike, and when they reached the landing Jennifer saw to her surprise that they were twins. One of the officers accompanying them was white, the other black. Jennifer couldn't help thinking that she didn't know when she'd seen such a racially balanced group before. They were like a road show for Mendel's theory of genetics.

One of the detectives came forward, his hands in his coat pockets, and said to Jennifer, 'Sergeant Clay, ma'am. And this is Detective Clay.'

Both sergeant and detective were tall and smooth-skinned, with those flat, almond-shaped faces and slightly hooked noses that betray Arabian ancestry. They both wore shiny metallic mohair suits and black loafers. The only noticeable difference between them was that Sergeant Clay had one brown eye and one gray one; while Detective Clay's eyes were both brown.

'Mind if I take a look?' asked Sergeant Clay, and eased open the bedroom door. His twin followed him inside. The two uniformed officers waited on the landing, one of them assiduously penciling notes in his notebook, the other yawning.

'Well, they made some kind of a mess,' Sergeant Clay remarked. 'How much did they take?'

'That's the odd part about it,' said John from the doorway. 'As far as we can make out, they didn't take anything at all. They just broke the place up.'

Detective Clay crouched down on his haunches, balancing himself with the splayed fingers of one hand. His nostrils flared slightly, as if he were trying to distinguish some faint and equivocal odour.

'They broke *everything*,' put in Jennifer. 'There isn't one single item in this room that hasn't been torn or damaged or thrown around.'

Sergeant Clay stepped carefully all around the room, glancing at this, studying that. Eventually he said, 'How do you think they got in?'

'What?' asked John.

'I said, "How do you think they got in?"'

John made a face. 'I really have no idea. The garden door has been locked all day, and nobody could have come in that way this evening without us seeing them. All of the downstairs windows have security bars and locks. And apart from the fanlights in this room and Lenny's bedroom down at the end of the corridor and the john across the landing, all of the upstairs windows are closed and locked.'

'Have you looked around the house since this happened?'

John nodded. 'I haven't checked every room

downstairs, and I haven't checked the cellar, but as soon as we heard the noise we came running straight up here, and I really don't see how ...'

Sergeant Clay leaned sideways, his hands still in his pockets, so that he could see out the bedroom door. 'Officer Mulroony,' he said. 'Would you be good enough to search the ground floor – cellar, too?'

The officer stopped scribbling in his notepad, tapped his pencil on the peak of his cap in salute, and went downstairs.

Sergeant Clay said, 'Officer Sabido, would you be good enough to go down to my car and bring me my Polos?'

'Yes, sir.'

'Your Polos?' asked John. 'What are your Polos?'

'They're little round mints like Life Savers. I have a friend who brings them across from England. You can stick the tip of your tongue through the hole in the middle, and apart from the fact that I was called away from a double-hot chilli to go and I'm going to be breathing it at you every time I ask you a question, they help me to think.'

John glanced at Jennifer in bewilderment.

'You'd prefer it if I smoked a pipe and played the violin?' Sergeant Clay asked him with perfect politeness.

At that moment, Detective Clay began to sniff even more deeply, holding his breath for long, quivering moments and then exhaling.

'What's gotten into him?' asked John.

Sergeant Clay laid a hand on his twin's shoulder and said, 'He's very sensitive to different smells, you know what I mean? He can tell you what brand of cigarette you smoke just by sniffing your hair. He can tell what spices you've been eating, anything from bell peppers to fenugreek, and everything in between. He can tell if

19

you've recently been close to animals, and what kind. He can smell something now.'

Detective Clay carefully reached over and grasped the corner of the ripped-open comforter. He hesitated for a moment, still breathing deeply, then suddenly whipped it off the bed.

On the sheet underneath, a huge wet stain was spreading, smelling faintly acrid and tinged with yellow at the edges.

'Oh, my God,' said Jennifer, and clamped her hand over her mouth.

'I'm sorry ma'am,' said Sergeant Clay gently. 'We often get this kind of vandalism. For some of these sickos, breaking into somebody's bedroom is pretty much like rape once-removed. You're lucky they didn't do anything worse.'

'You mean I'm lucky that they only pissed on my marriage-bed, instead of shitting on it?' Jennifer demanded, her voice scratchy with shame and fury. Shame – almost as if this disgusting desecration were *her* doing.

John held her close. 'It's okay, Jenny. We'll get rid of it and start fresh. New bed, new sheets, new carpet.'

'It's not the same,' Jennifer wept. 'It's my marriage-bed. It meant so much.'

Detective Clay leaned over the bed and kept on sniffing, his eyes closed.

'One person, or more than one, what do you think?' Sergeant Clay asked him.

Detective Clay kept his eyes closed and didn't answer, but raised his hand to indicate that he was still concentrating.

'Any alcohol? Unusual foods? Coffee? Tea?' Sergeant Clay asked.

Still Detective Clay kept on sniffing.

'Come on, Norman, was it a man or a woman? Or

both?' Sergeant Clay turned to John and Jennifer and said, 'He can usually tell that, too. It's something to do with the proteins in the urine.'

Quite abruptly, Detective Clay went up to his twin and whispered something in his ear. Sergeant Clay blinked, frowned, and said, 'Are you sure?'

'What is it?' Jennifer wanted to know. 'What can he smell?'

Sergeant Clay rubbed his chin thoughtfully. 'I don't know, ma'am; I think he's making some kind of mistake.'

'Does he often make mistakes?' asked John.

Sergeant Clay shook his head. 'Never. Never known him to make a mistake.'

'So why do you think he's making a mistake this time?'

'Well, sir, because he says this is urine right enough, and plenty of it. But whoever did it must've had a bladder that was five times the usual capacity, and whoever did it wasn't human.'

'You bet they weren't human,' John agreed.

'No, sir, you don't quite understand me. Whoever did this *genuinely* wasn't human.'

John stared at him, baffled. 'You mean an *animal* did this?'

Sergeant Clay stared back at him with a concentrated frown. Behind him, his twin frowned, too.

'Then what?' John demanded. 'If it wasn't human, and if it wasn't an animal – what?'

Two

With grim persistence, John and Jennifer spent the whole of the following morning clearing out the bedroom and bundling up everything into plastic trash bags – sheets, clothes, shoes, drapes, broken pictures, everything. Together they rolled up the mattress, tied it with webbing straps, and carried it into the yard. It stunk even more strongly than it had yesterday evening – a kind of thick, sweet, skunky odor, with a rusty-metallic undertone. As soon as they had propped it up next to the garage door, ready to be driven to the city dump, Jennifer stepped back well away from it and took a deep breath of fresh air.

'Really hums, doesn't it?' John remarked, his nose wrinkled.

Jennifer said, 'It's disgusting. I wonder what on earth it was?'

'Well, you heard the good Sergeant Clay. He didn't think it was any kind of creature known to man.'

'He was high,' said Jennifer. 'They both were.'

'You think so?' asked John, mildly surprised.

'There's no other explanation, is there? The way that other one was sniffing like that. They were both as high as kites.'

'I don't know. They didn't seem like they were high to me. I thought they were very *rational*.'

'What's rational about saying that something

nonhuman has destroyed your bedroom? That's not rational at all.'

John made a face. 'Well, no, I guess it isn't. But on the other hand, what *happened* wasn't very rational, either, was it? Whoever or *whatever* it was, how did it manage to break into the house completely unnoticed, tear the whole bedroom to pieces, and get away without anybody seeing him? Or *it*?'

'He could have slipped out when we ran upstairs to see what was going on.'

'But how? All the door were locked.'

'There was a key in the back door,' Jennifer reminded him.

'Of course there was. But I checked the back door myself last night and it was *still* locked, from the inside.'

'Maybe one of the cops locked it,' Jennifer suggested.

'You mean he found it unlocked and didn't tell Sergeant Clay? That's hardly likely.'

Jennifer folded her arms tightly. 'If you really want to know the truth, I don't *care* how he got away,' she declared. 'That's up to the police to find out. He was probably an expert locksmith.'

'It wouldn't make any difference if he was Harry Houdini, he couldn't have relocked a two-inch-thick mahogany door from the outside, now could he?'

'So what exactly are you suggesting?' Jennifer demanded. 'The supernatural? *The Amityville Horror?*'

John smiled and shook his head. 'Let's just get this stuff cleared up, shall we?'

They dragged the last of the trash bags out into the yard. It was a crisp but sunny day; a purple martin fluttered onto one of their bay trees and bounced up and down on a branch, watching them inquisitively, John wiped his hands on his jeans, then said. 'How about a glass of wine?'

They sat on the brick wall in the sunshine with tall

tulip-shaped glasses of chilled Chablis. Although the yard was completely secluded, they could hear the bustle of Philadelphia all around them: the rushing of traffic up and down Front Street, the scratching of jets taking off from Philadelphia International Airport, the thrumming of feet on the sidewalks of Market Street, the distant racketing of air-hammers and pile drivers around Center City.

Jennifer said, 'The only thing that really frightens me is that he might come back.'

John sipped wine and set his glass down. 'I've thought about that. I've asked a security company to come over tomorrow and install a proper alarm system. They may recommend that we put bars on the windows, too.'

'What about tonight?'

'I've thought about that, too. Jack Pelling goes on vacation this afternoon; he said that we could borrow his house for as long as we want.'

'Well, that's sweet of him.'

'I wasn't planning on staying here tonight anyway,' said John. 'I mean, quite apart from the fact that I don't relish another sleepless night on that couch, it'll do us all good to get away for a couple of days. Did you see Lenny this morning? He looked like he hadn't slept in a week.'

'Did he have nightmares?' asked Jennifer.

John shook his head. 'I don't know. But he didn't say a word when I took him to school this morning. He just sat in the car and stared out the window.'

'Oh, poor Lenny. We'll have to make sure that he goes to bed early tonight.'

John said, 'Tomorrow afternoon we can go to Strawbridge and Clothier and choose ourselves a new bed. Then maybe we'll go to Gimbel's and pick some new wallpaper.'

25

'It's clothes I need, not wallpaper,' Jennifer protested. 'I don't even have any underwear.'

'You mean, underneath that dress, you're completely naked?'

'Yes, as a matter of fact.'

John put his hand on her knee and edged it a little way up under the skirt. 'Why didn't you tell me that before, you brazen temptress?'

She firmly pushed his hand away, then kissed him on the nose. 'Because we don't have a *bed*, that's why.'

'What's wrong with the couch? What's wrong with the rug? When we were first going out together, we did it in the office stockroom, for God's sake.'

She kissed him again, quickly, flirtatiously. He leaned over to kiss her in return, but at that moment the front doorbell rang.

'Rescued from ravishment in the nick of time,' she said with a smile, and went to answer it. John grunted in amusement, and leaned back against the wall, finishing off his wine.

Two or three minutes went by without Jennifer reappearing, and eventually John went to see what was going on. Standing in the front hall was Mrs Scuyler, Lenny's teacher from school; and there, too, was Lenny, pale and quiet, and looking more like his dead mother than ever.

'John, darling,' said Jennifer. 'Mrs Scuyler's brought Lenny home. It seems he hasn't been feeling too good.'

John put his arm around Lenny's shoulders. 'Hey, champ, what's wrong? Have you been sick or anything?'

'He wouldn't tell me,' said Mrs Scuyler. She was a fussy, motherly woman with wild gingery hair that refused to behave itself. This morning she was wearing a vivid green tent-dress that made her look even more gingery than usual. 'But Mr Dreyfus said he was very quiet in gym practice, and when I took him for math he started to cry, didn't you, Lenny? So I brought him home.'

'That's very nice of you, Mrs Scuyler,' said John. 'I don't know whether Lenny told you, but we had a break-in here at the house yesterday. I guess it must have upset him. It certainly upset *us*.'

'Oh, I'm so sorry to hear that,' said Mrs Scuyler. 'Was anything taken?'

'Nothing at all, but they did some pretty disgusting damage.'

Mrs Scuyler clucked two or three times in disapproval. 'They're savages, these days, some of these young people. Just like savages out of the jungle. Do you know what they ought to do? They ought to send them there, instead of trying to keep them at Juvenile Hall.'

'I'm sorry, Mrs Scuyler, they ought to send them where?'

Mrs Scuyler stared at John in bewilderment. 'To the jungle, of course. That would soon sort them out! A few weeks of trying to survive amongst their own kind. Anacondas, and black widow spiders, and orangutans.'

'Well,' said John, 'interesting proposition.'

Mrs Scuyler leaned forward and squeezed Lenny's hand. 'You just take care of yourself, young man, and we'll see you back in class when you're better.'

Jennifer said, 'We're spending a couple of days away. That should help.'

'Well, you don't have to rush back,' said Mrs Scuyler. 'Maybe we'll see you on Monday morning.'

'What do you say to Mrs Scuyler?' John prompted Lenny.

Lenny lowered his head and said nothing.

'Come on, Lenny, what do you say?' John repeated.

Lenny remained silent, his shoulders shivering.

'It doesn't matter,' said Mrs Scuyler, 'he's probably

not feeling well enough.'

Just as he spoke, Lenny twisted on one leg and collapsed to the floor. He lay on his back on the doormat, both hands raised, clawing weakly and jerkily at the air. His face was floury-white and his lips were blue, and he was breathing in short, harsh gasps. His eyes rolled up into his head so that only the whites were exposed.

'Lenny!' John shouted. 'Lenny!'

Lenny convulsed once, a muscular shudder that went all the way down his spine, then relaxed. Gradually his cheeks regained their color and his breathing returned to normal. His eyes closed, but after a few moments he opened them again, and he could obviously recognize everybody around him.

'Lenny, are you okay?' asked John.

Lenny nodded. 'I think I fainted, that's all.'

'Does your head hurt, anything like that?'

'I'm fine,' said Lenny. 'I'm just tired. I don't think I slept too good.'

'All the same,' John told him. 'I'm going to call Dr Hendriksen, Jenny, would you go get him a glass of water or orange juice or something, please? I'll give him a piggyback up to bed.'

'It's too early to go to bed,' Lenny protested. 'It's only lunchtime.'

'You're going to bed and that's that,' John ordered. 'You can get dressed later, when we go to Chestnut Hill.'

'What are we going there for?'

'We're going to stay at Mr Pelling's house – just until our bedroom's been fixed up. You'll love it; he has an indoor pool.'

'Oh, wow,' Lenny exclaimed. He jumped up on to John's back, and John held him tightly. He was long-legged, but he wasn't heavy. Virginia had always

28

told him that he would never be eaten by giants because there was no meat on his bones.

'*But wouldn't they grind my bones to make their bread?*'

'*That's only a story. Giants hate bread. Giants eat nothing but fruitcake.*'

John carried Lenny up to the half-landing. As he did so, Lenny twisted around and said, 'G'bye, Mrs Scuyler. And thank you.'

John smiled, pleased to hear Lenny acting polite, especially unprompted. 'Come on, champ, let's get you into bed,' he said. 'I'm going out in a couple of minutes, to take all our bedroom stuff down to the dump. How about some comics?'

'Thanks, Dad. And, Dad?'

'What is it?' John joggled Lenny all the way along the corridor to his bedroom, then swung him gently down onto the bed. The sun flickered through the white bedroom curtains; Lenny's blond hair shone in a bright childish halo.

'Dad, do you ever dream about Mom?'

John straightened up and regarded his son carefully. 'Sure I do. Quite often. I guess I always will'

Lenny glanced up at his father, but said nothing.

'Have *you* been dreaming about her?' John asked.

'Not exactly,' said Lenny.

'What do you mean, "not exactly"?'

Lenny thought for a moment, then said, 'It doesn't matter.'

'Come on, tell me,' John encouraged him. 'Have you been having nightmares about her? It's natural, you know. It's nothing to be afraid of.'

Lenny frowned and licked his lips. 'It's not exactly nightmares, either.'

'Then what is it? Come on, champ, if you can't tell me, who can tell?'

Tears began to sparkle in Lenny's eyes, and he

swallowed with difficulty. 'The thing is, I've seen her.'

'You've *seen* her? What do you mean, you've seen her?'

'I saw her last week, outside the classroom window at school. And then I saw her again on Saturday, when we stopped at the gas station.'

'You saw her when you were *awake*?'

Lenny nodded, and the fat tears began to roll down his cheeks. John hunkered down beside the bed, put his arms around Lenny and held him close.

'It happens all the time, when people lose somebody they love. They see somebody who looks like the person they lost, and they believe that it's them. They really believe it. And – well – it's kind of scary, and it's upsetting, too. But it's part of getting over their death. It's part of grieving.'

'But she waved,' Lenny insisted.

'Is that so strange? People do wave, you know. It's not against the law.'

'She was waving at me. She was right outside the classroom window and she was smiling and waving at me. And it was Mom.'

John squeezed Lenny tight. 'Oh, Lenny, I'm sorry. I'm really sorry. If I could bring her back to you, I would. But she's gone, champ, she's gone forever, and all we can do is try to be happy. You like Jennifer, don't you?'

Lenny nodded. 'She's okay.'

At that moment, Jennifer came into the bedroom with a glass of orange juice. 'Here you are, Lenny. I've called Dr Hendriksen and he's coming right over. He says to get into bed and keep cool.'

John stood up and watched her as she helped Lenny take off his T-shirt. She treated Lenny so gently and so naturally, giving him all the undemanding affection a mother would have given him, but not trying to elbow her way into that well-guarded central core of love and memory that was still Virginia's preserve, and always would be. It had been Jennifer's immediate unselfish liking of Lenny that had convinced John that they could be more than lovers.

It couldn't be easy, being Lenny. Lenny had been alone with Virginia when she had choked to death, unable to help her, unable to do anything. No wonder he thought he had seen her waving at him through the classroom window. No wonder he'd seen her at the gas station.

Lenny put on his pajamas and climbed into bed. Jennifer leaned against John and smiled at Lenny. 'Anything special you want for lunch, *signor*?' she asked him. 'Your father and I were thinking of cold pasta.'

'We were?' asked John. 'It was my distinct impression that we were thinking of hot steaks.'

Lenny said. 'That's okay, I'm not too hungry.'

'Well, you should eat something,' Jennifer admonished.

'Maybe peanut butter and jelly.'

'Peanut butter and jelly?' John demanded. 'Do you know what peanut butter and jelly does to your digestive system?'

'Sure,' said Lenny, grinning, 'it fills it up.'

'It's poison,' said John. He checked his watch. 'What time did Dr Hendriksen say he was coming?'

'Right away. He should be here in five or ten minutes.'

'In that case, I just have time to go across the street and get us some steak. And maybe a bottle of champagne, too.'

'John, we have nothing to celebrate! Our whole bedroom was ripped to pieces!'

John kissed her. 'Maybe I'd like to drink a toast to a

new bedroom, and to a marriage that's going to be happy there, no matter who tries to spoil it!'

John and Jennifer both gave Lenny a kiss, and left him propped up in bed, reading a *Spiderman* comic.

Lenny sat there for two or three minutes, quietly turning the pages of his comic. After a while, he began to feel cold, and he reached down toward the end of the bed and drew up the quilted comforter.

As he did so, he saw the seersucker curtains stirring, as if they were being blown by an unfelt breeze. He looked toward the window; his heart began to beat a little bit faster. All he could see were the tops of the trees, and the irregular rooftops of Society Hill, and – farther to the west – the cranes and the structural steel skeletons of Philadelphia's downtown rebuilding program, as well as the ornamental clocktower of City Hall, with its famous statue of William Penn standing on top. He thought the statue was sinister rather than inspiring: the dark, motionless shadow of a long-dead man, encased in bronze.

He opened his comic again. Spidey had a bad case of the grippe, and was sr.eezing so much that he nearly let go of his web. But then the breeze that wasn't a breeze at all ruffled the page and turned it over, and then the next, and then the next, faster and faster.

Lenny turned toward the window; and froze, speechless with terror. Right outside, her hands cupped above her forehead to shield her eyes from the sun, was his dead mother, peering in at him. When he turned, she smiled, and lifted one hand, and waved. It was her, there was no doubt about it at all. It was his mother, fair-haired, white-faced, and she was smiling at him.

A scream rose from somewhere inside his chest, silent at first, but then higher and louder, until he was sitting in bed with his fists clenched and his mouth stretched open and his eyes wide, screaming and screaming and screaming and screaming.

John reached the bedroom first. He burst in through the door and scooped Lenny up in his arms. 'Lenny! Lenny! It's okay! Everything's okay! It's Daddy!'

Lenny was hysterical. He gasped for breath, thin whining gasps, and his arms and legs were rigid and trembling.

Jennifer rushed into the room. 'My God! I heard him right down in the yard! Is he all right?'

John laid Lenny carefully on the bed, and felt his forehead. He was sticky and chilled, but he didn't seem to be running a temperature. 'There,' he murmured. 'Ssh, you're going to be fine. Ssh.'

At last, still trembling, Lenny quieted down. John said to Jennifer. 'Would you mind calling Dr Hendriksen again, just to make sure that he's on his way?'

'Sure,' said Jennifer.

John knelt close to Lenny's bed and clasped his hand. 'Are you feeling better now?'

Lenny whispered. 'Has she gone?'

'She's just gone to call Dr Hendriksen, that's all. She'll be back in a minute.'

'I don't mean Jennifer.' Lenny glanced quickly and with obvious fright toward the window. John didn't know what he expected to see there, but when he lifted his own eyes and peered toward it, he couldn't see anything except the usual view.

'There's nobody there, Lenny,' John said. He stood up and walked toward the window, opened it, and looked out, leaning his arms on the windowsill. 'Apart from the fact that it's nearly forty feet down to the yard, there's nobody in sight, anywhere.'

'She was there,' whispered Lenny. 'Daddy, she was there, looking in.'

'Lenny, nobody could have looked in. It's impossible. It's a sheer drop, and there isn't even a box to stand on, let alone a forty-foot ladder, which is what they would have needed.'

'It was Mommy and she was looking in.'

John closed the window and returned to the bed. 'Come on, champ, you're not too well, are you? Why don't you close your eyes and try to get a little sleep before the doctor gets here?'

'I don't want to stay in this room,' Lenny begged. 'I'm too scared. Can't I come downstairs?'

Jennifer returned. 'The doctor just left. Only a few more minutes. How are you feeling, Lenny?'

'Fine,' mumbled Lenny.

'He wants to come downstairs and rest on the couch,' said John. 'He says it's too scary up here on his own.'

'Well, that's fine,' said Jennifer. 'I'll carry the comforter, John, and you carry the patient.'

John gave Jennifer a meaningful look, but she shook her head quickly in a gesture that meant *not now*. She must have overheard Lenny saying that he had seen his mother looking in at his bedroom window. That wasn't the kind of experience that was going to be easy for them to discuss. It was a little more complicated than deciding what they were going to have for lunch.

They took Lenny downstairs, his long legs swinging under John's arms, hard curly head pressed close against the back of John's neck. They tucked him up on the couch, like a young Victorian invalid. 'There you go,' John said, grinning. 'You can watch *As The World Turns* now. That'll do wonders for your education.'

John went through to the kitchen, where Jennifer was preparing the pasta: cold *conchiglie* with bacon, peas, and ricotta. The kitchen door swung shut behind him, and he stood by the tiled counter for a moment in silence, watching Jennifer pour oil and lemon juice into the bowl of pasta.

'He says he saw his mother.'

Jennifer stopped tossing the pasta shells and slowly put down her fork and spoon. 'I thought so,' she said, in a tone implying that Lenny's terror might well have something to do with her having married his father.

'She was looking in at the window,' said John. 'She was looking in at the goddamned window, that's what he said, and waving at him.'

Jennifer slowly shook her head. 'Hallucinating. It happens sometimes, when they have a temperature. My niece Alice saw a roomful of cats once, when she had the mumps.'

'He's not running a temperature,' said John. 'At least, I don't think so. His forehead's quite cool.'

Jennifer briskly chopped up bacon. 'It doesn't take much. Just a couple of degrees over.'

John said, 'You're not upset?'

'Why should I be upset?'

'Well ... him thinking about Virginia so vividly. I don't want you to think that Lenny doesn't love you. That he resents you being my wife or anything.'

Jennifer leaned across the counter and kissed him, slowly and softly, on the lips. 'He lost his mother. Who can blame him for thinking about her? And I can never replace Virginia. I wouldn't even try.'

John dragged a stool across to the counter and sat down. 'He says he saw her in the schoolyard last week, waving at him. And last Friday, at the gas station.'

'He'll get over it. He probably feels strange at the moment – not sure what role he's supposed to be playing. Not sure where he fits in.'

John watched her finish the pasta and arrange it on three blue-rimmed plates. In her yellow open-necked shirt and her designer jeans, she looked young and fresh and very pretty. The fine blond hairs shone on her arms; he stroked them with his fingertips.

'What are you doing? You'll make me spill it.'

'I'm in love with the hairs on your arms.'

'You make me sound like Popeye.'

John laughed; and then the doorbell rang.

'Dr Hendriksen,' said Jennifer.

Dr Hendriksen came out into the hallway, thoughtfully rubbing the back of his neck. He was a stocky, fiftyish man with short-cropped hair and a bulldog face like Teddy Roosevelt's. Despite his disproportionately deep chest and his short, bandy legs, he always wore perfectly tailored suits. Jennifer thought he would have made a better politician than a family doctor.

'I can set your mind at rest on one thing,' he said. 'There's nothing physically wrong with Lenny. No infection, no temperature. I've had two or three cases of tuberculous meningitis this year: I was worried it might be that. But Lenny is perfectly clear. He's a little listless. Maybe *preoccupied* more than listless. But there's no sign of fever or vomiting, no headaches. I'd say that, physically speaking, Lenny is one healthy young man.'

'That's twice you said physically,' Jennifer remarked.

Dr Hendriksen closed his bag and snapped the clasps. 'Well, we know what happened to his mother; and we know that he suffered shock and grief and a strong sense of personal guilt, even though it wasn't his fault.'

'So you think it might be some kind of delayed reaction to Virginia's death?' John said.

'It's possible. That break-in you had yesterday might

have contributed to it – caused a crisis of nervous tension.'

'What do you suggest we do?' asked Jennifer.

Dr Hendriksen smiled. 'Well, I'm not going to prescribe any medication, certainly not yet. Children get quite enough drugs in their breakfast cereals without doctors giving them any more. But you might consider taking him away for a week or so, just to calm him down.'

John opened the door for the doctor. Sunlight and noise streamed into the hallway. 'As a matter of fact, we're borrowing a house up at Chestnut Hill for a couple of days.'

'Nice area,' said Dr Hendriksen. 'Listen – keep him calm, that's my advice. When he talks about seeing his mother, don't over-react, just accept it quietly as part of the recovery process. I have some patients who lost husbands or wives twenty or thirty years ago, and they still haven't completely recovered.'

Dr Hendriksen collected his homburg, lifted it courteously to Jennifer, and walked across the sidewalk to his huge twenty-year-old Rolls-Royce. 'Call me, if you need to,' he told them, then climbed in behind the wheel and pulled away from the curb.

'There,' said Jennifer, kissing John quickly on the cheek. 'Nothing to worry about.'

'I'll go get that bottle of champagne,' said John.

'Nothing too expensive, okay? I'd rather spend our money on a new bedroom.'

They had only just finished their lunch when there was another ring at the door. John was in the kitchen, clearing up the plates, so Jennifer called, 'I'll get it!'

She opened the front door and found Sergeant Clay and Detective Clay standing outside.

'May we come in for a moment, Mrs Woods?' Sergeant Clay said.

She opened the door wider and they entered the hallway. Both were two heads taller than she was. Sergeant Clay wore a gray tailored suit, Detective Clay a bronze one, both from Sears. 'Is your husband home?' asked Sergeant Clay.

'We're all home today – my stepson, too. I guess we needed a day off.'

'I'd say so,' Sergeant Clay remarked.

The two detectives followed Jennifer into the sitting room.

'This is Lenny,' said Jennifer.

'Hi, Lenny,' Sergeant Clay nodded at him. 'You not feeling so good today?'

'He felt a little faint, that's all,' Jennifer explained.

'Well, that's not unusual, after what happened,' said Sergeant Clay. 'It's the shock, you know. You'll get over it.'

John came out of the kitchen, wiping his hands on a tea towel. 'Sergeant Clay? How are you doing?'

Sergeant Clay adjusted the small, tight knot of his necktie, looking up at the ceiling as he did so. 'Not too good, as a matter of fact, Mr Woods. We've had an interim report from the laboratory, and we've been discussing the whole pattern of what happened with our robbery and vandalism specialists, and on the whole we're inclined to the conclusion that there *was* no break in.' He stopped and lowered his eyes.

John stared at him, then let out a short, disbelieving laugh. 'What? You saw the bedroom for yourself, Sergeant. It was wrecked! And now you're trying to tell me that there was no break-in? Is this a joke, or what?'

Sergeant Clay shrugged. 'Mr Woods, the facts speak for themselves. Your house was secure last night; all the doors and all the large windows were locked from

38

the inside, and there was no sign of anybody having forced an entrance through any of the smaller windows. Your bedroom was ripped apart so totally that even a team of half a dozen angry and very energetic vandals couldn't have done it in less than a half hour; and I find it very difficult to believe that both you and Mrs Woods were in the house while this was going on and heard nothing at all until that loud bang that you told us about.'

'So what are you saying?' John demanded. 'You're saying that we did it ourselves, and made the story up?'

Sergeant Clay gave an almost imperceptible nod. 'We've had cases before, Mr Woods, where a husband and wife have torn their place up during a domestic confrontation, and then blamed some mysterious intruder.'

'Are you serious?' John asked, incredulous. 'Do my wife and I look like the kind of people who would systematically rip a freshly decorated bedroom to pieces?'

'Nobody looks like anything to me,' Sergeant Clay replied, trying to remain calm. 'I know a dear little old lady who sawed off her husband's head; and I know a Hell's Angel who gave the kiss of life to a half-drowned baby.'

'All the same, you're accusing us of having destroyed that bedroom ourselves?' John was furious now.

Sergeant Clay said, 'You tell me. There were no fingerprints in the room, apart from yours and Mrs Woods's. There were no unusual soil samples in the dust we vacuumed up from the rug.'

'And the urine on the bed? What about that – that urine you said was nonhuman?'

Sergeant Clay looked at John steadily. 'We were

right. It wasn't human. It wasn't even urine. It was simply a mixture of water and chemicals, including sulphur and iodine.'

There was a lengthy silence. John held Sergeant Clay's gaze for a moment, then glanced at his twin. Detective Clay was standing close to Lenny, frowning, his hand pressed to his forehead as if he were suffering from a headache.

John turned back to the sergeant. 'And that's what you think, is it? That my wife and I had an argument and smashed up our own bedroom and told you that it was vandals?'

'It's one of the possibilities,' said Sergeant Clay flatly. 'After all, you couldn't claim insurance, could you, if it was proved that you did it yourselves?'

'Oh, I see. We're guilty of perpetrating insurance fraud now, are we?'

'It's one of the possibilities,' Sergeant Clay repeated.

'And – do tell me, Sergeant – what are the other possibilities?' John demanded.

Before he could answer, Detective Clay came over and took hold of his brother's arm. He whispered something in Sergeant Clay's ear, nodded toward Lenny, then whispered something else. Sergeant Clay listened impassively, although his narrow Arabian-looking nostrils flared a little, as if he were breathing more deeply.

John looked from one twin to the other. 'What's all that about?'

Sergeant Clay checked his watch. 'I'm sorry, Mr Woods. We have to get back to headquarters. Something just came up.'

'Will you tell me what the hell is going on?' John demanded.

Sergeant Clay said, 'There's nothing going on, Mr Woods. Just a routine investigation.'

'So, what do you intend to do now?'

'We intend to go back to headquarters, that's all.'

'And you don't intend to make any further effort to find out who broke into my house and tore my bedroom to pieces because you think *I* did it?'

'Believe me, Mr Woods, the investigation is going to continue. But we have plenty of other work to do .The situation is that, whatever actually happened here, nobody got hurt.'

Jennifer came across and took hold of John's hand. 'Come on, John, he's right. There's no point in getting mad about it.'

John showed Sergeant and Detective Clay to the door. As they were leaving, Detective Clay whispered something else in his twin's ear. Sergeant Clay turned to John and said, 'Do you intend to stay here tonight?'

'We're staying at a friend's house on Chestnut Hill.'

'Maybe you should give me the address.'

'What for? You don't think this is going to happen again, do you?'

'Mr Woods, please don't make it difficult.'

'Very well, then,' said John testily. 'It's 1305 Fairmount.'

'Thank you, Mr Woods,' said Sergeant Clay, jotting down the address in his notebook. 'And there's one thing more.'

John said nothing, waiting with an exaggeratedly impatient expression for Sergeant Clay to tell him what this 'one thing more' might be.

'My brother says to lock your bedroom door.'

'Your brother says *what*?'

'It may sound impertinent, Mr Woods, but believe me, he knows what he's talking about.'

'Are you guys high?' John demanded.

'Mr Woods, what we're telling you is entirely for your own protection.'

41

'You're spaced out, both of you,' John retorted. 'I never met two such goddamned weirdos in my whole life. Well, you listen to me. If I get any more crap from you two, I'm going to call the police commissioner's office personally and make an official complaint. I'm not some bum living in a cardboard box, mister. You can't roust me, and you'd better not try.'

'We know who you are, sir,' said Sergeant Clay courteously. 'And we're still advising you to lock your bedroom door tonight. Not just for your own protection, but for the safety of your wife and son, too.'

John was about to snap out another caustic remark when Jennifer quietly laid a restraining hand on his shoulder. He turned around, and she smiled at him. He let out a long breath of resignation, and said, 'Okay, okay. Thank you, gentlemen. Let's just leave it at that, shall we?'

He closed the door, and put his arms around Jennifer, and kissed her.

'What do you think of that?' he asked her. 'They think *we* did it.'

Jennifer smiled. 'I love you when you're angry.'

'Angry? Goddamn it, I'm not angry. I'm just – I don't know – *mystified*.'

He went back into the sitting room and poured them both a last foaming glass of champagne.

'Here's to us,' he said. 'And here's to the confusion of our enemies.'

Three

As evening settled warm and cloudless over Chestnut Hill, John and Jennifer sat on the patio at the back of Jack Pelling's house and enjoyed a last glass of wine. Lenny was just inside the patio doors, playing with He-Man figures on the tiled floor of the sunroom.

John said, 'How about another toast? Here's to Jack.'

Jack Pelling was the chairman of the executive committee at the *Philadelphia News* group. Although he was eleven years older than John, and one of corporation's most senior executives, the two men had become friends almost at once. The immediacy of their friendship had had a lot to do with their mutual obsession with backgammon, but they were also remarkably alike, both in character and in looks. Jack saw in John the feisty young manager that he himself had been when he first joined the *News*; John saw in Jack the wise, experienced member of the board that he would like to grow into.

Chestnut Hill was one of the most desirable residential areas in Philadelphia, northwest of the city past Fairmount Park, and Jack Pelling owned one of its most dramatic houses. Jack's mother had been a native Neapolitan, and Jack adored Italy and everything Italian. He had built the house on three levels on a thickly wooded slope, its blue-tiled rooftops clustered together to resemble a small Italian village rather than a single house. There were cloisters and courtyards and ornamental fountains, and even a bell tower copied from a church in Siena, although its bell had been rung only once. Further campanology had been forbidden by the Chestnut Hill residents' association.

The patio was sheltered on its north and east sides by a spectacular rockery, densely planted with maiden pink and rockrose and snow-in-summer. An artificial stream trickled down through the rocks, and into a small circular pool at the patio's edge.

John and Jennifer had been too tired and a little too drunk to cook supper, so they had sat on Zarach stools in the stylish marble-countered kitchen and eaten a Chinese carryout, chow mein and sweet-and-sour-pork, straight out of the boxes. Now, an hour later, John was beginning to wish that he hadn't so doggedly finished off the last of the soft-fried noodles. He grimaced and thumped his chest with his fist.

'What's the matter?' Jennifer asked. 'You're not having a coronary on me, are you?'

'It's that Chinese food. I don't know how they do it. They chop it up into tiny little pieces, and when we eat it, we masticate it into even tinier pieces. So how come it's sitting in my stomach in one huge homogenized stomach-shaped lump?'

'That's because you ate so much, it's all been compressed back together again. They make chipboard the same way.'

John took a mouthful of tepid Chablis and swilled it around his teeth. 'Don't say things like that. I feel bloopy enough already.'

Jennifer swung her legs off her basketwork lounger, and came over to kiss John on the forehead. 'It's your own fault. You have too much *guilt* when you eat. You seem to think if you leave even the teeniest piece of noodle on your plate, you're going to upset the starving millions of Ethiopia or something. Well, John – I'm here to tell you that if you leave two spoonfuls of soft-fried noodles, it's not going to be a cause for international concern in Ethiopia or anywhere else.' She kissed him again. 'I still love you, though, you greedy hog.'

The corners of the patio were gradually filling up with shadows. The sky behind the treeline was the color of dying lilacs. Jennifer walked across to the pool and stood looking around, and said, 'Isn't this perfect? What a house.'

'I sure wish *we* could buy a house like this,' said Lenny.

'Well, maybe one day,' John told him. He looked at his watch. 'Hey, it's bedtime, champ. Upstairs and brush your teeth. You may not have school tomorrow, but you still have to get your sleep.'

Lenny went inside to brush his teeth. A couple of minutes later he came down one last time to kiss them good night.

'How are you feeling?' John asked, hugging him close.

'Okay,' said Lenny. 'Can I watch TV for a while?'

'Ten minutes, and that's all.'

'Okay, Dad.' He paused. 'Dad?'

'What is it?'

Lenny squinched up his face, the way he always did when he wasn't sure he ought to be asking what he was asking.' Dad, why did that detective say that to me?'

'Which detective? What?'

'That detective in the brown suit.'

'He didn't say anything; he only whispered. What are you talking about?'

'But he said something to me,' said Lenny.

'Well, I sure didn't hear him. All I saw him do was whisper.'

45

Lenny shook his head. 'He spoke out loud. It was real clear. He said, "Better watch out, kid. You're one of them."'

John felt a sudden pang of uncertainty. 'I sure didn't hear him say that. I didn't hear him say anything.' He turned to Jennifer. 'Did you hear that detective say anything? Not the sergeant; the other one, his twin?'

Jennifer slowly shook her head. 'I didn't hear him say anything at all, honey.'

But Lenny was adamant. 'He said, "Better watch out, kid." He said it real clear. "Better watch out, kid. You're one of them."'

'And that was all? He didn't explain what he meant?'

'That was all. He said it like I was supposed to know what he meant.'

John clasped his hand over his mouth for a moment. Then he said, 'I don't know. This gets wackier by the minute, I mean, if he'd said something out loud, if he'd said *anything* out loud, I'm sure I would have heard him. I was paying so much attention to the fact that he whispered all the time.'

Jennifer laid her arm around Lenny's shoulders, and smiled, 'I think you're suffering from Wearyitis. We've all had a bad night and a long day. It's easy to imagine things when you're tired.'

'But he *said* it,' Lenny insisted.

'All right,' said John. 'I'll tell you what I'll do. I'll call police headquarters tomorrow and talk to Detective Clay, and ask him what he meant. And if he denies that he said it, or if he doesn't want to discuss it, then I'll talk to the police commissioner in person.'

Lenny said, 'You do believe me, don't you? I'm not telling lies.'

'Sure I believe you. Just because *I* didn't hear him, that doesn't mean beans. I'm over forty now, champ, over the hill. The old eardrums are wearing out.'

Lenny went up to bed. John and Jennifer sat in silence for a while, their loungers pushed together so that they could hold hands, watching the stars come out.

A shooting star flared briefly, over toward Conshohocken.

'Isn't that supposed to be an omen?' asked Jennifer.

John nodded. 'Actually, it's a warning. If I don't take half a glass of Pepto-Bismol before I go to bed, I'm not going to sleep tonight, either.'

John woke up in the very smallest hour of the night and opened his eyes. For a long, disorienting moment, he couldn't think where he was. The window was on the wrong side of the room and something unfamiliar was shining on the opposite wall, and the bedcovers felt puffy and suffocating.

He sat up, and suddenly understood that he was in Jack Pelling's guest bedroom. Jennifer was breathing quietly and deeply just beside him. The shine on the opposite wall was nothing more than the moonlight, reflected in the glass of a large Italian print. *The Church of San Carlino by Borromini, at Daybreak.*

He looked at the digital clock on the marble-topped bedside table: 2:17 AM. He reached across for his glass of water, and drank almost all of it without taking a breath. He felt as if Chablis were oozing out of his pores instead of perspiration, and the roof of his mouth was coated with grease. The Chinese seemed to have perfected a special kind of grease that stuck to the roof of your mouth and wouldn't come off: Hong Fat, he thought wryly.

He lay back and stared at the ceiling. His stomach growled, but he knew he wasn't going to be sick. That feeling of nausea was just going to stay there until tomorrow morning.

47

He lay awake, his mind turning over like a flag-decorated Ferris wheel. He wondered if he could find a way to improve the *News's* distribution in Camden, on the Jersey side of the river, where they always ran second-best to the *Inquirer*. He began to think about a four-page supplement, folded around the outside of the paper, with a strong Camden lead on the front and Camden sports on the back.

After a while, his mind revolved around to thoughts of Lenny, and to Lenny's belief that he had seen Virginia. John guessed that Dr Hendriksen was right, and that Lenny was suffering from nothing more alarming than long-suppressed guilt and grief. All the same, it seemed strange that Lenny should have started hallucinating so suddenly, and for no apparent reason.

The fact that they had finished decorating the house might have had something to do with it. Maybe Lenny had finally come face-to-face with the fact that his mother was really gone forever, and that his new life with Jennifer was permanent.

All the same, there was still the bewildering vandalism of their bedroom to think about. For about ten seconds after they'd discovered it, John had entertained the possibility that Lenny hadn't really been asleep that evening, and that *he* had crept into their bedroom and torn it to pieces. But quite apart from the fact that he didn't have the physical strength to inflict all of that damage, especially in the short time that had been available to him, Lenny hadn't come out with any protestations of innocence – the kind that every father recognizes from his own youthful career of broken windows and stolen candy bars. The only time you could be sure that a boy had done something bad was when he took the trouble to tell you that he hadn't.

Then there was all this weirdness with the Clay twins. Had Detective Clay *really* spoken to Lenny, or had Lenny imagined it? And if he *had* said that – *Better watch out, kid, you're one of them* – what the hell was that supposed to mean? One of whom?

There you are, he thought with some satisfaction, *I can even be grammatical inside my own head.*

He felt a yawn coming on. He allowed his mouth to open slowly, his eyes to close, his back muscles to stretch. While he yawned, a soft thunder filled his ears, of rushing blood and rustlng bedclothes. But that thunder only partially blotted out the scratching noise from the corridor.

He stopped yawning instantly and lay there with yawn-tears still glistening in his eyes, listening.

There it was again, another scratch. Loose and hollow, like somebody dragging a garden fork along the wall. Closer this time, as far as John could make out.

'Lenny?' he called under his breath, trying not to wake Jennifer. 'Lenny, is that you?'

Silence. The scratching had stopped. John lay in bed with his heart beating hard and his toes stiffly curled and his ears listening so acutely that he could have heard a bird landing on the roof.

Maybe that was it, a bird scratching in the roof-space. Or squirrels. Squirrels were notorious for finding their way into lofts and tearing up insulation and paper to make themselves nests. He would have to tell Jack when the Pellings came home.

Krrrrrrrrrr. The scratching was repeated. This time it was much closer. And this time he knew it couldn't be squirrels because it was too long and too loud and in any case it wasn't in the roof, it was out in the corridor – right outside the door.

My brother says you should lock your bedroom door.

49

'Lenny?' he called, and this time his voice was loud enough to wake up Jennifer. She sat up beside him, with her hair tousled.

'What is it? John – what's the matter?'

'Ssh!' he said. 'Listen!'

'Listen to what? John – you woke me up!'

'*Listen!*'

They listened. There was nothing at all. No scratching, no movement. At last John said, 'I thought I heard something. Kind of a scratching noise, outside in the corridor.'

'It could have been Lenny.'

'Yes, well, maybe it was. But it didn't sound like Lenny.'

There was a very long pause. Then Jennifer said. 'Aren't you going to go check?'

John looked at her, then back toward the door, and then said, 'It's quiet now.'

'You ought to make sure. Perhaps he's sleepwalking.'

'Sure, you're right.' John pushed back the covers and climbed out of bed. He slept naked, but even though it was a warm night and there was nobody else in the house, he reached for his robe. Nobody relishes a nude encounter with the unknown.

'It's probably squirrels,' he remarked, tightening the knot in his sash.

Jennifer said nothing as she watched him go to the door. He put his hand on the doorknob, and hesitated.

'John?' asked Jennifer.

'I was just giving it one more listen. They have quite a few burglaries up here on Chestnut Hill. Last thing I want to do is run straight into a burglar.'

'My God,' said Jennifer, laughing. 'Vandalized and burgled, all in one week.'

John opened the door.

* * *

He opened his eyes again. It was still dark. He must have been dreaming. He lay still for a long time, and he was aware that the room around him was unfamiliar. It wasn't his own bedroom on Third Street: the window was on the wrong side. It didn't *smell* the same, either. This room smelled neutral and stuffy. No perfume. No wine. No hint of sex.

Somewhere nearby, he could hear voices. Somebody laughing. Then chimes, like a doorbell.

He felt peculiarly numb. He tried to lift his arms, but found that they wouldn't move. They were still there, lying by his sides, but none of the instructions his brain sent down to them seemed to be able to reach them. In fact, he couldn't persuade any of his body to move.

He began to wonder, vaguely, if he were dead.

But why should he be dead? All he had done was to eat supper in the kitchen with Jennifer and Lenny, and then finish a bottle of wine, and go to bed.

Perhaps he had died of alcohol poisoning. Perhaps he had vomited in bed and asphyxiated on his own vomit. Perhaps the giant prawns had been contaminated, and he had died of botulism.

Perhaps he wasn't dead, but simply paralyzed. His brain felt so anesthetized that it was difficult to work out which. He could feel himself slowly surfboarding in and out of sleep, over a dull, silvery-gray ocean that had no horizon.

Jennifer, he thought. Then, out loud, he said, 'Where's Jennifer?'

It seemed as if hours had passed him by, or possibly days. He was dimly conscious that it had been light, and then it had grown dark, and now it was light again. He could still hear the voices. Sometimes they were near, and sometimes they were very far away.

And, wave after wave, he surf-boarded over the silvery-gray ocean, on and on, as if his journey would never end.

He slept. He dreamed.

He dreamed he was reaching out for the doorknob. Jennifer said, 'Vandalized and burgled, all in one week.' He turned slowly back to smile at her, a glutinous movement like a man wading through syrup.

He said, 'It's squirrels, I'll bet you.'

And then the door was racketed open as if an express train were hurtling through it, and John was ripped across the chest by something that felt like red-hot wires, and was slammed speechless against the Italian bureau, hitting his head on the marble top.

Something huge and black rushed toward the bed, treading right on top of his pelvis so that the bone snapped like a broken dinner-plate. He experienced instant and over-whelming agony, and he screamed.

Jennifer was screaming, too, high and piercing, right through his head. And the huge black monstrosity tore the bedclothes off the bed with claws as sharp as kitchen knives, shreds of linen and feathers and silvered silk, and seized hold of Jennifer's naked body and raked her open from shoulders to thighs, blood bursting everywhere, gouting over the sheets, spattering the ceiling, raining hot and sticky on John's unprotected face. Shocked, maddened, he wailed like an injured animal.

He felt the huge black thing rush away again, leaving a cold vacuum of terror behind it. But all he could do was lie on his side on the blood-sprayed carpet, whimpering with pain.

He lost consciousness. When at last he opened his eyes, he saw Lenny's bare feet, close to his face.

'Lenny,' he whispered. 'For God's sake, Lenny, save me.'

Four

A nun in a white habit was waiting by his bed when he awoke. 'Mr Woods?' she said in the sweetest of voices. Her face was as smooth as a saint's. Her eyes were green and her lips were pale and her eyebrows were unplucked. The sun shone through the starched, upswept wings of her wimple. 'Mr Woods?' she said again, and reached out and held his hand.

Her fingers were cool and reassuring. He wanted to squeeze them, but couldn't. He couldn't move his hand at all.

'Was it a dream?' he asked, his speech still thick with drugs.

The nun shook her head. 'It was a terrible tragedy, Mr Woods, and terrible tragedies sometimes seem like dreams.'

'Then she's dead.'

A long silence. Outside the window, the sounds of the world going by. Airplanes and traffic and birds perching on the guttering. The nun squeezed his hand. At last she said, 'She's gone, Mr Woods, yes.'

His dream of opening the bedroom door had been so vivid that John had already suspected that it was real. But the confirmation that Jennifer was dead burst like a bomb inside his mind. A dark, silent bomb that blotted out everything with panic and grief and self-pity.

'I thought it was a dream. I thought it was nothing

but a bad dream.' The tears poured down the sides of his face and onto his pillow.

'In a way, Mr Woods, it was. You'll have to think of it like that.'

'Is my son all right?' asked John. 'He wasn't –?'

'Your son's fine. He's staying with your friend Mr Pelling. Now that you're awake, you'll be able to have him to visit.'

Again John tried to move his arm, but couldn't. 'And me? What about me? I feel so damned *numb*.'

The nun smiled at him sadly. 'You were lucky not to have been killed, Mr Woods. You were also lucky that Dr Freytag was still here when they brought you in. He is one of the most skilled neuro-surgeons in the country.'

John sniffed. 'If he's so skilled, why do I feel so numb? Look – I can't even move my arm.'

'Mr Woods, you've suffered some very serious injuries.'

'How serious?'

'Well …' Here she licked those pale lips. 'Your spinal cord has been damaged, and I'm sorry to say that …'

She paused, lowering her head so that all he could see of her was her wimple, like a snow-white seagull dipping toward the ocean.

'I'm sorry to say that you may not walk anymore.'

John closed his eyes. This was more than he could take. He didn't want to be here; he didn't want any of this to be really happening. He wanted to be right back in Jack Pelling's house with his hand on the doorknob, turning around to Jennifer and smiling and telling her that it was nothing but squirrels.

He didn't realize as he lay there that he was sobbing out loud.

The nun held his hand tightly. 'I'm sorry,' she repeated. The way she said it, it sounded almost like an Ave Maria. 'I'm sorry.'

'Oh, God,' he wept. 'Oh, God.'

The nun leaned over the bed, rustling and white and smelling of soap. She brushed away his tears with a tissue, and then unexpectedly she kissed him on the forehead. 'Dr Freytag thinks that with one or maybe two more operations, you should be able to move your arms. And we have a wonderful physiotherapy unit here. You have life, Mr Woods, think of that. And even the saddest life is full of possibilities.'

John opened his eyes. 'How – how long have I been –?' he asked. He was so miserable that his throat felt as if it were gripped by a tourniquet.

'Four days. They brought you in Friday morning, about four o'clock. It's Tuesday now.'

John lay for almost ten minutes in silence, trying to make sense of what had happened. His mind began to clear; and even though this was accompanied by the gradual worsening of a gripping pain in his back, he suffered the pain so that he could think straight.

...He remembered the scratching noise in the corridor outside the bedroom. He remembered opening the door. Instantly, something black and huge and powerful had raged into the room, ripping his chest open and crushing his pelvis. Then he had heard Jennifer screaming, and blood had spattered him like warm rain.

Then what? Lenny. He remembered Lenny. Just standing there, saying nothing.

'*Save me, Lenny. Save me. Lenny, for God's sake.*'

'Who's Lenny?' the nun asked.

John focused his eyes. He suddenly realized that he had been calling out loud.

'Lenny's my son. My son by my first wife.'

The nun said, 'Would you like me to call Mr Pelling and have him brought down here?'

John nodded. 'Yes, I'd like that. What time is it?'

'Almost lunchtime. Are you hungry?'

He glanced up at the dextrose drip that was hanging above the head of his bed. 'I think this'll do me for now. I'm feeling a little sick.'

'Any pain?' the nun asked.

'A sharp twinge in the back, that's all. It feels exactly like somebody's clamping my spine in a vise.'

The nun said, 'I'll find Dr Freytag and tell him you're awake.'

She went toward the door, but then she stopped, came back, and said, very gently, 'I'm sorry I had to tell you such terrible news. They teach us to be direct, you see, and to tell our patients the truth. There's no torture so bad as not knowing.'

'Yes,' said John.

'To lose your lovely wife, though, and to suffer such injuries ...'

John was unable to speak. He was crying again. This time, the nun cried with him. She bent forward to hold him close, giving him the comfort of starched cotton and human warmth. 'Oh, my poor man, you've lost everything,' she cried. 'But God will help you; God will protect you.'

They clung together for a long time. At last John said, 'I'm okay now. Thanks. I'm going to be fine.'

'Well, if there's anything you want ...'

'Who do I ask for?'

'Sister Perpetua. That's me. I'm always on duty at this time of day, and if I'm not, well, Sister Clare will help you just as well.'

'And you'd better call me John.'

Sister Perpetua smiled. 'John,' she said. 'The best of names.'

John lay there and looked at her. She was no beauty, but her love and charity made up for that.

'God will be with you,' she said.

John shook his head. 'I don't think so.'

She touched his cheek with cool fingertips. "If I take the wings of the morning, and dwell in the uttermost parts of the sea; even there shall Thy hand lead me, and Thy right hand shall hold me."

She turned and left, and he lay on his back staring at the ceiling and pouring out tears as if they would never stop.

Lenny came to see him at three o'clock. Grave, pale, wearing a gray cotton windbreaker that John had never seen before. He came into the room and stood with his hands in his pockets, looking at his father and biting his lip.

'Lenny?' said John hoarsely.

'Hullo, Dad,' said Lenny.

'Sit down; you can pull up that chair over there. How are things?' Did Mr Pelling bring you down here?'

Lenny remained standing. 'Mr Pelling told me you won't be able to walk.'

John attempted a smile. 'Well, maybe I won't and maybe I will. We're going to have to see about that. I talked to my doctor today and he seems to think there's a chance. Not much of a chance, but a chance.'

'Daddy,' said Lenny, 'I'm real sorry about what happened.'

'Well, me too,' John breathed.

Lenny came closer, and took hold of his father's hand. It was a strikingly adult gesture. 'You don't understand, I mean I'm *sorry*.'

'Listen, it wasn't your fault.'

'It was, Daddy. It was *all* my fault. I should have listened to that detective.'

John tried to lift his head, but couldn't. 'You mean that detective who was supposed to have said something to you but didn't?'

'You still don't believe me, do you?' Lenny protested.

John said, 'Forgive me. Will you forgive me? I'm more than a little crazy at the moment. Apart from that, they've given me every painkilling drug known to medical science. They could cut both my legs off and I wouldn't even notice.'

'He said I was one of them,' said Lenny.

John closed his eyes for a moment to calm himself down, then opened them again. 'Have you any idea what that means, "one of them"? When I was a kid, that used to mean that you were a faggot.'

'Detective Clay didn't mean that,' Lenny replied. 'It means – I don't know. I understand what it means, but I can't explain it.'

John looked at his son and smiled. 'You don't have to explain anything, and you don't have to apologize for anything.'

'But I *do*, Daddy. I have to explain. Otherwise it could happen again.'

'What do you mean, it could happen again?'

'Well, the first time it tore up your room, and the second time it killed Jennifer and made you a cripple, but what if it wants *more*? What if it's going to go on chasing you, until you're dead?'

John's voice was unsteady with emotion. 'Lenny, I love you, but this is nonsense. Whatever happened at Chestnut Hill was nothing to do with you and it was nothing to do with me. Somebody broke into the house and attacked us. That's all. It was just one of those acts of totally mindless violence. Sometimes people do things like that, for no reason that anybody can think of. You remember the guy who splashed gasoline on the people in a supermarket line and set them alight? Or the other guy who shot all those people at McDonald's? Mindless, totally crazy. They have some kind of personality disorder, and one day it just takes over and they start to believe that they're Rambo or Freddie Krueger or something. That's all.'

Lenny said nothing, watching his father with eyes that were unusually opaque. Then he turned and dragged the chair over, and sat very close to the bed.

'Daddy,' he said softly. 'I saw Mommy again.'

'Lenny,' John told him, 'I'm not sure I want to hear that stuff about Mommy anymore.'

'It isn't stuff, it's true. I saw her yesterday, at Mr Pelling's house, just before I went to bed. She was standing on the lawn and she was waving to me.'

John closed his eyes for a moment. Then he said, 'Lenny, will you please get it through your head that Mommy is dead. Jennifer is dead, too, and your daddy can't even look after himself right now, let alone you. You're going to have to come to grips with reality, Lenny, with real life.'

'Daddy,' Lenny insisted. 'I *saw* her. I keep thinking that she wants to tell me something.'

'It's a hallucination, Lenny. It's your mind playing tricks on you.'

Lenny was about to insist yet again that it wasn't; but then John winced and grunted, and even though he was only nine years old, Lenny realized that he was causing his daddy a lot of pain, both physical and mental. He lowered his head and said, 'Okay, Daddy. I guess you're right.'

John said, 'How are you getting along with Mr Pelling?'

'Okay. He's great. He lets me stay up to watch *Twilight Zone*.'

'You're not too homesick?'

Lenny hesitated for a moment, and then he said, his head still lowered, 'I cry sometimes.'

'Well, me too,' admitted John.

There was silence between them for a long moment. Then John said gently, 'Lenny … that night at Mr Pelling's house when Jennifer was killed – did you hear anything, or see anything?'

Lenny shook his head. 'I was asleep. I didn't wake up till I heard Jennifer screaming.'

'Then what did you do?'

'I ran into your bedroom, and you were lying on the floor and Jennifer was all bloody.'

'But you didn't see the man who did it? You didn't even get a glimpse?'

'No, sir.'

John lifted his head up a little, then let it fall back onto the pillow. 'Did the police talk to you?'

Lenny nodded.

'Who was it, Sergeant Clay?'

Lenny nodded again. 'Him and two others.'

'Yes, I guessed it would be,' said John. 'Sergeant Clay is supposed to come see me this afternoon.'

Lenny looked up, and his eyes were bright and serious. 'You won't be angry with him, will you, Daddy? Not like you were before. He understands what's happening.'

'Oh, really? And what *is* happening?'

But before Lenny could answer, the door opened and Sister Perpetua ushered Jack Pelling into the room. Jack was a big, heavily built man, a one-time quarterback for Philly U, with wavy iron-gray hair and a generous, German-ugly face. He approached John's bedside, laid his hand on Lenny's shoulder, and said, 'John … I don't know what to say to you. I just don't have the words.'

John said, 'You're looking after Lenny for me. That's a whole lot more helpful than words.'

'But Jenny…' said Jack. 'She was such a goddamned beautiful girl.'

'I know,' said John, and those hot tears started again. Lenny tugged out a Kleenex and dabbed at his father's eyes.

'The police have no idea what happened,' Jack explained. 'There was no sign of a forced entry into the house – the alarm system was still switched on, and nobody had triggered it. The way I understand it, those thick-headed flatfoots at Chestnut Hill were trying to pin it on you to begin with, until the hospital gave them all the details of your injuries. Let's put it this way: there is no way in the world that anybody could have done to himself what that maniac did to you.'

'And they still don't know who did it?' asked John.

'See for yourself,' Jack told him. He produced a folded copy of the *Philadelphia News* from his coat pocket. The second lead read, 'Chestnut Hill Slasher – Police Admit "We're Still At Square One."'

'They have no clues whatsoever,' said Jack. 'There were no footprints, no fingertrips, no tire tracks, no fibers, no apparent access to the house, and no apparent escape route. No authorized vehicles were seen in the vicinity, no vagrants, nothing. Whoever it was who attacked you, and whatever the reason, he came and went like a goddamned ghost.'

John said, 'I've been lying here trying to think who could have done it. I guess it must have been the same person who tore up our bedroom on Third Street. But *who*? And *why*? Neither of us knew anybody who hated us *that* much.'

Jack ran his hand through his hair. 'The police questioned Pete Marcowicz – you know, Jennifer's ex.'

'And?'

'He *could* have had some kind of motive for attacking her, I suppose. Jealousy, revenge, who knows? He was pretty stuck on her, wasn't he? But that night he was

63

staying with some friends in South Philly, and his friends all testify that he was totally smashed. He couldn't even stand up, let alone drive all the way to Chestnut Hill and murder anybody.'

John lay silent for a while. Then he said, 'Dr Freytag should be operating at the end of next week, if I'm strong enough. They're going to try to get my arms working. At least I'll be able to blow my own nose.'

'Don't you worry, John,' Jack told him. 'Nancy and I will be taking extra-special care of Lenny while you're getting well. And everybody down at the *News* is rooting for you.'

'What are they doing?' asked John with unconcealed bitterness. 'Taking up a collection to buy me a wheelchair?'

Jack gave him a wry smile. 'You're alive, John. That's what counts.'

John said, 'I'm not so sure. But thanks anyway.'

John ate a small lunch of corned beef and cabbage, fed every forkful by the saintly Sister Perpetua. It was exhausting, eating like this, with his head lifted up on Sister Perpetua's arm, and he was beginning to find his paralysis deeply frustrating.

At first, he had found the severity of his injuries peculiarly comforting. They were proof to everybody that he had suffered almost as terribly as Jennifer. In one sense, because he was still alive, he had suffered more, and he would certainly suffer longer. All this had helped to assuage the guilt that he had survived while Jennifer had died.

Being paralyzed also meant that everything was done for him. He was fed, he was washed, he was changed. He had been forced to surrender all of his adult responsibilities. He was a baby once again, the center of everybody's attention, and the focus of their pity.

But now he was beginning to understand the true horror of having an active mind in a helpless body. Even if he wanted nothing more than a sip of water, all he could do was to grope for his buzzer with his teeth, and wait for somebody to find the time to bring it to him.

As the hours went by and his pain began to ease, he began to think about the outside world once again, flickers and flashes of happy memory like an album of Kodachromes being tipped out onto the bed. The small agonies those thoughts brought were so intense that he forced himself to empty his mind and concentrate on the hairline cracks in the ceiling, or the time, or what Sister Perpetua must look like under her habit. Did she wear black stockings and a garter belt? Were her thighs fat and white?

So many pleasures that he had taken for granted were gone forever, even if Dr Freytag was able to give him back the use of his arms. He would never again be able to amble around Chinatown on a Saturday morning, elbowing his way into the Lung Fung Bakery. There would be no more visits to Reading Terminal Market for a giant hoagy from Di Gulielmo, to be eaten hot and crusty all the way down Arch Street while kicking a Coke can. And jogging around the East Park Reservoir was out of the question, as was his famous run through the Italian Market, on the same route that Sylvester Stallone had taken in *Rocky*, chased by crowds of small boys jeering, 'Rock-ee! Rock-ee!'

He would never know a woman again. He would never be able to make love. It would be a surgical miracle if he were capable even of masturbation.

God, he thought, his eyes filling with tears of frustration. A life sentence of wheelchairs and loneliness and adult-sized diapers and *Hustler* magazines. The awfulness of it was overwhelming.

* * *

He was still in a state of deep depression when Sister Perpetua came in with Sergeant Clay and Detective Clay. They stood behind her, tall and polite, both wearing sport coats, one blue, one brown, and permanent-press slacks to match.

Sergeant Clay said, 'We understand the seriousness of your condition, Mr Woods. We also want to tell you that you're not a suspect. So, if you prefer, we can come back to see you some other time.'

'That's all right,' said John in a clogged voice. 'I think I could use some company.'

Sergeant Clay drew up a chair and sat close to the bed. He and John looked at each other for a long time without speaking. John had never noticed before how fine the texture of Sergeant Clay's skin was. It was completely unblemished, like smooth milk chocolate, and if he shaved at all it didn't show.

'We want to tell you how sorry we are,' said Sergeant Clay finally. 'We feel like we failed you.'

John turned his face away. 'You couldn't have known that he was going to follow us all the way to Chestnut Hill.'

'Well, no, we couldn't, not for sure. But my brother had a suspicion, you see, and the fact is that we didn't take it any further. We talked about it, but we decided it would be better if we took no immediate action.' Sergeant Clay paused, and then he said, much more softly, 'As it turned out, we made the wrong decision.'

John turned back and frowned at him. 'You had a suspicion? *What* suspicion?'

Sergeant Clay glanced at his twin as if he were seeking approval for what he was going to say next. His twin, impassive, nodded his assent.

'We're going to have to ask you to believe some things that may be difficult to believe,' said Sergeant Clay. 'But if you'll hear us out, you can make up your own mind, and then maybe you can help us to prevent this happening again.'

John said, 'Go ahead. I've got all the time in the world.'

'You may have noticed that my brother has some unusual senses. He was born that way, with a highly developed sense of hearing, a highly developed sense of smell, and a highly developed sense of touch. He can hear dog-whistles; he can smell the difference between one brand of cigarette and another from twenty feet away. He can run his hand across a rug and tell you how many people walked across it recently, and what they weighed, and what kind of shoes they were wearing.'

'Can he tell me who killed my wife?' asked John bluntly.

'He can tell you who *didn't* kill your wife.'

'And what's that supposed to mean?'

Sergeant Clay inclined his head to one side. 'It means that he not only senses things in the physical world – smells, noises, that kind of thing – but he has a sixth sense, too. A feeling for the paranormal.'

'So?'

'So he sensed quite distinctly, Mr Woods, that whatever vandalized your bedroom on Third Street and killed your wife wasn't human. It was a *being* of sorts, he's certain of that. But it sure wasn't a human being.'

John responded with a high-pitched grunt of derision that was almost a laugh: *hih*! 'So tell me, Sergeant, where did this nonhuman being come from? Did it walk through the walls, or come down the chimney, or what?'

Sergeant Clay said, 'I didn't say that this would be easy for you to believe, Mr Woods. It's not so easy to explain, either. So give me a break, will you, and listen? When we came around to your house the day after the break-in, my brother detected a supernatural presence. A very strong presence, believe me. It was almost as strong as if somebody else was standing in the room. My brother was ninety-nine percent sure that this being came from your son, Lenny.'

John stared at him. 'What the hell are you trying to tell me? That my nine-year old son is capable of paralyzing me and murdering my wife? It's just not physically possible! He couldn't! And not only couldn't, he *wouldn't*!'

'Mr Woods,' Sergeant Clay said soothingly, 'we're not saying that your son committed these offenses. What we're saying is that something *came out* of your son; something *used* your son as a way to enter your house. Your son involuntarily acted as a medium, if you follow me. He was probably asleep when it happened and didn't even know.'

Behind him, Detective Clay nodded in agreement.

John said, 'You're detectives, right? Police officers?'

'That's right,' said Sergeant Clay.

'You have serious training in crime detection, right? And you're looking for a homicidal maniac? And you're talking about *ghosts*?'

'Listen, Mr Woods,' said Sergeant Clay, 'we haven't stinted on this investigation. We've pursued it by the book, all the way along the line. We've already interviewed more than two hundred potential witnesses house-to-house; we've run the *modus operandi* through the FBI computers. We've analyzed every scrap of forensic evidence, and the autopsy of your wife's body was carried out by one of the most thorough and respected medical examiners in the country. You can't accuse us on any count of being slapdash. No way. But the fact remains that this crime is totally extraordinary, and in our opinion there may be something to be said for trying to solve it by lateral thinking.'

'You accuse a ghost of killing my wife and call that lateral thinking?' John protested.

'You were the one who used the word 'ghost', Mr Woods. We prefer to call it the paranormal.'

'The paranormal?' said John, with almost as much skepticism.

'Well, what happened to you and your wife sure wasn't *normal*, was it? And we have to check out all the possibilities. A dangerous manifestation from a different plane of existence is one of the possibilities – far-fetched, I'll grant you, and not very easy to deal with, physically or mentally. But we have to consider it – especially since Lenny gives out strong psychic vibes. My brother could feel that the moment he met him. Your son isn't so much a medium, if you can understand what I'm saying, as a *carrier*. You could almost say that he's infected by some kind of psychic influence.'

John closed his eyes, trying to absorb all of this. He felt emotionally exhausted. 'Listen, Sergeant,' he said, his eyes still closed, 'all I want you to do is go out there and find the crazy who killed my wife.'

'I know you do, Mr Woods, but what I'm trying to tell you is that it may not be possible. The killer may not exist in the real world. That's one of the reasons I've come here today. I want your permission to put Lenny through some tests.'

John opened his eyes. 'Tests? What kind of tests?'

'We want to see whether he's in some sort of psychic communication with – well, with this different plane of existence I was talking about.'

'Is this official? Do you have the approval of the police department to do this?'

'To be quite frank, sir, no.'

'Have you even asked them?'

Sergeant Clay shook his head. 'Commissioner Lodge is not exactly an enthusiastic devotee of paranormal police work, sir. We did try to trace a missing woman once using a Dutch psychic called Piet van der Valk, and I don't think Commissioner Lodge was overly impressed with the results. Well, there weren't any results. We never found her.'

'Where would these tests take place?' asked John.

'At the University of Pennsylvania, in the Department of Paranormal Psychology, on Spruce Street. Professor Dianne Wesley has been conducting a whole series of tests on children's psychic abilities.'

'And what would Lenny have to do?'

'Well, he'd obviously have to recreate the experience that led to you and your wife being attacked. That's the only way we'd be able to find out what happened for sure.'

John said, 'Are you putting me on? You want my permission for my son to go through that whole experience all over again?'

Sergeant Clay looked serious. 'I honestly believe that it's the only way.'

'Well, I honestly believe that it's ridiculous and ill-considered and potentially very dangerous. I'm not at all surprised that Commissioner Lodge wouldn't allow it. That boy has been through quite enough, losing his mother and then losing his stepmother and having me crippled like this. You leave him alone. Good God Almighty, he's already having hallucinations that his mother's waving to him!'

Detective Clay lifted his head abruptly when he heard this, and leaned forward to whisper something in his twin's ear.

Sergeant Clay asked, 'Is this true? Lenny's been seeing his dead mother?'

'Three or four times,' John told him. 'Not that it's

anything to do with you.'

'Mr Woods, it could be everything to do with us. If Lenny has been seeing his mother, that means he could be the focus for some pretty intense psychic activity. You know what happens at séances, when people get messages from their loved ones in the spirit world, warning them about accidents or forthcoming financial problems or whatever? It's like a very high-powered version of that. Lenny's mother could well have been trying to alert him that something bad was about to happen.'

'Sergeant Clay,' said John, 'do you really believe all of this, or are you trying to make a fool out of me?'

'Mr Woods, my brother and I believe with complete sincerity that you were assaulted by some nonhuman manifestation. Has your son seen his late mother *since* the attack?'

'He claims to have done. I told him that it was just a hallucination.'

'And what did he say to that?'

'He agreed, I guess. What else could it have been? My first wife had been dead and buried for three years. It was a trick of the mind, Sergeant Clay. Lenny's under a whole lot of stress, so it's hardly surprising that he's seeing things.'

Sergeant Clay said soberly, 'You'd better call me Thaddeus.'

John looked at him, uncertain what the man was getting at.

'The thing is, Mr Woods,' Sergeant Clay continued, 'if your son's been visited by his mother *since* you were attacked, then you and I are going to be seeing a whole lot more of each other, and if we're going to be seeing a whole lot more of each other, we might just as well be first-name friends.'

'Sergeant Clay – Thaddeus – I'm not sure that I *want*

to be first-name friends. And besides, why should we be seeing each other anymore? The only time I want to see you is when you come in here and tell me that you've caught the lunatic who killed Jennifer.'

'That's understood, Mr Woods. But if Lenny has been visited by his dead mother since the attack on you, the likelihood is that history is going to repeat itself.'

'What?'

'You heard me, Mr Woods. It's going to happen again.'

Five

Jack Pelling spent most of the evening on the telephone, talking to his chairman in Venezuela. When he came out of his study, Lenny was ready for bed, sitting by the fireplace in the grandiose Italianate sitting room, while Jack's wife, Nancy, read him an excerpt from *Sea-Shore Fancies* by Walt Whitman.

Nancy was a handsome woman, with swept-back blond hair. Lenny always thought she looked like Krystle in *Dynasty*. Her voice was clear and inspiring, and he loved listening to her read, his back against the sofa, his legs tucked up inside the warm maroon robe that the Pellings had lent him.

Jack stood in the doorway, a glass of Jack Daniels' in his hand, and listened, too.

'''There is a dream, a picture, that for years at intervals has come noiselessly up before me. It is nothing more or less than a stretch of interminable white-brown sand, hard and smooth and broad, with the ocean perpetually, grandly, rolling in upon it, with slow-measured sweep, with rustle and hiss and foam, and many a thump as of low bass drums. Sometimes I wake at night and can hear and see it plainly.'''

'Some dream,' Jack remarked. He walked into the sitting room and sat down on the glazed-cotton sofa. Nancy closed the book and smiled.

'How's Todd?' she asked.

'Unhappy. He hates Caracas. But he should be through by Wednesday.'

Lenny said, 'Could I watch TV for a while?'

Jack checked his watch. 'Okay, but just for a half hour. Have you done your homework?'

'Yes, sir.'

Nancy got up from her lotus position on the floor. She was wearing a pantsuit of pale blue silk, which showed off her narrow-hipped figure. Jennifer had always said that Nancy was very well *groomed*. She hadn't meant it particularly kindly; but then she and Nancy had never gotten along particularly well. Their husbands had played backgammon together, and that was about all they had ever had in common.

'I'll take you up to bed,' she told Lenny. 'Jack, would you make me a champagne cocktail?'

'Sure thing,' Jack said, then reached out and scruffed Lenny's hair. 'G'night, champ. Sweet dreams.'

'Good night, sir,' Lenny replied, avoiding his eyes.

When Nancy returned, Jack had taken off his Gucci loafers and was stretched out on the sofa with his arms comfortably tucked behind his head. She sat down beside him and put her arm around his waist.

'You're marvelous with him,' Jack remarked.

'I hope you're not forgetting that we had two boys of our own.'

'No, but looking after Lenny, after all he's been through – this is different. This is *hard*.'

Nancy picked up her champagne cocktail and said, '*Prost!*' She took a sip. 'It isn't that much of a problem. He's very sweet, very helpful. Do you know what he said today? That he'd cook supper tomorrow night if I wanted him to. Isn't that sweet? I asked him what he could cook, and he said hamburgers and beans and toasted marshmallows.'

'My favorite,' Jack said, laughing. 'If only my stomach

74

could take it!'

They sat together for more than an hour, talking and drinking and laughing. Ever since Jack had been appointed chairman of the executive committee at the *Philadelphia News* group, they had seen very little of each other. The days were taken up with meetings and the evenings were devoured by telephone calls. They had come to value each other's company more than ever.

'You ought to retire,' said Nancy. 'We could live in a country cottage and walk around naked, just the way Walt Whitman used to.'

'Walt Whitman was a homosexual.'

'He wasn't a *practicing* homosexual.'

Jack swallowed whiskey. 'I didn't know you had to *practise* to be a homosexual.'

'Oh, you know what I mean,' said Nancy. 'But some of his descriptions of Philadelphia in the 1870s are absolutely marvelous. Do you know what he said about Chestnut Street in spring? "A myriad-moving human panorama." You ought to read it sometime.'

'I have enough trouble finding the time to read the weekly sales profiles, let alone Walt Whitman.'

They sat for a little while in contented silence. 'Do you want another drink.' Jack asked, but before she could answer they suddenly heard an odd, lopsided shuffle-bang upstairs, as if somebody had fallen over or were trying to move a heavy piece of furniture.

'What do you think that was?' Nancy asked. 'It wasn't Lenny, I hope.'

'Sounded like he fell out of bed,' Jack remarked. He put down his glass and stood up. 'I'd better go see.'

But Nancy suddenly snatched at his leg and said, 'Jack – be careful. Just remember what happened to John and Jennifer.'

'You don't think that he's going to come back, do you? That *would* be crazy.'

'Just be careful, that's all.'

Jack leaned forward and kissed her hair. 'I'll be careful, all right?'

He went through to the hallway and stood at the bottom of the stairs, listening. 'Lenny?' he called. He was darkly observed by an Italian painting of the Doge of Venice, hanging on a pale yellow wall. 'Lenny? Was that you? Are you okay?'

Nancy came out into the hallway, too, carrying her glass. 'Is he all right?' she asked.

'I'm not sure. I think I'd better go up and take a look.'

'Jack –' Nancy began, but Jack raised his hand to hush her.

'Whoever attacked John and Jennifer, honey, they wouldn't *dare* to come back. In any case, it's pretty clear that they were after John, not me. Didn't they follow him here from Third Street?'

Nancy bit her lip. 'Supposing he thinks that John is still here?'

'In that case, he's so crazy that he never reads a newspaper or looks at the television news.'

'Jack,' said Nancy, 'there *are* people like that.'

Jack couldn't help smiling, and kissing her. 'There are also people who don't like cheese-steak, but you won't find them in Philly.'

Confidently, he climbed the yellow-carpeted stairs. As he reached the half-landing he said, 'Don't look so *worried*. More than likely, Lenny went to the bathroom and tripped over the clothes basket.'

He reached the upstairs corridor and flicked the light switch, but the hall remained dark. All the bulbs had gone. 'Drat,' he breathed, and made his way toward the small guest room right at the very end where they had installed Lenny. On the way he passed the door to the guest room in which John and Jennifer had been attacked. It had already been stripped and cleaned, and Jack had locked it. All the same, he stopped and tried the handle, just to make sure. It was locked.

He flicked down the light switch halfway along the corridor, but that didn't work, either. Perhaps one of the fuses had blown. That occasionally happened on hot summer nights, when everybody in Chestnut Hill switched on their air-conditioning all at once, and created a localized power surge.

'Lenny?' called Jack. 'Lenny, it's Uncle Jack. Is everything okay?'

He opened the white-painted door of Lenny's bedroom. It was so dark in there that he might as well have been wearing a black felt executioner's hood over his head. He waited, listening. He thought he could make out Lenny's harsh, regular breathing; but he thought he could make out an *echo*, almost – as if somebody else was there, too, breathing in the same rhythm as Lenny to avoid detection.

Jack stood in the doorway and listened and listened, and still couldn't make up his mind whether he could distinguish one person breathing, or two.

'Lenny?' he whispered, and took a single step into the room.

It was then that he realized there was something there. Something cold; something huge. Something that wasn't Lenny at all; something that wasn't even human, but was somehow alive. He felt a cold shiver all the way down his back, and he dampened his shorts with a single involuntary squirt of urine. Fear, genuine fear. The kind of fear that paralyzes people when buildings collapse on top of them. His heart almost stopped.

'Who's there?' he demanded. His voice sounded weak and flat. 'Is there somebody there?'

The choice before him was terrifying. Either he could grope his way farther into the room to see what it was that was waiting for him here; or else he could retreat quickly and pretend to Nancy that there was nothing here at all, and then wait for it to do to Lenny whatever it had entered the house to do. But after it had finished with Lenny? Maybe them, too, if he didn't get them out of here quick.

'Listen, buddy,' he said out loud, in a voice that he hoped was confident and intimidating, 'I don't know who the hell you are or what the hell you're doing here, but my suggestion to you is that you get out of here pronto, the way you came in, and that you never come back here again. I called the police already. They're on their way. Give them three minutes, pal, and they're going to be clicking those cuffs on you pretty goddamned quick.'

He stopped talking. He realized that while he was talking, the resonance of his own words inside his skull prevented him from hearing what *it* was doing. He listened. Had it come closer? Was there anything in the room at all, apart from him and Lenny and his own abject terror?

But he was sure that he could feel a coldness, an emptiness; a vacuum of extreme hostility.

'I'm going to give you five,' he said unsteadily. *Five, why five? Why not give it five million and run like hell?* 'When I've finished counting five, you've got two choices, do you understand me? *Do you understand me?*'

Again, there was nothing but that light, constricted breathing – that breathing that might be nothing more than an echo of Lenny's breathing. *Only this and nothing more.*

'One,' he counted. From downstairs, he heard Nancy calling to him.

'Jack? Are you all right? How's Lenny?'

78

'Two,' he said, then shouted, 'Nancy, honey, don't come up! Everything's fine! I'll be down in just a moment!'

'Jack? What did you say? Jack!'

'Three,' said Jack.

He wasn't sure, but he thought he could feel the coldness intensifying. He thought he could see something rising in the darkness: huge, distorted, like a man's shadow when he stands in front of a lamp. Something that moved toward him with whispers of intolerable dread.

'Deep into that darkness peering, long I stood there wondering, fearing.

Doubting, dreaming dreams no mortal ever dared to dream before.'

'Four,' he said, and his voice was no more audible than a leaf turning in the wind.

'Five –'

And at that instant Nancy came marching purposefully along the corridor, saying, 'Jack, for goodness' sake, what *are* you playing at!'

Something slashed out of the darkness with an audible rush of air. Jack felt something brush his face, something cold and sharp, and stepped back in bewilderment. He turned to Nancy.

All that Nancy could see in the dimness was that his cheeks were hanging in inch-wide bloody ribbons and that one of his eyes had been split exactly in half. She said, '*Jack?*' unable to believe what she was seeing; but then Jack was wrenched back into the bedroom in a spray of blood, and Nancy screamed and screamed and dropped to her knees on the carpet.

'Jack! Jack! What's happening? Jack!'

There was a moment's dreadful pause. Then, from the bedroom doorway, something black and huge emerged. Nancy could do nothing but kneel in the corridor, staring at it in abject terror.

'Oh, God,' she prayed; and then the claws whistled like knives, and her head bounced from her shoulders and rolled all the way along the corridor, emptying out blood like an overturned bucket. The claws whistled again, and her blue silk pantsuit was torn into scarlet shreds.

Lenny's eyes opened suddenly, as if somebody had shaken him awake. He was trembling, and his pajamas were wet with sweat. He lay still for a very long time, not daring to lift his head.

His nightmare gradually shrank from his mind. The blackness. The power. The overwhelming urge to cut everything to pieces. He reached up and felt his face, and he was almost surprised to find that he was still the same boy.

But what if it had all been true? What if it had really happened – the way it had happened with Jennifer? He had dreamed the dream, and when he had woken up she was really dead.

He lifted himself up on his elbow and strained his eyes to see into the darkness. He found the bedside lamp, and switched it on. And then he saw the bright squiggles of blood on the corridor wall outside. A Jackson Pollock painting in human gore.

He licked his lips. They were dry as chrysalises. 'Mr Pelling?' he called. 'Mr Pelling?'

There was no reply. The house was silent. And even before he reached his bedroom door and saw Jack and Nancy ripped into bloody strings of meat, Lenny knew for certain that the nightmare had all been true.

Six

John was sitting propped up in a wheelchair in the hospital garden, enjoying the early-morning sun and the conversation of his fellow patients. There were five of them altogether, and their wheelchairs had been pushed out onto the red-brick patio overlooking the gardens, under the shade of a broad, dark Philadelphia cedar.

John was the most recently disabled. Next to him sat a twelve-year-old black boy called Toussaint who had contracted polio when he was seven months old, and had never known what it was like to walk. Toussaint was fine-featured and handsome and flip, and could play the acoustic guitar better than anyone John had ever heard.

There was Billy, overweight and bespectacled and clownish. Billy had once been thin and good-looking, but when he was eighteen he had overturned his secondhand TransAm and damaged his spinal column. He had been lucky not to lose his sight, too, because both of his eyes had come out of their sockets.

Billy was twenty-four. He would never dance, would never make love. He had nothing to look forward to but operations and chess and more operations, and an occasional part-time job working a lathe at Conrail. But Billy was always funny, always facetious.

There was Dean, who had lost both legs at Long Binh, and whose demeanor was permanently sour. Mean Dean, Toussaint had christened him. Mean Dean was thirty-six now, and smoked tiny, damp, hand-rolled cigarettes, perpetually sucking at three or four strands of tobacco with drawn-in cheeks. His eyes were as blank as pebbles. He rarely uttered more than two or three words at a time, and John had never seen him smile.

Lastly there was a young Korean, So Che-u, small-featured and oddly old-looking, with a close-shaved scalp and pointed ears, like Yoda. So Che-u's father owned a chain of Korean eateries throughout the Northeast, the Yi Dynasty Restaurants. Che-u had been born quadriplegic, and although he had been trained through years of therapy not to twist and writhe in constant athetosis, he was unable to willfully move any part of his body except his neck. He could paint, however, using bamboo brushes that he held between his teeth, and he wrote with the aid of an electronic typewriter. He wrote short, sad, mysterious letters, to nobody in particular, which he never mailed.

Billy was telling a joke, while the rest of them sat in their wheelchairs with their eyes closed againt the warm summer sun. The cedar berries, blue and bitter, bobbed in the southwesterly breeze.

'This guy walks into a brothel and pulls out a big roll of money and says, "Give me the ugliest girl you got." Well, the madame says, "Mister, for that money, you can have the very best." But he says, "Listen, lady, I'm not horny, I'm homesick." '

John gave a short laugh, just to be polite, but none of the others did. They had obviously heard the story before, or else they had read the same men's magazines in which Billy had found it. Mean Dean leaned sideways and spat tobacco juice into the pebbles that surrounded the cedar.

'Did you ever hear the one about the singing dick?'
Billy wanted to know.

But Toussaint said, 'Do you know what I feel like? I
feel like a big plate of charred barbecued ribs, with
hush puppies and buttered greens.'

'I could do with a cold beer,' said Billy. 'And a nude
woman with huge bazookas rubbing my back.'

'I'd settle for a stroll around the block,' John put in.

Che-u gave them a lopsided smile. 'Wishful
thinking, fellows. What you're going to get is Salisbury
steak and instant mashed potatoes, a bed-bath from
Sister Perpetua, and a whole night of lying flat on your
back until somebody remembers that you're still alive
and condescends to move you around.'

John said, 'You know, being so helpless – that's hit
me harder than anything else. And the way you have
to keep politely reminding people to do things for
you.'

Mean Dean relit his miniature cigarette with a huge,
flaring Zippo. 'It gets worse,' he remarked laconically.

'You become totally invisible.' said Billy. 'Little by
little, you vanish. First of all your family and friends
stop visiting you so frequent, and even when they *do*
turn up they spend most of their time talking to each
other like you weren't there.'

'Going out in the street, man, that's the worst,'
Toussaint told John.

'That's right,' put in Che-u. 'Even when somebody is
kind enough to wheel you out for a walk, people in the
street hurry past you as if you don't exist. They talk to
your *nurse*, sure. But they won't even look down at you
sitting there. Occasionally they might talk *about* you,
but they never ask you questions direct. I've even had
people spell out words to my nurse because they
thought I wouldn't be able to understand what they

were saying. Like, "Does he have very long to L-I-V-E?"'

Billy nodded. 'You know, that time Sister Xavier took me to see the flower show, some woman did that exact same thing to me. She was primping up this display of daisies, and she leaned right over in front of me and said, "I suppose he needs to wear a D-I-A-P-E-R." And I piped up and said, "Ma'am, I can use the doings as good as anyone else. I can sit on the seat without falling off and if it's an old-fashioned toilet I can pull the chain with my teeth. All I need is somebody like you with nice soft flower-arranger's hands to wipe my ass when I'm finished." And she stared at me like I was terrible and crazy, and how did I *dare* to embarrass her like that? Me, a cripple.'

'Well,' said Che-u, smiling 'you just have to be philosophical. In our society, physical perfection counts for so much.'

'Bullshit,' put in Billy. 'Physical perfection counts for *everything*.'

'I never realized that handicapped people felt so bitter,' John remarked.

'Bitter?' said Dean. 'Handicapped people are never bitter! They sing and they smile and they shout out praise the Lord! Just like the darkies in the Deep South. And just like the darkies in the Deep South, they're banned from buses and restaurants and theaters, and they're treated like they're only half-human. But that doesn't stop them smiling and singing, because if they stopped smiling and singing then they wouldn't be treated like they're even *half*-human. No, sir! Handicapped people aren't bitter, excepting amongst themselves, and in private, when they hide their faces and curse God.'

It was the longest speech that Dean had made in a week, and it silenced everyone. John closed his eyes.

84

He heard the wind, the rustle of the cedar tree, the traffic. Toussaint picked up the guitar and began to play a delicate, complicated melody, full of regret. John began to wonder what kind of world this was that he had entered.

His eyes were still closed when someone laid a hand on his shoulder and said, 'Mr Woods? John?'

He squinted up against the brightness. It was Sergeant Thaddeus Clay, in mirror sunglasses and a snap-brim hat, with his twin brother standing close behind him.

'John, may I talk to you in private for a while?'

John was devastated to hear that Jack and Nancy Pelling had been murdered. He sat in his wheelchair and trembled with grief. Thaddeus Clay must have warned Sister Perpetua that he was bringing John some catastrophic news, because she came in almost immediately and offered him a sedative. John shook his head. He couldn't control his body, but he wanted to stay completely in control of his mind.

He felt as if he had been pitched into an ice-cold ocean. Gasping, breathless, struggling to keep his head above water.

Thaddeus said, 'Your son's been taken to the Graduate Hospital suffering from shock. I'm afraid that Chief Molyneux now regards him as the prime suspect. We'll be questioning him later today. He can't be tried for homicide, of course, but there's a strong possibility that he could be committed into psychiatric care.'

John took a deep, painful breath. 'Goddamn this useless body!'

But Thaddeus said, 'You can still help Lenny, you know, even though you're immobile.'

'How? What can I possibly do? I can't even help myself.'

'You remember those tests we mentioned? The paranormality tests at Penn U?'

'What about them?'

'If you authorize us to go ahead, we may be able to establish that Lenny was under the influence of paranormal forces – that he was acting against his will.'

John raised his head. 'So now you think that he *did* do it?'

'Not me,' said Thaddeus. 'Not for one moment. But Chief Molyneux thinks he did it, so for us to *believe* that he's innocent just isn't enough anymore – we have to *prove* that he's innocent.'

'But you think now that he actually committed these murders – that he took out a knife or something and killed Jennifer, and Jack and Nancy Pelling – even though he was under the influence of these ... paranormal forces?'

Thaddeus lowered his eyes. 'I'm sorry, John. The circumstantial evidence is overwhelming. In all three incidents – the bed-slashing, the killing of your wife, the killing of the Pellings last night – the house was locked from the inside. Your son was the only person who was present at all three incidents, apart from the victims themselves, and nobody else could have gotten in.'

'Thaddeus,' John protested, 'you've seen him for yourself – he's a nine-year-old boy with skinny arms and legs like pipe cleaners! Are you seriously trying to tell me that he could have blasted into the bedroom and knocked me over and slashed Jennifer to pieces like that? And then killed both of the Pellings, too?'

'He was under a paranormal influence,' Thaddeus insisted.

'You mean that he was possessed by the devil?'

'Not exactly,' said Thaddeus.

'Then what, exactly?'

'I don't know. It's impossible for me to say. That's why I'd like your permission to send him to Dr Wesley.'

'Dr Dianne Wesley, ghostbuster?'

Thaddeus shook his head. 'She's a very serious and competent physicist, believe me. She won the Benjamin Franklin Award two years ago for her work in paranormal communication. She actually established that the human personality outlives the moment of death for anything up to a half hour, and that theoretically the dead can communicate with us.'

John looked at Thaddeus and lifted his eyebrows to indicate his skepticism. He was amazed how much he missed being able to wave his hands around to add expression to his conversation.

'All right,' he said. 'So the serious and competent Dr Wesley will try to show that Lenny didn't *mean* to murder anybody, that he was acting under the influence of a strange power from beyond the grave?'

'It could certainly be shown that he wasn't responsible for what he did.'

'And that would hold up in a court of law?'

'We're not talking about a homicide charge here,' said Thaddeus. 'Lenny is below the age of criminal responsibility. But what we *are* talking about is the danger of Lenny being sent to a psychiatric institution – particularly since his only surviving relative is a quadriplegic. I'm sure that's something that you don't want to happen.'

'No,' said John in a dry voice.

'So you'll give your permission for the tests to be carried out?'

'They won't harm him in any way, these tests?' John asked.

'As far as I know, they don't involve anything more dangerous than EEGs.'

John hesitated for a moment, then nodded. 'All right. You can give it a try. Is there any chance of my seeing him?'

'I don't think so, John, not just now. It's going to be difficult enough persuading Chief Molyneux to let us take Lenny to Dr Wesley. Maybe afterward, when things have quieted down.'

'Okay,' said John resignedly. 'Would you call Sister Perpetua on your way out and tell that I'd like to get back into bed?'

But Norman Clay stepped forward without a word, and wheeled John right over beside his bed. Then he drew back the rug that covered John's knees, bent down, and picked him up. In the whole of his adult life, John had never been lifted right up by another man, and he felt more helpless than ever. But Norman Clay laid him gently on the bed and drew up the covers, and somehow there was nothing patronizing nor even particularly kind in the way that he did it. He did it simply because John was another human being and it needed to be done.

'Thank you,' John said. Norman Clay didn't reply, but momentarily closed his dark, Arabian-looking eyes, in the way that a cat acknowledges a stroke under the chin.

Thaddeus said, 'We'll call you later today. And we're real sorry about the Pellings.'

'Yes,' whispered John, staring at the ceiling.

Lenny sat in the day room at the Graduate Hospital on Lombard Street, all alone, watching television. The room was furnished in browns and oranges and smelled of Lysol and cigarette smoke. Out of the window, there was a view across the airshaft of scores of windows, in each of which a small real-life drama was being played out – nurses coming and going, patients staring blindly out at nothing at all, visitors with bunches of flowers looking for their relatives.

Lenny felt lethargic and found it difficult to stay awake. When the paramedics had discovered him at the Pelling home late last night, he had been shivering and incoherent. They had immediately sedated him and brought him here, and he had slept dreamlessly until early afternoon.

Now he sat in a plain blue hospital robe, dully watching *Days of Our Lives* and thinking of nothing at all. There was nothing to think about, except black things that rose up out of somewhere deep inside him, with the cold, insatiable urge to kill, and he couldn't even begin to think about that. It was far too frightening.

He decided he was thirsty, but he didn't know what to do about it. After a while, he got up from his chair and shuffled across to the doorway and looked out into the corridor. It was shiny and bare and deserted. He waited for a little while, to see if anybody would come along, but when no one did, he let the door close on its pneumatic hinges and turned back toward the television.

To his surprise, a man in a doctor's coverall was standing by the window, looking out – a blond, thin-faced man, quite slight, with his hands in his pockets and a stethoscope hanging around his neck. Lenny stared at him, completely unable to understand how he had managed to get into the room. There were no other doors except the door out of which Lenny had been peering. And Lenny supposed that he could have slipped past him somehow; or maybe he had been here all the time.

The doctor turned and smiled at him in a friendly way. 'Hello, Lenny. How are things?'

'Okay, I guess,' Lenny replied cautiously.

The doctor held out his hand. Lenny hesitated, then shook it.

'I'm Dr Springer. I've been taking a close interest in you.'

'Oh, yes?'

Dr Springer looked out the window a little while longer. 'Look at all those windows. They look like televisions in a television store, don't they? A different soap playing on every set.'

Lenny said nothing, waiting for Dr Springer to tell him why he was here. Grownups always wanted to have a chat first, before they got around to the point, though Lenny could never understand how they managed to think of so much to say, or why they even wanted to.

Dr Springer said, 'Something pretty nasty has been happening to you, hasn't it?'

Lenny frowned. Did Dr Springer know about the nightmares? About the surging black thing that rose up inside of him and wanted to kill people? How could he know?

Perhaps I've been talking in my sleep. Perhaps I've told the doctors everything, without knowing it. And if the doctors know, they'll tell the police, and they'll take me away and lock me up forever.

Dr Springer came over and sat down on the arm of the chair next to Lenny, still smiling. He had one of those friendly Dr Kildare faces that puts everybody at their ease. Only his eyes were strange. They glittered, and they had no color at all, like pinballs.

'It's those nightmares, isn't it?' he asked. 'You keep having those nightmares, and when you wake up, they're real.'

Lenny didn't answer, but stood in front of Dr Springer in his hospital robe and shivered. He didn't know why he was shivering. He wasn't cold; he wasn't

90

frightened. But he had the feeling that he was in the presence of somebody momentous, somebody who knew absolutely everything. Somebody who understood the secret things that went on during the night.

'When did they start, these nightmares?' Dr Springer asked. 'Have you been having them long?'

'How did you know about them?' Lenny asked, shivering.

Dr Springer smiled. 'It's my job. I guess you could say that I work for somebody who has a strong interest in the well-being of children everywhere, and that includes you.'

'Do I have to go to prison?'

'What for?' said Dr Springer. 'You didn't do anything.'

'But they were all killed, and I killed them!' It was an incredible relief for Lenny to be able to shout it out. He had wanted to tell his daddy about it, but how could he, when Daddy had loved Jenny so much? And how could he explain what had happened at the Pellings' house? It sounded like madness, even though Lenny knew that he wasn't mad. Or *hoped* he wasn't, anyway.

Dr Springer laid his hand on Lenny's shoulder and smiled. 'Something is happening here, Lenny. Something very dangerous and strange. You see, there are many different worlds, one within another, like a box within a box within a box. And what has happened now, to put it simply, is that one box has opened a little crack – do you understand what I'm saying? – and something inside of that box is trying to lever open the lid so that it can get into *our* box.'

Dr Springer was silent for a moment, still smiling. 'This creature that is trying to get out is very dangerous, very vicious. It's like a kind of devil, if you can understand me, but it's not a devil with horns and a tail. It's not real in the same way that this room is real, or *you're* real. I suppose the best way I can describe it is to say that it is all of the bad things that children ever dreamed about, come to life.'

Lenny frowned. He couldn't grasp any of this. Boxes? Devils? It was like one of those intelligence-test puzzles they set you at school.

Dr Springer said, 'You've been having nightmares, Lenny, and those nightmares have been just a little too vivid for comfort. Wouldn't you say that?'

Lenny didn't reply. *Nightmares, yes, I've had nightmares. Nightmares about screams, and darkness, and chaos. Nightmares about blackness rising. Nightmares about Jennifer's skin, and how softly it fell apart at the touch of razor-sharp claws, revealing white fat, scarlet muscle, bone, welling blood. Nightmares about Nancy's head, flying from her shoulders like a spinning top. Nightmares about Jack Pelling's face, a carnival of ripped-open flesh.*

He could remember those nightmares with complete clarity. Yet how could he talk to Dr Springer about something like that? How could Dr Springer understand about killing and slicing and cutting off heads?

'The police haven't told you yet, but they're going to give you some tests,' said Dr Springer flatly. 'They're going to take you along to the University of Pennsylvania. They want to find out what it is that's been making you behave so strangely.'

'But can't *you* tell them?' Lenny asked. 'All about the creature in the box, and stuff?'

Dr Springer smiled. 'I'm afraid not. They have to find out for themselves. Even if I told them, they'd still want to double-check. It's hard for people to believe in creatures in boxes, Lenny. It's hard for people to believe in anything they can't actually see.'

Lenny stared at him.

'Lenny,' said Dr Springer, 'I want you to do everything you can to help Sergeant Clay. The chief of detectives thinks that you killed all those people; but Sergeant Clay is pretty sure it wasn't you, and he wants to prove it. Your father has already said that the tests are okay, that it's the best thing to do.'

'My father? Have you seen him?'

'Let's just say that I know where he is.'

'And you don't believe it was me that killed Jennifer and Mr and Mrs Pelling?'

Dr Springer smiled. 'You don't have to worry about that. I *know* it wasn't you.'

Lenny sat down. 'When will they let me out of here?'

'You'll have to be patient,' Dr Springer told him. 'But as soon as your tests are all finished, I'm going to see what I can do to get you away from here. You won't see me again until then. But keep an eye open for somebody you know very well.'

Lenny was about to ask who, but that moment the door of the dayroom opened and a nurse came briskly in.

'Lenny? It's time for your medication.'

Lenny turned back to Dr Springer – but Dr Springer had vanished. Apart from Lenny, the room was empty. There was nothing to suggest that anybody else had just been there. The sunlight angled through the space where Dr Springer had been standing and fell onto the carpet.

Lenny stood up and walked across the room, waving his hand from side to side in the air. There was nothing there. Nothing at all.

'Are you okay?' the nurse asked him with a grin.

Lenny turned and stared at her. 'Yes,' he whispered. 'I think so.'

The nurse put an arm around his shoulder and led him out. 'Looked to me like you were playing blindman's bluff.'

'Sure,' said Lenny. 'Something like that.'

Seven

John's wheelchair was lowered to the sidewalk on the electric elevator at the back of the ambulance, and then Sister Perpetua rolled him up to the entrance of the University of Pennsylvania building. She was having trouble opening the side doors and pushing him into the lobby at the same time, and a girl student came across to help her.

'Thank you, dear,' said Sister Perpetua.

The girl smiled. 'You're welcome.'

But John noticed that the girl didn't once look at him. Sister Perpetua might have been pushing a shopping cart full of groceries.

Billy was right. The handicapped were almost invisible. People were afraid to look at them in case their pity or their disgust might unwittingly show on their faces, and betray their lack of humanity.

The lobby was high and echoing, with a polished marble floor. Sister Perpetua wheeled John up to the reception desk. Sitting in his wheelchair, he couldn't even see over the top of it. He sat and waited while she asked directions to the Department of Paranormal Psychology, and he felt an unexpected lump in his throat.

Goddamn it, he thought, *stop feeling so sorry for yourself*.

But he couldn't help thinking about Jennifer and the

way she had smiled; and the way she had felt when he'd held her in his arms. He could almost smell her – that fragrance of soft skin and clean hair. She was going to be cremated the day after tomorrow at Chestnut Hill. Her father was flying in from Santa Barbara. He had retired there after Jennifer's mother had died.

And what consolation could John offer him? What possible condolences? His only daughter had met John and married him and died a bloody death.

Sister Perpetua pushed him along a side corridor, past rows of windows that looked out over a quadrangle lined with small maples. At last they reached a door marked *Parapsych Dept.*, *Dr Dianne Wesley*, and Sister Perpetua maneuvered John into an L-shaped waiting room. Thaddeus and Norman Clay were there already, sitting side by side, wearing identical powder-blue suits.

'Good morning, John,' said Thaddeus. 'Glad you could make it. Good morning, Sister.'

'Is Lenny here?' asked John.

'He's in with Dr Wesley,' said Thaddeus. 'She's giving him a preliminary once-over. You know – just to make sure that his pulse and blood pressure and respiration are okay.'

Sister Perpetua said, 'Would you care for some coffee? I noticed a machine in the lobby. I'm dying for a cup myself.'

'Sister,' said Thaddeus, 'you're a white man.'

While Sister Perpetua went to fetch coffee, John talked to Thaddeus and Norman. 'Did you have any trouble with Chief What's-his-name?'

'Molyneux,' said Thaddeus. 'No, not much. We told him that Dr Wesley is a psychologist, but we kind of accidentally-on-purpose forgot to mention the paranormal side of things. We said that you'd already considered having Lenny tested here, and that the tests could prove useful in deciding Lenny's future. He was pretty much in favor, as it turned out. All he wants is to have the case wrapped up, with no loose ends.'

'How about you?' asked John. 'Have you had any more ideas?'

'I'm keeping an open mind,' said Thaddeus. 'But Norman here picks up unbelievably strong vibes whenever he gets close to your son. He says it's like standing next to an electricity substation: strong invisible power that makes your hair crackle.'

'I don't like to be rude,' said John, 'but doesn't Norman ever speak for himself?'

Thaddeus glanced at Norman and grinned. 'He can, but he doesn't like to. He says that one mouth is enough for the two of us.'

Norman grinned back, nodded, and said hoarsely, 'Meanings are more important than words, you dig?'

Thaddeus said, 'We were born within twenty-three minutes of each other, Norman and me. We've always been close, always done everything together. Our father was a cop, so we wanted to be cops, too. We were brought up in South Philly, in the black quarter. They were tough times, believe me, but I'm not complaining, because we always had family. Our father wanted us to be concert violinists or twin Liberaces or something; but then I've never known a single cop who wanted his son to be a cop.'

John said, 'You could have been anything, with your gifts.'

'Yes,' agreed Thaddeus, 'But that's what they are, gifts. And when you have gifts, you ought to share them, to help everybody. Otherwise, you know – the world is a jungle.'

The door opened, and a tall, bespectacled brunette came in, reading from a clipboard as she did so. She hesitated, then took off her Ted Lapidus designer eyeglasses and looked around intently at everybody in the waiting room.

'You're all with Leonard, yes?' she demanded.

'Yes, ma'am,' said Thaddeus. 'This is Lenny's father, Mr John Woods. John – this is Dr Dianne Wesley.'

Dianne Wesley approached John and stood over him. Before his injuries, John would have stood over her, and smiled, and held out his hand. But all he could do now was sit tilted in his wheelchair and wonder whether he ought to nod seriously or crack a joke or try to act haughty. She had him at such a disadvantage that it didn't really seem to matter what he did. She was unnervingly attractive, with or without her eyeglasses. Her dark mahogany-brown hair was expensively bobbed. She had high European cheekbones and slanted eyes the color of chestnuts. She wore a lab coat over her red silk blouse, but even so John could see that she was very large-breasted – the kind of girl *Playboy* would have featured in its center spread as 'The Nudest Shrink.' Her legs were slender and ridiculously long (and he had always had a passion for black stockings), and when she came close he could smell Chanel No. 5, warmed to vaporizing point by her very smooth skin.

'How do you do,' he said with a grimace. 'Forgive me for not getting up.'

'That's all right,' Dianne Wesley replied. 'Sergeant Clay told me on the telephone what had happened to you.'

'How's Lenny?' asked John.

'He's very well. One hundred percent physically fit. No signs of any mental trauma or any abnormality in the brain. We're just about ready to start testing for paranormal activity.'

'Can I ask you what *you* think about this?' asked

John. 'I mean – about Lenny being possessed by some kind of demon?'

Dianne Wesley smiled without humor. 'We don't actually use the term "demon" here, Mr Woods. We're researching external psychological influences – EPIs, we usually call them. And while people might have called them "demons" in the Middle Ages – well, we're a lot more scientific about them these days.'

John said, 'I'm sorry – I didn't mean to suggest –'

But Dr Wesley turned away from him and said to Thaddeus, 'Perhaps you'd like to come through to the laboratory now. We're going to start with EEGs, and then we'll go into the sleep tests.'

Thaddeus stood up and took hold of the handles of John's wheelchair. Dianne Wesley blinked, then said, 'Yes – well, I suppose there's room for that.'

John was on the verge of shouting at her, *I may not be able to walk, I may not be able to wave my arms around, but Jesus Christ* – But Norman Clay came past him and laid his hand on John's shoulder and squeezed it, as if to say, *I understand how you feel, John, but stay cool. You will suffer far worse humiliations than this before you die.*

Thaddeus wheeled John through the laboratory door. The laboratory itself was almost sixty feet long and thirty-five feet wide, air-conditioned, painted eggshell-blue, with blinds drawn tight at every window. A battery of adjustable spotlights was clustered on the ceiling, picking out a bank of electronic monitoring equipment, a group of chairs, and a wide green-sheeted couch on which Lenny was lying, stripped to his shorts, nervously waiting for whatever was going to happen next.

John called, 'Lenny! Lenny!'

Lenny swung his legs down from the couch and rushed over. He took hold of his father's head and kissed his forehead. 'Daddy,' he said, and pressed his face close to John's, so that John could feel Lenny's tears sliding down the side of his cheek. At that moment, John would have given anything to be able to hold him tight, to hug him and tell him how much he loved him.

Sister Perpetua returned, handed a styrofoam cup of coffee to Thaddeus Clay, then seated herself on a chair, out of the way.

Dianne Wesley said, 'This is going to take a little time. Are you comfortable, Mr Woods?'

'Sure, I'm comfortable,' John told her.

'I mean – are you *comfortable*?' she repeated with lifted eyebrows. He suddenly realized that she was asking him if he needed to be taken for a pee. Anybody else could just slip out. A quadriplegic in a wheelchair would obviously cause a huge commotion, and jeopardize her tests.

She said in a soft voice, 'My father had a stroke. I've had a few years' experience dealing with people in wheelchairs.'

John flushed. 'I'm comfortable, thanks.' He didn't even want to mention the word "catheter" in front of a woman who looked like her. She turned away just a fraction of a second before he could give her his famous sarcastic stare.

'Come on then, Lenny,' said Dr Wesley. 'Let's get back on the couch and run some more tests. You remember we talked about those dreams you had? How we're going to try to get inside your head and track them down? Well, that's what we're going to do now. For this one, we're going to attach some of these little suckers to the side of your forehead. You won't mind that – okay?'

Lenny nodded. Thaddeus Clay checked his watch. Behind them Sister Perpetua rustled her starched habit, settling herself down like a swan on its nest to doze for a while.

John remained in his wheelchair, cramped and awkward, too proud to ask anybody to make him more comfortable. He watched suspiciously as Dianne Wesley connected Lenny to the machine and switched it on, then sat beside him, observing his responses, smiling at him from time to time, making notes. The machine beeped and clicked and hummed, and every now and then Dr Wesley turned around on her revolving chair and checked the printout.

'How long does this go on?' John asked Thaddeus after a quarter of an hour.

'Maybe a half hour longer. She's very thorough. She won't quit until she's satisfied.'

John checked his watch and caught Lenny's eyes. 'How're you doing, tiger?'

Lenny gave him a weak grin and said, 'Bored. And hungry, too.'

Dianne Wesley said, 'Don't worry, I'll send out for some sandwiches in just a while. And do please try to keep still.'

Lenny looked at his father for sympathy. *If only I could tear away that tangle of wires, pick him up, and take him home*, John thought, for one impossible split second. But all he could do was grimace. 'Got to be done, Lenny. I'm sorry.'

Nonetheless, he turned to Thaddeus and said, 'Do you really think she's going to find anything?'

'Who knows? If anybody can, she can. But we don't even know what we're dealing with here.'

'I should be out on the patio right now, with the rest of the charioteers,' John told him.

'Don't tell me you're starting to adapt already,' said Thaddeus.

John said, 'You should talk to those guys. There's Toussaint, he's only twelve, but he's the wisest, coolest young boy you could every imagine. And Che-u, he's

Korean – he's been crippled since birth, but his mind's like a knife. And Billy, and Dean.'

'All handicapped, huh?' asked Thaddeus.

John nodded. 'Sure. But real characters, full of fire. The kind of people who would have made their mark, if they'd been able to walk.'

'Well, maybe,' said Thaddeus. 'But sometimes it's precisely their handicap that gives handicapped people all that strength of character. Look at you. You've changed, since Norman and I first came around to see you. You've suffered a terrible tragedy, but you're a stronger man.'

John hesitated for a moment, then said, 'We'll see about that.'

At noon, a red-haired girl student brought in hot coffee and waffle sandwiches from The Other Rocking Horse restaurant on Pine Street. Afterward, Thaddeus had to take John to the bathroom. It was a simple act of help, without sympathy or sentiment, and accordingly, there was no embarrassment between them.

At three o'clock, with her tests almost complete, Dianne Wesley came across to John and said, 'Your son is beginning to doze.'

'That's not particularly surprising,' John said sharply. 'He's had two severe shocks recently, and he's been taken away from home. He's very tired. And most children fall asleep when they don't want to face up to things.'

'Mr Woods,' said Dr Wesley. 'I'm not fighting you. I'm trying to help.'

'In that case, you'll have to forgive me,' John said. 'I've been sitting in this wheelchair for less than a week. I'm still on painkillers because of the pain and I'm still on sedatives because I lost my wife. I'm trying very hard not to be grouchy and not to be depressed, but sometimes I find myself fighting a losing battle.'

Dianne Wesley looked down at him without saying anything. Then she licked her lips with the tip of her tongue, and said tautly, 'We could conclude these tests right now, Mr Wood. We could shred fifteen thousand dollars' worth of tests and throw your son on the mercy of the state. It's really up to you.'

'What are you proposing to do now?' John asked.

'A sleep test, once he falls asleep.'

'And what will that do?'

Dianne Wesley turned around and lifted her arm to indicate the whole of the laboratory and all of its electronics. 'With this new equipment we have here, we can do two things simultaneously. First, we can check on your son's vital signs while he's asleep. These can show us if he's receiving any paranormal influences over and above those he would normally receive during the course of the night. They can also reveal any hidden anxiety he might be keeping bottled up while he's awake.'

'And what else can it tell you?' John demanded. 'That he's *guilty*, because his mother choked to death right in front of him and there was nothing he could do about it? That he's *afraid*, because he opened the bedroom door and found his stepmother chopped into pieces? Or that he's totally *confused*, because everybody thinks that he murdered Jack and Nancy Pelling?'

Dianne Wesley tried to sound reasonable. 'Mr Woods – please – don't take any of this the wrong way. I'm on Lenny's side just like you are. But the way to help him the most is to prove what *I* believe to be the case – and that is that Lenny was influenced in his actions by an extremely powerful manifestation from another plane of cerebral existence. In other words, his body was like a puppet in the hands of a puppeteer.'

John made an effort to look deeply unimpressed. He hated jargon; and whatever they were, he wasn't prepared to believe in 'other planes of cerebral existence.'

But Dianne Wesley went on, 'We all receive a certain proportion of paranormal influx while we're asleep. Youngish people, especially, rather than old. On the whole, the influx is very slight, and so we wake up and say that we've had a good dream. At other times, however, the paranormal effect is extremely powerful, and that's when we say we've had a nightmare. Maybe you see your dead grandmother, alive, as if she'd never died. Maybe your childhood friends are all chasing you, and you're sure that they're going to kill you.'

John said nothing.

'We also have the capability for the first time of *photographing* your dreams,' Dr Wesley continued. She turned toward the computers. 'One of these computers can be directly linked to the part of Lenny's brain that decides what things look like. It gathers up the natural electricity of his thought-impulses and translates them into dots, rather like a wireless telegraph. The dots are analysed by the computer, and then printed out. They don't always make sense, of course, but we've had one or two remarkable pictorial records of people's dreams. I guarantee that in ten years' time, we'll be able to go to bed with contacts on our foreheads and a VCR running, and in the morning we'll be able to play back our dreams.'

John said, 'What if this wasn't a *paranormal* influence? What if Lenny wasn't dreaming at all? What if he *did* commit those murders?'

Dianne Wesley looked at him narrowly. 'Is that what you're afraid of?'

'What do you think?'

'In that case, Mr Woods, you'll just have to get him the psychiatric help that he deserves.'

John looked across at Lenny, dozing on the couch, one hand crooked and lifted the way he always used to lift it when he was little. Virginia used to say that he was holding the angel's hand. Then John turned back to Dianne Wesley, tears smarting in his eyes. 'He's my son, Dr Wesley. That's all I can say. He's my son, I'm supposed to be taking care of him, and I can't even walk.'

Dianne Wesley was about to say something; but then she changed her mind. She unlocked the brake on John's wheelchair and pushed him over to Lenny, as close as her banks of equipment would allow.

'Dad?' said Lenny, opening his eyes. He looked tired.

'Tell him,' Dr Wesley urged.

John hesitated, then said, 'Dr Wesley wants you to sleep for a little while. She has a machine that can print actual pictures of what you're dreaming about. Do you think you want to help her do that?'

'Do I *have* to?' asked Lenny. Not surprisingly, he had had more than enough of laboratories and computers for one day.

John said, 'No. You don't have to. But it's going to help us to track down that bogey you keep dreaming about.'

Lenny swallowed. 'Dad ... I'm frightened. It scares me.'

'I know,' said John. There was no use pretending.

Thaddeus came up and stood behind John, and gave Lenny a gentle grin. 'My brother Norman says that if you can show us what this thing looks like ... we can zap it. And that's a promise.'

Lenny bit his lip. Then, finally, he nodded and whispered, 'All right.'

'Thanks, champ,' John told him.

Dianne Wesley said, 'You're sure?'

Lenny nodded.

Dr Wesley went back to her computer consoles, perched on the edge of her chair, and punched out a long sequence of codes. Then she crossed over to Lenny, dabbed his forehead with alcohol, and began to attach one electrical contact after another.

'This won't hurt him, will it?' John asked her loudly.

She looked at him and shook her head. 'All children are precious, Mr Woods.'

Then she returned to her console and switched on her equipment, and sat down and waited like the rest of them for something to happen.

Four hours went by. John dozed on and off in his wheelchair. Close behind him, Sister Perpetua started to snore lightly. The sunlight faded behind the close-drawn blinds, and elsewhere in the building they heard doors closing and the sound of footsteps as students packed up their books and went home.

A young black student came in at eight-thirty with another brown paper bag full of sandwiches and coffee. 'Thank you, Marcus,' said Dianne Wesley, and handed around the sandwiches. 'Do you like pastrami, Mr Woods?' she asked.

'I think you'd better start calling me John,' he told her.

While they ate, they kept up their watch on Lenny. He had turned over twice, without waking up. John thought he looked rather pale, and he was disturbed by the way in which Lenny's legs trembled and kicked.

'He's dreaming,' Dianne Wesley explained. 'He's probably running or walking. That's why he's moving his legs. We can try checking with the electro-camera.'

Still holding a Styrofoam cup of coffee in one hand, she punched out a series of digits on her computer. There was a moment's pause, and then the printer softly chattered into action, printing out matrix dots for every electronic impulse that related to what Lenny could see in his mind's eye.

After several minutes, Dianne Wesley tore the sheet of paper out of the printer and came across to show it to them.

'Looks like nothing at all,' Thaddeus remarked. 'A flat line ... maybe those are clouds at the top there.'

John narrowed his eyes to focus on the picture more clearly. 'it looks like a landscape to me ... maybe a desert.'

But Dianne Wesley pointed to some dark, curved lines that ran across the center. 'I don't think it's a desert, I think it's a seashore. He's walking across a seashore.'

It is nothing more or less than a stretch of interminable white-brown sand, hard and smooth and broad, with the ocean perpetually, grandly, rolling in upon it.

John lifted his head and watched his young son sleeping. It was incredible to think that Lenny actually believed at this moment that he was there, that he was clearly imagining himself walking across this barren seashore.

'This is a very impressive piece of equipment, Dr Wesley,' he complimented her.

She smiled in appreciation. 'Why don't you call me Dianne?'

Another hour and a half passed. John stayed awake now, talking in a low murmur to Thaddeus and Norman Clay. 'Do you really think these tests are going to find out anything?' he asked Thaddeus.

'If there's anything to find, Dr Wesley'll find it,' Thaddeus replied.

'Supposing she *does* find something – what can she do to deal with it? I mean, if it's jumping out and slashing people to death, it's going to be something of a handful, right?'

'That's why we're here,' said Thaddeus.

Sister Perpetua snuffled in her sleep.

A few minutes before ten o'clock, Lenny suddenly started to moan. It was a low, suppressed whooping noise, the kind of noise people make when, inside their nightmare, they're screaming out loud.

Dianne Wesley approached Lenny and dabbed at his face with a wet compress. He relaxed for a while, and his moaning subsided. But just as she turned away, his arms and legs began to shiver and jerk, his head thrashing from side to side. Instantly, all the recording needles on the computer console started to jump wildly up and down, and the electroencephalograph indicator flashed red.

'What's happening?' John demanded. 'Is he okay?'

'A tremendous leap in brain activity,' said Dianne, concentrating on flicking switches on the console.

'It's not dangerous, is it?'

'It's unusually high, but I don't think there's anything to worry about just yet.' She leaned across and switched on the electro-camera. 'I'm going to start printing out pictures now, one fresh picture every ten-point-five seconds. That should give us some idea what he's dreaming about.'

John said to Thaddeus. 'Push me closer to the console, will you? I want to see what's going on.'

Thaddeus wheeled John right up next to the console. Dianne Wesley glanced at him quickly and said, 'Just make sure you don't touch anything. There's two thousand volts going through this console, and that wheelchair of yours looks like a pretty good ground.'

The first electro-picture came off the printer. It was totally black.

'What does that mean?' asked John.

Dianne Wesley held it up. 'Either he's not dreaming about anything at all, or else he's dreaming that he's in complete darkness.' She paused. 'There is the possibility, of course, that the EPI doesn't want us to see what it looks like, and has blacked us out.'

'Are you serious? It could really do that?'

'In paranormal psychology, John, you have to be prepared for *any* eventuality, no matter how extraordinary it may be.'

Lenny, on the couch, began to moan once more, and to flail at the air with outstretched hands. The needles on the computer console danced up and down, scribbling out a continuous record of the electrical impulses that Lenny was sending out from his cerebral cortex. The graph-paper was so thick with ink that it was coming out almost as black as the paper from the electro-printer.

'Something's happening,' said Dianne. 'I don't know what – but I've never seen brain activity like this before. The EEG's going crazy.'

'Don't you think you'd better wake him up?' asked John.

Dianne shook her head. 'Far too dangerous, at this level of subconscious activity. He could be traumatized for life.'

'Then what are you going to do?'

'There's only one thing I *can* do, and that's to take him through it.'

Thaddeus and Norman Clay stepped up to the console. Thaddeus said, 'Norman's picking up some very powerful vibes.'

John turned to Norman. The detective's face was covered with a sheen of sweat, his lips almost white. 'From Lenny, you mean? What kind of vibes?'

Norman whispered something in Thaddeus's ear. 'Hostile,' Thaddeus explained. 'Low-temperature, nonhuman, very hostile.'

'When he says nonhuman, what does he mean?'

asked Dianne, keeping her eyes on the EEG readouts.'

'Exactly what he says, nonhuman. No soul, no conscience, no feeling of any humanity. Something you couldn't reason with; something you couldn't scare. Like a spider, you know, or a scorpion.'

'Well, the EEG is certainly picking up *something*,' said Dianne. She reached across and tore off the next electro-camera image. 'But look at this – total blackness again. We're not getting any visual feedback at all.'

Sister Perpetua said, 'Do you think it's gotten *cold* all of a sudden?'

Dianne Wesley checked the ambient temperature. Although the air-conditioning was set at seventy, it was sixty-two degrees and dropping.

'That's a sure sign of paranormal activity,' she said. 'All EPIs induce a lowering of room temperature.' She crossed to the other side of the room and switched on her infra-red recording equipment. 'If there's any kind of paranormal presence, it should show up on the infra-red cameras as an *absence* of heat.'

Lenny continued to mewl and moan and paw at the air. Sitting in his wheelchair, John felt so frustrated and helpless that he wanted to beat his head against the computer console.

'Brain activity increasing,' said Dianne. 'It's so high now that it's practically off the chart.'

Thaddeus laid a hand on John's shoulder, and John looked up at him anxiously. 'Don't worry,' said Thaddeus. 'We'll take care of him.'

'Temperature fifty-eight degrees and dropping one degree per,' Dianne remarked.

'What does that tell you?' asked John.

'The quicker the temperature falls and the lower it goes, the more powerful the EPI.'

'And this one?'

She didn't even have time to look at him. 'This is the

most powerful EPI I've ever come across. This is way off the scale.'

Thaddeus unbuttoned his powder-blue coat and loosened his .38 in its shoulder-holster.

Dianne said quickly, 'I don't think we're going to need that kind of assistance, Sergeant. I'm conducting a strictly scientific psychological test here, not the gunfight at the OK Corral.'

'No harm in taking elementary precautions,' said Thaddeus.

'Well, just remember that there are people in this laboratory, not to mention several million dollars' worth of state-of-the-art equipment.'

'I will, ma'am,' Thaddeus reassured her.

Suddenly the overhead spotlights began to flicker and dim.

'Blackout?' said John.

'If it is, we have our own auxiliary generator,' said Dianne.

But the lights continued to flicker and, one by one, to die out. Soon they were left with no light except what came from the computer console. The rest of the laboratory was in total blackness.

'We should get the lights back in a minute,' Dianne told them. 'It's probably an overload.'

'Then why haven't the computers gone down?' asked Thaddeus. 'You said yourself they're running on two thousand volts.'

Dianne Wesley hesitated for a moment, then said, 'Do you have a flashlight, Sergeant?'

'Norman?' asked Thaddeus, and Norman passed over a police flashlight. Dianne shone it first of all on Lenny, who was still tossing and turning on the couch. Then she directed it at the electro-camera painter. Every ten-point-five seconds, a solid sheet of black came out. Black, and black, and black.

'Detective – would you mind finding the night porter and asking him to come check these lights?' she asked.

'Sure thing,' replied Norman hoarsely, and went to the door, 'Locked,' he said. 'Do you have the key?'

Dianne Wesley turned around. John could see her frowning in the faint green light from the computer console. 'It can't be locked.'

Norman Clay rattled the handle. 'Whether it's locked or not, it sure won't open.'

Dr Wesley left the console and went toward the door. But as she did so, the computers died completely with a whirring click, and all the remaining lights went out. They were left in seamless darkness, and intense cold.

'This is no fun at all,' said Thaddeus. 'Dr Wesley – can you reach the door?'

'I can,' said Dianne, 'but your brother's right. It seems as if it's been jammed.'

'Maybe we should wake Lenny,' John suggested.

'Not if we can help it,' Dianne cautioned. 'The effect would be worse than waking a sleepwalker. And there's no knowing what the EPI might do, especially if it's psychokinetic.'

'What does that mean?'

'In popular language – a poltergeist.'

Sister Perpetua murmured. 'Holy Mother protect us from all the forces of darkness and evil, amen.'

It was then that they heard a rustling sound, on the far side of the laboratory. Quiet, and soft, like something being dragged across the floor.

'Did you hear that?' asked Thaddeus.

'Yes,' said John. 'It sounds like there's somebody there.'

'Somebody?' asked Sister Perpetua.

'Somebody or something,' put in Dianne.

They strained their eyes to penetrate the darkness, but it was complete. Gradually, however, they became aware that there *was* something in the laboratory with them – something breathing, something cold, something hostile. Thaddeus groped for the flashlight that Dianne Wesley had left on the console, but when he switched it on it simply died away, the element of the bulb glowing for a second like an orange firefly.

'I'm drawing my weapon,' he announced. 'I don't want anybody to step in front of me.'

'But what about Lenny?' John retorted. 'You can't start firing in here, you could easily hit Lenny!'

Thaddeus hesitated, and then he put his gun away again. 'Okay – but everybody stick close.'

They waited, holding their breath.

'God,' said Dianne, 'if it's going to do something. I wish it would hurry up and do it.'

They waited one minute, two minutes, three. Then, without warning, there was a sudden rush of turbulent air, and John felt something catastrophic pass him by; something huge and terrible and strong. The rush was followed by a whistling swish, and Sister Perpetua let out a high, trilling shriek.

'Sister?' John called out. 'Sister Perpetua!'

He tried to turn in his wheelchair by wrenching his neck sideways and hoping that his body-weight would follow, but all he succeeded in doing was to knock his left eye-brow against the computer console, a sharp-edged blow that brought tears to his eyes.

He felt Thaddeus scramble past him. He heard Dianne Wesley cry out in fear. Then abruptly the lights blinked back on, and the computers click-*chirred* back to life, and they all looked around the laboratory, blinking, to see what had happened.

Sister Perpetua was standing next to the printer. From the chest downward, her white habit was drenched in brilliant red. Her face was ashy-gray, almost blue, and her eyes were staring. She swayed slowly from side to side, and they could see that she was just about to fall.

'Holy Mother,' she whispered in a bubble of shining blood. And then she reached down with both hands and drew back her blood-soaked habit as if it were the curtain of a marionette theater.

To John's horror, she revealed black stockings, runneled with dark red, and fat white thighs; but her stomach had been cut right open, with one razor-sharp slice, and the entire contents of her abdomen were hanging down between her legs like some grotesque kilt – bladder and pipes and stringy membranes, beige and blue and garish scarlet.

Thaddeus immediately stepped forward and caught her, then laid her down, covering her with her habit. 'Ambulance,' he snapped at Norman.

Dianne Wesley said faintly, 'There's a phone in the waiting room.'

Norman turned the doorhandle. This time the door opened with ease.

John turned his head away, feeling the nausea rise up in his stomach. As he did so, he saw Lenny sitting up on the couch, awake now, sensor wires still trailing from his forehead, staring at the grisly sight of Sister Perpetua lying on the floor.

He looked at Lenny, and Lenny raised his eyes and looked at him – and there was something in Lenny's expression that told John for sure. Fear, uncertainty – and wide-eyed guilt. Whatever it was that had risen out of the darkness to slash Jennifer to death, and had then taken its bloody toll of Jack and Nancy and Sister Perpetua, it had come from Lenny – and Lenny knew it. Whether Lenny was actively helping it or not, it was using his mind as a way of coming to life, and of killing whoever it happened to come across first. The creature was doubly frightening because it had killed without purpose, like a mad dog.

Eight

Thaddeus listened to Sister Perpetua's heart, then took her pulse. After two or three minutes, he lowered her wrist and said, 'She's dead, poor woman. Didn't stand a goddamned chance.' He stood up, and made the signs of the cross. *'Per Dominum nostrum Iesum Christum Filium tuum, qui tecum uiuit, et regnat in unitate Spiritus sancti Deus, per omnia saecula saeculorum, Amen.'*

Dianne stepped gingerly around Sister Perpetua's body, 'I've never known anything so powerful in my life,' she whispered. She was deeply shocked, and she couldn't stop trembling.

'It was the same thing that killed my wife, and disabled me,' John told her.

'I didn't see anything,' she said. 'Just blackness.' She walked unsteadily over to the computer and took out the very last electro-camera printout. 'And that was all the computer saw, too.'

She approached Lenny and cautiously put out her hand.

'I'm sorry,' Lenny whispered, shivering with fright. 'I'm sorry.'

'Lenny,' said Dianne, 'I don't think that it was your fault. Whatever comes out of you, it's very much stronger than you are. You couldn't control it if you tried.'

John called, 'Lenny – you were asleep when it

happened – but can you remember what it felt like? Can you remember anything at all?'

Lenny lowered his head and started to sob. Dianne held him in her arms, and the two of them clung together on the couch. All that John could do was sit awkwardly in his wheelchair like a painted dummy in a store window and watch them; unable even to console his own son.

After ten minutes, the ambulance arrived, followed by more police and the medical examiner. Thaddeus came over to John and said, 'I'm going to have to ask you to make some kind of statement, you know.'

John looked up at him. 'You want me to tell the truth?'

Thaddeus grimaced. 'I don't know. I'm not sure that anybody's going to believe the truth. Especially Chief Molyneux.'

'If I don't tell the truth, who gets the blame? Lenny couldn't have done it, not this time – he was all hooked up, and he couldn't possibly have taken off all of those electrical contacts, killed Sister Perpetua, and then put them back on again. Not on his own, not in the dark. No way.'

'Well, that's true,' Thaddeus agreed. 'But if we tell the truth, Lenny's going to be locked up in isolation. Chief Molyneux isn't going to risk this happening again. He's already had a call from the mayor's office, asking if the murderer's been caught yet. Understandable, I suppose, in "We the People" year.'

John said, 'Thaddeus, you listen to me – my son is more important than Philadelphia's tourist industry.'

'All the same, John, what are you going to do with him? When he falls asleep, something comes out of him that kills people. Are *you* going to sleep in the same room with him, until you know that it's gone for good?'

Just then, Chief of Detectives Molyneux came shouldering his way into the room. He was a thickset Irishman with explosive freckles all over his face and a moustache like a frightened porcupine. He wore a green-and-orange hounds-tooth sport coat, and a green-and-orange paisley necktie.

'Thadd, what in hell's going on here?' he wanted to know. His voice was thick Philadelphia Irish. 'You told me these friggin' tests were supposed to clear up these homicides for good and all. And now what – another one, right in front of the two of yez. Mayor Goode's going to kick my ass from here to King of Prussia.'

He peered into the blue body bag in which the paramedics were preparing to seal Sister Perpetua up, so that she could be carried cleanly away. He wrinkled up his nose at the smell of warm insides.

'A nun, too. That's going to make me popular down at St Ignatius, wouldn't you say? So where's your perpetrator?'

'That's the difficult part,' said Thaddeus. 'There *is* no perpetrator. Not in the conventional sense.'

'You're trying to tell me this was suicide? Hari-kiri or something?'

'It wasn't suicide,' put in John. 'Sister Perpetua was killed by what you might describe as a very powerful poltergeist.'

Chief Molyneux looked down at John as if he hadn't noticed him before. 'I beg your pardon?' He blinked.

'This is Mr John Woods,' Thaddeus explained hastily, 'Lenny Woods's father. He came here today to give Lenny some moral support.'

Chief Molyneux held out his hand; but John, of course was powerless to take it. 'I suffered nerve damage,' he told Chief Molyneux. 'All I can move is my head.'

'Yes,' said Chief Molyneux, 'I remember the report,

119

now you come to mention it. Well, let me tell you that I'm very sorry, and if there's anything the Philadelphia Police Department can do ...' He sniffed, wiped his nose, and then said to Thaddeus, 'So, what went down here tonight?'

'I told you,' John interrupted. 'Sister Perpetua was attacked and killed by a very powerful poltergeist.'

Chief Molyneux squinted one eye at him and cocked his head sideways. 'Is this a leg-pull? Because if it is, I can tell you right now that I don't consider it very amusing. A woman's dead here – the fourth slashing in ten days. That, to my mind, is not the stuff of hilarity.'

'Chief,' said John, trying to be patient, 'my son, Lenny, was brought here today to undergo tests in paranormal psychology. What Dr Wesley here was trying to establish was whether he was personally culpable for killing his stepmother and Mr and Mrs Jack Pelling, or whether he was being influenced by something paranormal, something outside of himself.'

Chief Molyneux slowly took out a pack of Philip Morris cigarettes, shook one out, and parked it between his lips, never taking his eyes away from John. 'Go on,' he said, snapping a match with his thumbnail and lighting up.

'You tell him, Dianne,' said John.

'Dianne, huh?' remarked Chief Molyneux.

'Well, what's your first name, Chief?' asked Dianne. 'We don't stand on formality here.'

'It seems to me that you don't stand on *anything* very much,' Chief Molyneux replied. 'In fact, nobody seems to have their feet on the ground at all.'

'Chief –' Dianne began.

Chief Molyneux raised his hand and said, 'Please – you want us to act informal – call me Bryan.'

'All right, then, Bryan. What happened here today

was Lenny was given a series of routine medical checks. Then he was hooked up to this EEG recorder and to this electrically activated visual-response decoder, which can actually print out people's thoughts as pictures. The idea was to let him fall asleep in the natural way, and then to see if any unusual brain activity occurred – brain activity that might indicate that he was being influenced by anything paranormal.'

'Such as a poltergeist?' said Chief Molyneux, smiling.

'Well, that's not the kind of word that *I* usually bandy around,' said Dianne. 'But, yes, you could say that we were looking for evidence that Lenny was acting as a go-between, if you like, between this world and the next.'

'And that's what happened? Something appeared from the next world, yes? And wasted this nun right in front of your eyes?'

'The lights went out. It was pitch-black.'

'So you didn't actually see this poltergeist at all?'

'No.'

Chief Molyneux nodded, and thought. Then he said, 'So, in theory, any one of you could have killed this nun and none of the others would have known?'

'Chief,' said John, 'at the time of Sister Perpetua's murder, this room was occupied only by myself, my son Lenny, Dr Wesley, and your own detectives, the Clay twins.'

'Oh, yes,' snapped Chief Molyneux. 'I hadn't forgotten about *them*. The all-singing, all-dancing Clay twins.'

Thaddeus said, 'At the time of the killing, sir, the door was jammed and Norman was holding on to the handle, so nobody could have gotten in or out.'

'Not jammed now?' Chief Molyneux turned around to look at it.

121

'No, sir. It loosened up again, right after it was all over.'

'Yes, Clay. And maybe you loosened up again, too.'

Thaddeus went on. 'Mr Woods is a quadriplegic, completely unable to walk or to use his arms. Dr Wesley was standing close to the door, and the only way she could have reached Sister Perpetua in order to kill her was by passing too close to where *I* was positioned for me not to have noticed her brushing past.'

'Well,' sniffed Chief Molyneux, 'Dr Wesley is certainly not the type of lady who could brush past *any* man unnoticed.'

Thaddeus said, 'Lenny was wired up to the EEG machine and couldn't have gotten free – let alone wire himself up again in ten seconds flat. So the conclusion has to be that *none* of us did it. And if none of us did it, and there was no access to the laboratory from outside – well, then, we have to entertain the idea that Mr Woods here might be right.'

'You mean that Sister Perpetuity, or whatever her blessed name was, was killed by a kind of ghost?'

Lenny, who had been listening and watching with pale-faced intensity, wordlessly shook his head. 'An EPI,' Dianne explained. 'An external psychological influence.'

'A ghost by any other name,' Chief Molyneux retorted.

'Bryan,' said Dianne. 'this was a highly advanced scientific study. This department is funded by the University of Pennsylvania and is regarded throughout the United States as being the most sophisticated and stringent of paranormal research units.'

'Well, yes, that's all very well,' said Chief Molyneux. 'But I have to file a report with the commissioner, and if you think I'm going to be saying that Sister Perpetuity was murdered by one of your poltergeists, then you've got yourself another thing coming. *You* may be allowed to believe in fairies, but I'm not.'

'What are you going to do with my son?' demanded John.

Chief Molyneux frowned at him. 'It seems to me that your son needs to be kept under strict observation. I'm going to take him downtown now, and apply to a judge for an order of protective custody.'

'Now, just a minute –' John began.

'Just a minute yourself, Mr Woods,' Chief Molyneux interrupted. 'Your son has been present at the commission of four homicides; and whether he committed them himself or whether some wacky ghost came popping out of him and committed them for him, he's still a danger to the community at large, and he's probably a danger to himself, too. So that's what I'm going to do – I'm going to keep him out of harm's way.'

'How about us, sir?' asked Thaddeus. 'Me and Norman, I mean.'

Chief Molyneux checked his watch. He was clearly very angry. 'You two will go back to headquarters and write a comprehensive report on what went down here tonight. Then you will surrender your badges and stay home until further notice. You're both suspended.'

'But, Chief –!'

Chief Molyneux turned on them. 'You didn't tell me what kind of mumbo-jumbo you were getting into, did you? Psychologist tests, that's what you said! And what do I find here? Dr Wesley's Flying Circus! And now another innocent person is dead, and I have no sane way of explaining it to anybody. What kind of story do you think the *Inquirer* is going to print about this? What the hell do you think the commissioner's going to say?'

Dianne said calmly, 'You can have an additional report from me, Bryan.'

'A statement will be quite sufficient, thank you, *Dianne*. One of my officers will talk to you in just a while. Girard! Nash! Come over here! Make sure this young man gets himself dressed, then take him downtown. And get in touch with that Mrs What's-her-face, from the Child Welfare Department.'

Two police officers went over and helped Lenny down from the couch. He came over to say good-bye to John and there were tears in his eyes. 'I'm sorry, Daddy. I didn't mean it.'

'Sure you didn't. Don't worry. I'll be talking to my lawyer later tonight, and we'll see what we can work out.'

Lenny leaned forward and hugged John around the neck. 'I love you, Daddy.'

'Hey, champ, I love you, too.'

'And, Daddy –'

'What?'

Lenny whispered close to John's ear. *'It was black and it was cold and it came right up inside of me, and it had claws like knives and all it wanted to do was slice people.'*

John leaned his head back and focused on Lenny more closely. Lenny was staring at him, willing him to believe what he was saying. *Daddy, you have to believe me. Nobody else does. And it's true.*

'Okay, Lenny.' He nodded. 'I'll talk to you later. Take care.'

Chief Molyneux looked down at John and sniffed. 'I guess you need somebody to take you back to the hospital.'

'It's all right,' said Dianne. 'If Mr Woods doesn't mind waiting until I've given my statement, I'll take him back in my wagon.'

'Suit yourself, said Chief Molyneux, and went over to talk to the medical examiner.

But when they left the university building, shortly after eleven o'clock, Dianne turned left instead of right, drove all the way round Rittenhouse Square, and went north toward Logan Circle.

'What's this?' asked John, who was tightly strapped into the passenger seat of her plum-colored Firenza Cruiser. 'The scenic route?'

Dianne adjusted her rearview mirror. 'I thought you might appreciate a night away from the hospital.'

'You mean you're taking me home?'

'That's right,' she said, and quickly grinned at him. 'I called your doctor, and he said fine.'

'Do I have any choice in the matter?' he asked.

'No, you don't. You have all your medication with you, don't you? It's not often I get my hands on a good-looking man who can't run away.'

John said, 'What's this? Sympathy? Pity? A night out in heaven for our boys who went through hell?'

Dianne drove around Logan Circle and headed northwest between the trees of Benjamin Franklin Parkway, which was unusually empty for this time of the evening. 'I'm sorry. If you want to go back to the hospital, I'll take you. But your doctor did say that you could cope. In fact, it might do you some good.'

'And you really want to take Raggedy Andy home with you?' They crossed the glassy water and the Schuylkill River and passed the waterworks, three classically styled brick buildings fronting the river, each with two crescent-shaped windows in the place of eyes and a down-curving arch where their mouths might be. They had always reminded John of stupid and tragic clowns. Jennifer had called them 'the Three

Miseries,' never knowing the misery that John would be suffering now when he saw them. Behind the trees rose the illuminated walls of the Philadelphia Museum of Art, pillared and pristine, like a Greek temple in a Victor Mature movie.

Dianne said, 'As a matter of fact, I wanted to talk to you in a lot more depth about what's been happening with Lenny.'

'You saw for yourself what's been happening with Lenny.'

'Well, I *witnessed* it, we all did. But we didn't actually get to *see* the manifestation, did we? The electro-camera showed us nothing at all. I can't tell if the infra-red camera registered anything until I have the film developed.'

'That night at Chestnut Hill, all I saw was darkness,' John told her. 'Something black, you know, and totally unstoppable, and *huge*.'

Dianne turned on to the Schuylkill Expressway, glancing behind her as she did so, and speeded up. 'Since I started this research,' she said. 'I've recorded fifty or sixty EPIs. That's *genuine* EPIs – paranormal influences that have definitely originated from another level of existence. One particularly strong one impressed me so much that I wrote a paper on it,' 'Paranormal Psychokinesis During Sleep.' The EPI came through a fourteen-year-old black girl, and do you know what it could do? It could riffle the pages of the Bible beside her bed. And I thought *that* was powerful.'

She was silent for a moment, concentrating on her driving. Then she said, 'Whatever it was that came out of your son this evening and killed Sister Perpetua, it was quite the most extraordinary paranormal phenomenon I've ever witnessed. In fact, it's probably one of the most devastating paranormal phenomena *anywhere*, at any time.'

'You mean this kind of thing has happened before?'

'Oh, yes, for sure. There are several authenticated cases of people being attacked by EPIs. There was a man called Hauser who was killed in Nuremberg in the 1930s by a mysterious "black-cloak'd man". Then there was the famous case in 1926 of a girl called Eleonore Zugun, who was half-strangled by an invisible assailant. There were witnesses who actually saw her neck muscles being squeezed in. The worst case was in Ventimiglia, in northern Italy, in 1761, when a peasant woman was literally ripped apart in front of her friends, even though they couldn't see anybody attacking her.'

'And you really believe that Lenny is acting as a medium for one of these things?'

'I can't say that conclusively, but it's hard to think what else it might be. Of course, there are endless disagreements about the true nature of EPIs. Some people like to believe that we're being attacked by invisible beings from flying saucers. But the research that I've been doing makes it pretty clear that there are several levels of existence parallel to the level in which we're living now. The sources of EPIs or poltergeists or whatever you want to call them are the minor charges of cerebral energy that occasionally stray from one level of existence to the next. It's rather like two couples playing tennis on adjacent courts, and every now and then someone accidentally knocks a ball into the other court. There's even some evidence to show that our thoughts are capable of intruding on the beings who exist on the level closest to our own – just as *their* thoughts are capable of intruding on us – and we don't even realize it.'

'You mean, if I dream that I'm killing somebody, I might actually be doing it, on another level of existence?'

Dianne nodded. 'Dreams have far more psychological substance than most people give them credit for. You've seen for yourself that we can actually print out pictures of what people see in dreams. The next stage will be to video-record them; and then, well, maybe to *visit* them, while we're still conscious. Dream travel.'

John looked at her. 'A week ago, I would have said you were crazy.'

'I'm used to it,' said Dianne with a smile. 'My last boyfriend said I was the flakiest thing since puff pastry. But at least the university faculty support me – most of them, anyway. They're very imaginative when it comes to funding. As long as I produce properly authenticated results, of course.'

They left the Schuylkill Expressway at the City Lane Avenue turnoff, and headed through Bala-Cynwyd toward Penn Valley. They drove between shadowy woods and moonlit tracts of farmland, although they weren't very far from Harcum Junior College and Bryn Mawr. Dianne eventually turned into the steeply sloping driveway of a small one-storey house set back from the road amongst overhanging oaks.

'Nice place,' John remarked.

'I bought it four years ago,' Dianne told him. 'I wanted a hideout – somewhere I could shut myself away.'

She lifted his wheelchair out of the back of the wagon and unfolded it. Wrestling John out of the passenger seat and into the wheelchair on the angled driveway was a difficult struggle, but at last she managed it, red-faced and panting.

'How much do you *weigh*?' Dianne demanded. 'If this relationship is going to continue in any shape or form, you're going to have to go on a diet.'

She pushed him toward the front door, turned the wheelchair and tilted it back, and lifted him backwards up the three stone steps.

'What relationship?' he asked, craning his head around.

'Hasn't it occurred to you that I like you?' Dianne said, 'I liked you the moment Sergant Clay wheeled you into the laboratory.'

'I'm a cripple,' John said flatly, deliberately choosing the most derogatory word he could think of.

'Maybe that's why,' she retorted in a tone of voice that told him she wasn't serious.

She unlocked the front door and pushed him into the hallway. It was dark and narrow, and smelled of wood-ash. She switched on the lights and wheeled him along the corridor to the living room.

The house was small but freshly decorated. The walls were painted white and hung with oil paintings of Indian tepees, all of them half-buried in snow, and the couches and chairs were heaped with Navajo blankets and thick furs. Over the fireplace, a huge feathered warbonnet was displayed, all spread out.

'I wouldn't have put you down as an Indian lover,' John remarked.

'I'm one-sixteenth Sauk and Fox,' Dianne told him. 'Not much of an Indian, maybe, but enough to be proud of.'

She went through to the kitchen and came back with a bottle of red wine. 'Are you allowed to drink?' she asked.

'Not really, I'm still on painkillers. But I guess one glass won't hurt.'

She poured out two glasses, then lifted one of them up to John's lips so that he could swallow some.

'Cheers,' she said, smiling, and raised her own glass.

John looked around. 'It must be pretty cozy here in the winter.'

'That's when I like it the most.'

'Don't you get lonely?'

Dianne shrugged. 'Sometimes. I used to be married. But I guess I'm one of those really self-sufficient people. I'm quite capable of looking after myself. *Too* capable, maybe. That's what my husband used to tell me.'

'Divorced?' asked John.

She nodded. 'Quietly. Amicably. But still painfully.'

'Do you ever hear from him?'

'No, not anymore. He was in Seattle, the last I heard, building a new hotel. He was a – what-do-you-call-it? – developer. Entrepreneur. But these days, it's just like we never met, let alone married. I don't think I have a single picture of him anywhere.'

'These paintings yours?'

'Yes,' said Dianne. 'They're not very good, are they? All I can paint is tepees and snow. But I guess they say something, in their own incompetent way. Something about being a free spirit, and standing up to hard times.'

She helped him to sip more wine. 'They're going to fix your arms next week, aren't they? Sergeant Clay told me.'

John said, 'They're going to try. Trouble is, I can't even keep my fingers crossed that they're going to succeed.'

Dianne smiled, and gave him a quick, unexpected kiss on the forehead. 'I'll keep mine crossed for you.'

Later, she helped him onto the couch, where he sat propped up with cushions. He still felt frustratingly helpless, but for the very first time since he had been injured, he began to feel that life could still be worth living, even though Jennifer had been snatched away from him, even though Lenny was threatened by forces that nobody could understand. Even though he himself was about as much use to everybody around him as a tailor's dummy.

He had to admit that this newfound confidence was mostly Dianne's doing. She hadn't just tolerated his disability, she had accepted it, and she had treated him from the very first moment as a complete human being. Her offhandedness in the laboratory hadn't been anything to do with his handicap. She had simply been treating him the way she treated everybody else.

She gave him no favors and offered him no pity. She made him feel like a man again. And that was why he found her so attractive.

When John was settled on the couch, she lit a log fire with crumpled newspaper; and while it crackled into life, she went to the kitchen to fix Denver sandwiches. 'They're my specialty,' she told him. 'I use chopped-up pickles as well as green peppers. And I let the egg soak into the bread so that it's *really* soft.'

She cut up his sandwich for him and helped him to eat. 'You know something,' she said. 'I still can't work out why the EPI should have chosen Lenny.'

'What do you mean? These things happen by chance, don't they?'

'Not at all. In every one of the cases that I've recorded in the laboratory, there's been some reason for strong EPI activity. Usually it's location. The subject moved into a house or a neighborhood that was associated with particularly stressful events, like a fire or a suicide or something like that. There are always unpleasant vibrations around locations like that, and even somebody with comparatively low psychic sensitivity can pick them up. Some people are aware of nothing more than a general sense of unease; other people get the whole works – blood dripping down the walls, screams in the night, unbearable smells.'

She jabbed at the fire with the long brass poker. 'You've told me all about Lenny's recent past, and I can't believe that he's particularly psycho-sensitive. He hasn't shown any of the usual characteristics of being a sensitive – none of the headaches, hearing voices, the psychokinetic phenomena. He hasn't made cups and saucers fly around the room and he hasn't set fire to the curtains just by staring at them. He can't speak to the dead. He can't do automatic writing. Yet for some reason, the most mind-boggling EPI that I have *ever* encountered has picked him out as a medium. Now, *why*, I ask myself. Why Lenny, and why here in Philadelphia, and *why now*?'

John swallowed his last mouthful of sandwich. 'Norman Clay said that he could pick up some sort of – what did he call it? – psychic vibes, when he got close to Lenny. He said he wasn't a medium, more of a carrier.'

'That's quite an accurate way of putting it. Lenny is harboring this EPI almost like a viral infection. Every now and then, the virus goes out of control – rather like having an attack of malaria.'

'So you're really saying that Lenny is *possessed*, in some way?'

Dianne poured out some more wine. 'It would be more scientific to say that he's host to a parasitical psychic influence.'

'God almighty,' said John. 'Why did it choose him? He's so darn *good*. His teacher gave him five merits the other day and said he was one of her angels.'

'I can believe it.' Dianne nodded. 'EPIs always seem to prefer to use the innocent and the good and the vulnerable.'

'But why Lenny?'

'That's what I've been trying to work out.'

She held up his head while he sipped a little more

132

wine. He was still strongly sedated, and he could feel the wine gurgling unpleasantly in his stomach.

'I don't think I want anymore, thanks. Cabernet and downers don't mix very well.'

'How about some tea?' Dianne asked.

'No, thanks.' He turned his head toward the window, where a hooked moon hung between the slightly parted curtains, almost as if somebody were standing in the yard dangling a silver-paper moon on the end of a fishing pole. 'Is there something we can do about it?'

'Do? Like what?'

'Well, can't Lenny be cured somehow?'

Dianne shook her head. 'I'm afraid I'm a research psychologist, not a psychotherapist.'

'What about exorcism? The power of prayer, and all that?'

Dianne looked doubtful. 'I don't think we have much chance of finding a properly ordained priest who would do it for us. The church is very reluctant to authorize exorcisms these days. They're bad press. The minute you mention 'exorcism,' the television people are after you, expecting to get pictures of Linda Blair with a green face and beds floating in the air.'

She paused, then continued, 'I've seen two exorcisms. One in New Orleans – that was a very elaborate affair, complete with candles and incense and all the mumbo-jumbo – and another one here in Philadelphia. Neither of them worked. In both cases, the EPIs remained reasonably passive while the priests were actually in attendance; but as soon as the priests had gone, out danced the EPIs, just as mischievous as they had been before.'

'At least they can dance,' said John, looking down at his useless legs.

Dianne got up, walked across the room, and slotted

133

a disc into her CD player. It was Nat King Cole, singing 'When I Fall In Love.' She danced slowly around the carpet, pretending that she was being guided by a man; at last she sat down cross-legged on the couch next to John and smiled at him.

'I was pretending that was you.'

John glanced at her. 'You wouldn't play games with me, would you?'

She was silent for a moment. She lowered her head. He could see the orange firelight dancing on her glossy brunette hair. 'Do you really think I would?'

'No,' he said in a hoarse voice, and longed to touch her.

She looked up. Her eyes were glistening. 'You haven't grieved for your Jennifer yet, have you? You're too busy trying to deal with what's happened to you.'

'I thought you said you weren't a psychotherapist.'

'I'm not. But anybody can see that you're keeping all that grief bottled up.'

'Is that bad?' he asked.

'It's not *wrong*, if that's what you mean. But you'll have to come to terms with it eventually; otherwise you'll crack up.'

John was silent for a while. He looked into the fire. Then he said, 'The thing is, Dianne ... I can't yet bring myself to believe that she's actually dead. I keep thinking that she's gone away for a couple of weeks, nothing more final than that. I simply can't make my brain accept that I'm never going to see her again.'

Dianne stroked his forehead. 'The day will have to come.'

'Well, I guess. But I'm not so sure that I want it to.'

At nearly two in the morning, the effects of two glasses of wine overwhelmed him, and he fell asleep. Dianne sat beside him for a long time, continuing to stroke his forehead. The CD player crooned, '... *it will be forever, or I'll never fall in love ... and the moment ...*' and the fire gradually lurched and dropped and died down, and a few last sparks went whirling up the chimney.

'Come on,' she said at last, 'Mommy says it's bedtime.'

She swung his legs up onto the couch and covered him up with one of her Navajo blankets. Then she switched off the light, and went to bed herself. She lay for a long time in the darkness, listening to the cicadas and the last spitting of the fire. Then she slept, too, dreamlessly.

Lenny woke up to find his mother sitting beside his bed. Smiling, calm, as if she had never died. He stared at her, both terrified and pleased, not daring to believe that she might be real. But she *looked* real. She was wearing the same low-waisted apricot dress that she had been wearing on the day she died; her fair, curly hair was just the same. And she smiled at him with the same radiance.

'Momma?' he said, his mouth dry.

'Hello, my darling,' she replied with a smile. 'Don't be frightened. It's only me.'

'Momma, are you alive?'

She reached out and touched his cheek, and he could feel her. 'I'm still here, Lenny; and I always will be, just as long as you need me.'

He knelt up in bed and put his arms around her. She felt strangely insubstantial, yet he was able to hug her close, and kiss her, and smell her perfume; and instead of crying he laughed, because he loved her so much, and here she was, back again, just when he was missing her the most.

'Momma,' he said over and over. 'Momma, Momma, Momma.'

At last his mother held him away from her and looked him in the eye, and said seriously, 'Lenny – we're going to have to get you out of here.'

Lenny stared at her. He still couldn't believe that she was really here. 'They won't let me go,' he told her. 'They said that I killed all of those people, but, Momma, I didn't, it wasn't me.'

'Honey,' she said soothingly, 'I *know* it wasn't you. That's why I'm here. We have to get out of here. You have to go to California. There's a man there who can help you.'

'California? but what about Daddy?'

'Don't worry about Daddy. We're going to help Daddy, too.'

'But you *died*,' Lenny said, trembling. 'You choked on that bone and you died.'

Virginia reached across the bedcover and took hold of his hand. 'Don't you understand that mothers always take care of their children, forever and ever, no matter what happens?'

She helped Lenny to dress, and stood beside him, smiling, while he brushed his teeth at the basin. Chief Molyneux had arranged for him to be held in one of the isolation rooms at the Graduate Hospital, the floor below the dayroom where he had encountered Dr Springer. The isolation room was sparsely furnished but not uncomfortable, with magnolia-painted walls and an angular view of Lombard Street. It's advantage, as far as Chief Molyneux was concerned, was that its outer door was reinforced by a second inner one, both of which had remained locked all night, and that nobody could enter or leave it without being seen by the policeman he had posted at the end of the corridor, next to the elevator bank. Chief Molyneux didn't believe in paranormal creatures that came roaring out of small boys and slashed nuns to death; but at the same time, he didn't believe in taking chances. His predecessor had taken a chance on a particularly persuasive psycho. The psycho had gone straight home and dismembered his mother with a chainsaw, and that was how the job of chief of detectives had become suddenly vacant.

By lunchtime, in any case, Chief Molyneux could have dropped the whole inexplicable business right in the lap of Mr Carlo Donatelli, the chief of the Juvenile Branch, and let *him* untangle it.

'Are you ready to go?' Virginia asked. Lenny nodded dumbly.

She approached the inner door and peered out the window to make sure that nobody was anywhere near. Then she simply passed her hand across the lock, and Lenny could hear the levers systematically clicking as they released themselves, one after the other. Virginia opened the door and whispered, 'Come on. We don't have much time. We're supposed to be catching the nine-fifteen flight from Philly International.'

Trembling, Lenny followed her. She passed her hand over the second lock, and that opened, too. She made sure that the corridor was deserted, then she led Lenny out, holding his hand.

They turned the corner – and only thirty feet away, tilted back in his chair, sat a uniformed policeman, reading the sports pages of the morning's *Philadelphia News* with almost comic concentration and covertly smoking a cigarette concealed in the palm of his hand. He didn't look up as they approached. The front-page headline read 'Nun dies in "Ghost-Laboratory" Slashing – Nine-Year-Old Held.'

Virginia led Lenny right up to the elevator bank and pressed the call button. The policeman glanced up at her briefly, then returned to his newspaper. Lenny's heart was hop-skip-jumping. The elevator arrived, and his mother led him inside. The doors closed, and they began to sink toward the lobby.

'He didn't stop us,' said Lenny, breathless. 'Why didn't he stop us?'

Virginia smiled and squeezed his hand. 'He saw us, but he didn't understand that he was supposed to be looking for us. Don't you remember *Star Wars*, when Obi Wan Kenobi told those storm troopers that they *weren't* looking for Luke Skywalker and Han Solo? Well, that was the same kind of thing.'

'You can do that?' asked Lenny, amazed. 'You can really do that?'

'My darling Lenny,' said Virginia, stooping to kiss him on the top of the head. 'I love you, and that means I can do almost anything.'

They left the hospital miraculously unnoticed. Nurses turned their heads away; receptionists caught sight of them, but immediately deflected their gaze. They might have been winds, or mirrors. The morning outside was bright but smoggy, and clamorous with traffic. A dilapidated yellow taxi was waiting for them; it didn't occur to Lenny to ask how somebody who was dead could possibly have called for a cab. They climbed into the backseat, and the driver immediately swerved away from the curb and headed west on South Street, toward the Schuylkill Expressway and the airport.

Virginia took hold of Lenny's hand. *Momma*, he thought, and his heart was bursting with love. *Momma came to rescue me.*

'How are you feeling, Lenny?' the driver asked as they crossed the river. The water was bright like beaten gold.

'Okay,' Lenny told him, although anybody could have detected a truckload of emotion in that one simple word.

138

The driver turned around. To Lenny's astonishment, it was Dr Springer, wearing a chauffeur's cap. He winked, and said, 'You're a good boy, Lenny. One of the best.'

'You're a doctor!' Lenny exclaimed. 'I saw you in the hospital!'

'Well, I'm not exactly a *doctor*,' Dr Springer admitted. I'm more like an odd-job man. You can call me Paul, if you like. Most people do. Well, some people do.'

Lenny didn't reply. He was only nine years old and he was far too intimidated. The way grown-ups behaved was always bewildering, and the re-appearance of Dr Springer was no more bewildering than anything else that grown-ups ever did.

'I'm going to take you to meet a friend of mine,' said Paul Springer over his shoulder. 'He lives in California, by the sea. You'll like him. His name's Henry, and he's going to be able to help you.'

'Is my mommy coming?' asked Lenny.

Paul glanced at Lenny in his rearview mirror. 'I'm sorry, Lenny. She can't come right away. But maybe you'll get to see her again later.'

Lenny turned to say something to Virginia – but she was gone. The seat next to him was empty.

He swallowed. He thought his heart was going to snap like a broken plate. He reached out and groped at the empty air.

'Momma?' he whimpered. Then he turned to Paul Springer, and his eyes were crowded with hot tears. '*Where is she?*' he shouted. '*Where is she?*'

Paul Springer said, 'Don't be upset. Your mommy hasn't left you. She's always there, always will be. It's just that you won't be able to see her and talk to her, not all the time.'

Lenny couldn't answer. He felt too desperate and frightened and too choked-up.

139

Paul Springer handed him a Snickers bar over the back of the seat. 'You must be hungry. They'll give you lunch on the plane. A stiff Johnny Walker, too, if you want one.'

'Aren't you coming?'

'In a way, yes.'

Lenny unhappily tore the wrapper off his Snicker's bar. 'Are you dead, too?' he asked Paul Springer.

Paul Springer laughed. 'Not exactly. You might just say that I'm not quite real.'

They reached the airport a half hour ahead of time. Paul Springer bought a ticket at the American Airlines desk for San Diego, then took Lenny to the coffee shop for breakfast. Lenny ate muffins and bacon and drank two glasses of 7-Up. Paul Springer seemed to be content with a small cup of black coffee, his silver-gray permanent-press slacks sharply creased, watching Lenny with a distant, amused smile.

'When you get to San Diego, you'll find a young man waiting for you. His name's Gil Miller. You'll like him.'

Lenny drained his glass of 7-Up to the bubbling, crackling bottom.

Paul Springer said, 'Gil will take you to a place called Del Mar. That's where Henry lives. Henry will take care of you and make sure that you're fed, and that you get some new clothes, and that you can call up your daddy whenever you want to. Henry's a good guy. You can think of Henry as a kind of grandpa.'

'How long do I have to stay there?' Lenny asked.

Paul Springer shrugged. 'It's difficult to say. It depends on those nightmares of yours.'

'Will Henry be able to stop them?'

'We sure hope so. Henry has tremendous power.'

'What's he going to do?'

Paul Springer reached across the Formica tabletop

and clasped Lenny's hand. One pale-faced nine-year-old boy with tousled hair; one thin, strange man with eyes that gave nothing away. 'You'll find out what Henry's going to do when you get to San Diego. It's a little too hard for me to explain right now. But, believe me, you're in very good hands. The best.'

Lenny finished his muffins, and then Paul Springer took him to Gate 12 and told the American Airlines stewardess that Lenny was traveling unaccompanied.

She put her arm around him and said, 'VIP, hey? Don't you worry, sir. We'll look after Lenny real good.'

Paul Springer shook Lenny's hand. 'Have a good trip, tiger. I'll catch up with you later.'

'Thank you, sir,' said Lenny, and followed the stewardess toward the reception desk.

He turned to wave good-bye to Paul Springer; but as he did so he glimpsed another familiar face, way back in the crowd of waiting passengers. His mother, in her apricot dress. She didn't wave back, but she smiled at him with such encouragement that he knew – in the words that she always used to use – that everything was going to come up roses.

Nine

John was just finishing lunch, fed by Sister Clare, when Chief Molyneux came to the open door of his room and knocked sharply.

'Mr Woods?'

John waited until Sister Clare had finished wiping gravy from around his mouth, and then said, 'Good morning, Chief. And what can I do for you?'

Chief Molyneux tried to enter the room just as Sister Clare was trying to take out John's lunch tray, and for a moment they did a little dance together in the doorway. Then Chief Molyneux stepped back to allow her out and bowed, with an expression that was almost a snarl, before finally entering the room.

'I'm looking for your son,' he told John, thrusting his hands into his pockets and fixing John with a hard, meaningful stare.

'My son is at the Graduate Hospital under your supervision, I hope?'

'Well, not exactly,' Chief Molyneux admitted. He rocked back on his heels. 'The point is that he seems to have left.'

'*Left*? What the hell do you mean, *left*?'

'Absconded, that's the word.'

'When? Wasn't anybody keeping an eye on him?'

'We had a police officer posted outside his room,' Chief Molyneux explained. 'But, well – somehow he managed to slip past him.'

John stared at Chief Molyneux in exasperation. 'I can't believe what I'm hearing.'

'Believe me – my face was never so red,' Chief Molyneux admitted. 'But we'll find him, don't you worry about that. After all, how far can a nine-year-old boy get with no money and no place to go?'

'You tell me,' John retorted angrily. 'You're the one who let him get away.'

'Believe me, Mr Woods,' said Chief Molyneux, trying to be conciliatory, 'this whole investigation is … well, damn it, it's very *mysterious*.'

'I never thought I'd hear a chief of detectives use the word "mysterious",' John replied tartly.

'What else would you call it?' Chief Molyneux appealed. He took his hands out of his pockets and held up two stubby fingers. 'Your son was locked up in an isolation room. Locked up, you got me? And there wasn't just one door, there was two. And there was a uniformed officer keeping watch by the elevator bank, and you can take it from me that he wasn't asleep.'

John said, '*You* decided to keep Lenny in detention. *You're* responsible – personally responsible. If you don't find him and find him quick, I'm going to have your head on a pole.'

'Mr Woods, I'm doing everything I can. You don't have to act unreasonable.'

'Unreasonable? Who's unreasonable? My son is nine years old and you were supposed to be taking care of him. Now he's out on his own – who knows where? And that's quite apart from the fact that anyone who comes near him could end up the same way as Sister Perpetua.' He paused, and took a deep breath. 'You saw Sister Perpetua for yourself.'

Chief Molyneux stood at the end of the bed for a long time without saying anything. Then he lowered

144

his eyes, and said, 'What you're telling me now is that Lenny *did* commit those homicides? Is that it?'

John stared at him in fury. 'I'm not telling you anything of the kind! What the hell do I have to do to convince you? Whatever killed those people, it came *out* of Lenny, yes. That's why anybody who stays close to Lenny is in serious danger. But it wasn't Lenny himself.'

Chief Molyneux let another long moment go by. 'Oh, yes. I forgot. It was a poltergeist, right?'

'Why don't you ask Dr Wesley? She'll tell you.'

'Dr Wesley? You mean *Dianne*? Sure, why not? She's the helpful sort, isn't she?'

John caught the slightly questioning note in his voice. 'And just what is *that* supposed to imply?' he demanded.

'You tell me. You spent the night at her place last night, all right, *si*?'

'Will you look at me?' John exclaimed. 'I'm totally helpless. I'm worse than a baby – I can't even suck my own thumb. And you're trying to make suggestive remarks about my spending the night with Dr Wesley? Don't you think you'd be better off looking for my son?'

'The entire Philadephia Police Department is looking for your son, Mr Woods. And I wasn't trying to be suggestive, not in that sense. What I was trying to discover was whether you and Dr Wesley might have been misguided enough to hatch some plan between you to spring young Lenny out of the hospital.'

John was about to shout back at Chief Molyneux; but then he let his head drop back onto the pillow and let out a long breath of resignation. Obnoxious as he was, the chief was only doing his job. And when Lenny had disappeared, his first suspicion must have been that his father had spirited him away.

145

The idea that anything intimate had happened between John and Dianne yesterday evening had come not from Chief Molyneux, but from John's own frustrated imagination. *Wishful thinking*, he thought with a surge of bitterness. *Just because you can't move your legs, that doesn't mean that you lose all desire to run. Just because you can't move your arms, that doesn't mean that you lose all desire to hold somebody's hand.*

Chief Molyneux went across to the window and tugged the pull-cord that altered the angle of the venetian blinds. He looked out at the hospital grounds, at the wide-spreading cedar, at the little cluster of handicapped men in wheelchairs.

'Friends of yours?' he asked John without turning around.

'We call ourselves the charioteers,' John replied.

Chief Molyneux nodded. 'The charioteers, huh?' Then he said, 'This isn't easy for me, Mr Woods, any of it. We have four homicides to clear up – messy, psychopathic homicides. We have a prime suspect in your son, sure, but I'm not so stupid or so insensitive as to assume that closes the file completely. As you pointed out yourself, Lenny is only a boy, and those four homicides were committed by somebody strong and determined and totally vicious.'

He paused for a moment, then added, 'I went over to Walnut Street first thing this morning and talked to one of our tame shrinks at the Psychology Center of Philadelphia. Dr Anderson, nice guy, very helpful. He showed me four authenticated case histories of children suffering from schizophrenia – you know, split personality – children who were quite capable of smashing up furniture and knocking down adults twice their size. One or two of them could easily have committed homicide.'

'Lenny didn't kill anybody,' John insisted.

Chief Molyneux turned around, and sniffed. 'Mr Woods, you and I have to accept the possibility that your son is suffering from schizophrenia, and that one side of his personality murdered all of those people without the other side being aware of it.'

'Now, listen, Chief –' John interrupted, but Chief Molyneux held up his hand to silence him.

'I said the *possibility*, not the certainty. The other two possibilities are that somebody else committed the homicides, somebody who went to a lot of trouble to make it look as if Lenny did them. However, *that* possibility is extremely remote, since no forensic evidence was found at the scenes of any of the homicides to suggest that anybody else had intruded, and the only individual who was known to be present at *all* of the homicides was Lenny.' He paused. 'The final possibility is that you and Dr Wesley are right, and that Lenny is harboring some kind of supernatural Jack the Ripper.'

'Well?' said John. 'What's your opinion?'

Chief Molyneux grunted. 'I'm not paid to have opinions. I'm paid to solve crimes, to arrest the perpetrators, and then to produce neat, tidy, comprehensible reports so that Commissioner Lodge can show the people of Philadelphia that they're getting crackerjack value for their tax dollars, and that they're not really being policed by a bunch of overworked eccentrics with views on poltergeists and beings from another level of existence.'

John narrowed his eyes and said, 'You're trying to tell me something.'

Chief Molyneux, with unexpected informality, perched himself on the side of John's bed. 'Yes, Mr Woods, I'm trying to tell you something. I'm trying to tell you that I personally have an open mind, and that I'm going to continue this investigation on two levels – the official level and the unofficial level.

'Officially, Mr Woods, I'm filing a report to Commissioner Lodge and to the District Attorney's Office and to the Juvenile Branch that all of the circumstantial evidence points to your son being the perpetrator of these homicides. In the same report, I'm going to add my personal recommendation that he undergo psychiatric analysis, with a view to corrective treatment.'

'And *unofficially*?'

'Unofficially, I'm going to ask you and Dr Wesley to continue to investigate this poltergeist idea of yours. I *was* going to make sure that you had access to Lenny – but, well, now that he's gone missing, you'll just have to do your best with him.' Chief Molyneux added, 'I'm sorry that we let him slip through our fingers. Do you understand what I'm telling you? But I'll find him, even if I have to go out and personally knock on every door in Philadelphia.'

He sniffed again; then he said, 'There's one thing more. I suspended Sergeant Clay and Detective Clay for two very good reasons. The first is that they failed to protect Sister Perpetuity from being murdered right in front of their eyes. The second is that I want them to work full-time with you and Dr Wesley tracking this poltergeist down and getting rid of it. I want it exterminated, exorcised, disinfected, whatever you do with poltergeists, before it kills anybody else. You got me?'

John could hardly credit what he was hearing. 'You *believe* in it,' he said slowly. 'You actually *believe* in it.'

'Let me tell you, Mr Woods, it isn't a question of blind faith,' Chief Molyneux replied. 'The simple fact is that when Sister Perpetuity was killed, your son was wired up like Frankenstein's monster. He was carrying eighteen different electrical contacts, all stuck into place with adhesive tape. He couldn't possibly have unfastened every single one of them, murdered Sister Perpetuity, and then returned to the couch and fastened them all back on again, in their *correct* locations, in pitch darkness, in fifteen seconds flat. Added to that, no murder weapon was found, and Lenny had no traces of blood on his hands – nor on his feet, which he would have done, if he had sliced her up like that.'

'But in your official report, you're going to accuse him of having done it,' John protested.

'I don't have any choice, Mr Woods. That's the only way we can keep the commissioner and the media and everybody else off our backs. That's the only way we can win ourselves some time. If the smallest whisper gets out that we're trying to track down a poltergeist – well, use your imagination. Dr Wesley will probably lose her funding from the university. The Clay twins will end up pushing brooms for a living. And me – well, Commissioner Lodge will hang me out to dry.'

John wished that he could reach out and grasp Chief Molyneux's hand. But all he could do was nod and say, 'I underestimated you, Chief. I'm sorry.'

'I don't want you saying you're sorry till I find your boy.'

'Do you think he's still in Philadelphia someplace?'

'More than likely. We're checking the bus stations and the railroad stations, and the homes of all of his school-friends.'

'You'll let me know when you hear something?'

Chief Molyneux stood up and laid his hand on John's shoulder. 'I promise. You'll be the first to know.'

Just then, Sister Clare appeared. 'Mr Woods? Your friends outside want to know if you're coming out to play Trivial Pursuit.'

'Trivial Pursuit,' said Chief Molyneux. 'That just about sums it up.'

* * *

Gil Miller was waiting for Lenny by the baggage carousels with a large cardboard sign that had GIL MILLER printed on it in green magic marker. He was a tall, thin-faced boy of almost twenty, with hair that had been cropped extra-short for the summer. Actually, he wished now he hadn't done it, because he thought it made his nose look too big, but his father had said it was 'excellent – just like the Marines.'

He wore a sleeveless sweatshirt with BORN TO SLEEP printed on the front, Adidas running shorts, odd socks, and sneakers that looked as if they ought to be taken to the city pound and humanely put down.

He caught sight of Lenny immediately, and enthusiastically waved his placard.

'Lenny? How are you? I'm Gil. How was your flight?'

The American Airlines stewardess who had escorted Lenny off the plane said, 'You're Mr Miller?'

'Here's my sign,' Gil told her. 'You want to see my social security card, too?'

Gil took Lenny out of the airport building and across the parking lot. It was a hot, cloudless day in downtown San Diego – glaring and dusty and almost fifteen degrees warmer than Philadelphia. Lenny followed Gil closely, feeling tired and jet-lagged after his journey, and very unsure of everything that was happening. He panted a little as he tried to keep up.

They walked around the chain-link fence that surrounded the parking lot, unable to talk because another jet was coming in, filling the afternoon with rippling thunder. Gill led Lenny across to a bright red '81 Firebird with yellow flames painted on the side. 'This is it, what d'you think? Friend of mine tweaked her up and she goes like a scalded cat.'

'She's very nice,' said Lenny in a whisper.

'*Nice?*' Gil burst out. But then he looked at Lenny

and saw how tired he was, and ruffled his hair. 'Come on, you look bushed. Let's get you to Uncle Henry's.'

They drove northward out of San Diego on 1-5, past the rounded green hills of La Jolla, and eventually out through the tawnier landscape of Carmel Valley. Gil drove fast, with the Firebird's exhaust blaring and the Beastie Boys on the stereo: '*You gotta fight, for your right, to par-tee!*'

They turned west toward Del Mar and the dazzling, sparkling ocean. But by the time Gil had jolted over the tracks of the Santa Fe railroad and squealed his Firebird to a halt outside Henry's beach house, Lenny was fast asleep.

'You poor little runt,' said Gill, grinning, and gently unbuckled him and carried him up to Henry's door with his skinny arms and legs dangling.

Henry came to the door wearing such peculiar clothes that his head didn't seem to belong to his body – as if he were being photographed at one of those fairground booths where you have to stick your head through a hole in a painted screen. He was gray-haired and professorial, with tortoiseshell eyeglasses, but he was dressed in a turquoise and orange beach shirt patterned with palm trees and hula girls and an oversized pair of safari shorts. Added to that, he wore navy-blue knee-length socks and basketball boots.

'Gil, you're late,' he said as Gil carried Lenny into the untidy living room. 'I was worried that maybe the police had spotted him. There – put him down on the couch.'

Henry cleared away a stack of magazines, *Philosophy Today* and *Turf* and *Sport Digest* and *Playboy*, and Gil laid Lenny on the couch, propping his head on a large, frayed cushion.

'Poor kid,' said Henry. 'Springer was here about an hour ago. He told me the kid was looking all-in.'

Gil said, 'You're going to manage okay?'

151

'You don't think I'm capable of looking after a nine-year-old boy?'

'I don't even think you're capable of looking after yourself. Look at the state of this place.'

Henry looked around as if he just been beamed into the middle of the room from the starship *Enterprise*. 'Looks all right to me,' he said, blinking. 'Maybe a little untidy. In any case, the maid comes tomorrow.'

'You don't need a maid, you need half a dozen Seabees with a bulldozer.'

Henry went through to the kitchen and opened the icebox. The front of it was dotted with novelty magnets in the shapes of cucumbers and melons and other oddities, and under each magnet a note was stuck: *Call Dr Weissman re Thursday's think-tank*! or *Laundry*!! or *Spinoza book – who borrowed it? Ask Gomez*!!!

'You want a beer?' he asked Gil.

'I thought you were still on the water-wagon.'

'I am,' said Henry, tossing him a cold Olympia. 'I'm having Gatorade.'

They returned to the living room, and Henry moved the magazines once again so that they could sit at the dining table by the window and look out over the promenade. The beach was wide, with pale gray sand; the ocean glittered like a chest full of fairy-tale diamonds. Gil popped the top of his beer can and swallowed almost half of its contents without taking a breath.

'I thought Springer seemed a little agitated,' Henry remarked.

'How, agitated?' Gil asked.

'I'm not quite sure. You remember the first time we met him, he seemed to be very expansive, very *confident*. All that talk of historical struggles and battles to save mankind. I don't know – this time, he seemed to be *diminished*, somehow. It's hard to explain. As if we might have bitten off more than we can chew.'

Gil wiped his mouth with the back of his hand. 'We won out againt Yaomauitl, didn't we?'

Henry nodded. 'I suppose so. But this time, I don't think Springer knows what it is that we're up against. It's something powerful, and very vicious; that's what he said. But he couldn't put a name to it. He couldn't even tell me exactly what it was. Black, he said, and strong, with no human feelings whatsoever.'

'Sounds like my basketball coach,' said Gil with a grin.

'Well, I don't know,' said Henry. He picked up a crumpled pack of Marlboros and discovered one last cigarette inside, as bent as a Charley Noble chimney stack. He carefully straightened it out, then lit it.

'Lung cancer,' Gil warned him.

Henry said, 'Yes. But I don't have the strength to hang up both crutches at the same time.'

'You should jog,' Gil told him.

'In these shorts? They catch so much wind I'm thinking of putting my name down for next year's Americas Cup race.'

'Oh, come on, Henry,' said Gil. 'Can't you wear different shorts? I mean, something with a little less acreage?'

'Then people would laugh at my legs.'

'Jesus, Henry, they *wouldn't*.'

'But *I* would, and I can't jog when I'm laughing. I can scarcely jog when I'm *not* laughing.'

Despite the difference in their ages, Henry and Gil shared a special rapport. Last year, they had both met the being who called himself Springer. With Springer's guidance, they had discovered for the first time that they were heirs to that secret and mythical brotherhood called the Night Warriors.

Even if they were never called upon by Springer to

153

become Night Warriors again, they would be bonded forever by the memories of battle. They were veterans, both of them, of the silent wars that rage during the hours of darkness. That made them special. That made them close.

Friends who saw them together could never understand how a down-at-heel professor of Philosophy from the University of California at San Diego could have formed such an easy and affectionate relationship with a young beach bum whose father owned a grocery store and who spent most of his free time bellowing up and down the Pacific Highway in his souped-up Firebird. There seemed to be no logic to it. Everybody knew that Henry wasn't gay; and Gil *certainly* wasn't gay.

None of their friends, of course, would have believed or understood the roles that Henry and Gil had adopted during the hours of darkness. Night Warriors, in imaginary armor, hunting the last vestiges of absolute evil through the landscape of human dreams.

They let Lenny sleep until four o'clock; then Henry went over and gently shook his shoulder. 'Lenny? Lenny, are you awake?'

Lenny opened his eyes, then rubbed them and yawned. Henry hunkered down beside the couch. 'How do you do, Lenny? My name's Henry.'

Lenny sat up and looked around. 'I was having a dream.'

'It must have been a good dream,' said Henry. 'What was it about?'

'I don't know ... I dreamed I was someplace nice ... by the sea.'

Henry laughed. 'You didn't dream it. You're here. You're right by the beach.'

Lenny blinked at Henry and then at Gil. 'Mr

Springer sent me. He said you were going to look after me.'

'That's right, Lenny,' Henry said. 'Welcome to the Hotel Watkins. I'm going to give you a bed to sleep in and a beach to play on, and if you don't object to chow mein to go and Big Macs every other night, I'm going to feed you, too.'

'Kid – whatever you do, don't let Henry feed you,' Gil put in, with a mock-serious face. 'You'll grow up weighing three hundred forty pounds, with a face that's one continuous zit. *I'll* feed you. The best of everything: fresh pasta, fresh tomatoes, charbroiled swordfish, prime rib, plenty of fruit. Believe me, my old man's in the food business.'

'Gil's too healthy for his own good,' Henry retaliated.

Gil checked his stainless-steel diver's watch. 'Look at the time, Henry. What do you say, *tempus fujiyama* or something? I have to get back to help Dad with the deli counter.'

'All right, Gil,' said Henry. 'I'll see you tomorrow, perhaps.'

'You bet. Are you going to be seeing Springer tonight?'

'I'm not really sure,' Henry admitted. 'He didn't tell me very much. I'm not even sure what I'm supposed to be doing – apart from taking care of our friend here.'

'Lenny,' Gil reminded him.

Henry laid his hand on Lenny's shoulder. 'That's right, Lenny.'

Henry and Lenny went out to the street to watch Gil drive away. Gil blew his horn – the first six notes of the national anthem, *Oh, say can you see* – and then he U-turned and headed back with burbling exhausts toward his father's store on the Solana Beach boardwalk.

'Are you hungry?' Henry asked Lenny. 'What would you like to eat?'

Lenny said, 'Is it okay if I have a Big Mac?'

Henry laughed. 'Of course it's okay. Don't take any notice of Gil. There's a McDonald's across the valley. You can have giant fries, too. And a strawberry milkshake. And ice cream to follow. Do you know what I always say?'

Lenny shook his head.

'I always say, "Goddamn the calories," that's what I always say.' Henry replied, shaking his fist. 'And goddamn Leibniz, and the irrefragable truth of individuation.'

'Sir?' said Lenny, frowning.

Henry flapped his hand. 'Oh, don't worry about that. That's philosophy. I'll explain it you over supper.'

After Henry had tucked Lenny into bed that evening, he went out onto the promenade that fronted his house to watch the fat crimson sun sinking into the sea. He leaned his elbows on the railings and smoked a cigarette. A warm wind blew across the beach and the gulls circled high over the sandstone cliffs, calling sadly.

A gray-haired woman in a floppy flannel hat came ambling past, walking her poodle. 'How are you, Henry?' she asked him, and he turned and smiled, and said, 'Fine, Marion, thank you.'

The truth was, however, that he felt edgy and anxious. Once last year's adventure as a Night Warrior had been triumphantly completed, it had been easy to look back on it as heroic – even fun. But when Springer had reappeared yesterday and told him that he might be called upon a second time, the old feelings of uncertainty had welled up again. He had been terrified, most of the time; and in the end he had nearly died. Suddenly his brief career as a Night Warrior didn't seem so damned glamorous anymore.

He shaded his eyes with his hand. The sun was almost gone now, but it was still dazzling. He thought he could make out somebody walking toward him across the sloping beach, a tall blond girl in a black swimsuit, carrying a pink towel and a pink beach bag. There were dozens of girls on this beach – schoolgirls, mostly, who came to swim and sunbathe after class – but there was something about this particular girl that caught his attention. Something familiar about the way she walked. He sucked his cigarette down to the filter, and then flicked it onto the sand. He couldn't suppress a feeling of deep dread as the girl came nearer and nearer, and at last came up the wooden steps and approached him.

She was as tall as he was, taller, and flawlessly beautiful. Straight nose, full pink lips, grape-green eyes. Her black latex swimsuit gleamed like a second rubbery skin, clinging to large rounded breasts and cut right up over her hips. She had legs that seemed to start at Henry's shoulder-level and go on and on and on, until they finally tapered into her ankles.

'Hallo, Henry,' she said, smiling.

'Hallo yourself,' Henry replied with a conspicuous lack of grace.

The girl came up close to him and leaned her back against the railings. 'How's Lenny?' she asked.

'Lenny's doing great, when you consider what he's been through. He stammers a little; he cries easily. But he's a terrific little boy. If Andrea hadn't been such a bitch, I could have had a grandson like that.'

The girl brushed hair away from her face. 'You were destined for other things, Henry.'

Henry shrugged. 'I didn't think that being a Night Warrior was compulsory. Otherwise I would have burned my draft card.'

'Are you frightened?'

Henry looked at her narrowly. 'More to the point, are *you* frightened?'

The girl turned around and gazed at the ocean. Her swimsuit was cut startlingly high at the back; the cheeks of her bottom were golden and perfect. If Henry hadn't known that she was nothing more than a collection of projected information, a living hologram, he would have found her very disturbing indeed. But she wasn't real in the same sense that he was real, and he knew from experience that she could just as easily have appeared on the beach as a man, or a child, or any one of a hundred personalities or shades of personality.

After a while, she said, 'We're not at all sure what's happening. Something is coming through from the other side, some very powerful and very malevolent force. It materializes in Lenny's dreams, and actually takes on substance in the material world. It kills at random, very cruelly. Then it vanishes.'

'Sounds like a must to avoid,' Henry remarked wryly.

The girl turned to him with a serious face. 'Unfortunately, Henry, you must do the opposite. You must not avoid it, but go to meet it head-on.'

'*Me*? You want *me* to confront this thing? I thought I was just doing a little baby-sitting here.'

'You're the charge-keeper. You carry the source of all of the power. I want you to enter Lenny's dream *before* this force has a chance to manifest itself, and destroy it.'

'On my own?' asked Henry.

The girl nodded. 'It is far stronger than anything we have come across before. You may very well need all the energy at your disposal. If you take the others with

158

you, you won't be able to use so much energy – because of course you will need quite a large proportion of it to get all of you back to the waking world.'

Henry thought about this, 'I don't know ... I'm not too happy about going on my own. I'd prefer to take Gil – or Susan, maybe, to watch my back. I'm not as young as I was. My reactions are a whole lot slower.'

The girl said, 'I'm sorry, Henry, the risk is too high. If you fail to destroy this force the very first time you encounter it, you will never get the opportunity to catch it by surprise a second time. It will immediately pursue you into the real world, and kill you without compunction.'

'Springer –' Henry began, but then he shook his head. 'Goddamn it, I wish I'd never set eyes on you.'

'It's your destiny, Henry,' said the girl called Springer, reaching out and touching Henry's arm. 'You can't avoid your destiny, no matter how hard you try.'

'So you keep telling me,' Henry complained.

'I will be watching,' Springer told him. 'All you have to do is to make sure that you enter Lenny's dream as soon as he falls asleep. Then hunt down that force and give it a charge of maximum power before it can take on physical shape.'

'I don't know,' said Henry. 'I can't say I'm particularly happy about all of this. You don't seem to have worked it out much in advance. No forward planning.'

'When we fought against the demon Yaomauitl, we knew just as little.'

Henry brushed back his windblown hair. 'That was different. Turning into Night Warriors was new to us then, a completely novel experience. It was *exciting*. And there were four of us, after all.'

The girl stood beside Henry without saying anything more, and meanwhile the sun disappeared into the ocean and the sky began to fade.

Henry took out another cigarette. He struck a match, and there was a momentary sharpness of burned sulphur in the wind. He smoked without taking the cigarette out of his mouth and kept both slitted eyes on Springer, as if he expected Springer to change into a man right in front of his eyes.

'I'll think about it,' he said at last. 'Meet me tomorrow, and we'll talk it over some more.'

'Henry, I'm sorry, you don't have any time to think about it. Lenny is asleep now. As soon as it gets wholly dark, the force that's hiding inside of him could take on material shape.'

'And then what?'

'And then it could kill you in your bed.'

Henry was silent for a while. Then he said, 'I don't even have a choice, then? That's what you're trying to tell me? I have to go after this force, whether I want to or not – kill or be killed? Thanks a million.'

'I'm sorry,' said Springer. A young boy in fluorescent pink and green jams with a surfboard under one arm and a James Dean haircut called out, 'Woo-ee, baby! Wanna boogie?' but Springer totally ignored him. She added, more gently. 'The Night Warriors have a historical duty, Henry. Choice doesn't enter into it.'

Henry turned to look at his beach house, and at the shuttered window where Lenny already lay asleep. In spite of the warmth of the evening wind, he shivered.

Ten

Norman Clay leaned over and whispered something in his brother's ear.

'Uh-huh.' Thaddeus nodded. 'Uh-huh. Uh-huh.'

'What's he saying?' John wanted to know.

Thaddeus circled the room, both hands held out as if he were feeling the texture of the air. 'He says it came from here – it came from the house. He can sense it.'

'Is it still here?' asked Dianne.

Norman shook his head, and whispered in Thaddeus's ear yet again.

Thaddeus said, 'It's gone now. But it was here for a very long time. Decades, maybe centuries. Ever since the house was built, maybe earlier.'

'You're trying to tell me the house was haunted?' John said.

Thaddeus pulled a face. 'Not exactly *haunted*. That's the wrong word. But the thing was here, no question about it; just like there's no doubt that now it's gone.'

At Dianne's suggestion, they had all gathered at John's house on Third Street. Dianne had argued that if they could possibly track the influence to its source, they might be able to discover what it was and how they could exterminate it. She and John had met up with Thaddeus and Norman Clay at the hospital, and they had all driven here in Dianne's station wagon.

'How old is this house?' asked Thaddeus.

161

'One of the oldest in the city,' said John. 'At least, *parts* of it are. Maybe not as venerable as Elfreth's Alley, but still pretty historic. The realtor told us that it predates the Constitution. So, what are we talking about? Two hundred years plus.'

'And this room?' Thaddeus wanted to know. 'This was original?'

'I guess so. It seems like it's central to the whole structure of the house.'

While they were talking, Norman was edging his way around the perimeter of the sitting room, touching the walls with his fingertips. Every now and then he paused and closed his eyes, as if he were listening to faraway music. Then he continued, occasionally moving chairs and tables away from the wall, even removing a painting, so that he could absorb the accumulated memories of two hundred years. All of the lives that had been lived out here, all of the human drama to which these walls had been witness. All of the crying, the laughing, the Christmases, the happy summers. And something else, too. Something black and secret and infinitely evil. Something that had been waiting here for Lenny to come along.

Norman reached a point by the window. In the daytime, there was an angular view out into the yard from here; but tonight the windows showed nothing but darkness and their own reflected faces. He stopped, one hand pressed flat against the plaster. He closed his eyes. Then he went on a little way – but he soon returned to the same spot by the window. He smoothed his hand over it, then bent forward and tentatively sniffed it.

'Anything?' asked Dianne.

'Smell it for yourself,' Norman suggested.

Dianne approached the place that Norman was

162

pointing out. It was about four feet up from the floor, on the right side of the window. There was an area no bigger than Norman's hand where the wallpaper was slightly discolored.

'Oh, yes,' said John. 'Jennifer mentioned that. It's a damp patch, something to do with water being drawn into the wall by osmosis. We were going to have it looked at by a builder if it got any worse.'

Dianne sniffed it, and immediately wrinkled up her nose. 'What a hideous stench! What is it!'

'I don't know,' said Thaddeus, 'but I think we ought to find out. John – do you have any tools any place? A hammer and chisel, maybe? And do you mind if we hack out this place in the wall, to find out what it is?'

'Go ahead,' John told him. 'The tools are in the garage.'

Norman spread newspapers on the carpet and knelt down in front of the wall. He tore off a wide strip of wallpaper, and began to chop away at the plaster with a hammer and a metal dog. The plaster came away easily in dusty lumps.

Thaddeus picked one of them up and hefted it in his hand. 'Looks like this part of the wall is original. You see this plaster? All horsehair and road-sweepings.'

Gradually, Norman widened the hole in the plaster until he exposed the bare brick. He rested back on his haunches for a moment or two, then attacked the mortar with the edge of the chisel, dislodging first one brick and then a small shower of them.

'Just make sure you leave some of the old place standing,' John told him.

Norman sniffed again at the hole in the wall. 'It was here,' said Thaddeus, watching his brother and interpreting every response. 'Whatever it was, it was right here.'

Dianne wheeled John a little closer so that he could

see what was going on.

'Do you have any idea what it was?' John asked.

'Not yet,' Thaddeus replied. 'But it was extremely evil. Norman says he never felt anything so evil.'

With a squeaking, grating noise, Norman wrested out two more bricks, with the chisel, opening up a large cavity in the wall. A soft draft blew out of it, a draft that had funneled through absolute darkness; and now they could all smell the sweetish odor of recent decay.

Norman unbuttoned his shirt cuff, rolled up his sleeve, and cautiously reached inside the cavity, until his arm had disappeared up to his elbow.

'Just be careful,' Dianne warned. 'Don't forget what happened to Sister Perpetua.'

'Now she reminds me,' said Norman, his arm deep inside the wall.

He groped around for a while, and then he suddenly wrinkled up his face in disgust and said quietly, 'Oh, shit.'

'What is it?' asked John. 'Did you find something?'

With an expression of total revulsion, Norman slowly withdrew his arm from the cavity. He hesitated for a moment, then dragged out a huge, slimy handful of something black, like rotting ox liver. Part of it was covered in a thin, black, wrinkled caul; the rest was glistening and putrescent and teeming with blowfly maggots. The smell was so strong that Dianne retched and had to turn away.

'Oh, my God,' said John, as Norman dropped it with a glutinous, splattering sound on the newspaper that he'd spread on the floor. 'What *is* that?'

Norman wiped his hand again and again on a crumpled-up sheet of newspaper. 'I don't know, man. Something dead.'

'Is it an animal?' asked John. 'I mean, *was* it an animal?'

164

But Dianne turned around and looked at the mess with deep distaste, and said, 'I know what it is. At least, I *think* I know what it is, I did midwifery once. It's an afterbirth.'

'An afterbirth?' said John. 'What the hell is an afterbirth doing in the wall?'

Thaddeus rose from where he'd been crouching near the newspaper, covering his mouth and his nose with his hand. Norman stood up, too, and whispered something in Thaddeus's ear. Thaddeus nodded. 'That black thing that killed your wife – the same thing that killed the Pellings and Sister Perpetua – Norman thinks it was born here,' he said.

'Here? In this wall? John demanded. 'How can any living creature be born in a wall?'

'John,' said Thaddeus, 'this is nothing but guess work. But we're not talking about anything human here, remember? We're talking about something that could have been waiting in this wall for two hundred years. An embryo, almost. Norman thinks that this cavity could have taken the place of a nest, or a womb, do you understand what I mean? The bricks inside are lined with slime. And here we have an afterbirth, or what *looks* like an afterbirth.'

'Burn it,' said John.

'No, no,' Dianne interrupted. 'Just scrape it into a plastic bag. I want to take it to the biology department. Seth Maxwell can analyze it for me.'

'Are you sure?' asked Thaddeus.

'Of course I'm sure,' Dianne insisted. 'Don't you understand how *important* this could be? If you're right – if this *has* been here for two hundred years – it could be the first genuine sample of real psychic ectoplasm that anybody has ever been able to take to a laboratory and analyze.'

John said, 'What worries me – supposing you *are*

right, and this is really the afterbirth of something that was born inside this wall – then can you imagine what that *something* must be like? And it's inside of my son, Thaddeus. It's actually inside of him.'

Norman went through to the kitchen and came back with a heavy-duty garbage bag. Together, he and Thaddeus picked up the slimy afterbirth and dropped it inside.

'Here you are,' said Thaddeus, handing the bag to Dianne. 'And you're welcome to it.' He checked his watch. 'Norman and me, we're going to go to the Historical Society on Locust and see if we can't check back on the history of this particular house. Maybe we can dig up something that will give us a clue to what this thing was doing in the wall.'

At that moment, the telephone rang. Thaddeus picked it up and said, 'Woods residence, who's calling?'

He listened, then said, 'I'll tell her,' and put the phone down again. 'Dr Wesley – that was your research assistant. The infra-red photographs have been developed.'

'All right,' said Dianne with brisk determination. 'Perhaps we'll get to see what this something actually looks like. Are you coming, John?'

'It depends whether you're going to push me or not.'

Dianne took hold of the handles of his wheelchair. 'Oh, I'll push you all right. You just watch me.'

Henry watched television for half an hour, then went through to the bathroom to shower. On the way, he looked in on Lenny in the guest bedroom. Lenny was fast asleep, his cheeks flushed, his left hand crooked. Henry sat down on the edge of the bed and stroked the boy's forehead. Lenny wasn't dreaming yet. He was

166

still overcoming the exhaustion of having been rescued by his mother from Philadelphia and flown here to the coast.

It was when his eyeballs started to shift under his eyelids that Henry would know that the dreaming had started, and that he was walking through the landscapes of the night.

After his shower, Henry made himself a mug of Ovaltine and went to bed. He had been reading Spinoza on the renunciation of the impossible, but he felt too tense to think about philosophy tonight. Instead, he rummaged around on the floor for a copy of *Reader's Digest*.

It was almost eleven o'clock when he switched off his bedside lamp, punched his pillow into a comfortable shape, and snuggled into the curled-up position in which he liked to sleep. A *sixty-year-old* fetus, he thought to himself. He sometimes thought that he ought to go looking for another wife, especially now that he had stopped drinking and his breath didn't smell like Seagram's distillery anymore. He often wondered how his friends had managed to put up with his breath, all those years. These days, he could tell at once if somebody had been drinking, from ten paces away.

It was hard to think what kind of wife would suit him at this age, however. Andrea had been intelligent, a brilliant conversationalist, but a mediocre cook and a chilly bed-companion. After his first adventure as a Night Warrior last year, bursting with newfound confidence and self-esteem, Henry had become entangled briefly with a waitress called Marcia. Marcia had baked heavenly ginger-cakes and made love to him so boisterously that he had sometimes feared for the survival of his divan-bed. But he had discovered that a man can eat only so much ginger-cake, and only make love so many times in a day; after that, a little small talk is usually required to fill in the hours before he starts feeling hungry and horny once again. Marcia had very little small talk, and no big talk whatsoever. Gil had called her his Darling Dipstick.

Henry missed Marcia's cakes sometimes, and at night he was frequently lonely. But he still remembered those endless afternoons sitting in silence, the two of them just smiling at each other. 'Did you know that Russell believed the world to be made up of atomic facts mirrored in the elementary propositions?' 'You mean *Kurt* Russel? Didn't he play Elvis in that movie?'

Marcia had almost driven him back to vodka.

A little after eleven-thirty, sleep washed over him like a dark wave; and almost immediately his dream-self rose out of his body and stood in the darkness, listening. All he could hear was the distant drumming of the surf along the shoreline and Lenny's high, even breathing. He waited for a few moments, then raised both hands, palms outward, and repeated under his breath the ancient incantation of the Night Warriors, words he'd never been able to forget: *'Now when the face of the world is covered with darkness, let me prepare myself here; let me arm and armor myself: and let me be nourished by the power that is dedicated to the cleaving of darkness, the settling of all black matters, and the dissipation of evil, so be it.'*

Gradually, the darkness in the room began to draw in toward him; and out of the atoms of the night a suit of armor began to form, Renaissance in style, with a wedge-shaped helmet, heavily plated shoulders, and hip-joints with overlapping scales like lobster-tails. Within two or three minutes, Henry had become Kasyx, the charge-keeper, the greatest and most powerful of all the Night Warriors.

He harbored so much energy that lightning crawled

and crackled across his shoulders, and sparks dropped from his arms like fireflies. He flexed his armored gloves. To feel all this energy flowing through him was exhilarating. It made him feel as if he were eighteen again – fit, alert, and fully in control of his mind and body.

Kasyx had no armament of his own, but the immense store of power that he carried with him could be used by his fellow Night Warriors to recharge their weapons during battle. Kasyx did, however, possess one ultimate sanction against the enemy: he could discharge almost all of his power in a single, devastating blast. *Almost* all, because he always needed to hold back enough to enable him to return to the waking world. Several times in the legendary history of the Night Warriors, in the days when demons had been rife and the Night Warriors were counted in their hundreds, charge-keepers had taken the heroic decision to destroy their evil enemies by releasing *all* of their power.

The consequences of total power discharge were that the charge-keeper's physical body remained comatose until he died of dehydration and malnutrition; and that his spirit remained imprisoned forever in an endless succession of dreams and nightmares.

Tonight Kasyx felt powerful and confident, but he still didn't relish the idea of either of those fates.

With a faint hum of psychic power, he moved across his shadowy bedroom and through the door, the molecules of his body blending with and flowing through the molecules of the varnished wood. He reappeared in the corridor and walked toward the guestroom, where Lenny still lay asleep. He hesitated, then approached the bed and leaned over it, a bulky, armored figure. Lenny's face was faintly illuminated by the dancing, quivering electricity that played across Kasyx's breastplate.

Beneath his blue-veined eyelids, Lenny's eyes were

darting from side to side. This was REM sleep – sleep with rapid eye movement. This told Kasyx that Lenny had started dreaming. He was moving through some imaginary world, and his mind's eyes were reacting to whatever he saw.

'All right, my boy,' whispered Kasyx. 'Let's see what you've been having all these nightmares about.'

Stepping back two or three paces, Kasyx raised his arms and directed his energy so that it flowed along his arms to his fingertips. Lightning jerked and jumped between one hand and the other, like a Van de Graaff generator. Kasyx methodically drew a flickering blue octagon in the air – an octagon of sheer power that remained hovering where he had drawn it.

He hesitated for a moment, then thrust both hands into the octagon and slowly tugged apart the substance of the waking world, opening up an entrance into the world of Lenny's dreams. He lifted the octagon so that it hovered over his head, and then gradually lowered it to floor-level.

He found himself standing in a bright, barren desert, with the midday sun high overhead. He switched his face-plate to anti-dazzle, and looked around him. There was no sign of Lenny anywhere, but he knew from experience that the dreamer doesn't always appear in his own dreams. He could see nothing but endless miles of heat-cracked rocks, tall fluted saguaro cactus, and dust-dry lizards, and a distant ripple of liquid air, rising off the hundred-and-twenty-degree desert and reflecting the peaks of shattered mountains.

Cowboy-land, thought Kasyx astutely. The unchanging Arizona of the Cisco Kid, Jeff Chandler, the Lone Ranger and Tonto. He lifted his hand to the side of his helmet, and adjusted his faceplate focus to infinity. As he turned slowly in a circle, he distinguished an Indian encampment in a shallow valley, about twenty or thirty lodges. He could make out several dozen brown-and-white palomino ponies, tethered close by, but no Indians. According to the scale on the side of his faceplate, the encampment was 9.23 kilometers off to the southwest. To the east, 5.8 kilometers away, he saw what looked like a small railroad town – a depot, a church, a dry-goods store, a two-storey hotel, a jail, and a scattering of houses. Smoke rose from the hotel's chimney stack and looped lazily into the air.

Well, thought Kasyx, *where there's smoke there's life, even if it's the kind of life you can only find in nightmares.*

He began to walk across the stony surface of the desert toward the town. Although he had a long way to go, he seemed to be able to cover the ground as quickly as if he were on horseback. The rocks and the gulleys and the towering cactus hurried and jostled past him at almost thirty kilometers an hour. His first experiences in dreams had taught him that progress varied wildly, according to the moods and frustrations of the dreamer; in this case, he guessed that young Lenny was recreating in his mind the way that all boys canter around the yard when they're playing cowboys – pretending that they're riding a horse.

He glanced behind him and saw that he was leaving a high trail of dust, just as if he were galloping on horseback.

The sun glared down out of a white sky. Every now and then Kasyx glimpsed a scorpion dancing across the rocks, or heard the *skrrrrrr* of a rattlesnake. These were definitely the badlands, he decided.

He reached a low ridge overlooking the town. Now that he was closer, he could see people promenading along the boardwalks and crossing the streets. An occasional rig clattered along the main street, and the drivers would wave to the men sitting outside the saloon, their boots propped up on the hitching-rail. A faded wooden sign announced that this was Gun Gulch, Ariz., Pop. 131. Presumably the law of the six-gun had caught up with the 132nd member of the populace. Beyond the wooden facades of the buildings, up on the hill, Kasyx could see a small cemetery, thickly clustered with wooden crosses.

He was about to walk down toward the town when his infra-red sensor began to go *meep-meep-meep-meep*. Backing quickly away from the exposed position on the ridge, he looked around to see what had set it going. Almost immediately, as if he had stepped out from behind a cardboard rock in a school play, an Indian appeared. He wore a huge warbonnet of eagle feathers, a buffalo-skin robe, and moccasins. His face was dark red, the color of freshly burnished mahogany, with high cheekbones and a hooked nose and a mouth that was so thinly drawn that it was almost lipless.

The Indian stared at Kasyx for a moment, and then he lifted one hand. 'How,' he greeted him.

Kasyx lifted a hand in cautious response. Did Indians *really* say 'How,' he wondered, or was it merely a myth from cowboy movies? However, this dream Indian had said 'How,' so Kasyx said 'How' in return.

'My name is Particular-Time-of-Day,' the Indian announced.

Kasyx bowed his head. 'Good to know you. My name's Kasyx.'

The Indian focused his eyes on the horizon. 'You are not from this place, Kas-Yx.'

'No,' said Kasyx, 'I'm just passing through, you might say.'

'You visit the white man's lodges?'

'I was considering it, yes.'

172

Particular-Time-of-Day clenched his right fist, then swept it downward with his fingers spread out. Evidently it was Plains Indian sign language, but Kasyx didn't understand what it meant. 'Bad,' said Particular-Time-of-Day. Then he pressed the heels of both hands together and opened them wide, so that one was pointing upward and the other was lying horizontal. 'Bad Shadow. You should not go there.'

'Bad Shadow? What do you mean by that?'

Particular-Time-of-Day simply repeated the two signs. *Bad. Shadow.* Then he waved his hand from side to side, indicating that Kasyx should approach the town no nearer.

'There is death there, Kas-Yx. There is death that walks through every lodge, and nobody can stop it.'

'Like an illness, you mean? Plague, or typhoid? Something like that?'

Particular-Time-of-Day shook his head. 'Bad shadow.'

Kasyx hesitated for a moment, then said, 'I appreciate your warning. But I have to go down there. I think this bad shadow of yours is what I've been looking for.'

'I cannot protect you,' the Indian cautioned him.

Kasyx glanced up at the glowing horizontal bar inside his helmet that told him how much power he had left. It was way up, almost one hundred percent. Enough psychic energy to demolish half of downtown San Diego. 'I think I'm capable of protecting myself,' he told Particular-Time-of-Day.

'Nonetheless,' the Indian replied, 'I will walk with you as your travelling companion.'

'Well ...' Kasyx demurred.

'You are a warrior of great strength,' Particular-Time-of-Day complimented him. 'But even warriors of great strength sometimes need eyes that look to all points of the compass at one and the same time.'

'All right, then,' agreed Kasyx. 'But when I tell you to get the hell out of the way, you don't even think about it, you get those moccasins motoring, you understand me? I'm going to be doing some major demolition here tonight, and I wouldn't like any part of Lenny's personality caught up in it.'

Particular-Time-of-Day frowned and made a sign indicating he was confused.

'Don't ask me to explain,' Kasyx told him. 'Just make sure that when I say *vamos*, you *vamos*.'

Side by side, they negotiated the stony incline that led down to the dream community of Gun Gulch.

In his first experience in penetrating dreams, Kasyx had been surprised that nobody seemed to find his bulky crimson armor at all incongruous or strange. He could walk into a roomful of people in evening dress, and they would treat him as if he were wearing a smart black tuxedo and a well-pressed dicky. It was only when Springer had explained that the people in dreams were not people at all, but creations of the dreamer's imagination, that Kasyx had begun to understand why. They were incapable of independent thought; and provided the dreamer was not disturbed by Kasyx's entrance into his dream-world, the characters who peopled it would not be disturbed, either.

Kasyx and Particular-Time-of-Day walked side by side along Gun Gulch's dusty main street. On one side was Chisholm's hardware, with barrels of nails outside and saws and plow blades and rope hanging in the window near a placard announcing *Dynamite*; on the other was Hickock's Gun Emporium, with racks of Winchesters and glass cases crowded with Starrs and Colts and Derringers.

Tinkling piano music reached their ears as they came close to the Lucky Shot Saloon. Three or four boys in dusty serge pants and buttoned-up coats sat on the steps outside, playing with buffalo-bone dice. One of the boys glanced up, and Kasyx saw that it was Lenny.

For a moment, Kasyx thought that Lenny might recognize him; but Lenny returned to his game without a second look.

They reached the McSween Hotel. It was a square, weatherboarded building painted sun-faded green, with a large veranda and ostentatious mahogany doors that had probably been specially ordered from the East. An elderly couple were sitting on the veranda drinking coffee and playing an innocuous game of cards. As the old woman rocked backward and forward in her rocking chair, one lens of her wire-rimmed spectacles reflected the light like a silver dollar. Kasyx mounted the veranda steps and nodded to them, and the old man lifted his wide-brimmed going-to-meeting hat.

Kasyx guessed that they were Lenny's grandparents, both long dead.

He pushed open the hotel's doors and entered the lobby, with Particular-Time-of-Day following behind. It was cooler inside the lobby. A brass fan revolved slowly on the ceiling, causing the potted palms to dip and curtsy with each revolution. There were couches and easy chairs in worn green velvet, and a table with newspapers and magazines. A young woman in a starched blouse stood behind the mahogany desk, writing in a large accounts book with marbled pages.

She looked up. She was young, brisk, her brunette hair tied in a ribbon at the back. Kasyx guessed that she was Lenny's math teacher.

'No Indians,' she said sharply.

'I beg your pardon?'

'No Indians. We don't allow Indians.'

Kasyx turned to Particular-Time-of-Day; but the Indian simply shrugged as if he were used to it. 'I wait outside, *kemo sabe*.' He went back out onto the veranda, and Kasyx approached the counter.

'Did you want a room?' the young woman asked him.

Close up, he could see that she was older than she had appeared at first. Her skin was pale and freckled and there were lines around her eyes. She was quite pretty, but her prettiness had been spoiled by hard work and a vexatious personality. She was wearing some kind of cologne or hairdressing that smelled strongly of violets.

'I'm looking for somebody,' he told her.

She stared back at him with defiance. 'You're not a bounty hunter? We don't allow bounty hunters.'

'No Indians, no bounty hunters. Whom do you allow?'

She wasn't amused. 'This is a hotel for clean, decent citizens.'

'That means they have to wash off the trail dust before we allow them between the sheets,' another voice interrupted. Kasyx turned, and saw a small, voluptuous girl in a red and white candy-striped satin gown, just coming down the stairs. She had curly black hair, mountains of it, all pinned up with tortoiseshell combs, and a black beauty spot on her upper lip. Her plump, soft breasts were barely contained by her low-cut gown; the pink areolas of her nipples were exposed, and Kasyx thought that she would only have to sneeze once to be completely topless.

He wondered for a moment what a nine-year-old could be doing, dreaming about a 'soiled dove' like this. But then he recalled his own heightening interest in girls at about the same age, especially in Paulette

Goddard, God forgive him, and those bosomy floozies in cowboy movies, so Lenny was excused.

'I'm looking for somebody,' said Kasyx.

'Well, I sure hope it's me,' the soiled dove replied, winking at him with blackened eyelashes.

'We don't care for strangers,' said the woman behind the counter.

Kasyx said, 'This – person, this thing I'm looking for – it's black.'

'You mean a Negro? We definitely don't allow Negroes.'

'No, no. He dresses black. The Indians call him the Bad Shadow.'

'Wow-ee,' said the soiled dove, impressed. 'The Bad Shadow! Sounds like my kind of man.'

'To tell you the truth, I'm not entirely sure that he's a man,' said Kasyx.

'Oh, *that's easy* to find out,' the soiled dove remarked with a laugh, and prodded his chest with a red-painted but well-bitten fingernail. Lenny's idea of a bad girl must be one who bit her nails.

Kasyx said, 'Do you mind if I check your rooms? It's possible that he could be hiding here.'

The woman behind the counter shook her head. 'You're not the sheriff, I can't let you do that.' Her eyes darted from side to side, oddly anxious and shifty. 'I'm sorry, you'll have to leave.'

'Supposing I book a room?'

The woman let out a short, exasperated breath. 'Very well, then. How long do you want it? A half hour? An hour? All night?'

'A half hour is okay, thank you.'

'And Katherine, too?'

'Only five dollars,' said Katherine, winking and waggling her hips.

'No, thanks,' Kasyx told her.

'All right, then, four dollars. And a clean hand-towel thrown in.'

The girl behind the counter swiveled the register book around so that Kasyx could sign it and turned to the hooks behind her to select a key. Kasyx quickly glanced down the list of guests who had signed into the McSween Hotel in the past two days. Most of them were famous cowboys – Wyatt Earp, Bat Masterson, Wild Bill Hickock, Buffalo Bill Cody – although these were interspersed with the names of people who must have been no more legendary than Lenny's school-friends: Peter Schreiner, Jimmy Phipps, Angela Ehrenbach. The very last guest in the register, however, had signed his name in uneven, spidery writing, as if he had pressed the pen far too hard.

Malasombra, Miguel; Nacozari de Garcia, Sonora, Mexico.

Malasombra – Spanish for 'Bad Shadow.' Kasyx raised his eyes. The woman behind the counter was waiting for him. In a strangely coquettish way, she was dangling his brass room-key from the end of her finger. Kasyx signed – *Cassicks, Henry; San Diego, California* – swiveled the register back around, and held out his hand for the key.

'I want no trouble, Mr Cassicks,' the woman told him. Her eyes gave nothing away.

'I won't give you any,' Kasyx told her.

The girl Katherine was waiting for him at the foot of the stairs. She had raised one arm to lean against the mahogany newel post, and one breast was now completely bared, rounded and white, like a well-shaped milk-pudding onto which had been dripped just the merest tinge of red currant jelly.

'Are you coming, *hombre*?' she asked, smiling.

'I'll be one minute, I have to talk to my Indian friend.'

He went outside. To his surprise, it was already night-time. The elderly couple had gone, and the veranda was in deep shadow. Across the street a lamp was alight in the window of the dry-goods store, and music was still tinkling from the saloon, but apart from that the town was unlit and deserted.

A sad night wind blew across the desert, sending tumbleweeds rolling across the street.

'Particular-Time-of-Day?' Kasyx called.

'I'm here, Kas-Yx,' said a calm voice from out of the shadows.

'I think Bad Shadow is here. In fact, I'm certain of it. There was a Mexican name on the register, Miguel Malasombra. In English, that means Michael Badshadow.'

'You must run for your life,' said Particular-Time-of-Day. 'The Bad Shadow will surely kill you.'

'Listen, friend, if the Bad Shadow doesn't kill me here then he's going to kill me someplace else. I have to get him now.'

'Then we should burn down the hotel. That will be safest.'

The idea was tempting; but Kasyx wasn't at all sure what the consequences would be. A full-scale fire, inside of Lenny's sleeping mind – a fire that surely would destroy many of the living images that he had created in his dream – who could imagine what subconscious trauma that might inflict on him? And Kasyx knew in his heart that even if they razed the building to the ground, the Bad Shadow would most probably escape unhurt. The Bad Shadow was not Lenny's creation: it was an influence of its own that had invaded Lenny's sleeping mind, just as Kasyx himself had. A fire started with dream matches in a dream hotel would have no effect on it. The only thing that could effectively destroy the Bad Shadow was the psychic power that Kasyx had carried into the dream with him.

Kasyx stepped out into the street and looked up at the hotel. All of the windows were in darkness. One of them reflected the curved moon; a dream-image of the same curved moon that had shone through Dianne Wesley's window in far-off Philadelphia. Kasyx said, 'Particular-Time-of-Day, here's what I want you to do. I want you to climb up that drainpipe to the balcony, and let yourself in through the middle window. If I've worked it out right, that faces the top of the stairs. I want you to stay there while I check out all of the rooms. If you see something try to escape or try to come after me, then I want you to yell.'

'Is that all?' asked Particular-Time-of-Day, his face in darkness. The night wind ruffled the feathers of his warbonnet. 'I have a knife, I could kill it if you asked me to.'

'Believe me, my friend, you wouldn't stand a hope in hell.'

Particular-Time-of-Day said, 'In that case, what then, when I have yelled?'

'Then you jump. And I mean jump. And when you hit the ground, you run like you're caught on a railroad track and there's an iron horse pounding up the track right behind you.'

'Iron horse?' said Particular-Time-of-Day, frowning.

'Well, shit, you know what I mean. Locomotive. Choo-choo.'

'Ah,' acknowledged Particular-Time-of-Day.

Kasyx left him in the street and went back through the double mahogany doors into the hotel. The woman behind the counter looked up and said sharply, 'Have you quite finished discoursing with your Indian friend? Katherine's upstairs waiting for you, Room Six. You paid for half an hour, no more. You have only twenty-six minutes left.'

'Thanks,' Kasyx told her. 'That's all the time I'm going to need.'

He climbed the stairs with their worn carpeting. All the way up the stairs, on both sides, hung the fleshless skulls of deer and coyotes and mountain lions, jagged and empty-eye-socketed, mounted on wooden plaques. The brown floral wallpaper reminded him of his Aunt Mary's black parlor in her tiny, claustrophobic house in Chicago. He could almost smell her burned teacakes, and the bug powder she used to sprinkle around, and the cancer that had eventually wracked her to death.

He reached the landing. It was dark, except for a single N-shaped angle of moonlight coming in through the window. There were eight doors altogether, four on each side of the landing. All of them were closed, and there were no lights showing underneath them.

He stood still for a moment, getting his breath back. Then he switched on his infra-red probe, searching the rooms for any sign of life. Five of them were definitely occupied, all by more than one person. The sixth he wasn't so sure about. There seemed to be some kind of glimmer there, but it might be nothing more than a heating stove, or a hot chimney leading up from the kitchen.

A rapping at the window made him start and turn. It was Particular-Time-of-Day. He had managed to climb up onto the balcony and reach the window, but it was locked from the inside. Kasyx walked along the landing as softly as he could, twisted the catch, and heaved up the sash. It gave a disconcerting rumble; both of them paused and listened.

'It's okay,' said Kasyx at last. 'At least five of these rooms are occupied. I have to check them out one by one. Just make sure that nobody gets away, or tries to jump me from behind.'

'I understand, *kemo sabe*.'

'Way to go, Particular. And please stop calling me *kemo sabe*. It comes from *The Lone Ranger*, and it means "he whom nobody knows who he is."'

Particular-Time-of-Day was silent for a long moment. Then he said, 'Well, *kemo sabe*, I don't know who you are.'

Kasyx didn't even attempt to answer that. He helped Particular-Time-of-Day to swing his legs in through the window. Then he padded back along the landing to the first door. The floorboards squeaked and groaned under his weight.

He approached Room One, hesitated, and then knocked. There was no reply. He knocked again, louder this time, and said, 'House detective, open up!'

Again, there was no reply. He licked his lips and looked toward Particular-Time-of-Day. The Indian, concealed deep in the shadows beside the window, called, 'Maybe it's open.'

Before he tried the handle, however, Kasyx checked his infra-red sensor again. The head-up display that appeared on his faceplate indicated that there were two people lying in the room, but for some reason they didn't register as brightly as they had before. They were losing body heat.

Kasyx reached up to the complex power switch on the right side of his chest. It was like an oversized D-ring, with finger-grips on it and a safety catch. If it was tugged out, like tugging the rip cord of a parachute, Kasyx released a devastating blast of naked energy, that would drain his entire power reserves in slightly less than three seconds. It was up to Kasyx to release the switch if he didn't wish to use up every single ounce of his power.

'All right,' he told himself. 'Here goes nothing.'

Psychic energy fizzed and crackled along his arms as he reached for the brass door-handle. Slowly, very slowly, he turned it. He could hear the spring squeaking as the bolt was eased back. Thin fingers of lightning crept from his gloves onto the doorplate and showered softly on to the floor.

Holding his breath, Kasyx pushed the door open. The room was totally dark. He waited for a moment, then called, 'Is anybody in there? Hello? Are you awake?'

There was still no reply. He switched on the lamp on top of his helmet, and flooded the room with brilliant, tungsten-bright illumination.

What he saw made his skin tighten with shock. In the middle of the bedroom stood a high four-poster bed with faded brocade hangings. On the bed itself, two human figures were sprawled, a man and a girl, but they were scarcely recognizable as human. They had been slashed wide open from crotch to neck, and their intestines were piled in two gradually intermingling heaps of glistening purple. The embroidered pillows were soaked dark red with blood. Blood dripped from the fringes of the bedspread onto the carpet. Blood was streaked diagonally across the daguerrotypes on the wall: General William Tecumseh Sherman with a bloody and gradually lengthening moustache.

'Oh, God,' Kasyx whispered. 'It's started already.'

He backed out onto the landing. 'They're both dead,' he warned Particular-time-of-Day. 'Don't say anything. Don't move. He's still here somewhere, in one of these rooms. God knows which.'

Particular-Time-of-Day – although Kasyx had told him that it would be futile – took out his sawtooth bowie knife. It glinted brightly in the moonlight.

Kasyx knocked at Room Two. Again – no reply. *Dear*

183

God, he thought, *it looks as if he's killed them all*. He pushed open the door, and what he saw in Room Two was a grisly repetition of what he had encountered in Room One. The only difference was that the girl had obviously tried to escape. She was sprawled over a bedroom chair, almost as if she were kneeling at a prie-dieu, her dark, tangled hair covering her face. Her red satin basque had been slashed open at the back, twice, and with her last breath her lungs had inflated out of the wounds like gruesome gray water wings.

Now Kasyx knew that there was very little time. If the Bad Shadow had finished its slaughter at this hotel, it would probably be ready to manifest itself next in the real world, stepping into Henry's house and cutting up the first human being it came across – which would be *him*.

He flung open the door of Room Three. Blood everywhere: butchery and blood. Room Four. Blood. Room Five. Blood. Room Six – and there was Katherine, standing in the middle of the room in her black, wasp-waisted basque, clutching her hands over her breasts and juddering with fear.

'*Don't!*' she shrieked when Kasyx pushed open the door. '*It's in here!*'

Kasyx forced the door wider; but then something immensely powerful racketed the door shut again, and there was a deep, catastrophic thundering noise that filled up the whole world, like a jet passing ten feet over Kasyx's head.

He pushed at the door again, trying to force it open, but it wouldn't budge. Either the door was solidly locked, or whatever was keeping it closed from the other side was so strong that it was immovable.

All right, you dark-hearted bastard, thought Kasyx, and pressed the palm of his hand flat against the door panels. *One burst of oscillating psychic energy, and this whole door is going to shake itself to sawdust. Then I'll have you.*

His heart racing with terror, his arteries surging with adrenaline, Kasyx switched on oscillating power. But the instant he did so, the door burst open again, and that terrible blackness came hurtling out in a rush of freezing cold air, huge and roaring and totally overwhelming.

Kasyx was flung violently back against the opposite wall of the corridor. His armor hit the wooden dado with a crash like somebody sledgehammering a packing case. His right glove was still switched to oscillate, and as he tried to grab at a door-handle to pull himself up from the floor, there was a sharp vibrato *skkreeek* and it burst into fragments of glittering brass.

Stunned, half-concussed by his own power, Kasyx tried to focus on the huge, dark being that filled the landing. Lightning poured out of his fingertips and crawled like electrocuted snakes across the carpet. All he could see was blackness, thundering blackness. The entire hotel shook to its roots.

Then Particular-Time-of-Day stepped into the N-shaped angle of moonlight, his eyes wide, his bowie knife lifted.

'*No!*' Kasyx bellowed. But Particular-Time-of-Day crouched and parried and then lunged at the overwhelming blackness.

'In the name of all the spirits, I defy you!' he shouted. 'In the name of my fathers, and my grandfathers, and all of my loved ones, *I defy you!*'

Kasyx struggled to his feet. As he did so, something swept across the landing, something that rumbled like Dracula's cloak, like a storm cloud rushing across a midwestern landscape, like death and chaos and old night. It momentarily blotted out the moonlight. When it swept away again, Particular-Time-of-Day was still standing by the window, but the upper part of his body had been diagonally sheared away, from his right shoulder to his left hip, and a faint wisp of pungent steam was rising from his gaping abdomen.

'*Bastard*!' roared Kasyx, even though he knew that Particular-Time-of-Day hadn't been real, hadn't existed as anything more than part of Lenny's nightmare. But the blackness had viciously destroyed a small part of Lenny that was loyal and kind and helpful; and if it went on doing that night after night, Lenny would eventually change. Lenny would end up as soulless as the shadow itself.

Grim but decisive, Kasyx yanked at the D-handle that activated his energy-release. His armor spat and fizzed with pent-up power. He took two steps toward the blackness, held out his right hand stiff and straight, and squeezed the release switch.

The burst of psychic energy was instantaneous and blinding, an explosion of power like the core of the sun. The entire hotel detonated around them – the weatherboard walls bursting apart and crashing into the street, the shingled roof scattering into the night sky, the staircase twisting and collapsing with a volley of wrenched-out banisters. Doors tumbled into the darkness; beds fell; bodies fell. Kasyx was slammed backward against the wall, then dropped straight through the floor to the hotel kitchen. Deafened, unable to see, he still managed to take his finger off the switch before his entire energy reserve was emptied.

I've done it, he thought, stunned, as he lay amongst the debris of fallen timber and shattered bricks. Shreds of ragged brown wallpaper blew in the breeze like torn shrouds; bricks still dropped, one by one, from the tilting chimney stack. One of the coyote skulls had fallen next to him, and grinned at him like a fleshless omen of death.

'*I've done it.*'

But even as he whispered the words into the closeness of his helmet, a great black shape rose up in front of him, and the air sang with the *wheeoow, wheeoow* of razor-sharp claws. Kasyx realized at once that the Bad Shadow was still alive, still virulent; and that he had discharged nearly all of his psychic energy to no purpose.

The thing that had signed itself *Malasombra* had survived an explosion of energy that could have brought down the Empire State Building, and was looming over him with claws that could slice their way through anything – armor, clothing, skin, muscle, bone.

Kasyx could make out two dull reddish gleams that could have been malevolent eyes, and a tangle of night-black skin tissue.

Close to panic, he quickly checked his power-meter. He had less than four percent of his energy left. Maybe the Bad Shadow whatever it was, was wounded. Maybe that last four percent would do it. But if he discharged everything he had, he was going to be trapped in this dreamworld forever; he would never be able to escape, and his real body would lie comatose and unattended in his bed at home until it died.

On what was only his second mission as a Night Warrior, he was confronted with the choice that charge-keepers had always dreaded: survival or self-sacrifice.

Better to back off, he told himself. *Better to go back and muster up reinforcements. We can try again tomorrow night, all four of us – Tebulot and Xaxxa and Samena. I can't fight this son-of-a-bitch all on my own.*

He stumbled backward across the wreckage of the hotel. The shadow swept after him, huge and dark and sinewy. He pressed the switches that prepared his power unit for returning to the waking world. 'Next time, you bastard,' he whispered.

But at that moment, out of the corner of his eye, he saw Katherine appear out of the splintered timbers of her smashed-apart bedroom. How she could have survived the discharge of Kasyx's energy, he couldn't imagine – forgetting in his panic that this was nothing but a dream, and that Katherine was nothing more than a figment of Lenny's unconscious mind.

She was stunned, naked, her white shoulders lacerated and bruised. She looked around as if she couldn't remember who she was or what she was doing here. She lifted one arm and smeared dust away from her forehead with the back of her arm.

'*Katherine!*' shouted Kasyx. But the shadow had already seen her, and was turning toward her with an earth-quivering rumble, its claws upraised. Katherine suddenly caught sight of it and screamed, and tried to scramble to her feet, but Kasyx could see that she was going to be far too slow.

Without thinking, he ran forward across the rubble, his heart pounding and his breath screaming inside his air system. Just as the shadow's claws swooped down toward Katherine, he roared out, '*Ashapola!*' and wrenched at his D-ring, and discharged his last four percent of psychic energy.

There was a crackle of power, a zigzag of lightning that flickered at the shadow and then grounded itself like an incandescent caterpillar down the hotel's water-pipes. Kasyx was thrown heavily onto his back, sliding down seven or eight feet of crazily angled staircase and demolished plaster. He scrabbled at the railing; and managed to stop himself from sliding any farther. Then he climbed to his feet, gasping for breath, and looked up to see what had happened to the Bad Shadow.

It had vanished. There was nobody left in the wreckage of the McSween Hotel but himself and Katherine. She fell whimpering in the torn-apart framework of her room, her eyes glassy with shock. Kasyx made his way toward her, and hunkered down beside her.

'It's gone,' he told her. 'You're safe.'

He reached out and stroked her hair, to calm her down. But even as he did so, she began to change. She grew smaller and thinner. Her arms and legs began to shrink. He kept on stroking her, but right in front of his eyes she turned into a young girl of eight or nine, with long hair like corn silk and wide, mysterious amber eyes. Between her narrow shoulder blades, two buds of skin began to form and to grow larger and wider, until at last they peeled open to reveal moist, sticky wings, iridescent like dragonfly wings.

'You're a fairy,' he said increduously. But this was a dream, after all, wasn't it, in which nothing had any permanence; a landscape that could endure only as long as Lenny remained asleep, imagining it in his mind?'

The Katherine-fairy fluttered and stretched her wings. They made a dry, shivery sound. She smiled at him enigmatically and said, 'You always were beautiful, my darling,' and then she rose and turned away, thin and long-legged and almost translucent in her nakedness, and launched herself into the air.

Bruised, exhausted, Kasyx rose slowly to his feet. Dawn was beginning to break. The cowboy town seemed to have melted away, removed by the soft-footed scene-shifters who could change Los Angeles into Rome, or the Taj Mahal into a Dunkin' Donuts, or childhood into old age. The Katherine-fairy was now flying high above him, caught by the sunlight that had not yet reached him, the way that an

189

eastbound plane is caught by the sun as it flies over plains and cities that are still nestling in darkness.

You sentimental, senile old fool, he told himself. *You sacrificed yourself for nothing. You gave up your last chance of returning to the real world for the sake of a woman who wasn't even a woman.*

He remained where he was, watching the sun creep gradually over the rim of the desert, until his crimson armor flared with dazzling reflected light. He was so stunned by what he had done that he couldn't move. In any case, there was nowhere for him to go. His real body lay in its bed in Del Mar – comatose, unwakeable. And this landscape would remain only for as long as Lenny stayed asleep.

During the day, while Lenny was awake, he would be consigned to a foggy limbo, a world without shape or form in which the only spark of conscious life would be his own imprisoned awareness. At night, however, when Lenny fell asleep, Kasyx, would find himself embroiled in whatever dreams or nightmares Lenny happened to conjure up. He had no choice; and no matter how frightening or threatening those dreams and nightmares turned out to be, he would be unable to escape them – not even to the dreams of someone else. His psychic energy was totally drained, and he was powerless.

All he could hope for was that his last burst of energy had succeeded in destroying the shadow forever. Otherwise, he would have to confront it again tonight, when Lenny started to dream, and he had nothing left with which to fight it.

However, he was guardedly confident that he might have won that last desperate skirmish. If the shadow *hadn't* been vaporized – if it had escaped – there was only one way in which it could have escaped from Lenny's dream, and that was to have manifested itself in the real world – in Lenny's room, in Henry's house. And if it had managed to do *that,* the odds were high that it would have instantly attacked Henry's sleeping body.

Since Kasyx was still alive in Lenny's dream, his waking body clearly hadn't yet been harmed. So the chances were good that the shadow *hadn't* escaped to the waking world, and that Kasyx's self-sacrifice hadn't been wasted.

I suppose that's some consolation, he thought. *Nothing more depressing than being a failed martyr.*

The desert began to tremble and shimmer and break up into waves like an ocean. Kasyx knew the signs. Lenny was dozing restlessly now, almost ready to wake up. Kasyx stood with his head bowed, and offered a prayer to Ashapola, who was God and all the gods, and to everyone who had ever known him and cared for him.

He felt that he was looking down on himself from a tremendous height: a tiny figure in shining red armor, ankle-deep in a glittering desert that was no longer a desert, but the gradually dissolving substance of a boy's dreams. He knew that this was one of the moments from which the enduring legends of the Night Warriors were fashioned, and that even here, on the lonely shores of the human imagination, he would never be forgotten.

That same night John had dreamed of Jennifer – so vividly that he could touch her, and kiss her, and talk to her. He was able to walk, and he took her back to Bread and Co. on South Sixteenth Street for Sunday brunch. Laughter, sunshine, heaps of crispy bacon and scrambled eggs, and glasses of Chandon champagne.

She smelled of his favorite perfume, Chanel No. 5, and the sun glowed in her hair.

'What's happened to Lenny?' she asked him.

'Lenny?'

The sun died; the conversation in the restaurant became suddenly muffled and hostile. Jennifer stared at him with undisguised hostility, and his croissant turned to ashes in his mouth. Real ashes. He had been eating his own son's cremated body.

He screamed and screamed, but when he woke up he was making no sound at all. It was 3:05 in the morning. The plastic-soled sneakers of the night nurses were squeaking up and down the corridor outside his room. He was sweating and trembling, and tears were running down the sides of his face.

He groped for his buzzer with his teeth, and pressed it. After a few moments, Sister Clare appeared.

'What is it, Mr Woods?' Against the light from the corridor, she looked in her wimple as if a huge seabird had settled on her head.

'Nightmare,' he told her, his mouth dry.

Sister Clare came into the room and stood close beside him. She had a round, ruddy-cheeked, Irish-looking face. 'These have been difficult times for everybody, Mr Woods. But God will see us safely through them, don't you doubt it.'

'I dreamed about Jennifer. The worst part about it was, she seemed so real.'

'She always *will* be real, Mr Woods, just so long as you remember her the way you do.'

Unexpectedly, John found himself sobbing out loud. 'I miss her,' he gasped, over and over again. 'Oh, God, Sister, I can't tell you how much I miss her.'

Eleven

Dianne Wesley came into his room shortly after he had finished his lunch of fried chicken, peas, and grits, and waited patiently by the door until Sister Theresa had wiped his face and straightened the bedclothes.

She was wearing a primrose-yellow summer suit, and she had pinned her hair back. She made John feel more like a cripple than ever. He hadn't noticed the few small freckles on her nose before.

When Sister Theresa had closed the door behind her, Dianne held up a manila folder. 'Guess what this is? The pathology report on that gloppy stuff we found in your wall. Seth Maxwell really did a number on it.'

'And? It's not going to make me nauseous, is it? I just ate lunch.'

Dianne sat down on the edge of the bed. 'He took all kinds of slides and samples, and he tested them for everything you could think of.'

'And were you right? Was it an afterbirth?'

She nodded, although she didn't look too pleased about it. 'It was definitely placenta-type material, with the obvious function of filtering nutritional material from the outside world to what – for lack of a better word – one can only describe as a fetus.'

'Was there any indication what kind of a fetus it might have been?' John asked.

Dianne licked the tip of her finger and turned the first

page of the laboratory report. 'Don't let's get ahead of ourselves. The afterbirth itself displayed some very unusual and interesting characteristics. For one thing, it contained cells that resembled nothing so much as brain cells.'

'*Brain* cells? In a placenta?' John frowned.

Dianne nodded. 'Seth was puzzled by that at first. But then he did some quick research on fetal development, and he turned up several authenticated cases of babies having acquired *knowledge* from their mothers while they were in the womb. Sometimes the mother had died in childbirth or before the baby was technically of learning age – so there was no other way in which the child could possibly have acquired the knowledge, except through mother-baby communication in the uterus.'

'So?' asked John. 'Where does that take us?'

'You may well ask.' Dianne replied. 'But Seth postulates that the afterbirth had the function not only of filtering food to the fetus in the form of proteins and carbohydrates and what-have-you, but that it was also capable of feeding it with thoughts and emotions. In other words, while it was clinging to the wall of your house, it fed its growing baby on anything that managed to penetrate through to that cavity in the brickwork. Not only the rats and the bugs and the fungus and the birds that fell down from the eaves; but human feelings, too – all the happiness and anger that it could absorb through the wall. Quite literally, it was a cuckoo, a parasite that was nourished by the lives of everybody who lived in the house.'

John was silent for a moment. Then he said, 'All right, it fed off everybody who lived in the house. But what was it? Did your friend have any ideas?'

Dianne closed the report. 'He took a sample of the cells and tried some biological extrapolations on the computer, using a model based on Dr. Leakey's work on prehistoric bones found in Africa.'

'And?'

'The computer went bananas, to tell you the truth. It identified the cells as belonging to a form of life that hasn't physically existed on this planet for two hundred and fifty million years.'

'What do you mean, *physically*? You mean it exists in some other way?'

'According to the University of Pennsylvania mainframe computer, it does. You see, during the early stages of evolution on this planet, some forms of life were successful in developing, while hundreds of others failed. There were scores of different fish and mollusks and lizards and insects, most of which died out. But this particular form of life, when it was faced by extinction, developed an extraordinary way to survive. It evolved its brain so that when it was threatened, it could escape into the minds of its enemies. It could literally disappear into their imaginations, like a conjuring trick.'

John swallowed, but said nothing. He had seen too much to be skeptical. He had seen his bedroom door crash open and something black roar into the room like a whirlwind, something that had sliced Jennifer open with one sweep of its claws. He could easily believe in something that lived inside the human imagination.

'From there,' said Dianne, 'Seth did some further research, using resources of the Department of Paleobiology at the Smithsonian and the Peabody Museum at Yale. Apparently, there have always been legends about a "shadow-creature," and these legends were particularly strong in North Africa in the 1100s, and among a number of Indian tribes in America in the eighteenth century. The Sauk and Fox have a very colorful story about the "mind-monster."'

'So, what are you trying to tell me – that you think these legends could be true?'

Dianne leaned forward and kissed him on the forehead. 'This, I'm afraid, is where we leave the cultivated pastures of serious research and start hacking our way through the undergrowth of wild speculation. But what we're up against is pretty wild, too. I told Seth only half of the story, and he thought *that* was wacky enough. But he was prepared to sketch out a serious theory, using all the available facts, and I have to admit that it seems to fit what's been happening to Lenny.'

'Go on,' John urged her.

'Well – remember, this is only theory. But Seth believes that when intelligent human life appeared on the scene, about two million years ago, the shadow-creatures discovered that they had been blessed at last with a perfect host. You see, up until the time that man appeared, they could only enter their enemies' imaginations when their enemies were actually *imagining* something – like at moments of critical danger, when a giant lizard or a saber-toothed tiger was after them, thinking *blood, blood, blood*. With man, however, who had a much more advanced imagination, the shadow-creatures could spend most of their life cycle inside his mind. They only needed to materialize in the real world to hunt, or to give birth to their offspring. By the Pleistocene epoch of the Quaternary period –'

'The what?' John demanded.

'That was the time that man appeared,' Dianne explained. 'And by then, the shadow-creatures' DNA structure had already evolved into something that was part imagination, part flesh – able to change within certain limitations from one to the other, and back again. Now they could live far more safely – unseen, well-fed, probably hermaphroditic, two sexes rolled into one. Whatever conceived that creature inside the wall, it most likely fertilized it, too.'

'But – in a wall in Philadelphia, for two hundred years?'

Dianne shrugged. 'Classic parasitic survival pattern. Give birth to your offspring and leave it someplace totally safe – someplace where it needn't hatch out until it's pretty well fully grown, and able to defend itself.'

'But if they were such highly evolved parasites, why did they *need* to defend themselves? Why didn't they take us over years ago? How come there's only *one* of them, and he's inside of my Lenny?'

'John, please I know how you feel.'

'Not a chance, princess. You don't know how I feel. You'll never know how I feel.'

She reached out and took hold of his hand. 'Don't be upset. They'll find Lenny, I know they will, and when they do, we can try to get rid of that thing that's inside of him, for good and all.'

'You still haven't answered my questions,' said John.

'John – I just don't know. Seth doesn't know. We were flying kites, that's all. Trying to work out something that made some sense.'

John was silent for a moment. 'Okay. Sure. I appreciate what you've done. But I don't really see how it brings me any nearer to finding Lenny and destroying that goddamned disgusting monster that's inside of him.'

Dianne squeezed his helpless hand. 'John, if we're right – if it *is* a shadow-creature – then there must be a way of getting rid of it. Those questions you were asking – like, how come they didn't take over the whole world, and how come there's only one of them left – if we can find the answers to those questions, then the chances are that we can use those answers to get rid of it.'

'Have you had any ideas?' asked John.

'I've been up all night, just working out what we've managed to get together so far.'

'Sure,' said John. 'I'm sorry. Sometimes it gets too frustrating to bear, just lying here, while everybody else is rushing around. I was always so goddamned active. You know, Jennifer used to say –' He paused, and swallowed.

Dianne said softly, 'Tell me, John. Jennifer used to say what?'

'Jennifer used to say that I was hyperactive. That I rushed around too much. "You're never still," that's what she used to say. Now look at me.'

Dianne smiled at him. 'I guess you have every right to feel sorry for yourself.'

John shook his head. 'Nah. Nobody has the right to feel sorry for himself.'

'What are you going to do this afternoon?' Dianne asked him after a pause.

'Go out and play with my crippled buddies, I suppose, under the cedar tree.'

Dianne got up and walked across to the window. It was a hot, hazy afternoon. She opened the slatted blind and looked out at the yard. 'Yes, I see them. A black kid and a guy with a shaved head.'

'That's Toussaint and Dean. Toussaint had polio when he was young; Dean lost his legs to a Claymore in Vietnam. We call him Mean Dean. You'll see why when you meet him.'

'Do you want me to push you outside?' asked Dianne.

''Preciate it if you would, ma'am.' He was trying to be flippant, but his heart was still heavy for Jennifer.

And he didn't dare think about what might have happened to Lenny.

Dianne called for a nurse, and between them they lifted John into his wheelchair. As Dianne was pushing him along the corridor, John asked, 'What happens now?'

'We have to find Lenny, of course, that's the first priority.'

'I mean – is there anything we can do to get ourselves ready to kill this creature? Even before we find Lenny?'

Dianne eased the wheelchair down the step that led to the brick-paved garden. 'We need to do some serious research into the shadow-creature's life cycle, and also its evolutionary history. That could take weeks, maybe months. But I have some friends at the Museum of Comparative Zoology at Harvard, and also in the Department of Vertebrate Palaentology at the Museum of Natural History in New York.'

'So you're in with some pretty serious eggheads?' John remarked.

'You wouldn't say that if you saw them. The guy at Harvard does fire-eating in his spare time, and the guy in New York is gay and loves Italian cooking.'

Dianne pushed John under the cedar tree. Toussaint was playing the theme from *All in the Family* on his guitar, and Mean Dean was reading a *Death Rattle* comic.

'Morning, gentlemen,' said John. 'Here's somebody I'd like you to meet.'

Dianne stayed for almost an hour, talking about her work and her career. Sister Theresa came out with a tray of hot coffee and cookies, and after a while they were joined by Billy and Che-u.

John looked at Dianne sitting on the brick wall under

the tree, her face lit by sunlight, and felt genuine gratitude for knowing her. God wasn't always censorious and vindictive. In another time, under other circumstances, he could have loved her.

She made all of them laugh, especially with her story about the family in Levittown who had tried to claim insurance compensation for the furniture they had damaged during a family fight by blaming a poltergeist. When Dianne had been called in by the Cigna Corporation to test the claim, the family had faked a poltergeist manifestation by making saucepan lids dance up and down on nylon fishing lines thumbtacked to the ceiling, and by paying the next-door neighbor's eleven-year-old son to throw plates through the kitchen window. 'And all the time they kept grabbing my arm and saying, "Look! look! Everything's flying around! Ain't it frightenin"!'

After Dianne left, the five of them sat in their wheelchairs in the warmth of the afternoon and played mental poker. This was one of the games they had devised to keep their brains sharp; and already John found that he could remember whole pages out of books that he had read, and almost every telephone number of everybody he knew. He depended a great deal on the telephone. Fewer and fewer people found the time to visit him; and at least when he called them on the phone, they didn't have to sit in the hospital and look at his drawn face and his helpless body.

John was just about to raise Che-u by $500 when he became aware of a shadow falling across him. He turned his head as far as he could manage, and saw a lean, pale-faced man standing close behind his wheelchair. The man was wearing the kind of shiny 1960s mohair suit that Rod Serling used to wear when he introduced *Twilight Zone*.

He smiled and nodded to John, and said, 'I wouldn't

raise him if I were you. You ought to see the hand he's holding.'

John had been concentrating so hard on remembering his imaginary cards and trying to calculate the imaginary cards that everyone else was holding that it didn't occur to him straight away that the pale-faced man had just done something that was totally impossible. He said to Che-u, 'I'll raise you five hundred,' but then he frowned and turned back to the man in astonishment. 'How the hell did you know I was going to raise him? How the hell did you even know we were playing cards? And how the hell could you tell what kind of hand he's holding?'

The stranger smiled and walked into the middle of their circle. 'I was showing off, I'm sorry to say.' He nodded to each of them in turn, and named them. 'Billy, Che-u, Toussaint, Dean, and John. It's good to meet you. My name's Chet Springer.'

'What's that, some kind of mind-reading act?' Dean demanded, one eye closed against the smoke that rose from his cigarette.

Billy said, 'I had a dog once that could tell the time. You know – you'd say, "What's the time, Fido?" and he'd say, "Arf Parf!"'

'Can it, man,' groaned Toussaint.

But Che-u looked up at the stranger called Springer, and there was an odd look in his eyes, almost of recognition.

Springer rubbed his hands together. The palms were dry, and they crackled with static electricity. 'I'm sorry that I came to see you unannounced. But the truth is that I have very little time.'

'That's all right, man,' said Toussaint. 'We always appreciate visitors.' He plucked a few random chords, then propped his guitar against the side of his wheelchair.

Che-u said nothing, but didn't take his eyes away from Springer for a moment.

Springer walked over and laid a hand gently on John's shoulder. It was not the kind of gesture that John usually liked, but there was something unusually soothing about the touch of Springer's fingers.

'I don't suppose that any of you have ever wondered what brought you here,' he said.

'Two smartass corpsmen,' growled Dean.

'A stupid and preventable disease,' put in Toussaint.

'Fate,' said Che-u.

Springer turned to Che-u and smiled. 'Yes,' he said. '*Fate*, or rather destiny. It was your appointed destiny, all of you, to gather together here. It has been your destiny ever since you were born.'

'Are you a preacher?' Billy demanded. 'Because if you are, buddy, I'm going to warn you here and now that we don't take too kindly to preaching. Quite apart from the fact that Dean here is an atheist, and Toussaint is a Black Muslim, and Che-u is a Buddhist, and John is a Baptist, and I myself used to be a Mormon but quit on account of the fact that they gave up polygamy and they didn't give Green Stamps.'

'I'm not a Baptist,' John interrupted.

'Sorry,' Billy told him. 'I could have sworn you were John the Baptist.'

Springer shook his head. 'I am not a preacher, my friends. But I am a messenger from a place that you could describe as the House of the Lord.'

'In other words,' said Billy, 'you're a total fruitcake.'

'Hey, give the man a break,' Toussaint said.

'He's a messenger from the House of the Lord?' scoffed Billy, 'I'd prefer a messenger from the House of Pancakes.'

Springer said, 'I come from the one called Ashapola, the greatest of the great ones. Ashapola needs your help.'

'What help?' said Billy. 'We're the most helpless bunch of people you ever met. We can't help ourselves, let alone this Ashcan character.'

'Ashapola,' Springer corrected him.

'Same thing, Ashcan, except it's in Polish,' Billy gibed.

Springer said, 'You didn't laugh so much the day you turned over your TransAm, did you, Billy?'

Billy reddened. 'Who told you that? Dr. Freytag? One of the nuns?'

'You didn't laugh at all,' Springer persisted. 'Especially since you thought you could overtake that Exxon truck on the inside, didn't you? And then you found that it was squeezing you nearer and nearer to the guardrails, and the driver couldn't see you because you were too close.'

'Who told you that?' Billy snapped. 'Who the hell *told* you that?'

'And you,' said Springer, turning to Mean Dean. 'You told the medics you were out looking for VC, didn't you? But in reality you were going back to Long Binh to collect all that liberated liquor, weren't you? Eleven cases of Johnnie Walker Red Label, two cases of Smirnoff.'

Mean Dean didn't say a word, but narrowed his eyes as if he were aiming at Springer through a gunsight.

'I come from Ashapola,' Springer repeated, more forcefully this time. 'Ashapola is the God of gods. He is every god of every creed, in one. He is the creator and the father of your race. We are all his servants.'

Billy was about to interrupt again, but John said, 'Hush up, Billy, let's hear what he's got to say.'

'Thank you,' said Springer. 'As I said before, your destiny has brought you here. All five of you share one thing in common, apart from the fact that you are handicapped. You are all descendants of a great and invisible army that once protected the earth from evil. That army is scattered now, and the sons and daughters of those who were numbered in its ranks have no way of knowing that within their veins there flows the blood of legendary heroes. Great heroes! Heroes of the night! Because all of you – all five of you – are direct descendants of Night Warriors, the chosen soldiers whose task it was to exorcise evil from the minds of all humanity.'

'What did I tell you?' snarled Billy. 'Solid fruitcake, from ear to ear. Night Warriors! D'you ever hear such crap?'

Springer stepped up to him. 'You, Billy, your great-great-great-grandfather was Arkestrax, the night-engineer. You're a talented lathe turner, aren't you? That's why. Even when you are awake, you exhibit some of the skills for which Arkestrax was renowned.'

He turned to Toussaint. 'You, Toussaint – you are a descendant of Lyraq, the music-sniper. Lyraq was capable of bringing down hundreds of enemy soldiers with a single perfectly pitched note. Instant death in F-sharp – fascinating, isn't it? And you could play melodies that would turn men's minds.'

He walked around the tree and appeared behind Dean's wheelchair. He was still smiling, although his voice was serious. 'Dean, you are the heir to the one they called Themesteroth, the rocketeer. Your ancestor was capable of destroying tanks, walls, bridges, castles. A fierce hero, with maximum firepower.'

Dean scowled, as if he could happily grasp Springer's throat with his over-developed hands and choke the air out of him. But Springer passed him by, and addressed himself to Che-u.

'Che-u, you are descended from Ex'ii the discus-thinker. Ex'ii wore a remarkable helmet arrayed with different discuses, which he could shoot at tremendous velocity simply by looking at his targets and *thinking* the discuses at them. An extraordinary skill, known only to Night Warriors in the Orient in the centuries when they were fighting against the demons known as the Shui Mu and the Hminza Tase and the Tengu.'

Lastly, Springer returned to John.

'You're not telling me that *I* was descended from a Night Warrior?' said John, almost ready to laugh.

Springer nodded. 'You are probably the best qualified of all for the task we have to face. Two hundred years ago, your great-great-grandfather William F. Woods was Reblax, the runner, fleeter of foot than any of the other Night Warriors.'

John said with a grin, 'You have a terrific imagination, Mr. Springer.'

Springer laid his hand on John's shoulder again. 'I wish I could tell you that this *is* imagination, Mr. Woods, but we have a crisis on our hands. A serious and very dangerous crisis.'

'Have you thought of calling the police?' John asked him sarcastically. 'Try Chief of Detectives Molyneux.'

'Mr. Woods,' Springer insisted, 'this crisis involves your son.'

The grin drained away from John's face like water draining out of a basin. 'Lenny? This is something to do with Lenny? Do you know where he is?'

Springer said, 'Yes, I do, and he's safe. At least for the time being. But every time he goes to sleep, every time he dreams, he constitutes a terrible risk to the people around him, and to himself, too.'

'Goddamn it,' John swore, straining at every numb nerve in his body, trying to move, trying to work a miracle.

'Mr. Woods, please – calm down,' said Springer.

'You won't do yourself any good if you get upset. And you won't be helping Lenny, either.'

'Where is he?' John shouted. 'Have you got him? I want to know where he is!'

'Please, Mr Woods, stay calm. Lenny was flown to San Diego yesterday morning, and now he's staying at Solana Beach with a family I know. They're good people, the best. Their son Gil is a Night Warrior himself.'

'Night Warriors! Night Warriors! For Christ's sake, stop talking this gibberish about Night Warriors! I want Lenny back here in Philadelphia, and I want him back *now*. Otherwise, believe me, the very first thing that I'm going to do is call the police.'

Springer paused for a moment, and then he said, 'Mr. Woods, we haven't kidnapped Lenny. He's not locked up, and the last thing we want is a ransom. We took him away from Philadelphia because we were worried about him going into state care. That *thing* that's inside of him could kill anyone who's trying to look after him; and eventually it could kill Lenny, too. Not physically, but mentally. Mr. Woods – we don't want Lenny to end up as a soulless zombie. I'm sure you don't, either.'

John took a deep, steadying breath. 'You know about the ...?'

'The shadow-creature, yes. That's what Dr. Wesley calls it, isn't it? Yes, I do. I don't know what it is, or why it's chosen your son as its host. But I do know that it's evil, and cruel, and very powerful indeed.'

John looked at Springer for a long time without saying anything. Beside him, Mean Dean smoked and sniffed and occasionally spat. Che-u, too, stared at Springer, and it was obvious to John from the expression on Che-u's face that he thought Springer was telling the truth, and that he believed the Night

Warriors to be real. Toussaint glanced at Billy, but all Billy could do was to shrug.

Springer said, 'Something tragic happened last night, and that's why I've come to see you today. Lenny stayed at the house of a university professor called Henry Watkins, at Del Mar. Henry Watkins is a Night Warrior, too. *Was* a Night Warrior, rather. He was Kasyx, the charge-keeper, the warrior who carries the vast reserves of psychic energy his fellow Night Warriors require to reload their weapons systems. Last night, he went into your son's dream in pursuit of the shadow-creature. We were hoping that he could destroy it inside your son's mind before it manifested itself in the real world.'

'What happened?' asked John.

'We're still not sure,' Springer replied. 'But when I went to his house at Del Mar this morning, I found Lenny making his own breakfast and Henry still asleep. Henry wouldn't wake up – *couldn't* wake up. His spirit is still trapped inside the dreamworld. His physical body is still breathing, which means that his spirit is alive. But he could be injured, or trapped, or imprisoned ... or, worst of all, he could have run out of energy.'

'Is that bad?' asked Dean. 'Running out of energy, I mean?' John couldn't tell whether he was ribbing Springer or not.

Springer said, 'It simply means that he has no way of returning to the real world. It also means that before any of *you* can enter the dream-world to hunt down this shadow-creature, I have to locate and recruit another charge-keeper.'

Dean pinched his cigarette out from between his lips between finger and thumb. 'Let me get this straight. You want *us* to track this shadow-thing down? *Us*?'

Springer nodded.

Billy put in. 'In case it's escaped your attention, good buddy, my friends and I are immobile to a man. We can't even go to the can by ourselves, let alone hunt down monsters.'

'In dreams,' said Springer quietly, 'you will discover that everything is very different.'

'Aw, come on,' jeered Billy. 'You guys don't *believe* this bullshit, do you? Night Warriors, Schmight Warriors! He's pulling our legs – at least, everybody's legs except Dean's. You know what you are, mister? You're just another one of those sickos who get their jolts out of tormenting helpless cripples. What are you going to do for an encore, Mr. Springboard, release the brakes on our wheelchairs and send us rolling off down the hill? That'd be good for a few yuks.'

Without a word, Springer approached Billy and stood over him, unsmiling. Billy said, 'Come on then, sicko, hit me. That's what you do for kicks, isn't it?'

Springer raised his right hand, as if he were giving the pledge of allegiance. There was a moment's hesitation, and then the thinnest thread of blue electricity flickered from the open palm of his hand and connected with the armrest of Billy's wheelchair.

Billy stared at it, wide-eyed and open-mouthed. 'What the hell's that? What are you doing? You trying to electrocute me or something?'

In complete silence, Billy's wheelchair rose from the ground, until it was suspended in the air two or three feet above the bricks. Billy gripped the armrests tightly, and peered over the side in terror. 'What are you doing? What the hell are you doing? Don't let me drop! For Christ's sake, don't let me drop!'

Springer made a gesture in the air as if he were wiping a window, back and forth, and Billy's wheelchair started to revolve. It went around and around, faster and faster, with Billy clinging on, grim-faced, white-knuckled.

John said, 'Let him down.'

'He doesn't *believe* me,' Springer replied tightly.

'I believe you for Christ's sake!' Billy shrieked out.

'Let him down,' John demanded. 'Come on, Springer, we're convinced.'

Gradually, Springer slowed down his window-wiping, and Billy's wheelchair slowed and stopped spinning. As silently and as carefully as he had raised him into the air, Springer brought Billy down again.

Billy was gray-faced, his upper lip was popping with perspiration. 'Jesus,' he said, wiping his face with his sleeve. 'How the hell did you *do* that?'

Springer essayed a smile. 'It was the power of Ashapola, channeled through me. It took no effort on my part at all.'

John said, 'If Ashapola is so powerful, why can't he deal with this shadow-creature himself? Why does he need us?'

Springer looked back at John, clear-eyed. 'He cannot struggle with the earth's evils face to face, nor does he wish to. The earth is his own creation, and the evil that has evolved here is as much a part of his creation as the good. He expects you to overcome the evil through your own efforts, because only by doing so can you raise yourselves out of ignorance and brutality and reach that high state of perfection that your church-leaders call Paradise. Ashapola can, however, assist you to confront and vanquish anything that threatens you.'

'Supposing we don't want to confront and vanquish anything that threatens us?' Mean Dean demanded. 'Supposing we tell you to go shove your Night Warriors right up that place where the sun never shines?'

Springer turned around and looked at each of them

in turn. 'You have no choice. It is your duty. No man can avoid his duty, no matter how hard he tries to resist it. And besides – I think that when you have experienced what it is to be Night Warriors, you will think very differently.'

Dean shook his head. 'It's going to take more than a couple of conjuring tricks to convince me, fella.'

'How about you, Billy?' asked Springer.

Billy was still trembling. He didn't say anything at all, but lowered his head, looking hunted and frightened.

Toussaint said in a clear voice, 'I'll give it a try. Man – there's nothing else to do around here, except poker in your head, and telling jokes, and not knowing whether you'd like it better if you was dead.'

Che-u spoke up. 'You are speaking the truth, Mr. Springer. I have seen you already in a dream. I recognized you when you first approached.'

Springer's face seemed to undergo a curious melting, as if they were looking at him through running water. 'I must leave you now,' he told them. 'I have to find a charge-keeper who will give you the energy you need to carry into battle. But I shall call you tonight, when you are asleep, and summon you to the nearest key location.'

'Nearest *what*?' asked John.

'It's what you might describe as a psychic gas station,' Springer explained. 'There are nine hundred key locations, all across the continental United States. They are the places where Night Warriors can tap the power of Ashapola Himself.'

'I'm imagining this,' said Billy. 'I've been drinking too much surgical spirit. My frontal lobes have gone.'

Springer laid his hand on Billy's shoulder. 'Wait until tonight, Billy. Then you will understand for the first time the power that lies sleeping inside you. You will never feel the need to drink anything again.'

Silently, Springer faded. He didn't walk away; he simply faded. The five of them found themselves confronting each other, shaken and baffled and, mostly disbelieving. Only Che-u was quiet; but then Che-u believed that he had seen Springer before.

'That was nothing but a trick, lifting up that wheelchair,' Dean insisted. 'Total crapola. I seen it done a thousand times. There was a Chinese magic show in Saigon, they were always levitating stuff – chairs, swords, naked women, even a cageful of monkeys once.'

Billy seemed to be recovering from his fright. 'Did I ever tell you the one about the magician who was looking for a job in Vaudeville? He says to the producer, "I can saw a woman in half." And the producer says, "Forget it, thousands of magicians can saw a woman in half." And the magician says, "Sure they can, but *lengthways*?"'

John said, 'Billy, that was no trick.'

'Oh no? You're not trying to tell me that Springer's for real?'

He lifted you up in the air, Billy! He scared you half to death! Then you saw him disappear, *pff!* just like that, right in front of your eyes.'

'That was a *trick*, for Christ's sake,' said Billy dismissively. 'David Copperfield walked straight through the Great Wall of China, one side to the other, in front of twenty million TV viewers. You're trying to tell me he *really* did that?'

'Billy, this wasn't television. You went right up in the air.'

Che-u said, 'John is right, Billy. Whoever he is, or whatever he is, Springer has great power.'

Dean gripped the armrest of his wheelchair and leaned forward with a grimace of pain and frustration and anger, angrier now than John had ever seen him

211

before. 'The only power that matters to *me*, fella, is the power to walk. And nobody can give me that, *nobody*, not even that fancy conjurer.'

At that moment, hearing them arguing, Dr. Freytag came across the yard. He was short and stocky, with a close-shaved head and thick black-rimmed spectacles. He always reminded John of a mad professor out of a Bugs Bunny cartoon. He usually wore a taupe gabardine suit that always stayed so perfectly pressed that John couldn't imagine that he ever sat down in it, or unnecessarily flexed his arms.

'Well, now,' said Dr. Freytag. 'Is this a private argument, or can anybody join in?'

'We were discussing the war between Iran and Iraq,' Billy replied.

'No, we weren't,' put in Troussaint. 'We were talking about the Night Warriors.'

Dr. Freytag took off his spectacles and stared at Toussaint with proturberant blue eyes. 'Night Warriors? What are Night Warriors?'

'*We* are,' said Toussaint. 'I'm Lyraq – I can kill people with music, right? And Che-u is Ex'ii and Billy is some dude called Arkestrax, and I forget the rest. But that's who we are, Dr. Freytag, so I'm telling you now, don't you try messing with us, man because we're something else.'

Dr. Freytag gave them a vague, thick-lipped smile. He was used to his patients acting oddly. Being imprisoned in a wheelchair often caused crises of stress and frustration that ordinary people couldn't begin to imagine. To have a mind that could walk but a body that couldn't, that was the greatest tragedy of all.

'We're all ready for your big operation, day after tomorrow,' he told John, completely ignoring what Toussaint had just said. 'I've been studying the X-rays, and the chances of restoring some movement to your arms look better than ever.'

John nodded. It was strange, but after Springer's appearance, and after the news he had been given about Lenny, Friday's operation didn't seem so critical. More than anything else, he wanted Lenny safe. Not only safe, but released from the tyranny of that black shadow that was hiding inside his mind.

Che-u said, 'Dr. Freytag – what do you think about psychic forces?'

Dr. Freytag blinked. 'I don't know. Psychic forces? Is that some kind of trick question? I never thought about it.'

'Well, perhaps you will soon have the opportunity,' said Che-u.

Dr. Freytag replaced his spectacles. 'Che-u, my friend, I always said you were too inscrutable for your own good.'

That evening, it rained. One of those heavy summer storms, out of a single charcoal-gray cloud, in a sky that was otherwise achingly clear. The streets of Philadelphia were slicked with wet; in the tarmac of Market Street, the rear lights of the yellow cabs trailed their reflections like the crimson tailfire of Buck Rogers space rockets. On top of City Hall, the statue of William Penn gazed solemnly out over a rain-freshened city of glistening rooftops and clustered traffic and office workers fleeing from the Curtis Center with newspapers covering their heads.

A tanker hooted across the Delaware River, a long, inconsolable moan.

John, in his bed, could hear the rain pattering against the window. He thought with a deep surge of nostalgia of evenings after work, sitting in Harry's Bar or the City Tavern, drinking and laughing. He thought of dinners with Jennifer, a table for two at Le

213

Champignon on Lombard Street, candlelight, hands held across the table.

He had been watching television, but his eyes were starting to ache, so he gripped his buzzer between his teeth and called Sister Clare to come and switch it off.

'There's such heathen nonsense on the television, I'm not surprised,' said Sister Clare fussily. 'Have you seen that Alf, for goodness' sake?'

'Sister Clare,' he asked, 'do you believe in anything greater than God?'

Sister Clare tugged his covers straight, though there wasn't any need for it. He couldn't move, so he never rumpled them up.

'You'll have to ask Father O'Rourke about that,' Sister Clare replied. 'It's my job to minister to the deficiencies of your body, not to the shortcomings of your faith.'

'But could you believe in a God of gods, a God who is *all* the gods, all rolled into one? Jesus and Buddha and Shiva and all the rest of them?'

'Sure and a funny-looking sort of God *that* would be,' Sister Clare retorted.

John smiled. 'Yes, Sister, I guess you're right.'

Sister Clare finished tidying up his room and tucking him in, and then John was alone, paralyzed, staring at the ceiling and listening to the rain, his mind churning like a concrete-mixer.

He was desperately anxious about Lenny; all afternoon he had been sorely tempted to tell Sister Clare to alert Chief Molyneux for him, so that the FBI could go to Solana Beach and pick Lenny up.

The only thing that had stopped him was the possibility that Chet Springer might have been telling the truth. If there really *were* such people as the Night Warriors, he wouldn't be doing Lenny any favors by calling the police. He would simply be exposing Lenny and anyone who was assigned to take care of him to critical danger.

He decided that he had very little choice but to wait and see if Springer was bona fide, or whether he was nothing more than a charlatan with a sick and sadistic sense of humor. And that meant waiting out the night.

He was still lying awake when there was a quick rapping at the door of his room, and Thaddeus and Norman Clay came in.

'Hope we're not disturbing you, John,' Thaddeus said.

'Come on in, I wasn't asleep.'

Thaddeus held up a manila envelope. 'We spent a few hours at the library, and another two or three at the Historical Society. You're just not going to *believe* what we've found out.'

'I think I'm ready to believe anything. Some guy came around to the hospital this afternoon and told me that Lenny's been taken to California.'

'California? Who took him there? Is he okay?'

'As far as I know. I'm still waiting for more news.'

'Who was this guy? Somebody you know?'

John said, 'There's a lot I can't tell you at the moment. I'm not sure whether he was on the level. But I should find out tonight.'

'Lenny's safe, though?' asked Thaddeus.

'I think so.'

'Well, take a look at this,' said Thaddeus. He dragged a chair across from the other side of the room. Norman remained standing, his hands clasped in front of him, looking pleased with himself. 'We discovered some real old street plans of Philadelphia, and your section of Third Street in particular. This one here dates right back to 1784.'

He held up the photocopied street plan so that John could see it clearly.

215

'Here, look at this – a plan of all that row of houses, drawn by somebody called Amos White, September 1784. The names of their occupants, too. The family who lived in your house were called the Grants.'

He rummaged in his envelope, and came up with a sheaf of notes. 'It took us a while to track the family down, but in the end we discovered a facsimile of a diary that had been kept by a man who lived three doors south of the Grants. His name was Arnold Logan – no relation to James Logan, who was William Penn's secretary. He says that in March 1787, the Grant house was the center of what he calls "a grate commotion." '

'Did he say what this "grate commotion" was?' asked John.

Thaddeus shook his head. 'No – although he does mention it once more, on the first Wednesday of March 1789. That was the day the Constitution came into effect. He talks about Gouverneur Morris, the guy who actually wrote the Constitution, and says, "Gouverneur Morris declar'd himself to be well pleas'd, and to me confided his sentiments that the Blacknesse at the Grant house had been thoroughlie confounded."'

'Blackness?' said John. 'Do you think he meant that thing in the wall?'

'You're getting ahead of me,' Thaddeus told him. 'We went to the Historical Society and looked through everything we could find on occult or magical events that have taken place in Philadelphia over the past two hundred years. There weren't that many. Philadelphia is obviously not what you might call the supernatural center of the East. In fact, there seemed to be twice as many spooks and poltergeists in Camden as there were in Philly. Something about that soupy New Jersey air, if you ask me.'

'Did you find anything?' John asked.

'Did we ever. According to this book here, *A Yearbook of Philadelphia*, the Grant family were well known on South Third Street for their weird behavior. They had moved to Philadelphia from Salem, Massachusetts, in 1785. As far as we were able to discover, there was Nathan Grant, the father; Hilda Grant, his wife; and two daughters, Nora and Kathleen, who were very rarely seen, but *"whose appearance was of retards, with sloping foreheads and slack mouthes and dragging gait."* When they *were* glimpsed – usually in the back of the Grants' carriage – they were always wearing "plain gray sacklike dresses, button'd up to the neck."'

Thaddeus turned over two or three pages. 'We found out, too, that the Grants moved into the house under the cover of darkness, and that from the day they moved in, neighbors complained of strange noises coming from the house, screams and rumbles and echoing sounds "as if the interior of the house were as huge and as empty as a cathedral."

'Of course, everybody thought that the Grants were practicing black magic or something like that. Children used to cross the street so that they wouldn't have to walk in front of the house, and the story was that the Grant sisters killed and ate the neighborhood cats and dogs. No evidence to substantiate *that*.

'What we *do* have evidence for is that Gouverneur Morris took a particular interest in the Grants. He was even supposed to have written a book or a pamphlet about them, but it seems that it was never published, and his executors had the manuscript burned. But look at this essay here, written in 1787 by Leopold Powell – "Objections to More Perfect Union." In this, Powell says that Nathan Grant caught hold of Gouverneur Morris outside of the Independence Hall Assembly Room, and threatened him with a dire catastrophe if he pressed ahead with his work on writing the Constitution. He told Morris that the nation belonged to "Its Originalle and Anciente Denizens" and that the Constitution was an affront to "Naturalle Law."'

John raised his eyebrows. 'That's something they don't mention in *The World Almanac*.'

'That's something they don't mention *anywhere*, my friend.'

'Did you find out how Morris reacted when Nathan Grant threatened him? Surely he thought he was nothing but a crank?'

'Oh, no. Leopold Powell says that Morris was very worried, and that he regarded Nathan Grant's threat as "extremlie grave." Morris only had one leg anyway, and after Grant talked to him he became quite ill and refused to go to sleep at night, unless he was heavily drugged with laudanum. He was obliged through sheer exhaustion to stop work on the Constitution – but after a while he was visited by Rufus King, the delegate from Massachusetts, and it seems they had a long talk. For some reason, King immediately went to Salem. We don't know what he did there, or who he went to see, but he came back almost straight away and told Morris that it was safe for him to continue work on the Constitution, "because he had recruited a companie of arm'd vigilantes who could deal with such as Nathan Grant and his familie."'

Thaddeus paused, and then he said, 'That, apparently, was when "the grate commotion" occurred. King went round to the Grant house "with his staffe." There were terrible noises from the house. One neighbor said it was like a battle. There were flashing lights and bolts of lightning, and screaming, and grotesque shadows appeared at the windows. The shutters and the doors were torn off the front of the house and hurled into the street. In the end, it all went quiet. When the neighbors ventured inside to see what had happened, they found the Grant family lying dead on the floor, "verie whyte in the face, but with no sign whatever of any injurie." I think the verdict was that they had died of fright in the presence of a supernatural manifestation.

'A whole bunch of papers were found in Nathan Grant's sitting room, describing how he considered himself to be the chosen agent of the old ones, the Mistai, or "America's Anciente Shaddowes," as he called them. Does that ring some bells? The neighbors also found a *waxobe*, or medicine-bundle, of the Osage tribe. It was made out of woven straw, and it contained the head and shoulders of a hawk, two human scalps with braided hair, an eagle's claw, and part of a buffalo's tail. It didn't look as if the *waxobe* was simply a souvenir, because it was unrolled when the neighbors found it, as if Grant had been using it.'

Thaddeus folded his notes and put them back in the envelope. 'We talked to Dr. Wesley on the telephone about a half hour ago, and she told us what *she* had already come up with – those shadow-creatures or mind-monsters or whatever. *Mistai* is actually Cheyenne lingo for ghosts. It looks very much as if Nathan Grant had found a way to conjure up these monsters, and that Morris had to send somebody to exorcise them. Morris obviously thought that they had succeeded in wiping them all out. But nobody realized that one of the shadow-creatures had left its offspring inside the wall.

'We don't know why it chose to come out now. Maybe it's something to do with the two-hundredth anniversary of the Constitution. Maybe you simply disturbed it by moving in. Maybe it sensed Lenny's vulnerability, and latched on to him. Who knows? It doesn't seem like we're dealing with anything rational here. I mean, this shadow-creature behaves like the craziest of crazy killers. It kills you because you happen to be there, and that's the bottom line.'

John said, 'You mentioned that Rufus King recruited some armed vigilantes.'

'That's right,' Thaddeus nodded. 'But it's a funny thing about that. Although the description of the "grate commotion" is very detailed and accurate, it doesn't make any mention of armed vigilantes at all. Maybe they didn't show up, or maybe they weren't needed.'

John thought for a moment. Then he said, 'I think they *did* show up.'

Thaddeus frowned at him. 'What makes you think that?'

'Something that happened this afternoon. Something somebody told me.'

'You're being extra-mysterious,' Thaddeus complained.

'I'm not really. It's just that I'm not sure yet if it's truth or bunkum.'

'You're not sure if *what's* truth or bunkum?'

'I'll tell you tomorrow. And listen, I'm really impressed with all that detective work.'

'Don't thank us, thank the Pennsylvania Historical Society. They have stuff in their archives that would make your hair stand on end.'

'I think I've had enough of that for one lifetime,' John told him.

Thaddeus leaned over and gave John's shoulder a comradely squeeze. 'We're all in this together, man. You sleep good, and we'll see you in the morning. And I sure hope that Lenny's okay.'

'Thanks, Thaddeus. Thanks, Norman. Me, too.'

When Thaddeus and Norman left the hospital it had stopped raining, and the night was warm and airy.

'How about a drink before we crash out?' Thaddeus suggested.

They were close to Silveri's, so they crossed Twelfth Street and went in for two beers and two shots of Jack Daniel's. The bar was crowded and noisy, but they managed to find two seats in the corner.

Thaddeus swallowed some beer and wiped his mouth. 'What do you make of John saying that he knows where Lenny's at?' he asked Norman.

Norman shrugged. 'Maybe some friend of his sprung the kid out of the hospital without him knowing, and he doesn't want to tell us too much about it until he's sure that his friend's lying low. After all, if the guy's taken the kid to California, that's a federal offense.'

'By rights, we should tell the chief,' said Thaddeus.

'You're not seriously suggesting we should?'

'What do you think?'

Norman knocked back his whiskey. As he put down the glass, he suddenly shivered and looked around.

'What's wrong?' Thaddeus asked. 'Jack Daniel's too strong for you?'

'Something's here,' said Norman, his eyes darting from face to face, all around the bar. 'Something *heavily* psychic.'

'In *here*?' queried Thaddeus. He turned around in his seat. 'What kind of psychic?'

'I'm not sure … it doesn't feel hostile. But it's not human, I can tell you that.'

Thaddeus took another look around. 'Man – I don't see *anybody* here who isn't human.'

At that moment, a pretty young girl with heaps of blond, curly hair came through the crowded bar toward them, turning heads as she did so. She wore a short, tight miniskirt and a white cotton sweater and lots of cheap, jangly jewelry.

'We're here,' said Norman, rising to his feet as she approached.

She smiled and nodded, making her earrings jingle. She smelled of some strong flowery perfume like Anaïs Anaïs. 'Well, Detective,' she replied in a breathy East coast accent, 'you're even more sensitive than I gave you credit for.'

Norman pulled over a chair from the next table and helped the girl to sit down.

Thaddeus looked from Norman to the girl and back again, baffled. 'Do you mind telling me what's going on here?'

'This young lady is the source of the psychic disturbance,' Norman explained.

'You mean –?'

'I mean she's not human. She's not even a girl. She's a collection of psychic information, that's all.'

Thaddeus stared at her. 'You're pulling my leg, right? This is some kind of practical joke that you and this flaky brother of mine have worked out between you.'

The girl shook her head. Reflected light danced in her colorless eyes. 'No joke, Sergeant. I am exactly what your brother says I am. You can call me Jennifer Springer, if you wish.'

'All right, knock it off,' said Thaddeus. He turned to Norman. 'You fixed this, didn't you? Just when you knew that my head was going to be full of ghosts and shadow-creatures and mind-monsters.' Looking back at Jennifer Springer, he said, 'What would a very dishy collection of psychic information like to drink?'

She showed a mouthful of sparkling white teeth. 'I'll have what you're having,' she said.

Thaddeus raised his glass. 'You mean Jack Daniel's?'

Jennifer Springer nodded. As she did so, the whiskey remaining in Thaddeus's glass rose up in a perfect amber sphere, right over the rim, and then slowly floated toward her, fifteen inches above the tabletop, until it reached her mouth. She kissed it as it touched her lips, and it burst into a fine spray, and dissipated in the smoky atmosphere.

A man who had been sitting with his head resting drunkenly on the bar blinked at her in disbelief. Then he sat up straight, tapped sharply on the bar with a dime, and called out in a blurry voice, 'Barman, bring me another one of those old-fashioneds, and quick!'

Thaddeus peered into his empty glass, and then set it down. 'Who are you?' he asked her. 'What the hell do you want?'

Twelve

John at last sank into sleep. He slept dreamlessly at first, breathing so lightly that when Sister Clare came to check him on her eleven o'clock round, she had to lean over his bed and listen close to his mouth to make sure that he was still alive.

In Solana Beach, California, in his room over Miller's Mini-Market, Lenny stood by the window looking out over the backyard fences toward the ocean. It was only eight o'clock, and he had slept so heavily last night that he didn't feel like going to bed yet.

He had never seen the ocean look so pale and colorless. It was almost white. A coastal fog had been predicted for the morning, and it looked as if it were gathering already.

Lenny was beginning to miss his daddy badly. Mr. and Mrs. Miller had been warm and friendly; they had bathed him and fed him corned-beef hash and lent him a Popeye T-shirt and a pair of boxer shorts to use for pajamas. But he still yearned to see his daddy's face, and to hear his voice saying, 'Come on, champ, you can do it.'

For some reason, Gil had told his father and mother that Lenny was the younger brother of a college friend of his, whose parents had been urgently called to Mexico because this college friend had been injured in a motorcycle accident.

Lenny didn't know why he had to lie. His daddy had always told him that lying was as bad as homicide: 'When you tell a lie, you murder the truth.' He had to pretend that his name was Sammy Gerber, and that he lived on a road called Manchester Avenue, and that he had a sister called Grace (who was staying with some other family) and a spotted terrier dog called Rasputin.

But Mr. Springer had arrived at Mr. Watkins's house early yesterday morning and taken Lenny away, even before Mr. Watkins had woken up, and Mr. Springer had told him that he *had* to pretend to be Sammy Gerber, at least for a little while; otherwise his daddy would get into serious trouble and so would he.

Springer had acted so anxious and so upset that Lenny had done what he was told. But now he had read all of Gil's old *Secret Wars* comics and watched television for a while, and there was nothing to do but kneel on the checkered blue cover of the bed and stare out the window at the cluttered yards behind the restaurants and stores along the Solana Beach boardwalk, and wish that he were back in Philadelphia.

The sun began to sink toward the sea. Lenny swallowed a lump in his throat, and felt the tears crawling slowly down his cheeks.

John opened his eyes. Yet, strangely, his eyelids were still closed. He could see the room all around him – the fan-shaped shadows that the venetian blinds threw across the ceiling, the dull gleam of his bedhead and his drip-stand, the picture on the wall of summer fields, printed in bilious green and yellow-ocher. Enough to give anyone a relapse, that picture.

Then, slowly, he stretched his fingers, one hand at a time. And he could move them.

He lay still, hardly daring to think that this could be true. He stretched his fingers again. Then he wiggled them. After a moment or two, he raised his head and looked down at himself lying in the bed. He wiggled his fingers again. Yet – oddly – the bedcovers didn't move.

I'm hallucinating. I'm going out of my mind. Either that, or I'm having a nightmare.

But then he lifted his left hand, and it appeared *through* the bedcover, like the hand of a phantom. He shouted out, '*Ah!*' in shock, and dropped his hand again. But then, cautiously, he raised it once more, and turned it from side to side, and he knew then that what was happening was real, and that Springer had been telling them the truth.

He sat up in bed, without any difficulty at all. After so long lying paralyzed, the feeling was extraordinary, and he laughed out loud, or what he thought was out loud. *He was dreaming, he was dreaming about himself. Could anybody see him? Could anybody hear him?* He stretched his back and flexed his arms, and then he swung his legs out of bed – *through* the bedclothes – and stood up.

On the bed, his earthly, paralyzed body remained asleep. He peered at himself closely and thought how drawn he looked, how gray. He hadn't realized that his head was quite so flat at the back. Odd, to see himself as other people saw him; quite unnerving. He tried to imagine what would happen if he suddenly woke up and found himself face to face with himself. *Frighten myself to death, probably.*

He walked around the end of the bed and went to the window. Outside, he could see the cloudy night sky and the twinkling buildings of Philadelphia's Center City. An airliner flew diagonally over the Schuylkill River, its navigation lights flashing. John stood motionless for almost a minute, breathing deeply and regularly, relishing the feeling that he was part of the world's activity again.

He glanced at the clock beside the bed. It was 11:41. He wondered what was supposed to happen next, where he was supposed to go. Springer had talked about a key location, but hadn't told them where it was or how to get there.

He was thinking about trying to leave when a very pretty girl appeared, standing quite close beside him. She was slightly built, with extravagant heaps of curly blond hair, and she wore an elaborate black velvet ball gown, sewn with diamond-patterns in silvery thread and seed pearls, and cut extremely low at the front. What was more remarkable than the fact that she had appeared was the fact that he was completely unsurprised to see her, and that he recognized her at once as Springer, in another guise.

'Ah,' she said smiling. 'I see you're ready. I thought you might be the first.'

He felt a little awkward, standing in front of this exotic creature in nothing but his backless hospital nightshirt, but he managed to smile back at her. 'It's true,' he told her with a mixture of amusement and triumph and relief. 'Everything you said about the Night Warriors was true.'

Springer nodded. 'Come along. We have to collect the others. Then we can go hunting.'

She led the way through the door and along the corridor. They passed three or four night staff, but to waking eyes they were invisible. The nurses stared directly at them but didn't see them, which John found deeply unsettling. Only once did a nurse look up from her lamplit desk and frown, disturbed by the rush of molecules that had roiled through the empty corridor as John and Springer passed by.

They reached Che-u's room. Che-u was lying on his bed waiting, his expression one of complete helplessness. He had never walked in his life, so his body was unable to respond to what his mind expected of it.

'Hello, Che-u,' said Springer gently, and John understood why she had chosen such a soft and feminine manifestation to arouse them for the first time.

Che-u whispered in quiet desperation, '*I don't know what to do.*'

'Don't worry,' Springer told him. 'All you have to do is *think* yourself upright. Your real, physical body will remain in bed, so there's no chance of you falling and hurting yourself. All you have to do is *rise.*'

'Come on, Che-u,' John coaxed. 'It's fantastic.'

Che-u took a deep breath, and then slowly sat up. He looked around him. He pressed his hands against his chest to check that he was actually upright. With great caution he swung his legs off the bed, and stood up on the floor. He was surprisingly tall when he stood up unaided; John had always imagined that he was tiny.

He turned to Springer, and there were tears in his eyes. 'I never knew what it was like,' he said, his voice choked with emotion. 'All my life I've tried to imagine it … what it was like to run, what it was like to dance. But this … it's wonderful. I didn't have any idea.'

Springer laid a hand on his shoulder and kissed his cheek. 'There will be better things to come, I promise you.'

They moved up to the seventh floor to find Dean. John had been secretly wondering about Dean. *I mean, the man has no legs – how is he going to …?* but when they passed through the door of his room, absorbed through the atoms of the wood like warm soup pouring through a strainer, they found Dean standing by the window, looking out over the city just as John had looked out, complete with legs.

'Hey, Springer, you sumbitch, or whatever your name is,' he said, turning around with a sly, gratified grin. 'I take it all back. That wasn't no conjuring trick, was it? You *meant* it, every last word of it.'

'I knew you would change your mind, once your legs were restored,' said Springer with unconcealed self-satisfaction.

Dean reached down and rubbed his thighs. 'I don't know how the hell you did it, but I'm sure happy that you did.'

'*I* didn't do it, *you* did,' Springer told him. 'You could always feel your legs, couldn't you, even after they were amputated? And you always had legs in your dreams. You're dreaming now, so it doesn't matter whether your physical body has legs or not – as long as your dream body is complete.'

'You're something else,' said Dean.

'Yes,' Springer agreed. 'You could probably say that I am.'

They moved on – to find Billy wandering along the corridor in his nightshirt, looking bemused but pleased. 'I woke up and I could walk, goddamn it! It didn't even hit me until I was halfway across the room.' He stared closely at Springer. 'You're a girl,' he declared. 'Were you a girl before, or was I seeing things?'

Springer took his hand. 'You will always see what you want to see; nothing more and nothing less. And I will always be what you want me to be.'

It was Toussaint who impressed John the most. They crowded into his room to find him dressed in a long 76ers T-shirt, dancing. His eyes were closed. 'Killer' was thumping tiny and tinny from his bedside tape-player, and his bare brown sandy-soled feet were

230

hopping and skipping and moonwalking all around the vinyl-tiled floor.

Springer nodded toward the tape-player and it switched itself off. Toussaint opened his eyes to find them all standing around him, smiling at him.

'For a cripple, you sure can boogie,' Billy chaffed him.

'Hey, I just got up and I could *dance*,' whooped Toussaint. He did a quick spin around the floor, pummeling his fists in the air like Mike Tyson, the world champion boxer.

Springer raised her hand. 'There is very little time to waste. Here in Philadelphia we are three hours ahead of California, so Lenny is not yet asleep. But as soon as he slips into unconsciousness, the shadow-creature will be able to emerge yet again. We must do everything we can to destroy it before then.'

John said, 'Thaddeus and Norman Clay found out a whole lot more details about the shadow-creature from the Pennsylvania Historical Society. Apparently, some weird character by the name of Nathan Grant –'

Springer interrupted him by laying a hand on his shoulder. 'I know all about it, John; and in a very short while you will see why. Now it is time for you to come with me to the key location, where you will take on the identities that destiny has always intended to be truly yours.'

'Do we take a bus, or what?' asked Billy. 'Hey, can you imagine it – five ghosts in a cab!'

Springer smiled, but shook her head. 'All you have to do is to rise.'

'*Rise?*' queried Billy.

Billy tried it first. He simply imagined that he could float, that the air could absorb him. He found himself drawn through the ceiling of Toussaint's room, then rising through room after room until he passed clear

231

through the hospital's rooftop water tank and out into the night. He looked around, elated, and he could see both the Delaware and the Schuylkill Rivers, black and glossy and sparkling with reflected lights, and between them the brilliantly glittering lights of the city itself, Rittenhouse Square and City Hall; and farther to the west the colonial spire of Independence Hall, where the Pennsylvania Convention had argued the Constitution into being.

He turned and dived, and circled the hospital at the level of the fifteenth floor, just as the rest of the newly recruited Night Warriors rose out of the roof like shadowy balloons untethered into the night.

Springer came last of all; but she quickly drew them all toward her, and led the way over the city toward the rich trees and elegant colonial houses of Germantown.

They gradually sank lower over Wissahinnock Avenue, descending below tree-level as they reached Tulpehocken Avenue between Germantown Avenue and Greene Street. John was concentrating too hard on his flight through the night to concern himself with his fellow Night Warriors, but he imagined that they must all be experiencing the same extraordinary sensation that they were being *soaked in* by the atmosphere, that their own molecules were no different from the molecules in the air.

They arrived at last at a small Georgian house, stone-fronted, with brown shutters at the windows and a brown-painted second-storey balcony all the way around it. The house was surrounded and mostly hidden by ancient overgrown oaks, and it looked unkempt and uninviting compared with most of the houses around it, which had been meticulously restored.

Without hesitation, Springer led them through the

tiled roof and into a large empty room on the second storey. They sank to the floor, and looked around them. The room had two tall windows on either side, two overlooking the road and two overlooking a weedy and unkempt garden. The windows were so grimy that it was almost impossible to see out. The room smelled of dust and years of neglect.

Billy said, 'I don't think much of Ashapola's hospitality lounge, I have to tell you.'

'It is impossible for us to keep all nine hundred locations in good repair,' Springer replied. 'Also, we do not wish to draw attention to ourselves.'

'What happens now?' asked John.

'We are waiting for one more arrival,' Springer explained. 'You will remember my telling you that all Night Warriors require a charge-keeper – somebody to transport the huge stores of psychic energy they need for reloading their weapons-systems, and also for traveling in and out of dreams.'

'You said that you'd lost your charge-keeper,' put in Toussaint. 'What was his name – Kasyx, or something?'

Springer said, 'Kasyx, that's right. We still have no word; and I am already having to concede that we have lost him forever. Still, we have one consolation, and that is that I have been able to locate another charge-keeper – in fact, two charge-keepers – who will be able to give this force of Night Warriors more power when they enter into dreams than any equivalent force in the history of the armies of Ashapola.'

Springer raised both hands; almost immediately the room began to hum and the windows to rattle and vibrate in their frames – a buzzing noise that went right through John's teeth. There was a moment's pause, and then down through the ceiling came Thaddeus and Norman Clay, to stand side by side at the opposite end of the room.

233

John was startled. 'Thaddeus, Norman – *you*?'

Thaddeus came forward and took hold of John's hand. In spite of the fact that they were invisible and insubstantial to the rest of the world, their dream-selves could still touch each other, still feel each other. Thaddeus said, 'I guess you could say that we were pretty confused at first. But, you know, once we'd gotten over the initial shock, the idea of being Night Warriors kind of *appealed*.' He turned to Springer and added, 'So did she, or he, or whatever she is, once we'd gotten over the initial shock of *her*.'

'So you're descendants of Night Warriors, too?' asked John.

'It's not so surprising, when you think about it,' Thaddeus replied. 'Norman has always been psychic ever since he was born; and our mother always used to tell us that we were descended from "special people." Springer says our great-great-great-grandfather was Oromas, a charge-keeper from the east coast of Africa. Seems he was responsible for exterminating some African demons called the – what were they called, Springer?'

'The Maskim,' said Springer. 'The demons of Sumeria. There were seven of them, and for hundreds and hundreds of years they swept the entire African continent with plagues and slavery and droughts and bloodshed. Oromas defeated them single-handed. He was one of the greatest and the bravest of the charge-keepers.'

'Well, I'm really glad to see you,' John told Thaddeus, and shook Norman's hand, too. 'It looks like you're boldly going to go where no police detective has ever gone before.'

Springer said, 'We have very little time. Thaddeus and Norman – I'm going to energize you now, and then you can pass on your energy to your fellow Night Warriors.'

'What are we going to do?' asked John. 'Lenny's in California – how can we possibly help him from here?'

Springer stepped back, her long velvet ball gown swirling like a pool of oil. 'You have the power to reach California almost instantaneously, especially since you have *two* charge-keepers. You will use a technique called the dream shift, using the dream of Gil Miller, the Night Warrior who is looking after Lenny. Gil is Tebulot, the machine-carrier. He will be entering Lenny's dream with you, as a guide.'

Springer beckoned to Thaddeus and Norman to approach her. One of them stood on each side of her, while the others watched and waited. She laid a hand on each of their shoulders, closed her eyes, and whispered, *'Ashapola ... I ask for your power.'*

A deep vibration went through the house, as disturbing as a distant earth tremor, and for a moment John felt the odd seismic sensation of having the floor pulled out from underneath him like a rug. Fingerlike patterns of lightning crawled from Springer's hands and danced all around the Clay brothers' heads and shoulders. At the same time, the room was filled with the burned odor of electricity and heated metal.

Right in front of John's eyes, huge and complex suits of armor began to form out of the air and build themselves around Thaddeus and Norman. In a matter of moments, they were complete, and Thaddeus and Norman themselves had taken on physical substance, so that they looked as solid as any human being. Their armor was shiny midnight-blue metallic, with narrow wedge-shaped helmets, giving the twins a sharklike appearance. Each twin had a chrome grille on the front of his suit of armor, and this grille constantly flickered and crackled with blue-white energy. Thaddeus's grille protruded to the left side of his breastplate, Norman's to the right.

'Thaddeus,' said Springer, stepping away from them, 'you are Oromas I. Norman, you are Oromas II. As you are in everyday life, that is how you shall be as Night Warriors – able to fight independently of each other, but also capable of coming together and forming a force that is greater than the sum of your individuality.

'Each of you carries thousands of volts of psychic energy. Each of you, on your own, can support all of the other Night Warriors here. You understand that you have no weapons of your own, but that in critical circumstances you can discharge a large proportion of your energy, with devastating effect. If you are ever tempted to do that, however, think first of your fellow Night Warriors. Without your reserves of energy, they will be unable to return to their waking bodies.'

Springer drew the twins close together, and showed them how their power grilles could be connected by means of three chrome levers. The grilles fitted perfectly, and the heavy levers closed with a satisfying click-*kachunk*. Instantly, the flow of psychic current that had been sparkling around each individual grille began to circulate around the entire double structure, with an even louder hum of latent energy.

'Interconnected like this, you can command up to three times the power that you have at your disposal individually. If you were ever to discharge this power, it would have the equivalent effect in a dream of a ten-megaton nuclear bomb in real life. Of course, psychic energy discharges have no fallout; but you must remember that the consequences of such a discharge in the world of dreams could be as disruptive as they would be in real life. You would shake the psyche of everybody within a hundred-mile radius.

'Even more seriously, you could destroy the

dreamer himself, as he appears in his own dream. And if you do that, the dream will collapse on you, and you will be lost to the real world forever.'

'Sounds moderately dangerous,' Dean remarked.

Springer smiled. 'On a percentage scale, the enemies you will encounter in dreams will be about two hundred percent more dangerous than anything you ever had to face in Vietnam.'

'The worst thing I ever had to face in Vietnam was friendly fire,' Dean retorted.

'That is the way of all wars,' said Springer, 'and no less true of the wars of the night.'

Billy said, 'I'm beginning to think I'd prefer to sit this one out.'

Springer held out her hand toward him. 'You will soon find your courage when you feel the power of Ashapola. Come forward.' Billy was reluctant, and Springer had to take his hand and lead him up to Oromas II as if she were tugging a shy date onto the dance floor at a graduation ball.

'This isn't going to *hurt*, is it?' queried Billy, cautiously laying his hand on Oromas II's shoulder-plate.

Springer shook her head. 'We will see you now as Arkestrax, the night-engineer. Close your eyes and let the energy flow into you.'

Billy wiped sweat from his forehead with the back of his hand. 'You're really sure you need me?'

'The part you have to play is crucial,' said Springer. 'Without you, an enemy such as the shadow-creature can never be defeated.'

John had been watching Springer, the way her face constantly changed and shifted. Sometimes she looked more masculine than feminine. Sometimes she looked so smooth-faced and neutral that she could have been either, or both. Her clothes changed, too. Sometimes

237

the back of her dress was dotted with thousands of shining seed pearls; at other times it was plain.

Billy swallowed, and grasped Oromas II's shoulder as tight as he could. 'Oh, well, here goes nothing. Give it everything you've got, good buddy.'

Again, there was a smoldering crackle, and a smell in the air of burned copper and ozone. Billy gritted his teeth, threw back his head, squeezed his eyes tight shut, and shivered all the way down his body as the power of Ashapola flowed into him. Gradually, a shining, domed helmet materialized on his head, a helmet with three different instruments fitted to the brow so that they could be swung down in front of Arkestrax's eyes whenever he needed them.

Arkestrax wore an armored breastplate in the same flawless chromium and a molded chromium codpiece. His muscular legs were bare, but he wore knee-length boots of some malleable metal, just as shiny as the rest of his armor. Around his waist, he carried an extraordinary collection of tools – speed-wrenches, reversible-ratchet spanners, hammers, gauges, micrometers, drills and welding torches.

Springer approached him, and smiled. 'The night-engineer,' she said with satisfaction. 'It is over two hundred years since I have seen a Night Warrior such as you.'

Arkestrax reached up and touched the instruments on the brow of his helmet. 'What are these doodads?' he asked.

'Your surveying and planning equipment,' Springer explained. 'This large one here, with the multiple lenses, this is a laser-array that makes it possible for you to calculate the precise distance and height of any object, building, or topographical feature. This – next to it – is a psychic compass, which works out the discrepancy between magnetic north in the real world and the dreamer's perception of north – which, of course, can often be wildly at variance. And here, lastly, is your structural theorizer, which is a visual-display unit giving you an instantaneous pictorial plan of the best structure you can build to solve any given engineering problem, whether it's a bridge or a fortress or a pier, or some completely imaginary construction to match the strategic situation in the dream.'

Arkestrax said, 'What about weapons? Don't I have any weapons?'

Springer told him, 'You will have very little time for fighting, Arkestrax. The others will be depending on you to prepare the way for them. But you have a knife that is capable, quite literally, of cutting through any substance, whether it is real or imaginary.'

Now it was Che-u's turn. He approached Oromas I and laid a hand on his shoulder. He said nothing, but serenely closed his eyes as Ashapola converted the boy who had been born as a helpless quadriplegic into one of the most graceful and powerful of his Night Warriors. In a swirling of molecules, a huge samurai-style helmet materialized on his head, arrayed with eight discs in complicated metal racks.

The rest of his armor was just as magnificent. It was made from heavy strips of blue-black leather embossed with gilded curlicues and dragons, and had upswept epaulets crested in gold and a heavy leather kilt. Che-u was now Ex'ii, the discus-thinker.

Springer released one of the discs from Ex'ii's helmet. It was about six or seven inches across and brilliantly polished so that it gave off rainbows, not unlike a compact disc. It hummed very slightly, because it contained power of its own.

'All you have to do, Ex'ii, is to stare unwaveringly at your enemy and *think* one of your discs at him. You will soon learn the different functions of the various discs. One of them oscillates in flight, so that it can cut through armor; one of them curves around like a boomerang and attacks your enemy from the rear; one of them gives off dense and acrid smoke; one of them burns; one of them radiates dazzling light. One of them is capable of passing through anything and anyone without causing any damage until it reaches the target you have chosen.'

'Better than a neutron bomb,' remarked Billy.

Ex'ii bowed to Springer. 'I accept my duty as an honor. I will not disgrace Ashapola, nor the name of the Night Warriors.'

'Give a slant a weapon and, believe me, you're in trouble,' said Dean. 'I'm thanking my stars that he's on *our* side.'

Springer said sharply, 'Dean – there will be no derogatory remarks passed between you. You are Night Warriors. In battle, you will depend on each other totally. One night, you may have to look to Ex'ii for your life.'

'Just joshing,' said Dean with a tight grin.

Toussaint now stepped forward, a little nervously, to lay his hand on Oromas II's shoulder and feel the influx of energy that would change him into Lyraq, the music-sniper. There was a high keening noise in the room as his armor gradually appeared around his body, the kind of noise that makes neighborhood dogs prick up their ears and windowpanes suddenly crack. Toussaint was dressed in a hard, ribbed, shell-like material that was almost translucent. It curved around his chest and over his shoulders in a way that reminded John of conch shells, with two rows of spiny knobs all the way down his back. His legs were protected by jointed sections of the same material, so cunningly articulated that he could move as smoothly as if his legs were bare. Instead of a helmet, he wore a tight white skullcap made of fine-grained leather.

However, it was Lyraq's music-rifle that impressed them all the most. It was nearly seven feet long, a thin, attenuated instrument that was more like a stretched-out sitar than a rifle. There were dozens of strings along its neck, each of which could be adjusted by an arrangement of steel pegs and cogs, and each fitting into the multi-barreled muzzle like a panpipe. Attached to the left side of the music-rifle's stock was a binocular sight with a brass mask instead of eye-cups, so that it fitted over the music-sniper's face. At the sides of the mask were two earphones made of the same shell-like material as Lyraq's armor, so that the music-sniper could *hear* what he was aiming at, as well as see it.

Springer helped Lyraq to fasten the sight to his face. 'The sight enables you to aim with both senses. When you have your enemy in sight, you can tune your rifle so that it sends out a musical note that matches exactly the cadence of his heartbeat or any other of his biorhythms, destroying him instantly. There was a great battle in the eighteenth century in Germany, in the recurring nightmares of Marianne Kirchgessner, a blind virtuoso on the glass harmonica. Even Mozart's nightmares became entangled in the battle, because he knew Fraülein Kirchgessner well and had written music for her. That was a time when the music-rifle proved itself to be one of the deadliest weapons in all the Night Warriors' armory.'

Lyraq raised the long barrel and swung it around.

'It's not properly tuned at the moment,' said Springer. 'But try it and see what happens.'

Lyraq pressed one of the triggers. There was a sound like a soft cloth being rubbed against a stiff and unyielding surface, but enormously amplified. It made

John feel as if every nerve in his body had vibrated. Instantly, a lump of plaster dropped from the ceiling cornice on the opposite side of the room and clattered to the floor.

'Properly tuned, that could have blown the roof clean off the house and into the Schuylkill River,' said Springer.

Lyraq removed the mask and lowered the rifle, impressed. 'Man – this beats your ghetto-blaster any day of the week.'

It was Mean Dean's turn to step forward now. He walked stiffly on legs that were nothing but memories of legs, but he stood next to Oromas II with a self-assurance that was almost cocksure. 'Come on, friend, let's have it. Full power.'

Oromas II transmitted the energy that changed Dean into Themesteroth, the rocketeer. His armor was massive and slabby and jet-black, with an octagonal helmet and an angular breastplate. On his back he carried a rack of nine sharp-nosed rockets, black and wicked-looking, and protruding from the right side of his helmet was a rectangular box containing the rockets' guidance system. On each thigh, Themesteroth carried a heavy metal box that contained the components of nine more rockets.

Dean looked out through the green-tinted faceplate. 'How the hell does this work?' he demanded in a muffled voice. 'There's about a hundred gadgets and flashing lights in here. It makes Caesar's Palace look like an outhouse.'

Springer said, 'These rockets are devastating in effect, but they are comparatively simple to launch and direct. Your suit will do most of the work for you. The rockets do not home on heat, but on latent aggression. If you come across anybody in a dream who might do you harm – even if they would only *consider* launching

242

an attack against you – a warning light will flash immediately and ask you if you wish to take pre-emptive action. It's like knowing in advance that a man approaching you along the street is disposed to mug you, and having the chance either to take evasive action or to hit him first.

'Once you have decided to attack, your guidance system will automatically take over, and the rocket will pursue your enemy at high speed. When one of your rockets hits its target, it will *implode* rather than explode, creating a temporary point of infinite gravity – a miniature black hole, if you like. Your enemy will not be blown apart, but compressed beyond all imagination. Needless to say, the Night Warriors have yet to encounter any dream-manifestation that is capable of withstanding Themesteroth's awesome rocketry.'

'Thanks for the compliment,' said Themesteroth.

Springer lifted a warning finger. 'Each Night Warrior who carries the name Themesteroth has to earn his reputation.'

'I earned my reputation already, in 'Nam, without all this junk,' said Dean.

'A reputation for dishonesty?' asked Springer, arching one perfectly plucked eyebrow. 'Or for sheer folly?'

'A reputation for doing what was necessary, Ms. Springer. Like, if this sensor here suddenly told me that *you* were a latent aggressor, I wouldn't have any qualms about jabbing the zap button.'

'Well, my dear, that shows just how little you've learned,' said Springer airily, turning her back on him. 'I am not a sensate being nor even a dream-creation of a sensate being, so your equipment will never register anything at all.'

John looked at her smooth-skinned triangular back,

now bare, and thought, *How can the holographic messenger of an unseen God have anything so desirable as a single mole on her right shoulder blade?*

He didn't know whether Springer was capable of reading his mind, but she turned at that moment and gave him a curious flickering look that made him feel for an instant as if his soul had been exposed.

'Now,' she said, 'we have just one more – you, John. Please step forward.'

John walked up to Oromas I and held out his hand. Oromas I clasped it, a tight and brotherly handshake.

'It seems like this is one battle we were fated to fight together,' said John.

Oromas I nodded, his face half-hidden by his chisel-shaped helmet. 'It's one we're going to *win*, though, John, believe me. For Lenny's sake.'

John laid his hand cautiously on Oromas I's shoulder. He felt at once as if his entire circulatory system were effervescing, as if power were surging through his body, fizzing through his muscles and his veins and his nerves, right down to the soles of his feet. His body began to develop and to fill out. His chest deepened. He felt strength and confidence like he had never felt before.

Around his head, a sleek, lightweight helmet materialized, teardrop-shaped, not unlike the helmets worn by high-speed cyclists. His chest and upper arms were covered in a tight, stretchy skin of shimmering electric-blue.

'Energy-armor,' Springer explained. 'It has no molecular weight whatsoever, and it will protect you against glancing blows and random fire.'

'What about a direct hit?' John asked.

Springer ran her finger along the muscular outline of his shoulders, and her fingertip spat tiny sparks. 'Reblax the runner is the fastest of the Night Warriors.

He runs faster than anyone has ever dreamed possible, and that means that no enemy has yet been able to hit him. You should need no more protection than this.'

Reblax looked down. The lower part of his body was encased in a sleek semi-transparent material like thin latex, and he wore running shoes that were little more than thin slippers.

He was not going to be weaponless, however. In the palm of Reblax's right hand, a thin curved piece of metal began to materialize, like a flattened pistol-grip. It fitted into his hand perfectly, as if it had been molded from an impression of his own palm. This curve of metal was attached at its lower end to the thinnest of metallic wires, and the wire was wound around Reblax's wrist.

Springer explained, 'As you run, release your grip on the crescent and spin it around and around, so that the wire unwinds. You can whip it around your head, or in any direction you choose. It is more devastating than a scythe. It can take a man's head off his shoulders, or even cut him clean in half.'

Springer took two or three paces back, and lifted her arms. 'You are Night Warriors now. You are ready to join Tebulot in our battle against the shadow-creature. Before you leave, however, you must repeat the ancient chant of the Night Warriors. It will be your protection and your creed, throughout the battles of the night.'

One by one, in that upstairs room in Germantown, Philadelphia, the Night Warriors knelt, and bowed their heads, and repeated the pledge that every Night Warrior had made since men and women had first ventured into the world of dreams to fight the evil that dwelt there.

'Now when the face of the world is covered with darkness, let us prepare ourselves here at this place of our meeting; let

us arm and armor ourselves; and let us be nourished by the power that is dedicated to the cleaving of darkness, the settling of all black matters, and the dissipation of evil, so be it.'

'So be it,' the Night Warriors repeated.

On Springer's instructions, they formed a circle, hands gripping hands, facing outward. Springer said, 'The dream-shift works on exactly the same principle as the séance, where people sit holding hands in order to share and to circulate their spiritual sensitivity. Of course, the dream-shift is millions of times more powerful than the séance. If anybody were able to tap in to the same psychic energy that *you* will be using, they would be fried in their seats.

'You are facing outward because the center of the dream-shift is pure psychic power, and to look at it, even through your masks and faceplates, would blind you.'

Reblax thought that they looked like the most extraordinary collection of warriors he had ever seen; but as he gripped hands with Ex'ii and Themesteroth, he felt pride and strength and determination. *There should be music,* he thought, *deep, dramatic, belligerent drums. This is the moment when the forces of light come out to make war against the forces of darkness. This is the moment when the Night Warriors march.*

'Now,' Springer told them. 'And may Ashapola guide you all.'

From Oromas I and Oromas II – their power-grilles connected – a wave of immense energy surged around the circle of Night Warriors. The current was so strong that all of them jerked in muscular spasm, and Arkestrax actually cried out. But the current did not subside. Instead, it built up stronger and stronger, around and around, like molecules racing around a linear accelerator. Reblax felt as if his entire being had been dragged out of his body and circulated at high speed all the way around the circle – and as if the beings of Ex'ii and Themesteroth and Arkestrax and Lyraq and Oromas I and II were being circulated through *him*, veins, arteries, capillaries, and nerve-ganglia faster and faster, one after the other, like a carnival carousel that had gone deliriously out of control.

Behind their backs, in the center of the dreamshift circle, a bright light began to shine. It was tiny and intense at first, like an arc lamp. Then it gradually stretched and grew, until it was a single dazzling pillar, so bright that if any of them had glimpsed it even for an instant, their retinas would have been printed with a dozen green after-images, the dancing pillars of blindness.

Unseen, the light began to take on a shape – the shape of Tebulot, the machine-carrier, which was Gil Miller's identity during the hours of darkness; helmeted, armored, and carrying over his shoulder the huge energy-weapon that gave him his name.

Tebulot looked like an embryo, half-formed and sheathed in light, because this manifestation was not really him, but his dream-energy bridging the distance between Philadelphia and Solana Beach. It was his soul, which had arrived in this house tonight to guide the seven new Night Warriors across the darkening curve of the American continent.

Outside the house on Wissahinnock Avenue, a sixty-year-old man in golfing slacks and an Arnold Palmer sport shirt was walking his poodle. For an instant, in the second-storey windows, he saw a flash of light so bright that the oak trees surrounding the house looked as if they had been cast out of soldering flux and the grass was bleached white.

'Holy Jimminy,' he said, standing stock-still, staring. He knew the house was empty. He had often complained to the Germantown Historical Society about its peeling shutters and unkempt garden. But that light had flashed like a bomb. Or maybe it wasn't a bomb. Maybe it was aliens. He had read something in the *News* about aliens landing.

'*Renoir!*' he shouted hoarsely. But his poodle had slipped its leash and run for the bushes. Dogs could feel the presence of Night Warriors, even if their masters couldn't.

If he hadn't turned away to look for his poodle, the man would have seen one other sign of supernatural activity: a few brief flickers of light above the roof of the old Georgian house, as the Night Warriors were taken instantaneously to California. They left the room dark and bare, except for Springer, who stood alone, her hands lightly cupped together, her forehead furrowed in anxiety.

Springer knew the risks of sending inexperienced Night Warriors against a manifestation that was as old and as emotionless as the earth itself. But she had been given no choice. There *were* no experienced Night Warriors, apart from Kasyx and Tebulot and Samena and Xaxxa, who had fought the demon Yaomauitl. But Kasyx was dead now, or trapped in the limbo of Lenny's dreams; and without Kasyx, their chosen charge-keeper, Tebulot and Samena and Xaxxa were powerless to go into full-scale combat. Like 'old sweats' in the First World War, all they could do was help the raw recruits on their way to the front.

Springer turned to the window and looked out at the night. She could remember the years when the world had been teeming with demons; when the Night Warriors had gone out every single night on massive campaigns; when their war-banners had flapped in the unfelt winds that had blown through the dreaming consciousness of the entire human race. They had battled over every imaginable terrain, through every imaginable nightmare, never knowing what the next night was going to bring. But they had cornered the last of the demons, one after the other, and destroying them or imprisoned them forever with the seals of righteousness; and there had been no need for Night Warriors anymore.

Only Springer remembered; and Springer wasn't even real. She lowered her head and closed her eyes as if she were asleep, and gradually she faded from the room and disappeared.

Thirteen

Reblax opened his eyes. They were still standing in a circle, but now the circulation of energy had died away. Everything seemed quiet.

Reblax had been conscious of leaving the ground, of flying at a great height, so high that he had seen the curvature of the earth, and the stars, and the spattered lights of sleeping America. But 'flying' was not enough to describe the experience fully. It had been like falling; it had been like exploding; it had almost been like dying.

The Night Warriors looked at each other, and then at their surroundings. They were standing in a shabby upstairs room in a house that obviously had once been elegant. The room was lit by a single naked bulb. The plaster was hairlined with cracks, and the floorboards were swirled with grit.

'Seems like Ashapola's property maintenance leaves a lot to be desired,' Arkestrax remarked. He hitched up his belt, and all his tools clinked and clattered.

'He's a god, not a landlord,' Ex'ii retorted.

Lyraq unshouldered his music-rifle. 'What do we do now? I thought we were going into action.'

Oromas I lifted his hand to quiet him. 'Ssh. The one they call Tebulot is here. The least you can do is show some respect.'

Tebulot appeared through the unopened door. He

251

wore no helmet, but his chest was protected by white armor with shining white wing-plates. In one hand he carried a massive piece of machinery shaped like an M-60 machine gun but larger and longer, with all kinds of complicated switches and clips and slots on it.

'Welcome,' he said. 'My name is Tebulot, the machine-carrier.'

'Good to know you,' said Reblax. He shook Tebulot's hand. 'I understand from Springer that you've been taking care of my son.'

'Lenny? Yes,' said Tebulot, smiling. 'And don't worry about him – he's fine so far. All we have to do is make sure that we hit that shadow-creature that's hiding inside of him, and hit it quick.'

He looked around at the assembled Night Warriors. 'Some great dogfaces you've got here,' he said. 'Oromas I, Oromas II – Ex'ii, right? – Arkestrax, Lyraq, and Themesteroth.'

'Dogface yourself, friend,' Themesteroth snapped back. 'This isn't goddamned Fort Meade.' Obviously he still resented his experience at the U.S. Army Training Center in New Jersey, where they had shaved off his hair, marched him up and down, and made some kind of soldier out of him.

'Hey, come on, man,' said Tebulot, clapping his hand on Themesteroth's arm. 'We're all in this together. Nobody's pulling rank.'

Themesteroth pushed Tebulot's hand away. 'I don't need to be patronized, friend. Just because you've done this before.'

'Whatever you say,' Tebulot told him. It was clear that he wasn't canvassing for a fight.

But Lyraq put in, 'Don't take any notice of him, man. He was in Vietnam, thinks he's tough. Spent most of his time ripping off liquor and hustling girls.'

'You want your ass blown off?' Themesteroth

retorted. 'Because I can oblige.'

'Enough!' said Oromas I. 'We're Night Warriors now. We haven't come here to argue among ourselves. We've come here to fight the shadow-creature.'

Themesteroth shrugged, sniffed dryly, and turned away. Tebulot gave him a sharp look, but then turned to the others and said, 'Listen, we don't have very much time. Lenny has only just gone to sleep, and he was pretty tired, too, so under normal circumstances you could expect your full eight hours. But he's been upset, you know, and he's pretty unhappy away from his dad, so there's a serious risk that he could wake up at any time. I'll take you to him now, and we can get straight into his dreams. But I have to warn you – they're real unstable, and you'll have to keep a weather eye out for the slightest sign that he's waking up. In which case, we need to get out of there pronto.'

Tebulot rose out of the house, and one by one they followed him. Reblax saw that the dilapidated house stood by itself in an overgrown garden, but that all around it was a small seaside community typical of the southern stretches of the Pacific Highway – Leucadia, Encinitas, Cardiff-by-the-Sea – a jumble of beach houses and souvenir shops, Mexican restaurants and rinky-dink hotels. The Pacific Ocean crawled up to the shoreline, noisy and dark.

Together the Night Warriors were carried through the night in loose formation, as light as dandelion puffs, keeping the ocean on their left. Tebulot led them northward up the Pacific Highway, only sixty or seventy feet above the road, then down toward the Solana Beach boardwalk and the small store with the steel-shuttered window and the Pepsi-Cola sign that read *Miller's Open Late*.

Reblax's mouth was dry with anxiety and anticipation as they sank through the shingled roof and into the bedrooms above the store. They found themselves gathered in one of the smallest rooms, where Lenny lay asleep. Reblax knelt down beside the bed, taking off his streamlined helmet so that he could get a closer look at his son.

To his relief, Lenny looked fine. He was hot, his cheeks flushed; but then the night was hot, even with the window open and the sea breeze blowing in. Lenny's hand was crooked up; he was holding hands with his guardian angel.

Reblax turned to Tebulot, and his eyes glistened in the darkness of the room. 'Thank you,' he whispered. 'It looks like you've taken care of him real well.'

Tebulot said. 'We like him a lot. My mom would probably adopt him if Dad would let her.'

'May I touch him?' asked Reblax.

Tebulot shook his head. 'Better not to. He's beginning to dream. We should be getting ourselves ready.'

Reblax slowly stood up, and looked around at his fellow Night Warriors. 'Well,' he said, 'I guess we'd better do it.'

Oromas I and Oromas II raised their hands. Between them, they drew two overlapping octagons of brilliant blue light. These octagons remained in the air, unwavering. Oromas I reached inside them, and while the rest of the Night Warriors watched – all mesmerized by this procedure except for Tebulot, who had seen it done many times before – he literally parted the fabric of waking reality with his hands, and opened up the world of Lenny's dreams like an amateur theatre production.

Through the eyeglass-shapes of the double octagons, they could see a wide, windy beach, in bright but cloudy daylight, and a distant ocean churning along the shoreline.

'There is a dream, a picture, that for years at intervals has come noiselessly up before me. It is nothing more or less than a stretch of interminable white-brown sand, hard and smooth and broad, with the ocean perpetually, grandly, rolling in upon it ...'

Oromas I and Oromas II raised their arms in unison, and the octagons rose up above them and shimmered in the air just below the ceiling, over their heads.

'Keep close together,' Tebulot warned. 'And don't shoot at anything until I tell you to. You're going to find that nothing is what it seems to be.'

'Let's just get in there and kick some ass,' Themesteroth complained. With the return of his mobility, he had recovered his intolerance, too.

Tebulot turned to him and said, 'Listen, Themesteroth, the way Springer tells it, your ancestors were always spoiling for a showdown. But try to cool it, will you? The whole thing about dreams is that they're imaginary. They're unstable. They're like nitroglycerin, you know, all you have to do is stumble or trip, and up they go. Just entering them is dangerous enough. So use some self-control, okay? Otherwise you could end screwing up the whole deal. And screwing up the whole deal means that lots of people get hurt – us, Lenny, and however many people this shadow wants to get out and kill.'

Themesteroth took a tight breath. 'Whatever you say, Mr. Tebulot, sir.'

'All right,' said Tebulot to their two charge-keepers, 'let's get this show on the road.'

Between them, Oromas I and Oromas II lowered the octagons down to floor-level, until the beach scene surrounded the Night Warriors on all sides. They looked around them. They were inside a dream, but they could feel the damp, salty ocean breeze blowing, and they could smell the wrackweed that swirled in the surf.

'Any idea where we are?' Tebulot asked Reblax.

Reblax frowned. The beach was completely unfamiliar. 'Any reason why I should?'

'You're his father, Reblax. If Lenny ever visited this place in his waking life, then you're the one who would know about it. Did you ever take him on vacation someplace that looked like this? Do you recall seeing a place like this on television, or in a movie, or in a book, even?'

Reblax shook his head. They could have been anywhere, although the beach had the general appearance of the less-populated stretches of the Jersey shore between Ocean City and Cape May. The sky was whitish and overcast, the color of Andrew Wyeth's dry-tempera skies. Off to the west, a line of low dunes lay like dead or sleeping camels. The sea beat against the beach with the sound of muffled drums, and the drumming was echoed by the dunes.

Oromas I switched on his sensors and turned slowly in a circle, his bootheels making curved impressions in the brown-white sand. 'I'm not picking up any signs of life,' he remarked.

Nonetheless, Tebulot drew back the T-bar of his machine and checked the glowing bar, which told him that it was fully charged. Lyraq lifted his music-rifle, too, and tuned it to the whistling of the wind.

Oromas II, even though he hadn't switched on his sensors, said. 'There's something here. Something out of key. Something that doesn't *belong* in this dream.'

'Can you work out *what*?' asked Tebulot. 'And *where*?'

Oromas II pressed his gauntleted hands over his face. 'It's running. I don't know what it is, or where, but it's running.' He hesitated for a moment, and then he said urgently, *'It's running toward us!'*

They whipped around, looking in every direction – but all they could see was the ocean and the beach.

'Maybe it's invisible,' Ex'ii suggested.

'Invisible? Jesus!' Themesteroth cursed. 'How are we supposed to fight this thing if we can't even *see* it?'

But Oromas II kept his hand pressed over his faceplate, using his own psychic perceptions rather than the sophisticated direction instruments that had been given to him by Ashapola. Gradually, showing some uncertainty at first, he lifted a right hand, palm toward the ground, and pointed toward the northeast. 'There – it's coming from that direction, just about there – and it's coming *fast!*'

'For Christ's sake, man, I can't see anything at all!' Arkestrax shouted, and the fear in his voice was as prickly as a mouthful of sewing pins.

Tebulot said, 'I'm picking it up now. You were right when you said it was fast. God almighty – it's coming straight at us like a goddamned *train!*'

The Night Warriors instinctively formed a defensive semicircle. Themesteroth armed his rocket-array, and all the way around the edges of his rocket pack, tiny red telltale lights began to blink. Ex'ii adopted the traditional knees-bent, arms-upraised kung fu posture of his oriental grandfathers. Arkestrax hefted his huge bowie-style knife.

Reblax let the metal crescent slip from his hand and unwound two or three meters of cutting-wire, listening to it whistle as it sliced up the wind.

He prayed that he wouldn't lose his nerve – that whatever creature they had pursued into Lenny's unconscious mind could be killed easily and quickly, without any casualties, without any bloodshed. He kept thinking of horror movies he had seen on late-night television – stabbings, and stranglings, and decapitations. But these images were only a mental defense against the most hideous image of all – the monstrous black shadow that had come rushing into the bedroom and sliced Jennifer open with one terrible sweep of its claws. The hideous darkness that had enveloped Sister Perpetua, and eviscerated her without any hesitation at all.

Darkness, he thought. *Darkness!*

So dark in every essence that they should have been able to see it coming from miles and miles away, on a beach as brightly dirty-white as this. So uncompromisingly black that it could never be completely invisible.

So where was it? How could it be invisible, unless dreams obeyed no logic whatsoever? And he refused to believe *that*.

Ex'ii had cocked back the catch on his discus-helmet, preparing to shoot at whatever might (or might not) suddenly appear in front of them. Themesteroth had armed his first rocket and eased himself down on one knee, rather like a medieval knight waiting to feel the touch of a king's sword on his shoulder, anticipating the word to fire.

Suddenly the answer occurred to Reblax.

John had taken Lenny to Atlantic City about two months before Virginia died, and the sun had been so fierce that Lenny had started to burn. To protect Lenny, John had dug him a little hollow in the sand, and they had pretended that it was Lenny's cave. The sun never shines in caves, Lenny. Caves are always dark.

'Under the ground!' he shouted at the Oromas twins. 'Look for him underground!'

They didn't have the chance. As Oromas I hastily fumbled to adjust his sensors, something huge and black came detonating out of the sand right in front of them, and the daylight was instantly drowned out.

The beach became a chaos of darkness and terror and stinging sand.

Claws whistled at them through the boiling, abrasive murk. Lyraq screamed shrilly. Reblax felt something slice past his shoulder, so close that he felt the wind of it, and saw furrows in the dust-cloud. Then another slice struck him a glancing blow on his shimmering blue energy-armor, and he was knocked to one side, colliding with Tebulot, who was juggling the muzzle of his machine-weapon from side to side in a hopeless attempt to see what he was aiming at.

He thought for one jagged moment that they were all going to die – that the shadow-creature was going to slash them all to ribbons.

But then Themesteroth fired. Reblax saw the blast of magnesium-bright flame out of the corner of his eye, heard the brief ripping thunder of Themesteroth's rocket. The shadow-creature was almost on top of them – a black, tempestuous cloud like thunder, or locusts – and the rocket's implosive warhead went off instantaneously, creating a nexus of ultimate gravity that flashed darker than the shadow-creature itself.

Reblax felt the creature *shudder*, and momentarily yield.

'*Another!*' he screamed at Themesteroth. '*For Christ's sake, Themesteroth – another!*'

Themesteroth fired again; and a second rocket ripped from the rack on his back. With a dull, unyielding thump like a bowling ball dropped on a hardwood floor, another black hole blossomed darker than dark, and there was no doubt this time that the shadow-creature flinched.

Scrabbling to recover his balance, Tebulot lifted his machine and hosepiped a stream of pure psychic energy at the shadow-creature. It glittered and sparkled in the darkness; but while it looked spectacular, it appeared to have no effect on the shadow-creature at all. In fact, the shadow-creature appeared to *absorb* the energy, and recover itself, and roll forward again.

'Get back, ya mother!' Themesteroth yelled at it, and fired a third rocket. The implosion was so close that their eardrums popped with negative pressure, and Reblax felt his eyeballs tugged in their sockets.

The shadow-creature swirled for a moment, and then withdrew, the same way that a black silk opera cloak slides off a marble tabletop, and vanished surrealistically into a slit in the sand.

The beach was suddenly bright again, and empty.

Reblax turned around, alarmed and distressed. Lyraq was sprawled face down on the sand, with Tebulot already kneeling beside him. There was blood everywhere, a fine spray all over one side of his seashell breastplate.

'Is he bad?' asked Reblax, hunkering down.

Tebulot lifted Lyraq's arm, feeling his pulse. 'He'll live. But he'll carry a scar. One of the claws caught him just between his breastplate and his upper arm, cut the muscle. Listen – Oromas II can take him back into the waking world. We'll go on. Oromas I will have enough energy to get us back.'

'We hope,' said Themesteroth, lifting his faceplate and wiping his forehead with the back of his hand.

Ex'ii said, 'How can we follow the creature, when it has gone under ground?'

'Blast our way in,' Themesteroth suggested.

Arkestrax swung his surveying lenses down in front of his eyes and switched the mechanism on. On his screen, he could see a cross section of the composition of the beach that stretched in front of him. The others watched him as he adjusted the dials, the illuminated diagram of the sands casting a rippled pattern across

260

the upper part of his face.

At last he said, 'The whole geological substructure of this beach is riddled with holes. It's more like a sponge, or the inside of somebody's body.'

'Can we gain access?' asked Tebulot.

'There's a fault line running roughly east to west; we could try blasting it with a couple of rockets. If you can give me a couple of minutes, I can run the whole scenario through my theorizer.'

'No time,' said Tebulot. 'Oromas II – you take Lyraq out of this dream. Themesteroth, get blasting.'

'I've picked it up,' Oromas I said suddenly. 'It's heading north, under the sand, very fast.'

Arkestrax turned northward. 'And there's a natural outlet right over there, about six miles north-northeast, right between the dunes. I'll bet you a sawbuck that's where the creature's headed.'

'It's going too fast,' said Oromas I. 'We'll never catch it.'

'Let me try,' Reblax suggested. 'I'm supposed to be the dream equivalent of Carl Lewis.'

'It's worth a try,' Tebulot agreed. 'Maybe you can keep it holed up just long enough for us to hit it from behind.'

Oromas II was already creating the shimmering octagon that would take him and the wounded Lyraq back into the waking world. He didn't look too happy about missing all the action, but he held out his hand to his twin brother and said, 'Take it easy, man, you hear?'

The octagon slowly descended around Oromas II and Lyraq, and they disappeared from sight, as if they had stepped through an invisible trapdoor.

Reblax left the others and started to run toward the dunes. He started off at an easy jog; but he soon realized that he had never felt like this before. His legs seemed to move with incredible smoothness and power, without any real effort at all. His thin-soled shoes gave him extraordinary sureness of foot, without gripping. He looked back and saw that he had already covered two hundred meters, and he was barely warmed-up. He lowered the purple-tinted visor of his helmet and began to run faster.

He was astonished by the way he picked up speed. He accelerated from jogging to running as if he were jet-propelled. Then he was doing more than running, he was sprinting. But not with the jerky, furious movements of an Olympic sprinter. His arms and his legs were still working with perfect smoothness, almost unhurried; yet he must have been running at nearly fifty miles an hour.

He crossed the beach like a human arrow, his feet pelting so lightly across the surface of the sand that he scarcely marked it. The slipstream whistled past his teardrop-shaped helmet and slithered around his skintight running-costume. To anyone watching, he would have looked like a high-speed, two-legged machine, strong and tireless and perfectly coordinated. Reblax, the runner.

He had already covered half the distance to the dunes when a dull thump caught up with him: Themesteroth's rockets, dislodging the sandstone crust that covered the caves into which the shadow-creature had fled. He looked over his shoulder and saw a wind-twisted pillar of dust, and his fellow Night Warriors disappearing into the surface of the beach as if they were climbing down into a cellar.

He ran on, his arms and legs flying. He felt he could run at this speed forever without losing his wind. Three and a half miles, four – all in slightly less than six minutes. And he was still going at full speed as he passed the five-mile mark, only a mile away from the natural outlet that Oromas I had perceived with his viewer.

He lifted the communicator on his wrist. He had been warned by Tebulot that these were not infallible: the Night Warriors had only to enter a dream in which somebody had imagined a wall of electrical static, or that radio waves were very different from what they actually are, and they could find themselves unable to speak to each other. That was why Night Warriors almost always fought close together, within sight of each other. And there was no telling when a dream might suddenly change.

'Tebulot,' he called. 'Tebulot, come in, please!'

There was a blurry crackle, then a few indistinct words, although he could definitely recognize Tebulot's voice. '... flesh ... be careful ... that shadow ... any moment ...'

'Tebulot!' Reblax shouted. 'Tebulot – do you read me? Are you guys okay?'

'... not here ... what ... collapse ...'

'Tebulot!'

But now there was nothing but static, as if somebody were maliciously crumpling cellophane directly into Tebulot's communicator.

'All right,' breathed Reblax with determination, and slipped the metal crescent out of the palm of his hand. As he ran, he began to swing it slowly around and around and around way above his head, like a lethal propeller, flashing in the dull-bright light – the only thing that did. The wire whistled softly at first, *whew, whew, whew.* But as Reblax put on a last burst of speed and spun the crescent even faster, the whistle built into a moan, and then a scream, and then an ear-splitting shriek; *eeeeeeeeeee – hooeeeeeeeee.*

He was running through dunes now. They were soft and sliding and sparsely tufted with grass, but they hardly slowed him down at all. He gazelle-jumped from one dune to another, still spinning his crescent, still keeping his eyes on the natural outlet that lay just ahead.

This 'natural outlet' turned out to be a roughly triangular cave in the side of one of the larger sand dunes. Reblax paused outside it, knees slightly bent, eyes trying to penetrate the darkness, his crescent whistling round, and round, and round.

He could see nothing inside; it was too dark, but he could sense a warmish draft, as if something huge were approaching. It occurred to him how *gigantic* this shadow-creature had grown since he had first encountered it that night at Chestnut Hill. It seemed to have spread to ten times its previous size.

Almost as if –

He hesitated, his crescent whistling *fwip, fwip, fwip* above his head.

Almost as if it took strength from everybody it slaughtered. More strength. More darkness.

'Tebulot?' he called, trying the communicator again. But all he got back was a high-pitched whistle, the same noise the TV made when you fell asleep on the couch and inadvertently left it switched on.

He wasn't sure what he ought to do. Should he wait here, out in the open, to confront the shadow-creature if and when it appeared? Or should he go in after it?

When Springer had invested him into the order of the Night Warriors this evening, he had felt confident and nerveless. He had believed that he would no longer feel fear. Now, however, he stood amongst these windblown sand dunes, inside his own son's nightmare, dressed in nothing but weightless armor and clothes that were next to nakedness, swinging a thin wire and praying to God and Ashapola that the most malevolent thing that had ever existed would stay where it was, inside that cave, and never come out.

His whole body tingled with dread, and although his high-speed six-mile run hadn't exerted him in the least, his breathing was short and stressful.

'Come on, you bastard,' he whispered under his breath. 'Come on, you bastard.'

Without warning, the cave gaped wider and the ground dipped beneath his feet, and Reblax found himself falling toward it – then *into* it. Instantly, he allowed his crescent to snap back into the palm of his hand and the wire to rewind itself around his wrist. Inside this churning mass of dark, fleshlike softness there was not room to swing it; and he was afraid that it might get snared on something and tear off his arm.

'Flesh,' Tebulot had reported on the communicator. And that was what this cave felt like: deep, ribbed, slippery flesh, like the inside of somebody's stomach. It was totally dark and overwhelming, and the cave mouth closed behind him and was lost.

For a moment he panicked. He felt as if he were going to be suffocated in flesh. But he managed to struggle to his knees, then his feet, and wade through the yielding, quivering tissue, feeling its mucus skidding against his skin-tight suit. It was like trying to walk across a waterbed in the dark.

Then, gradually, the flesh became more rigid and drier, and although it was still difficult for Reblax to walk, he was able to grope his way through it more quickly. He reached up and tentatively felt around the rim of his helmet, eventually locating a small depression. He didn't fully understand how he had known it was there and what it was for. Maybe it was a hereditary memory, one of the silent instructions passed down by generations of Night Warriors. But he thumbed the depression, and his helmet illuminated, sending out a diffuse but powerful light. Now he could see that he was making his way along a dry, coral-pink tunnel, between walls of what appeared to be atrophied muscle. The tunnel stretched as far ahead of him as he could see, and ahead there was nothing but darkness.

There was a strong, sweet, pungent smell that he couldn't quite place. Arum lilies? Orange blossom?

He hurried on. He felt like the White Rabbit in *Alice in Wonderland*. The tunnel went on and on; there must have been miles of it. *I'm late, I'm late, oh my paws and whiskers!* As he hurried, the tunnel became smoother, until it wasn't a tunnel at all but a corridor. A corridor in an unfamiliar house, with walls rag-rolled in Italian peach. His feet in their running slippers pattered along a floor of pale oak parquet. There were no pictures, only mirrors in gilded frames, hung symmetrically at head-height on either side, so that every time he passed a pair of them he was two reflections of himself.

At last he reached a door at the very end of the corridor. It was painted glossy black, with a decorative brass handle. He turned the handle, but it was locked. He rattled it, and tugged at it, but it was held fast by the will of the dreamer, as well as a lock. Lenny didn't want it opened. Lenny didn't want to see what might be lying beyond it.

Reblax turned around. Behind him, the corridor had disappeared, and he was faced with another door, identical, glossy black, with a brass handle. He tried that handle; it, too, was locked.

'*Lenny!*' he shouted. He knew that if he appealed to Lenny directly, there was a risk of waking him up, and of the dream collapsing on them – on Tebulot and Arkestrax and Ex'ii and Themesteroth and Oromas I, and himself, too. But there was something in Lenny's mind that he didn't want to confront – something he didn't want his *father* to know about.

'*Lenny!*' he shouted. '*Open the door, Lenny! Open the door!*'

There was a long silence. Not even a heartbeat. Reblax stood between the two black doors, his chest heaving, upset now, and anxious, and increasingly short of oxygen.

To die of suffocation in his son's own dream, that would be something. Sister Clare would try to wake him in the morning, and he wouldn't be there, not even his soul.

He didn't call out to Lenny again. He simply waited, knowing that there was nothing else he could do.

And, after three or four minutes, the lock-levers in one of the doors clicked like a quick burst of castanets.

The door sprang open, just an inch. And remained open.

Reblax hesitantly put out a hand, and opened the door wider. As he did so, it vanished like windblown smoke. Outside, it was nighttime. The sky was unnaturally black, and a wild wind was blowing. Reblax found himself standing on a curved patio of knobbly granite flagstones, most of them felted over with lurid green moss. He looked up. Beyond the patio, a narrow, stone-balustraded staircase led down to an unkempt ornamental garden. There were beds of veronica and japonica and Jew's mallow, tangled and weedy and with the borders overgrown. All around the garden, at the conjunctions of various paths, stood marble statues, most of them nude, most of them blind of eye and with broken arms.

Reblax slowly walked down the staircase to the main garden. There was something important here, something meaningful. The wind blew coldly through the stunted shrubs. The grass rustled as if it were crawling across the borders like crippled crabs.

There was a secret here, a clue. Reblax was sure of it. He could sense Lenny's unconscious reluctance to admit him here; yet he could also sense that Lenny wanted him to understand.

A black door. A deserted garden. What the hell did it all add up to?

Reblax walked slowly along the pathway that led to the center of the garden. He paused by a mutilated Venus, and laid his hand on her cold marble toes. A black door. A garden. What did it mean? He turned his face to the wind and felt its bone-dryness. Not a sea wind; an inland wind, a wind that had lost its moisture to dry prairies and dry fields and dry people.

He walked a little farther. As he negotiated a shriveled carpet of Saint-John's-wort, he stopped and froze. Somewhere in the blowing of the wind, he thought he had heard another sound. A soft dragging sound, like somebody pulling a thick cloak across a grassy lawn.

He remained absolutely still, holding his breath. The dragging sound stopped for a moment, then continued. It was coming closer. Not only that: he could hear the faint clicking of claws – claws as sharp as knives. Claws that could slice a human body open with one upward sweep. He felt a tingle of panic all the way down his back, as if a centipede were crawling inside his armor.

On the other side of the garden, between the criss-crossed pathways, he glimpsed a fleeting shadow. He released the metal crescent from his hand and began to swing it around, lengthening the wire with every swing. *Ssffeww, ssffeww, ssffeww*, around and around, until he was wielding nearly ten feet of wire. He stepped cautiously forward, from one path to the next, between pallid weeds and shriveled hedges and mutilated statues.

Behind a high stone sepulchre, he glimpsed the shadow again. He quickened his step, dodging on his running slippers through thorn and bramble. He reached the sepulchre and carefully stepped all around it, still swinging his crescent. The stone of the sepulchre was riven with cracks, and grass had grown through the crumbled base. On the side of it were carved large letters: OM; and underneath, the smaller letters YE VA SH.

Reblax hesitated, looking all around him. The wind blew fitfully through the grass. Beyond this garden was total darkness: no landscape, no trees. He felt as if he were standing on a stage set rather than in a real garden.

It was cold, and growing colder, although the wind remained dry.

Cold as death.

Reblax walked around the sepulchre one more time. The shadow-creature seemed to have vanished. He hoped that it hadn't left Lenny's dream and materialized in the real, waking world. He slowed down the swinging of his crescent, and allowed some of the wire to wind itself around his wrist.

Ssffew, ssffew, ssffew, whistled the wire.

Then he turned another corner of the sepulchre and the shadow was there, black and gigantic, and the whole garden shook with its thunder. He saw claws gleam, narrow and hooked. He saw eyes that flared with demented viciousness.

He thought, *It's beserk, this creature, it's totally beserk!*

He whipped his crescent faster, stepping back across tussocks of grass and snares of briar. The shadow-creature lunged at him, and he breathed in a sickening deathlike smell, like bad pork defrosting in an icebox.

He ducked to one side and lashed his wire straight toward the center of the shadow. The creature flinched, jerked, recoiled horribly, like a live eel dropped into scalding water. A fragment of darkness tumbled to the ground and immediately divided into spiderlike creatures that scurried away through the grass.

Reblax feinted, dodged, and ran around the sepulchre to slash at the shadow-creature from behind. As he did so, he let out his wire to its longest, thirty feet of sharp, sizzling, high-tension titanium.

Ssa-ffewwfff! sang the wire. But the shadow rolled away, and the wire lopped the head from a blind-eyed marble statue and wound itself tightly around a bramble bush.

The shadow-creature came rumbling forward again. Its claws lashed out, narrowly missing Reblax's shoulder and screeching against the stone of the sepulchre. It lashed again, and again; each time Reblax managed to dodge out of the way; but he was caught by the hand. He couldn't yank the wire free from the bramble bush, and he couldn't release it from his wrist.

'Tebulot!' he yelled. *'Anybody!'*

Suddenly a powerful white light was switched on. The garden was immediately floodlit, and every shadow was banished, including the shadow-creature. Reblax blinked and looked around, shading his face with his left hand. The garden was no longer a garden at all, but a brightly lit living room in the apartment in Newark where they used to live when Lenny was small. Brown carpet, brown furniture, a lamp with a yellow pleated shade, a large Montgomery Ward television, and a black metal magazine rack with colored balls for feet. His wire wasn't caught around a bramble bush at all, but around the arm of one of the chairs.

270

Carefully he untangled the wire and rewound it around his wrist. He crossed over to the window. The floorboards squeaked in the old familiar way: Beethoven's Fifth. Below him in the street lay a sunlit memory of Newark through Lenny's eyes. All the automobiles were giant versions of Lenny's favorite toy cars, and the sidewalks were crowded with the diverse population found in his toybox – shiny-faced soldiers and railroad engineers and milkmaids with pails and Indians in massive warbonnets. The sky was bright blue and cloudless, as if it had been carefully colored in crayon.

Reblax stood by the window for a moment of nostalgic contemplation that he couldn't really afford. Lenny's memory was more like Newark than Newark was itself.

He was still standing there when the door opened behind him. He turned around, spinning his crescent on a short, controlled leash of wire. But to his astonishment, it wasn't the shadow-creature, or any of the Night Warriors. It was Virginia, his dead Virginia, dressed in a turquoise summer-dress with black polka-dots on it, the same dress that he had bought her all those years ago.

She smiled at him, amused at his surprise. 'John?' she said. The sound of her voice almost broke his heart. 'John – what's the matter?'

He opened and closed his mouth. 'I didn't expect – I don't know, I just didn't expect it.'

She came up to him, so close that he could smell her gardenia perfume. Her eyes were bright, her hair shining. He slowly rewound the wire around his wrist, staring at her, unaware that tears were streaming down his cheeks.

'I heard you calling,' she said. 'Your friends were too far away to help you.'

'You *know* about the Night Warriors?'

She nodded. 'They were all separated when the dream began to change. But it won't take them long to get here.'

'Are you *alive*?' John asked.

She shook her head. 'Not in the same way that you are, my darling. But nobody completely ceases to exist as long as there is one person left alive who can remember them. And nobody completely ceases to exist as long as there is one person left alive who still needs them.'

She took hold of his hands. She felt peculiarly insubstantial, and yet her skin was soft and warm and he could feel her pulse. 'Lenny needs me,' she said gently. 'And as long as Lenny needs me, I will always be here.'

John wiped tears away from his mouth. 'Virginia – Virginia. I loved you so much.'

She kissed him. 'And I loved you, too, and always will. I was so sorry about your Jennifer, and I was so sorry about your injury.'

'It's hard to think about that, when I can walk quite easily.'

She looked up at him with a sad smile. 'If only this was real, and reality was nothing but a dream.'

He couldn't hold himself back any longer. He put his arms around her and hugged her tightly. She felt just as good as she always used to; and yet she gave him an indescribable sensation of impermanence, as if she might slither out of his arms like a deflating balloon and vanish forever. 'Oh, Virginia … I never imagined that I would ever be able to hold you again. Oh, God, I love you. Virginia, Virginia.'

She let him keep her in his arms for just a moment, but then she drew away from him and said, 'John, I love you, too. But you'd better find your friends and get back to your own body. That creature has escaped from Lenny's dreams. It's in the real world now.'

'Are you sure? How do you know?'

'That was how I saved you. I talked to Lenny. I called to him. I made him forget that nightmare about the garden and dream about Newark instead.'

'And the shadow-creature got out into the real world?'

'That's how it does it. It hides inside one of Lenny's nightmares, and then breaks into the real world when he starts dreaming about something else. It doesn't always do it, not every night, and I don't know *why* it does it, or how. But it seems to be able to break out of Lenny's unconscious and into the real world just at that moment between one dream and the next.'

'Virginia –' John began.

Virginia put her fingertip up to his lips and shushed him. 'You may not see me again, my darling, especially if you manage to kill this creature. I am not a Night Warrior. I am nothing more than your wife, now dead, and Lenny's mother. I am helpless against the shadow-creature, but I will do everything I can to guard you against it – and Lenny, too.'

She smiled, such a wistful smile, and added, 'You two … you're my men.'

At that moment, they heard heavy footsteps coming up the stairs. Reblax stepped in front of Virginia protectively, but the first person to come racketing into the room was Themesteroth, his hand tightly gripping his rocket-launching switch. Oromas I was close behind, followed by Ex'ii and Arkestrax, with Tebulot bringing up the rear.

Oromas I switched off his infra-red detector. 'We thought it was you,' he told Reblax with relief. 'Have you seen the shadow-creature anywhere?'

Ex'ii went to the window and peered out. 'This is so

strange, this place. Yet it is somehow so familiar.'

Reblax said, 'I'm sorry – I went after it. I caught up with it, too. But I think it's gotten out into the real world.'

Tebulot stared at him. 'You mean – it's escaped into my parents' house?'

'I'm sorry, Tebulot. I did *try* to stop it.'

'Oromas!' barked Tebulot. 'We've got to get out of this dream right now! And I mean *now!* Jesus Christ, if that thing's touched my parents –!'

Oromas I immediately switched to full power, and drew a glowing octagon in the air, right in the middle of the living room.

'Come on, Reblax,' he ordered.

Reblax turned to Virginia. 'Isn't there any way at all that you could …?'

She shook her head. She was crying. 'I'm dead, my darling. I can't come back with you. This is my world now, dreams, and fantasies, and memories of things that happened a long time ago.'

'I love you,' Reblax told her.

'Reblax, get your ass in gear,' Tebulot snapped.

Reblax stepped quickly toward the octagon. Virginia stood watching, her hands by her sides, as the octagon sank to the floor all around them. In a few seconds they were gone, and she was left alone in a dream-Newark that had never really existed, and didn't exist now, and never would. The sun shone. The pennants flew on top of the office buildings opposite. Toy cars came and went.

'John,' she whispered, in a voice clotted with pain.

Phil Miller opened his eyes and listened. He couldn't hear the sea: he had lived next to it for so long that he was deaf to its endless drumming along the shoreline, just as city dwellers grow deaf to the thunder of traffic.

But he heard something else – a sharp, distinctive sound like somebody scratching the wall at the top of the stairs. This was followed by a shuffling, dragging noise. Then more scratching. Then silence.

He sat up in bed. He listened and listened, but the noises weren't repeated.

'Gil?' he whispered. He waited. But there was no reply.

He swung his legs out of bed, glancing back at his wife to make sure that she was still asleep. She hadn't stirred. She put in a long day every day, helping him to run the Mini-Market, and she usually slept so deeply that he could have practised his euphonium in the bedroom without waking her.

He opened the drawer of the bedside table, hesitated for a moment, and then took out the .38 Police Special that lay inside. He didn't like guns; but the Mini-Market had been burgled four times in a year, and one night they had woken up to find a naked black man in their room, holding a knife. Fortunately, the black man had been too stoned to put up a fight.

Wearing only his pajama bottoms, Phil went to the bedroom door, and listened again. 'Gil, is that you?' he whispered.

Again, no reply.

Well, thought Phil, *maybe it's young Sammy, gone to find himself a drink of water*. He felt sorry for the poor kid. There was something vulnerable and fraught about him, something that made Phil feel that Gil hadn't taken him in simply because his parents had rushed off to Mexico.

Maybe his parents had been beating up on him. Maybe it was something worse. But Phil hadn't asked any personal questions, because he trusted Gil, and he knew that if there was anything about Sammy that Phil needed to know, Gil would have told him already.

Gil had changed last year, after he had found that girl's body on the beach and met up with that professor person, Henry Watkins. He had gained some depth, some emotional maturity. He said some pretty weird things, too; things that seemed to suggest that he had *traveled* somehow, although Phil couldn't work out how, when as far as *he* was aware, Gil hadn't been much farther than Knotts Berry Farm to the north and Tijuana to the south, and not much farther inland than Escondido.

He lifted his gun and opened the bedroom door. 'Gil?' he whispered. 'Sammy?'

It was just past three o'clock in the morning. The moon had already set, and the landing was in total darkness. Phil strained his ears; he was sure that he heard a shifting, dragging sound, but then there was nothing but the ocean, drumming on the shoreline, and he scarcely heard that at all.

He stepped out into the corridor and quietly eased the bedroom door shut behind him. No point in alarming Marjorie. He waited for a while, trying to make out the shape of the banister-rail and the top of the stairs. Sammy's bedroom was straight ahead, Gil's off to the right. Phil could just about distinguish the doorway of Sammy's bedroom, because the door was slightly ajar.

On tiptoes he crossed the landing to Gil's door. He leaned his head against it and called, 'Gil? Are you awake there, son?'

There was no reply. He tried the doorknob, but Gil had locked it. He hadn't locked it for quite a while now – not since last year, when he had first met Henry Watkins. At that time, he'd locked it almost every night, God alone knew why.

'Gil!' Phil called, and knocked; but there was still no response.

'Damn-fool boy sleeps like a hog,' Phil grumbled. He lowered the gun and made his way to Sammy's bedroom. The door was already ajar, so he eased it open and peeped inside. Sammy lay fast asleep amid his tousled blankets, his face illuminated by a quadrant of streetlight from the highway. Phil looked at him for a moment, then shrugged and turned back to the darkened landing.

Instantly, out of the darkness, a huge black shape reared up. Phil, in absolute terror, dropped his gun. The shape hung over him for a moment, as high as the ceiling, softly rumbling and stinking like death. Then it sliced him with an upward sweep of a single curved claw, from testicles to breastbone, and he felt the hideous sensation of all of his insides dropping out onto the floor.

He couldn't scream. He couldn't cry out. He couldn't even breathe. He reached out and grabbed at the huge black shape, and it was like taking a handful of musty black fabric, rotten and thick with dust. He thought of churches and monks and funerals and death; and then his mind emptied, and he was falling, sliding down some long black funnel, falling and falling until he dwindled away to nothing at all, not even the tiniest of specks.

Marjorie Miller, white with terror, snatched open her bedroom door. At that instant, Lenny woke up and sat straight up in bed, and the black shape vanished as if it had never existed. Marjorie called hysterically, 'Phil! Phil!' and switched on the landing light. Phil lay on the floor with his arms upraised like a begging dog, his carcass almost empty, his viscera heaped on the carpet.

Marjorie stared at this grisly display for only a second. Then she turned back to her bedroom, her face clenched, unable to catch her breath.

She heard nothing, saw nothing. She didn't even hear Gil's key furiously rattling in the lock of his door, or his anguished cry of *'Dad!'*

Fourteen

Springer was waiting for them when they reappeared in the upstairs room of the old house at Del Mar. He was a man now, with a bald head and small, serious features and a long white robe without any decoration whatsoever. Springer had been a princess when they were going off to battle. Now that they had returned defeated, he was a priest, a confessor, and a nurse.

Oromas II and Lyraq were already there. Lyraq was looking gray-faced, and a thin scar ran all the way from his left shoulder to his left nipple, but apart from psychic shock he was generally unharmed. All of them, however, were badly shaken by their encounter with the shadow-creature, and by the wildly unpredictable landscape in which they had just been trying to fight.

Springer greeted them soberly. 'I have tragic news,' he said, his eyes as translucent as agates. 'The shadow-creature escaped from Lenny's dream and materialized in the Miller household. There was nothing that could be done. Tebulot's father was killed.'

'Oh, my God,' said Reblax. 'Is Lenny all right?'

'He's very distressed, quite understandably, and I think he's going to need all the sympathy and help that we can give him. But Mrs. Miller has called the police, and we may find that Lenny is taken into care.'

'But the shadow-creature could do the same thing tomorrow night, and the night after. Lenny can't cope with that! And Tebulot – oh, God, it killed his father. For Christ's sake, Springer, we have to go in there and exterminate that creature, and we have to do it now.

Springer looked toward the darkened window. 'It is already dawn in Philadelphia, and you will have to return to your sleeping bodies. Otherwise the hospital staff will try to wake you, and that could be injurious.'

'But we can try again?' Reblax insisted.

Springer nodded. 'What happened tonight was partly my fault. You were all too inexperienced. It is difficult enough for you to cope with dreams, the way they shift and change and trick you, without having to cope with one of the most powerful adversaries that I have ever encountered in the wars of the night.'

He pressed his thin fingertips against his hairless forehead. He was so thin and delicate that he looked as if he had been made from bisque porcelain. 'Ideally,' he added, 'I should never have sent you. But of course I had no choice. There were no other descendants of Night Warriors who would have been as motivated to fight this shadow-creature as you were.'

He turned away. Reblax could see that he was gravely unhappy.

Themesteroth said, 'The rockets hurt it. No question about that.'

'Well, that's one of the tactical aspects of this battle that we will have to consider during the day,' Springer told him without turning around. 'I will come to you later, when you have returned to your waking bodies, and perhaps we will be able to draw some lessons from tonight's disaster.'

'How are we going to return?' asked Ex'ii.

'You have the power within yourselves,' Springer told them. 'Oromas I and Oromas II will connect their power grilles; then all you have to do is allow yourselves to rise up toward the eastern horizon. Oromas I and Oromas II can use their guidance systems to get you back.'

'Springer,' said Reblax, 'we didn't do very good tonight. In fact, we hashed it up badly. But I think we've all learned some lessons; and as for me, I'm beginning to get some ideas what this shadow-creature actually is.'

He paused and took a deep breath. He was sorely distressed by the death of Tebulot's father, and by what might now happen to Lenny. 'This fiasco tonight – well, let me put it this way: it's not going to happen again. No way.'

'I second that, man,' said Lyraq. 'Didn't even get the chance to use my music-rifle. Didn't even get the chance to pull the *trigger*.'

'Very well,' said Springer. 'Go now, before it gets too late. I will see you later today in Philadelphia. Meanwhile, I have to go to Tebulot, to Gil. This is one of those occasions when even those who are awake need the care of Ashapola.'

'Give him our sympathy, okay?' asked Lyraq.

And Ex'ii said, 'There is a Korean saying that the best wood for coffins is that which is grown in your own garden. I am very sorry for Tebulot. I wish him well.'

With these words, they each touched Springer on the shoulder, and then formed again the circle that would circulate their psychic energy and take them back to their sleeping bodies in Philadelphia. Reblax closed his eyes as he felt their combined personalities flowing through his nerves and his arteries; and behind his eyelids he saw memories that were not even his. Memories of pain, mostly, of being disabled. Memories of longing, and of endless days spent staring at the passing clouds.

* * *

He opened his eyes. He tried to lift himself up and found that he couldn't. He felt a wave of panic. *I can't move! I can't even lift my hand!*

The reality of his paralysis hit him with such force that he thought his brain was going to explode with the frustration of it. He hadn't anticipated that he would return from his dreaming adventures as a Night Warrior to be faced so ruthlessly and so forcefully with arms that wouldn't respond, legs that wouldn't even budge.

He swallowed, and swallowed again. His stomach was churning and his mouth was flooded with saliva. The room seemed unbearably hot and stifling. He twisted his head to one side, groping with his teeth for his call-button. He touched it, missed it, then pushed it out of reach.

By the time Sister Clare came around with his early-morning grapefruit juice, he was sobbing uncontrollably, like a child who has lost his mother in a supermarket. Sister Clare put down the juice, knelt by the bed, and took hold of his head and kissed him and hugged him.

'John, John ... why are you so upset? What on earth is the matter?'

He took a deep quivering breath and tried to suppress his misery. How could he tell her that only a few hours before he had been one of the fastest runners ever known? That he had fought his way through unimaginable landscapes? That he had challenged one of the most terrible evils that had ever beset America?

And now here he lay, useless, paralyzed. Unable to help anybody, especially his precious son.

'John, what is it?' Sister Clare cooed, stroking his hair.

'If I told you, Sister, you wouldn't believe me.'

'Now then, John, you know me better than that. Haven't I always held the faith? If I can believe in the Lord Jesus Christ, then I can certainly believe in one of His blessed creations such as yourself.'

John hesitated for a long moment. Then he said, 'I had a dream, Sister, that I could move.' He paused, then added, 'Not just move, Sister ... that I could run. I was so fast that nobody could catch me.'

'Hush, John,' Sister Clare soothed him. 'You're not the first to have such dreams. Che-u had dreams of running, and he has never known in his whole life what it is to run. Dreams are a gift from God, John. They are a vision of better things. You should not let them upset you.'

She helped him to drink his grapefruit juice. Then she sponged his forehead and chest with cool water, and brushed his teeth. 'It's a *very* hot day today,' she told him. 'You'd be better off staying inside, where it's cool.'

She was about to leave when there was a knock at the door, and Chief Molyneux came in, his face the color of rare beef and sweat clinging to the furrows in his forehead like glass beads strung along an abacus. He was followed by Thaddeus and Norman Clay, both looking tired, and wearing identical seersucker suits.

'Mr. Woods?' said Chief Molyneux, dragging across a chair, and straddling it with tight-trousered thighs. 'Thought you ought to know that we've located your son.'

John glanced at Thaddeus; but with the subtlest flicker of his eyes, Thaddeus indicated that he should say nothing.

Chief Molyneux cleared his throat. He was obviously going to make a meal of this. 'Your nine-year-old son somehow managed to make it all the way to a small burg just north of San Diego, California.

How he did that, we don't know yet; but we intend to find out. We haven't excluded the possibility of collusion by you or by some of your friends.'

John said nothing, waiting numbly for Chief Molyneux to tell him what he already knew.

'It seems that he was staying with a storekeeper, a man named Philip K. Miller, of Miller's Mini-Market, Solana Beach. About three-thirty this morning, Pacific time, it was reported to the local police that Philip K. Miller had been found dead.'

Chief Molyneux inspected his stubby, well-clipped fingernails. 'He was slashed, Mr. Woods. Disemboweled, if you want to know the grisly truth. The medical examiners didn't know which was guts and which was carpet. Exact same modus operandi as the death of your wife and the deaths of Mr. and Mrs. Pelling and the death of Sister Perpetuity.'

'Where is Lenny now?' asked John.

'He's in the care of the San Diego juvenile branch. They'll be flying him back to Philly when they've finished questioning him. In the company of two juvenile officers, I hasten to add.'

John said, 'You found the murder weapon?'

Chief Molyneux shook his head. 'No murder weapon. No trace of blood on the suspect's hands or clothing. No circumstantial or logical evidence that a nine-year-old boy with puny arms could eviscerate a forty-four-year-old man who also happened to be armed with a fully loaded and cocked .38 Police Special.'

He watched John for a while, his pale eyes peering out from under sandy eyebrows, and then he said, 'Mr. Woods – John – I told you before that my mind is open to all kinds of possibilities. But I have to produce some coherent kind of report. Something that the people who pay my wages can understand.'

John said, 'I realize that. But let me tell you this. We're making some progress. In two or three nights – I mean, two or three days – we can probably wrap this whole case up for good. I hope sooner, before anybody else gets hurt.'

Chief Molyneux turned to confront Thaddeus and Norman. 'You never told me nothing about this. What's going on?'

'Chief,' said John, 'it's weird and it's hard to understand. We don't fully understand it ourselves. But we do seem to be getting somewhere. So, please, if you can give us a little time … and meanwhile, if you can make sure that Lenny is kept alone at night, in a locked room, with no supervisory staff –'

'So that you can spirit him away again? Come on, John, I'm beginning to worry about my job here.'

'Chief Molyneux, if you allow any supervisory staff to get anywhere near Lenny while he's asleep, there's a strong possibility that they could be killed, too.'

Chief Molyneux looked glum. 'And not by Lenny?' he asked, although he knew what John would say.

'No,' replied John. 'Not by Lenny.'

'By this – supernatural crow-crackling of yours?'

Thaddeus said, 'I'm sticking my neck out here, Chief, but it ain't crow-crackling. It's as real as you and me.'

'You've seen it?' Chief Molyneux demanded.

Thaddeus lowered his eyes. How could he explain that he had seen it only in a dream? And not his own dream, either, but Lenny's?

'I know it to be real, Chief,' he replied.

'But you can't give me any proof?' Chief Molyneux challenged him. 'Not courting proof?'

'No, sir. Not yet.'

Chief Molyneux lifted himself off the chair, and replaced it against the wall. 'I'm sorry, fellows, but

Commissioner Lodge wants some answers that he can understand. You're free to carry on your investigations, whatever it is you're doing, and I hope to God that they bear some fruit. But Lenny will have to go through the whole juvenile procedure, and there's nothing that I can do to stop it.'

John tried to lift his head. 'Please, Chief – just try to make sure that he spends his nights on his own, securely locked up.'

Chief Molyneux said, 'I'll try.' He nodded to Thaddeus and Norman, gave John one last look, and left.

Thaddeus approached John and said, 'How're you feeling?'

'Pretty bad. I almost feel like I murdered that poor Phil Miller myself.'

'We were so goddamned disorganized,' said Thaddeus. 'I think back on it now – we should have made sure that we hit that thing and hit it hard and went on hitting it. The big mistake was to let it get away.'

'I want to do some thinking about it,' said John. 'Certain things happened in those dreams, certain images appeared ... it's like they *remind* me of something, and I'm not sure what. Listen – do you think you could call Dianne for me, and ask her to come over later this morning?'

'Sure thing,' said Thaddeus. 'In the meantime, Norman and I are going to do some more digging in the library.'

John said, 'Keep in touch, won't you? We're going to have to go into Lenny's dreams again tonight. In fact, we're going to have to go *every* night until that thing's been exterminated.'

The Clay brothers clasped John's shoulder in a gesture of friendship and sympathy and solidarity.

Then John was left on his own again. But for once he appreciated the quiet and the lack of visitors. He lay back, watching the clouds sail past through the venetian blinds, and listening to the endless whispering of the air-conditioning, and he tried to piece together some of the things that he had encountered during the night's conflict.

The black door. The shriveled garden. That's what he remembered most. They had been the strongest images in the dream. And what was particularly intriguing was that Lenny had tried hard to keep them locked away.

He tried to remember if he had ever seen a black door like that before, or if they had once visited a garden that looked anything like that. But the images were so sinister that he was sure he would have recognized them straight away.

Maybe in a movie, he thought. *Maybe Lenny's seen them on television, in a comic book, or something like that.*

Wherever the images had come from, they were full of dread. He could picture them now, and the feeling of darkness and claustrophobic terror had not diminished at all.

There was something else he remembered: the lettering that had been carved on the side of the cracked-open sepulchre. OM ... YE ... VA ... SHA. Not words in themselves, but parts of words that had been divided by the splitting marble.

He wished he could move his hands, in order to sketch the door and the garden on paper, and the words too. But as long as he could describe them, maybe somebody would recognize what they represented. Maybe – once Lenny was brought back to Philadelphia this afternoon – John could ask Chief Molyneux to let him talk to him about it.

He closed his eyes and, without intending to, fell asleep.

When he woke up, the sun had moved around the room, and Dianne was sitting beside the bed, smiling at him.

'I hear it went badly,' was the first thing she said.

'Who told you?'

'Springer. He's here. Or rather, *she's* here. She wants to talk to you later.'

John licked his lips. He had been sleeping with his mouth open, and his tongue felt as rough as sandpaper.

'Do you think you could get me a drink of water?'

'Sure thing,' she said. She brought him a glass of mineral water and held his head up while he drank it.

When he had finished, she eased his head back on to the pillow. 'I saw Dr. Freytag on the way in. He's pretty optimistic about your operation tomorrow.'

John shook his head. 'I can't go through with an operation until we've destroyed this shadow-creature. I have to go back into Lenny's dream tonight and every night, if it's necessary.'

Dianne said, 'You actually saw it, Springer says. Can you tell me what it was like?'

John shook his head. 'Black, huge. Like some kind of robed figure, I guess. But it was so dark that it was impossible to see very much. I saw claws, I think, and a split-second glimpse of glowing eyes. Or they may not have been eyes at all.'

Dianne nodded. 'I've been doing some more research with Seth. We went off on a couple of tangents, did some brainstorming. Seth called a friend of his at the Widener Library at Harvard, an expert on ancient languages; and he suggested there could be a positive link between the "mind-monsters" of the Pleistocene era and the "shadow-creatures" or Mistai that the Indian tribes used to talk about.'

'Go on,' said John.

'Well ... some hieroglyphics were found in a cave in Maine in 1953. They were almost certainly inscribed by Wabanaki Indians more than three thousand years ago. Their message isn't entirely clear, but they suggest that "all the great creatures of the earth and many of the tribes were eaten by darkness." The hieroglyph for darkness that was used by the Wabanaki was almost identical to the Egyptian hieroglyph – rather like two dishes and a curved moon. That not only supports the theory that the eastern regions of America were once colonized by the ancient Egyptians, but it also gives us some idea of what we might be fighting.

'The Egyptians wrote whole books about "black animals that jumped at men and entered their heads and drove them mad." And we can go even *further* back, and find evidence in several ancient locations throughout the world of battles to the death between prehistoric creatures in which the fossilized footsteps of one of the creatures abruptly and mysteriously vanished in mid-track. There's a famous example at the Grand Canyon – trochosaurus tracks, and the tracks of something unknown. The inference being that the unknown creature vanished in the middle of a fight by leaping right into the mind of the trochosaurus.'

'But come on, Dianne, this is fascinating research stuff, sure, but it's all historical,' John protested. 'We're talking about today, now – *tonight*.'

'Of course,' Dianne agreed. 'But we've been looking all through recorded history, and time and time again we've found stories and folk songs about people being killed by clouds of darkness, and dozens of the stories have been backed up with real, hard evidence. About six years ago, archaeologists found nine Finnish villagers who had been preserved in a peat bog, all of them cut wide open. They found out that for *centuries* there had been a legend in the region that nine men had slept with the village harlot, and that each of them in turn was attacked and disemboweled by a "murky black cloud." A tenth body was discovered next to them, that of a young woman of about seventeen. She had been ritually strangled and thrown in the bog while she was still alive.'

'All right,' said John, 'supposing you're right. Supposing these various historical darknesses were all the same kind of darkness that we're fighting now. How does that help?'

'Because of one word,' Dianne told him, her eyes bright. 'In Maine, in the cave of the Wabanakis, they found *this* symbol.'

She held up a piece of paper. On it was drawn a squarish shield-shape with four horizontal lines.

'It's the Wabanaki character for *terror*. The Egyptian hieroglyph is almost the same. And the name the Finns gave to their "murky black cloud" was "Dark Terror."'

'I'm still not following this,' John told her.

'The same thread runs through all recorded history,' Dianne explained. 'In the very beginning, in prehistoric times, the shadow-creature was real, it was completely physical and external – as real as a tiger or a bear. Other creatures were afraid of it, but only as an *external* threat, not as a fear within their own minds. Gradually, however, it learned to fight by attacking their minds as well as their bodies.

She tapped her forehead with her fingertip. 'When man arrived on this planet – man, with his highly developed imagination – the shadow-creature quickly evolved into a beast that was almost entirely psychic.

'John – to begin with, man was not *naturally* afraid of death. He always saw death as it really is: another stage on the long journey of his existence. Only when the shadow-creature came into his mind did he begin to lose that certainty in a life beyond life.

'It was when we looked up the Indian legends about the Mistai, the ghosts, that the whole thing fell into place. Indian medicine men would perform potent and elaborate ceremonies to banish the Mistai, and to keep them away from their lodges and their young braves in particular.

'The great medicine man White Bull just about said it all: "The ghost-darkness is what the white men call "fear," from the smallest darkness which is the smallest fear to the greatest darkness which is the greatest fear; and the greatest fear is the fear of death. We banish the *Mistai* because we do not wish our young men to fear death in the face of the white man, because a man who fears death is a man who is already as good as dead."'

Dianne said, 'It was White Bull who saw the great vision of a warbonnet that protected Chief Roman Nose from bullets. Roman Nose rode through fusillades of rifle fire from the U.S. Cavalry and never got hit. Not until 1868, when he broke the taboo prohibiting a warrior from eating with a metal fork before battle. Then the fear of death got into him, the shadow-creature, the mind-monster, and he was shot the same day at Beecher's Island, in Colorado.'

'But this was all primitive magic,' John protested. 'Can you really believe it?'

Dianne looked at him seriously. 'Can you really believe that you can go into dreams, and run and fight, and then come back again? You may not be able to believe it, but you can do it. So the evidence we have about the shadow-creature isn't conclusive, not yet. But that afterbirth we found in the wall of your house – that's taken our research *years* forward. It proves that the shadow-creature *does* exist in some physical shape, that it isn't *all* hallucination.'

'So what we're up against is simply the terror of dying? The real, living, breathing fear of death?'

Dianne nodded. 'That's our framework theory. We still have a long way to go. But ever since I've been working on external psychological influences, I've suspected very strongly that many of the feelings that we assume originate within our own minds are in fact the result of influences from other levels of existence. Rage, for instance. How many times have you seen people lose their temper, and then blink and frown and say, "I just don't know what came over me." They genuinely feel that for a few moments they were possessed by something that wasn't *them* at all.'

John was silent for a long time. Then, dry-mouthed, he said, 'How do we fight it? How can anybody fight the fear of death?'

'Are you afraid of dying?'

'Sure, aren't you?'

'Yes, I am. Even though I know full well that I don't have to be. We've grown used to fearing death, when we shouldn't. After this life, there are other lives, other ways forward. I know that for sure because I've seen them.'

'So what's the plan?' John asked.

'The plan is, tonight I stay here, next to your sleeping body, and I use my electronic sensing equipment to take pictures of what *you* see inside Lenny's dream. Then – even if you don't manage to destroy the shadow-creature – we may be able to see what it looks like, or discover a different way of attacking it.'

John said, 'You realize that every time Lenny goes to sleep, somebody else stands a good chance of getting slashed to death? I wonder how long the authorities are going to be able to tolerate that? What would you do, if you were the police commissioner?'

Dianne shook her head. She didn't want to consider it.

'If *I* were police commissioner,' John told her, 'it wouldn't be long before I'd start thinking ways to arrange a little accident. Overdose of sedatives, something like that. Some way of dealing with Lenny for good and all. Come on, Dianne, it could happen. They may feel they don't have any choice.'

He paused. 'Quite apart from that, every time that goddamned creature comes to life inside of Lenny's mind, it destroys a little piece of *him*.'

Dianne leaned over the bed and kissed him. They looked closely into each other's eyes, and all kinds of questions were asked and some of them were answered. Dianne said gently, 'My mother always told me to beware of men like you.'

The Night Warriors met beneath the cedar tree, their wheelchairs parked close together. Springer sat on the brick wall beside them, in her elegant female persona, but dressed less ostentatiously than yesterday in a thin dove-gray dress with a skirt as flared as a convolvulus flower.

The day was crushingly humid and hot, and even Mean Dean was fanning himself with the *Philadelphia News* to keep himself cool. Heavy gray clouds hung low over the city, the same sort of oppressive weather that had prevailed for weeks in 1887, when the Pennsylvania Convention had been arguing over the Constitution.

Thaddeus and Norman Clay were there, too. Norman had brought a cooler crammed with 7-Up and Coors Lite and orange juice.

Toussaint had almost completely recovered from the shock of his injury. But all of them were grave and subdued. They knew that if they failed to exterminate the shadow-creature tonight, another life might be taken. Not to mention the high risk that they might lose their own lives.

Springer said, 'Dianne Wesley's research into the nature of the shadow-creature may be able to help us tonight. We suspect now that it could be Fear, the actual emotion of Fear, that has been resurrected in its original physical form.'

'You're the messenger of Ashapola,' Dean remarked caustically, his cigarette waggling between his lips. 'Doesn't Ashapola know everything? The god of gods?'

Springer turned on him. 'My dear Dean, Ashapola cannot see those things that men choose to conceal from him. Why do you think many churches have a rite of confession? It is only in voluntarily revealing your sins to your god that you can find forgiveness. The confession would be meaningless if your god could already read your mind.'

'But Ashapola is the creator,' Toussaint argued.

'Your father created you, Toussaint. But does he know those things that you choose to keep secret from him? The progress of the human race would be meaningless unless man had the choice between secrecy and confession.'

'And men have kept secret from their god their fear of death?' asked Che-u.

'Most people fear death in one way or another,' said Springer. 'But what we seem to be confronting now is the last appearance of *the fear of death incarnate*. Fear as it originally evolved in the world, as an actual creature, rather than the *memories* of fear that shape our responses now. These days, we are afraid of death simply because we have inherited fear from the days when these creatures dominated humankind.'

'The question is – how do we waste it?' Billy wanted

to know. 'The only weapon that seemed to have any effect on it was Dean's rockets.'

'Yes,' said Springer, 'and I think I know why. The shadow-creature feeds off the power of normal weapons, because they are instruments of fear. The more fearfully you react to it, the more power you give it. It feeds off the fear of the people it kills, it even feeds off the darkness inside their bodies. That's why it slices them open, to steal their darkness. But Themesteroth's rockets have the effect of *imploding* rather than *exploding*. They create a nexus of ultimate gravity – a momentary black hole – into which the darkness is compressed.'

Billy popped the top of a can of Coors, and sucked noisily at the moisture-beaded aluminum. 'Compressed darkness, that sounds more like my brain.'

But John said, 'If I'm following you, Springer – what you're going to suggest now is that we set up a very much *bigger* implosion, and compress the shadow-creature for good.'

'Total energy.' Springer nodded. 'I tried it when I sent Kasyx in search of the shadow-creature; but at that time I had no idea what the shadow-creature actually was. I regret to say that Kasyx actually *fed* the creature with energy, rather than hurting it. And, sadly, I lost Kasyx.'

Dean said slowly, 'I thought you said that if we used up all of our energy, we wouldn't be able to get back.'

'That's true,' Springer agreed. 'So you will of course use only a proportion of your energy – eighty percent or so. With two charge-keepers, Oromas I and Oromas II, you should be able to exterminate the shadow-creature without any difficulty.'

Thaddeus put in, 'We're going to have to be real accurate, though, right? We're going to have to hit that thing right where it lives, dead center.'

Springer touched her braided blond hair. She looked faintly Germanic, as if she ought to be sitting in a field of edelweiss in the Bavarian Alps with the wind stirring her thin gray dress. But there was no wind in Philadelphia, only heat and humidity and overwhelming clouds.

'If you use up eighty percent of your energy and you fail to destroy it, then I have no doubt that *it* will destroy *you*,' she said. 'Instantly, this time. It is probably waiting for you even now.'

Springer stood up, and walked around the circle of wheelchairs, 'I believe that Dianne Wesley is right, and that this is the last remaining creature of darkness from a time very long ago. They were a race of demi-demons, all-powerful in the days of magic and superstition. But they were gradually exterminated by succeeding generations of Night Warriors, and perhaps they were exterminated most effectively of all by man's own faith in himself and in his own future, however unsteady and unreliable that faith sometimes showed itself to be. However, one dark enemy remained – just one – and for some reason this shadow-creature was nurtured by the man Nathan Grant and his family, and brought to Philadelphia at the time of the Pennsylvania Convention.'

She turned, and smiled slightly. The dampness made her dress cling to her slender, small-breasted figure. 'The fear of death incarnate ... that was what Gouverneur Morris was threatened with, when he was writing the Constitution. We can only guess that the forces of evil saw the Constitution as a serious threat to their future survival. Among many other things, some good, some mediocre, the Constitution was a guarantee of freedom from oppression, freedom from fear. Another nail in the coffin of the old, dark ways. Somehow, Morris defeated the shadow-creature, with

296

the help of Rufus King and King's knowledge of the Night Warriors. But at some time the shadow-creature had managed to secrete its offspring in the wall of your house; and two hundred years later that offspring entered Lenny's mind. And that is what we have to fight against tonight.'

She hesitated, and looked toward the Center City skyline, its taller buildings cushioned in gray cloud. 'Tonight, and every night, if necessary, until we have finished the job that the men who drew up the American Constitution started to do, all those years ago.'

Later that afternoon, with the permission of Dr. Freytag, Dianne arrived at the hospital with two young lab assistants and set up her monitoring equipment in John's room. Dr. Freytag had been asured that she was running tests on parapsychological cures for paralysis and coma conditions, and that she would need to bring in 'just a few odds and ends.' By the time she had finished installing her psychic sensors, however, there was scarcely room for John's bed; and Sister Clare made it quite clear that she found the whole business extremely inconvenient and annoying.

'All these buzzing and humming contraptions in a man's sick room, as if he's not suffering enough!' she muttered, but John calmed her down by saying that she could wheel him to mass tomorrow before his operation.

At seven o'clock, Chief Molyneux called, and Dianne switched on John's telephone amplifier.

'Mr. Woods? John? This is Chief Molyneux. I'm out at the Odd Fellows' Orphans Home at Melrose Park. They've agreed to take Lenny here for a few days while the Juvenile Branch decides what action to take next. I've had a talk with Lenny this afternoon. It seems like he's pretty tired and upset, but I thought maybe you'd like to tell him good night.'

'Are you going to lock him up?' John demanded.

'He'll be isolated at the opposite end of the building from all the other orphans and all the staff. I'm going to have two officers guarding his door. I don't want any kind of repeat of what happened last time.'

John said, 'No. Sure you don't.'

Then Chief Molyneux put Lenny on the line. Lenny's voice sounded very weak and childish and high, and John's eyes filled with tears as soon as he heard it.

'Daddy? I hate it here! I want to see you!'

John sniffed and swallowed. 'I'm sorry, champ. I'm sorry about everything.'

'It wasn't your *fault*, Daddy. It's this black thing inside of my head.'

'I know that, son. But don't you worry about it. I've been working with some real good people, and they all want to help you.'

'But, Daddy, what if it happens again? What if it happens again tonight?'

John cleared his throat. 'I have a pretty confident feeling that it's *not* going to happen again, that's all.'

'But, Daddy –'

'You listen to me, champ. We're going to lick this thing, and we're going to lick it good. And you can help by sleeping deep and sweet, and not eating too many pickles before you go to bed.'

'Daddy ...?' He puzzled, 'You want me to *sleep*? All I want to do is to stay awake. I don't want to go to sleep. When I'm asleep, I have these awful dreams, and I really hate them, some of them, all of them. They make me feel like I'm some kind of terrible person.'

John hesitated, and glanced up at Dianne. She gave him a quick, encouraging smile. 'Ask him what he dreamed about last night,' she murmured.

John asked him, but all Lenny could say was, 'I don't remember.'

'Are you sure? You don't remember any of it?'

Lenny didn't answer, but John was pretty sure that he had signaled his denial with a firm shake of his curly head.

'Don't you remember the beach?' asked John. 'Don't you remember that smooth browny-white sand?'

Dianne touched John's shoulder. 'John – I'm not so sure that it's a good idea for you to let Lenny know that you can perceive his dreams. You could easily disturb him, make him suspicious. I don't think we want that kind of background emotion in tonight's dream, do we?'

But Lenny interrupted, 'The beach …? Daddy? How did you know about the beach?'

'Inspired guess, I guess. People often dream about beaches. There was something about it in a book I read.'

'That beach …' whispered Lenny, so softly that John could scarcely hear him. 'That beach was in a story that Mrs. Pelling was reading me … it was about a man who kept dreaming about this beach. And then *I* kept dreaming about it.'

'There was something more, Lenny. A black door. A black door with a decorated brass handle.'

'A door?' Lenny queried, obviously shocked.

'A door that led into a garden. You know the door. And the garden was all dried up and there were statues everywhere, and there was a big marble tomb with letters carved on it.' John could hear Lenny sniffling.

Dianne said, 'John – no! Don't go on! You'll upset him too much! He may not sleep at all!'

There was a clattering noise as Lenny dropped the receiver, and immediately afterward Chief Molyneux came on the line and said, 'I'm sorry, John. He's very upset. He doesn't want to talk about things of that nature. He wishes you a very good night, I'm sure, but let's leave it at that for now, shall we? I don't want the boy to have nightmares.'

My God, thought John, *if you only knew*.

When Chief Molyneux had hung up, Dianne sat down on the side of the bed and took John's pulse. 'I hope you haven't upset the applecart,' she said.

'I think that garden holds the answer to everything,' John insisted. 'I wanted to see if Lenny could give me some clues about it – anything that might give me an indication of what it means, or where it is, I don't want to go into tonight's dream as unprepared as I was last night.'

'Well, when you go into the dream, see if you can locate it,' Dianne suggested. 'I'll be taking sensory pictures every eleven seconds throughout the course of the night, so if you manage to find it, and if it makes a sufficiently vivid impression on your cerebral cortex, then we should get ourselves a picture of it.'

John lay quiet while Dianne prepared the sensors that would be stuck to his temples while he slept. Outside the window, the oppressive summer sky changed from heavy gray to deep, dark plum, and then to black. The temperature was still up in the high eighties; the humidity was worse. A single fly circled and circled the fluorescent light on the ceiling. In that summer two hundred years ago when the Pennsylvania Convention had been arguing about the Constitution, one visitor had written that 'a veritable torture during Philadelphia's hot season is the innumerable flies which constantly light on the face and hands, stinging everywhere and turning everything black because of the filth they leave wherever they light.'

300

At last, at about ten-thirty, John was fully wired up and beginning to feel drowsy. Sister Clare came in to give him his medication, and to make sure that he was settled for the night.

'I'm sure I hate to leave him sprouting all these wires,' she complained. 'If he doesn't look like a veal chop on a bed of spaghetti.'

John, half-dozing, smiled. Then the door closed and the room was darkened, and there was nothing to see but the ceiling, faintly figured by the lights from Dianne's instruments, and nothing to hear but the irregular scratching sound of EEG needles as they danced across their endless rolls of paper.

He managed to lift his head a little. He could see Dianne leaning over her camera equipment, the faint light shining on her hair. 'See you tomorrow,' he said hoarsely.

She looked up and smiled. 'Sweet dreams,' she said, and blew him a kiss.

They gathered just after eleven o'clock on the second storey of the house on Wissahinnock Avenue.

Springer appeared to be highly agitated. She paced from one end of the room to the other and kept primping and patting her hair, as if she couldn't arrange it properly. She wore a dress very similar to the gray dress that she had worn that afternoon, except that this one was white with flecks of silver.

'It is absolutely essential that you locate the shadow-creature immediately when you get into the dream,' she insisted. 'Then you must use whatever wits you have to find a way of cornering it, isolating it, and finally exterminating it.

'We are working on the theory now that the shadow-creature actually *benefits* from being attacked. It is actually nourished by any positive power that you

301

discharge at it with hostile intent. So – everything you do to retaliate against it must be *negative*. You must reverse your usual feelings. You, Ex'ii – you must think only the finest and most generous of thoughts when you release your discuses at it. You, Lyraq – don't attempt to destroy it by tuning your music-rifle to the creature's own biorhythms – try music that is sweet and pure.

'And then – when you have the shadow-creature cornered – Oromas I and Oromas II must join together and *reverse* their power-discharge to create an implosive negative field. That should have the effect of reducing the shadow-creature to a single indivisible atom of infinite mass. So tiny that it cannot be seen; so heavy that it will simply drop through the fabric of the universe.'

'To where?' asked Ex'ii, fascinated.

Springer laid a hand on his shoulder. 'There are places beyond; and there are places beyond beyond. If I could explain it to you in the certain knowledge that you would understand a single word of what I would tell you, then I happily would. But wherever that single atom eventually comes to rest, it will be very far away from your understanding.'

Somewhere on the other side of Germantown, a clock struck the quarter-hour. The Night Warriors gathered in a circle, their armor shining dully in the bare lamplight, and knelt, and intoned the sacred words of Ashapola. *'Now when the face of the world is covered with darkness, let us be conveyed to the place of our meeting, armed and armored ...'*

They rose through the roof of the house, flickers of light like the aurora borealis, and this time the old man in the Arnold Palmer golfing shirt was standing right opposite and saw them clearly. He stood for a very long time with his mouth open, watching them turn above the treetops toward Melrose Park.

'Holy shit,' he whispered to himself. '*Ghosts*.'

The seven Night Warriors were absorbed through the hot, oppressive clouds, circling at last above the jigsaw-puzzle rooftops of the Odd Fellows' Orphans Home. Oromas II guided them down toward the wing where Lenny was being kept. He could sense Lenny's presence with such certainty that Reblax felt a twinge of paternal possessiveness. *Lenny's my son, how come you can detect him so clearly?*

They descended one by one, until they found themselves assembled around Lenny's bed. Reblax looked around the room. Sparse, utilitarian, its walls painted powder-blue, on the wall a framed print of palomino ponies at play. No wonder Lenny hated it here and wanted so much to be reunited with his father.

Oromas I and Oromas II connected their power-grilles. 'Just remember,' said Oromas I, 'we have to locate the shadow-creature immediately, no matter where we find ourselves. Then both of us charge-keepers are going to need all the defensive fire we can get.'

'Let's just cut out the chin-music and do it,' Themesteroth complained.

Oromas I and Oromas II drew their glowing octagons in the air. Dazzling blue light illuminated Lenny's soft, crimson-flushed cheek as he lay asleep. Reblax could have bent over the bed and kissed him; but this was not the time. Besides, he would soon be far closer to Lenny than a kiss. He would be right inside his dreams.

The twin charge-keepers parted the air within their octagons, and revealed a rain-lashed parking lot. The Night Warriors looked at each other in concern.

'Where the hell's this?' Arkestrax wanted to know, peering into the darkness and the wet.

Reblax had recognized the place right away. 'Lenny's

school,' he told them 'It looks like we're going back to class.'

Without any further hesitation, Oromas I and Oromas II raised the octagons above their heads and let them slide downward, so that the Night Warriors entered the dream. The rain was a steady, cold, persistent downpour, misting their faceplates and trickling down their armor. And they were alone: seven of them, on a deserted asphalt parking lot, on a wet night, outside of Benjamin Franklin Grade School on Sixteenth Street in Philadelphia.

The parking lot was surrounded by a sagging chicken-wire fence. The street beyond it was deserted, except for a few parked automobiles. The school itself was a gloomy five-storey brown-brick building, with grimy stone lintels above the windows. In the rain and the darkness it seemed even more forbidding. Oromas I immediately switched on his infra-red detecting equipment and scanned the area for any sign of life.

'Something in the building,' he said.

'Human, or what?' asked Arkestrax, jingling his tool-belt.

'It's a negative reading ... that means it's intrinsically colder than the ambient temperature.'

'Can you give us a location?' said Ex'ii.

Oromas I adjusted the tuning of his sensor, frowning as he did so. 'It *twitched*, kind of. I get the feeling that it knows we're here.'

Themesteroth activated his rocket-rack. Tiny crimson lights glowed all around it, and an amber *ready* light began to wink steadily on and off.

'Third storey, in back,' confirmed Oromas I.

'All right, then,' said Themesteroth. 'You know what they say in *Hill Street Blues*. Let's do it to them before they do it to us.'

The seven Night Warriors fanned out and advanced

quickly across the parking lot. They went through to the playground, with Lyraq and Ex'ii ducking beneath the swingset. The school stretched taller and taller as they approached; and by the time they reached the front doors and gazed upward, their eyes flinching against the tumbling rain, it seemed to tower over them fifty stories high, a dark brown cliff of wet glistening brick. That was the effect of Lenny's dreaming mind, distorting the school so that it looked the way he felt about it.

If we ever get out of this, thought Reblax, *I'll take Lenny out of Benjamin Franklin straight away. I never knew it frightened him this much.*

Oromas I said, 'Okay, are we ready? We go in quick, we locate the shadow-creature, we blast it.'

Arkestrax tried the double doors. 'Locked,' he announced.

'That doesn't surprise me,' said Reblax. 'Lenny's always complaining that they make him wait outside on rainy days.'

'No sweat,' said Arkestrax. 'I have a little something here that Lenny was never lucky enough to have. Not that his teachers would have approved.' He unclipped from his belt a shining stainless-steel gadget that looked like a giant nutcracker. Working with the swiftness of psychically inherited skill, he connected the head of the gadget to the two doorknobs, and squeezed in the handles.

With a sharp crunching noise, the locks were wrenched out of the doors. They dropped clattering onto the wet red tiles of the porch. Oromas II stepped forward and kicked in the doors, revealing a dark hallway that smelled of school: blackboard chalk, stale school food, pencils, and sweaty sneakers.

The Night Warriors advanced into the darkness, their feet squeaking on the composition flooring, and paused.

'Some goddamned nightmare,' whispered Themesteroth. 'How could you send your son to a shithole like this?'

'It's not as bad as this in real life,' said Reblax defensively. 'Besides, it has a terrific academic record.'

'Yeah, so did Alcatraz,' Themesteroth retorted.

Oromas II, who was sensitive to noises that were right on the edge of human hearing, suddenly said, 'Ssh! Listen!'

They listened. At first, they could hear nothing but the rain, sheeting across the playground. Then they heard voices, children's voices, reciting something by rote, over and over and over.

'It's upstairs,' said Oromas II. 'Let's go check it out.'

Oromas I lifted his hand. 'This is it, friends. Good luck, and shoot to kill.'

Fifteen

Swiftly, their feet pattering on the concrete, they climbed the wide gloomy staircase. The only illumination came from a tall window at the top of the stairs. The window was glazed in yellowish hammered glass and protected from stray baseballs and accurate stones by rusted metal mesh. Although they had plenty of lighting between them, including Reblax's helmet, they decided that it would be safer to make their way forward in the dark.

When they reached the second-floor landing, Oromas I stopped to check his sensors again.

'I'm still getting that strong negative signal from the third floor back ... But there's quite an array of smaller signals from the second floor, and they're all negative, too.'

'Let's check those first,' said Themesteroth. 'I'm not particularly in love with the idea of going farther upstairs without covering my ass first. That's what Charlie used to do – hide in tunnels and foxholes while we advanced through their lines; then jump up out of nowhere and zap us in the rear.'

'So you *did* learn some soldiering in 'Nam,' Arkestrax remarked.

'I learned more goddamned soldiering than you ever learned about driving cars.'

'Is that supposed to be funny?' Arkestrax snapped back.

Reblax laid a hand on Arkestrax's armored shoulder. 'Relax, will you? We're supposed to be going after the shadow-creature, not each other's throats. Now, come on, we don't have much time.'

He led the way on his thin-soled running shoes along the landing and down the corridor. Along the right-hand side, there was a row of identical classroom doors, each with a square window in it. The light from the windows shone on the opposite wall like dim and empty picture frames. All the time, the recitation grew louder, young boys' voices repeating hollow words, over and over.

Reblax glanced quickly inside the first classroom. It was dark, deserted, with lines of empty desks. The blackboard, however, was densely covered with tiny, illegible writing. Reblax turned to Oromas I and said, 'Can you read that? What does that say?'

Oromas I focused his telescopic view finder on it. He read only the first few words, '"We, the people of the United States, in order to form a more perfect Union ..."'

'The Constitution,' said Ex'ii.

'That's right,' replied Themesteroth. 'That bit of paper that makes sure that even slants like you get protected by the law.'

'Not to mention legless rednecks like you,' Lyraq put in.

Reblax nodded impatiently to indicate that they should continue, and led the Warriors to the next window. The boys' voices were very loud now, although Reblax still couldn't make out what they were saying. He glanced in at the window; and what he saw made him duck back at once.

'That's the one,' he told Oromas I. 'Check it out for yourself.'

One after another, the Night Warriors looked into

the classroom. It was shadowy, but they could see that all the desks were occupied by small black figures, their heads covered with hoods, like dwarfish monks. Each figure had a sheet of paper in front of it and was chanting from it, one after the other, one verse at a time.

It was the monstrosity that stood beside the blackboard that horrified Reblax the most, however. It was like a gigantic praying mantis, pale and gleaming and shuddery, with long, sticklike claws and feelers. Yet at the very end of its attenuated head there was a small human face with black darting eyes and the skin texture of uncooked chicken. It danced awkwardly from one side of the classroom to the other, even more frightening because of its unpredictable jerkiness, and it was obviously conducting the recitation. As it turned around, Reblax saw that its jointed body was knotted around with clothing – a twisted shirt, an inside-out coat, a stringy necktie. It looked as if, by tying clothes around itself, it had tried wretchedly and unsuccessfully to make itself look more like a human being.

Reblax recognized the stuff of nightmares: this mantis-teacher was Lenny's dream impression of Mrs. Scuyler, his math teacher. And what the little black figures were reciting, over and over, was a garbled version of their times-tables.

'Once once is once,
Nunce nunce is nunce;
Never nines are fit to fight
Ten tents are a thunder and sticks.'

With an extraordinary pang, Reblax was reminded of his own unhappiness in math lessons, of his childhood inability to make any sense at all out of the numbers that had seemed to pour out of his books like thousands of black ants. And he remembered, too, just how much he had feared and disliked his own math teacher.

'I'm getting a strong negative reading from this class

room,' said Oromas I.

Reblax turned to Oromas II. 'Is Lenny in there? Can you sense him at all?'

Oromas II nodded. 'He's sitting center front.'

Themesteroth said, 'What do we do? Blast 'em?'

'I'm not sure,' said Oromas I. 'I'm not sure what they are, what they represent. It's hard to tell if they're any kind of threat to us or not.'

'One way to find out,' said Reblax. 'Go into the classroom and ask them. But for Christ's sake, if any shooting starts, watch out for Lenny. If we hurt his dream-presence, we could very well kill him – and ourselves, too.'

'Got you,' said Themesteroth.

Carefully, Reblax turned the doorknob and opened the classroom door. At once, the chanting of tables died away. There was a chilly rustle, and all the black hooded figures turned around at their desks. Oromas II had been right. Lenny was sitting center front, white-faced, although he didn't appear to recognize his father at all. As for the other figures, however, it was impossible for Reblax to see their faces. They were completely buried in shadow.

He was struck by the chilliness of the air, and a sickly smell like dying flowers or rotting meat. In the gloom of the room, the mantis-teacher clicked and clattered its claws and stared at him with emotionless eyes.

'What do you want?' it whispered in a voice that sounded half-choked by a hairball. 'You could have had the grace to knock.'

'Mrs. Scuyler?' Reblax asked. Behind him, he felt Themesteroth pushing forward; and he could hear the high-pitched whine of Themesteroth's launch mechanism building up to full power.

There was a second's hesitation, and then 'Mrs. Scuyler' came lurching across the classroom toward

310

him. *'You're late, child, late! You'll have to be punished!'* Her claws scraped on the classroom floor.

'Reblax!' warned Oromas I. 'Negative feedback just surged up!'

Reblax stepped quickly backward. As he did so, 'Mrs. Scuyler' slashed a claw at him, and slit open the shining blue armor over his chest like a fisherman's knife slitting open a trout. He felt a thrill of utter cold, and then a surge of pain.

Instantly, the dwarfish black figures swarmed out of their places and came rushing across the classroom.

'Fire!' shouted Oromas I, and Themesteroth launched a thunderous rocket from his backpack that hit the classroom ceiling and ricocheted back into the crowd of figures. There was a dull thumping implosion, and three of the figures were sucked into oblivion.

Hastily the Night Warriors retreated from the classroom and back along the corridor, but the black figures came hurrying after them. Themesteroth stopped, turned, and prepared to launch a second rocket, but one of the figures caught up with him, and sliced at his legs with glinting claws.

'What the hell!' he roared as the claws raked into unprotected thigh-muscle. He kicked out in all directions as more black figures clustered around him, their claws lifted, their feet scurrying.

Lyraq had reached the landing. He knelt down on one knee and lifted his music-rifle, clamping the mask to his face. His fingers played deftly over the strings. Reblax, who was right beside him, heard a musical note rise from deep, vibrant inaudibility to C-natural to F-sharp, reaching a pitch of utmost clarity and sweetness – so sweet that it was almost unbearable to listen to.

The four or five dwarves who were slashing with such fury at Themesteroth's thighs and ankles stopped suddenly, and turned, transfixed by the pitch of Lyraq's

311

rifle. Without hesitation, Lyraq pulled the trigger, and the musical note screeched out of the rifle's multiple panpipe barrels with a sound like a banshee. The black figures imploded, one after the other, in rapid succession in a jumping blizzard of dust and shredded black cloth.

'Bo-day-*shuss!*' shouted Arkestrax. Themesteroth meanwhile was able to kick away another black figure and limp-hop-hobble back to the landing.

There were seven of the small black figures remaining. Behind them, the pale insectlike 'teacher' dragged its claws along the corridor, head swaying uncontrollably from side to side. Reblax was chillingly reminded of the noise he had heard outside his bedroom that night that Jennifer had died.

Oromas I said, 'Do we have any idea what these half-assed bastards *are*?'

Reblax nodded. 'I can guess what's happened. Last night when I was fighting the shadow-creature, I cut a piece of it away – and that piece turned into lots of small pieces and ran off like spiders. It's the same thing that happens to plantar worms, isn't it? You try to chop 'em up, but each piece grows into another worm.'

Lyraq tuned up another note, and fired at the figures again. One of them burst inward in a shower of shredded cloth, but the others rushed forward before Lyraq could adjust his aim.

It was Ex'ii's turn now. He stepped toward the advancing figures with consummate grace and control, his hands raised in the hawk positions of kung fu. One of the discs on the front of his samurai-like helmet was gleaming in readiness, filling the corridor with reflected rainbows.

For one long heart-stopping moment, Reblax thought that Ex'ii was unable to summon up the psychic energy to launch his disc. He released the metal crescent from his hand and began to swing it on a short wire, in case Ex'ii failed.

'Ex'ii!' bellowed Themesteroth, struggling to reset his rocket-launcher. 'Hit 'em, for Chrissake!'

Themesteroth lurched forward, but Oromas II lifted a hand to restrain him. Oromas II had sensed the perfection of Ex'ii's technique; he could feel the complicated psychic vibrations that Ex'ii was giving out, and knew that Ex'ii would choose exactly the right instant to concentrate them all into firing his thought-disc.

The dwarf-figures surged forward, then hesitated. Behind them, the 'teacher' cried out, *'Punishment! Punishment! That's what they deserve!'*

But at the instant that the dwarf-figures shuffled closer again, Ex'ii let out a cry of *'Hai!'* and the rainbow-shining disc whipped from his helmet, cutting diagonally through the cluster of black figures, then diagonally back again, faster and faster, chip-chopping them into thousands of black fragments right in front of their eyes.

The disc flew so quickly and so precisely that in less than three seconds, the dwarf-figures fell into a soft cloud of shadowy dust, as if they had never existed. Every cut had been mentally planned, and the disc had followed Ex'ii's mental programming to the last millimeter.

'Look at that,' Arkestrax breathed. 'This joker ought to get a job at Benihana.'

'Don't leave the dust!' cautioned Oromas I. 'You heard what Reblax said – if you tear the shadow-creature into pieces, it could regenerate itself!'

Ex'ii raised his hand. 'I had no intention, honorable warrior, of leaving the dust.'

The rainbow-shining disc had been wobbling unsupported in the air, just above the remains of the black dwarf-creatures. Ex'ii frowned at it, and it began to wobble even faster, faster and faster, until it formed a gleaming hourglass shape in the air. All of the grayish dust that was scattered on the floor of the corridor was sucked up by the vacuum that the spinning disc had created, and compressed in the narrowest part of the hourglass shape, smaller and smaller, until it winked darkly once, and vanished.

Ex'ii snapped his fingers, and the disc slowed, described a lazy, graceful curve in the air, and returned to his helmet.

All this time, the insectlike figure had been clattering and clashing from one side of the corridor to the other, eyes swiveling, head swaying, although it had made no further attempts to attack.

Now that its black brood had been destroyed, however, and it was outnumbered by the Night Warriors seven to one, it began without warning to change. Its face melted like pink wax, its limbs thickened, its knotted clothes unwound themselves. Claws reassembled themselves into hands; feelers shrank into ears. The jointed thorax shrank and shriveled. In a few moments, he had metamorphosed into a human – an emaciated, shortish man, with a forehead as large and pale as a lamp and lank black hair. A man in disheveled, old-fashioned clothes and a tightly knotted cravat.

Arkestrax said. 'Holy criminentlies – Edgar Allan Poe on his day off.'

Lyraq had been tuning his music-rifle to exterminate the mantis-creature; but now he stood up in bewilderment, took two paces back, and looked to Reblax and Oromas I for guidance on what he should do.

'Just hold it a minute,' said Reblax. He was still spinning his metal crescent on a short ten-inch wire. He pushed past Lyraq and Themesteroth, and approached the man as close as he thought was safe.

314

The man had been looking down at the floor. As Reblax approached, he raised his eyes, and stared at him.

'Night Warriors,' he said in a husky whisper. 'I thought that I might have seen the last of your kind.'

'Who *are* you?' Reblax demanded. 'What are you doing in my son's dream?'

The man gave a slanting smile and kept tugging at his cravat as if he had a nervous compulsion. 'With dreams, *mon ami*, it is sometimes difficult to determine who is in *whose*.' His smile disappeared. He clasped his hands behind his back and cracked his knuckles, one hand after the other. 'Is Lenny dreaming me, or am I dreaming Lenny? Or are you dreaming both of us? Or none of us? Dreams within dreams, *mon ami*.'

Oromas I interrupted, 'Reblax – I'm picking up increased negative feedback from the third storey back. Drop in temperature, minus twenty-two Celsius.'

The man in the old-fashioned black suit laughed, showing off brown stumps of teeth. 'The principal!' he cried out. 'Do you want me to send you to the principal?'

'We'll find him ourselves, thanks,' Reblax told him.

'Maybe you will,' the man said, grinning. 'But you didn't come properly equipped, did you? I wouldn't feel confident about going to the principal, if I were you, not without a book down the back of your pants.'

Oromas I said, 'Come on, Reblax, we're wasting time. This fruitcake isn't going to tell us anything.'

'All right,' Reblax agreed, without taking his eyes off the man in the black suit. 'Let's get up to the third floor.'

'Unwise,' the man warned them, wagging a chalky finger. 'Very unwise.'

'For Christ's sake, Reblax,' said Themesteroth. 'Zap him, and let's get moving.'

Reblax hesitated. 'Just a minute,' he said, and approached the man closer. The man held his ground without flinching and leered up at Reblax with rheumy eyes. 'What do you mean, we didn't come properly equipped?' he demanded.

The man sniffed, and abruptly laughed, so that mucus sprayed from his nose. He wiped it away with the back of his sleeve, and said, 'Innocents! Not like the Night Warriors used to be. Wise and tough, in the old days, you people used to be! Wise and tough! But I knew you were tyros the moment I saw you. Not properly equipped, *mon ami*, and now it's death for you and no mistake.'

'You've known Night Warriors before?'

The man looked sly. 'Wouldn't you like to know? But why should I help you? Too pure and saintly, you are, just like that Gouverneur Morris. Just like that Rufus King.'

'Come on, Reblax, for Christ's sake,' Themesteroth gripped.

'Reblax, he's right – *please*,' Oromas I insisted. 'That negative feedback – it's moving, it's coming toward the third-storey landing.'

But Oromas II came up and laid a hand on Reblax's shoulder. 'You are right to question this man,' he said, and his voice was very soft and very steady. 'You sense in this man what *I* sense.'

Reblax stared at the man steadily. 'Nathan Grant,' he said quietly, but with great confidence. 'You're Nathan Grant.'

The man's eyes bulged, and he sniffed and blew spit. 'Nathan Grant! You believe that I'm Nathan Grant? How dare you! I am all that *remains* of Nathan Grant – but I am not Nathan Grant in flesh and blood and holy spirit amen! Oh, no! Nathan Grant in flesh and blood and holy spirit was sizzled by the Night

316

Warriors! Sizzled, sizzled, sizzled, like raw beefsteak! And his wife, too, and his saintly daughter!'

'Reblax, man come *on*!' Lyraq yelled at him.

'Daughter?' Reblax persisted. 'What do you mean, daughter? You had *two* daughters, didn't you? Nora and Kathleen.'

Nathan Grant lifted one leg and danced a little jig around the corridor, amusing but frightening at the same time, the dance of a spirit possessed. 'Yes, yes! Two daughters, two daughters! Nora the one, Kathleen the other! And slow from birth, both of them, slow, slow, slow! But good for trading, in their way! Helpful and obliging! Both took the Mistai's seed quite happily, no complaints, and bore their burdens to Philadelphia, no complaints. Both big with shadow-child! Ha, Ha! And would have borne them, too, except for Rufus King and you Night Warriors, curse your sanctity, chasing them here and chasing them there, awake and dreaming, no place to escape! Except of course for clever, clever Kathleen, hiding herself in the wall-place we'd made; and we plastered her up! Plastered her up! And she knew that she'd die, but smiled about it, and kept herself awake so that the Night Warriors wouldn't find her; but cleaved to her bigness, didn't she, my angel Kathleen!'

He was hopping more slowly now, hopping like a man in a fit. But the tears for his lost Kathleen were trickling down his chicken-skin cheeks. 'Ah, but it was all worthwhile, wasn't it?' he asked. 'For his lord and master is back now, isn't he? Good as ever. *Bad* as ever! And nothing that *you* can do can stop him!'

Themesteroth bellowed, 'Sic him, Reblax, ya turkey!'

'My God,' said Reblax, stunned by what Nathan Grant had told him.

'Kill him, will you!' Arkestrax shouted. 'We've got to get out of here!'

Reblax hesitated. He knew that they had to destroy the shadow-creature, and destroy it quickly. But there was so much more that he wanted to ask Nathan Grant.

Nathan Grant grinned at him. 'Come on, *mon ami*, you can kill me if you want. Much good may it do you.'

The school building began to shake and tremble. Pieces of masonry dropped from the sides of the staircase and shattered in the hallway below.

'He's coming!' shrieked Nathan Grant. 'The principal! Ha, Ha! Now you'll be punished! Now you'll be sorry! And you're not *prepared*! Not prepared at all!'

Reblax allowed three more feet of wire to lash out from his wrist. He spun it faster and faster until it shrieked; and all the while the school rumbled and shook, and windows shattered, and desks careened from one side of the classrooms to the other; and with an ear-shattering crack a huge lightning-jagged split appeared in the side of the building, right up to the massive yellow-glazed window. The rain poured in through the split, and misted the stairs with wet.

Oromas I clutched at Reblax's arm. 'Reblax! Come on! We've lost the initiative! We've got to fight this rearguard! Reblax! It's *coming*, for God's sake!'

Reblax released as much wire as the narrowness of the corridor would allow and spun it – so fast that it would have taken off a man's hand if that man had been foolish enough to reach out to touch it.

And just at the moment that he was ready to whip off Nathan Grant's head, Lenny's dream-personality came running out of the classroom, white-faced and crying, and Nathan Grant snatched Lenny's cloak and spun him around and lifted him up, *heyyy!* and pressed his cheek close to his. Champ, champ, don't you run off now, champ. Grinning, loving every moment of it, smooth nine-year-old skin pressed suction-tight up against withered long-dead chicken-skin.

'Come on, *mon ami*!' Grant laughed. 'Take my head off! Take my head off! Chop, chop, chop, my fine-feathered Night Warrior – just the way your ancestors sizzled me! But Lenny's head will go, too! Two heads with one stroke! One stroke, two heads! What a story that could make!'

Lenny screamed and kicked, his eyes wild; but there was nothing that Reblax could do. He kept on whipping the wire around and advanced on Nathan Grant step by step; but Nathan Grant taunted him, and laughed, and kept Lenny's cheek squashed tight against his.

'Take my head off! Take my head off!'

And at the same time, the concrete landing creaked and grated, and started to tilt sideways. *Something* was descending the upper part of the staircase from the third floor. Something dark; something huge. Something that dragged itself along the flooring with a noise like thirty canvas sacks crammed with drowned dogs.

Something with claws that scraped along the walls, stripping off ribbons of olive-drab paint.

The Fear of Death, the grisly principal of Lenny's nightmare school.

Oromas I frantically checked his sensors. 'It's on its way down! It's after us! Come on, Reblax, we need to get out of here – and fast!'

Oromas II grasped Reblax's left wrist. 'It's all right, you don't have to worry about the boy! It's only a dream – Grant can't hurt him! The only person who can hurt him is *you*!'

Lenny fought hysterically against Nathan Grant; but Grant clasped Lenny tighter still, kissing him with liver-colored lips, licking his cheeks with a long tongue that seemed to have an existence of its own.

Reblax shouted, 'No!'

But Oromas II tugged him back, and snapped at

him, 'If you don't come – *now* – I'm going to drain down your power.'

From upstairs, the sound of dragging grew thunderously louder. It began to descend the stairs. Lightning flashed through the gaping cracks in the collapsing school building; and for one split second it illuminated a gigantic black-cloaked shape on the rainswept stairway, with curved claws as long as swords and a body that was tangled black gristle and eyes dull red like raging sores.

Then darkness again, and the thunderous dragging, and the cold drenching sensation of absolute fear.

Reblax took one last desperate look at Lenny, struggling in the grip of Nathan Grant, and then he turned away. Lyraq and Arkestrax were already halfway down the stairs, and Themesteroth and Ex'ii were close behind. Oromas I shouted, 'We'll regroup – set up an ambush! Then we can make sure that we hit it dead center!'

Nathan Grant, instantly realizing that his play to make Reblax kill Lenny's dream-personality had failed, threw Lenny aside. Lenny tumbled over and over in the air, and miraculously tumbled himself into a bright blue ball, which bounced along the corridor with a happy spanking sound. Grant, however, came tearing after Reblax in a hissing fury.

As Nathan Grant ran, claws opened out from the skin of his chest with a sickening tearing sound, his neck stretched out, and his face was pulled back into an insectlike mask, with teeth upon teeth. He jumped onto Reblax's back, and clung there, scratching and biting.

Reblax twisted and turned and scrabbled behind him in a frantic effort to dislodge this insect-Grant from his shoulders. But Grant dug spiny quills into Reblax's skin and gripped the back of his helmet between two layers of teeth; and even when Reblax backed up and crushed him against the wall, again and again, with a ghastly crunching sound like treading on grasshoppers, Grant refused to relax his grip.

'*Reblax!*' shouted Lyraq. '*Turn around again! Turn around!*'

Reblax staggered around, gripping the banister-railing for support. His shoulder muscles stung as if they had been lashed with razor-wire, and Grant was beginning to bite and snap at the back of his neck. And all the time, the shadow-creature was dragging itself down the stairs, stair after stair, so that its darkness began to blot out the light from the huge yellow-glazed window.

Lyraq lifted his music-rifle, fitted the sight-mask onto his face, tuned, and fired.

Reblax heard an extraordinary shriek of pure music, fifty sopranos, two hundred violins. On his back, the insect-Grant jerked and shuddered, and then abruptly exploded in a spray of hairy shell and pints of glutinous yellow liquid.

'A-y-y-y one!' Themesteroth bellowed. 'Now let's *haul ass!*'

Close together, they sprinted down the slippery wet stairs, skidding on the composition flooring in the hallway. They jostled out of the school's main doors into the pouring rain and jogged across the playground.

It was only when they reached the swingset that they turned around and looked at the collapsing school building. Dark brown against a darker sky, it crumbled and fell. Huge chunks of masonry dropped into the playground and burst apart. Lintels, guttering, chimneys, windows, it all came down, with a sound like the ocean shattering on the shore.

And then, behind the yellow-glazed window, they saw the darkest of shapes. The shadow-creature, bloated on human terror, nourished on human darkness, reared behind the glass, and was momentarily silhouetted by lightning.

'God almighty,' said Arkestrax.

The yellow-glazed window exploded. Glass fragments blew slow-motion into the rainy night, turning over and over.

'*Back!*' ordered Oromas I. '*I want you all the hell out of here!*'

Nobody questioned his command. But when they turned to run, they discovered that the swingset had somehow transformed itself into a complicated metal barrier, a puzzle-fence of poles and bars and chains.

'We're trapped!' said Lyraq.

But Ex'ii lifted his hand and said, 'Wait! This is only a maze, and all mazes can be penetrated.' He pressed his fingertips against his forehead and closed his eyes, and one of his discs began to glow. He released it; and it flew from his helmet with a soft *zzhhapp*! and twisted and turned its way through the fence of metal poles, leaving behind it a glowing after-image.

'All we have to do is follow the disc,' said Ex'ii 'There is no combination of metal shapes that was not known to the ancient Chinese. The disc has all the knowledge of the ancients, as well as all the technology of today.'

Arkestrax was already clambering through the metal poles. Themesteroth grumbled, 'Could have blasted them, just as easy.'

'Yes,' said Ex'ii with a smile. 'But rockets use a great deal of psychic energy, and that is what we must conserve, above all.'

They clambered through the bars of the swingset, and then ran across the parking lot, their feet splashing in the puddles. Even as they ran, however, the dream began to alter and shift, and they found that they were running along a wide corridor with mirrored walls, so that it looked as if endless teams of Night Warriors were all running together toward the same objective.

At first the corridor was bright, but as they ran forward it became narrower and dimmer, and its gradient became steeper, until at last it was too steep for them to climb.

Arkestrax said, 'Hold on,' and braced himself against the wall and switched on a powerful flashlight that was attached to his shoulder. The flashlight revealed a corridor that sloped up at more than a sixty-degree angle until it reached a black six-paneled door with a shining brass handle. But the door was more than two hundred feet away. 'What do we do now?' asked Lyraq. 'We can't go back. That black thing is going to have us for breakfast, with a side-order of grits.'

Arkestrax lowered his structural theorizer in front of his eyes and punched a complex arrangement of buttons on his left chest, almost like a miniature accordion. Leaning close to Arkestrax, Reblax could see Arkestrax's screen light up and a plan of the sloping tunnel appear, in holographic 3-D. Immediately, the screen projected a picture of a spiral, rather like the core of an Archimedes screw; and beneath the picture a box appeared, crammed with technological data.

'Can you do it?' asked Oromas I anxiously.

'No sweat,' Arkestrax replied.

He reached behind him and unhooked from his belt a heavy cylindrical instrument that looked like a flashlight. He adjusted two slide-switches on the side of it, and then he knelt down and aimed it at the wall of the sloping corridor.

A sickly wind began to blow along the corridor, and Ex'ii retched. 'Death,' he said. 'It smells like death.'

But Arkestrax's instrument was glowing now; and out of its muzzle a thin silvery beam of pure energy began to stream, following the same spiral path that his structural theorizer had plotted. It came out slowly at first, but then it poured out faster and faster – until with one final spin it had created a perfect spiral of shining metal, all the way up to the black door.

'Cool tool, huh?' said Arkestrax, holding up the instrument, then clipping it back onto his belt. 'Takes any metallic content out of the air and makes it into usable metal.'

'Well, great,' said Themesteroth. He jerked his head toward the spiral. 'But how does *that* help? That – half-assed Disneyland ride?'

Without answering, Arkestrax reached into the bag that he carried around his waist, and tossed to each of them a small bracket-shaped piece of shining copper-colored metal. 'All you have to do is attach that to your belt, right round at the back, and connect it up to the metal spiral. That's all. The power of Ashapola will do the rest.'

Oromas II went first. He seemed to have developed a quiet assurance during the course of this second dream, and a closer understanding of what they were doing. The world of dreams might have turned out to be a world of madness, but at the same time it was still bounded by the limited parameters of the human imagination. What was unimaginable couldn't be dreamed. What was imaginable could be dealt with, one way or another.

Oromas II slotted the copper bracket into the back of his armor, then moved carefully backwards until it connected with the metal spiral that Arkestrax had laid up the angled corridor. 'Okay, go,' said Arkestrax.

Without any hesitation Oromas II slid up the spiral, around and around, until he reached the black doorway at the top. He braced himself against the sides of the corridor like a rock-climber, and called back, 'Fann-tastic! Come on up!'

Quickly, one by one, they spiraled their way up the

324

corridor until they had all joined Oromas II by the door.

Arkestrax connected a complicated arrangement of stainless-steel levers to the door-handle, and forced it open without any effort at all. Oromas II raised the door cautiously, like a manhole cover, and immediately they felt a freezing wind blow down the corridor.

'Nighttime,' commented Oromas II. 'And damned cold, too.'

They climbed out of the doorway to find themselves standing in a bleak, gale-tossed garden. Reblax recognized it at once. It was the garden he had seen last night: the garden in which he had fought the shadow-creature. He wished that there were some way in which he could contact Dianne, and make sure that she was photographing everything that he could see: the ink-black sky, the sour and shriveled grass, the crisscross pathways, the sightless statues.

He walked ahead of the rest of the Night Warriors, the grass stinging against his legs. *Where had he seen this garden before? Where had he seen that door before?* It was all so familiar, in spite of its coldness. It was somewhere that he and Lenny had been together: it must be. But where? It wasn't Fairmount Park and it wasn't the Brandywine Valley and it wasn't even Neptune, New Jersey.

Oromas II came up close behind him. 'This is the place, isn't it?' he asked. 'The place you mentioned from yesterday's dream?'

Reblax nodded. His eyes scanned the black horizon for any sign of the shadow-creature. 'It's here somewhere. I swear it.'

'Have you ever been in this garden before?' asked Oromas I, looking around him as he approached.

'No,' said Reblax. 'But it's familiar, for some reason. Don't ask me why.'

Oromas I switched on his sensors. 'You're right – it

is here. Three hundred meters south-southwest.'

Arkestrax double-checked that bearing on his own equipment. 'You're right. Lenny's perception of north is spot-on true north.'

Oromas II said, 'The shadow-creature knows we're here. It knows we're trying to hunt it down.'

'How can you tell a thing like that?' Themesteroth demanded.

Oromas II tapped his helmet. 'I can sense it. It's mad. It's been waiting for two hundred years, and now we're trying to kill it. I mean – wouldn't *you* be mad, if that happened to you?'

'I don't give a shit whether it's mad or not, I'm going to waste it,' Themesteroth told him.

With a lopsided smile, Oromas II went back to talk to his twin. Oromas I was already suggesting that they should fan out and make their way through the garden separately. Reblax could tell that by the way he kept sweeping his arm from side to side.

He sat down on the corner of one of the marble graves. He was feeling exhausted, especially after seeing Lenny threatened so lewdly by Nathan Grant. He knew that Lenny hadn't been physically or mentally harmed – after all, Lenny was still dreaming this dream, which he wouldn't have been able to do if he were hurt. But all the same, Reblax was beginning to feel the strain of fighting a battle in which he was so closely involved. His emotions were stretched out like high-tension wires.

Oromas I came over and hunkered down in the grass. 'We've decided to search this garden by sections, the same way we do in Philly in the Italian district, when suspect somebody of harboring a felon.'

Reblax said, 'There's a key to the whole damned business somewhere here.'

'Yes, well, maybe there is,' said Oromas I. 'But right

now we've got ourselves a shadow-creature to kill.'

'All right,' said Reblax. 'Tell me what you want me to do.'

They powered up their weapons and started to search the garden systematically. It was pitch-dark, and nerve-wracking. All they could see was the light from their own helmets, sometimes close, sometimes far away, and the pale, blind statues that stood at every intersection.

From time to time they called to each other with echoing voices, but most of the time they were silent and tense as they patroled through sepulchres and tombs, their weapons raised at the ready. Their lights dipped and bobbed like the lights of fireflies, weaving a pattern through the night.

Oromas I said, 'I've lost it. I'm still scanning. It could be anywhere.'

'Thanks for the backup, pal,' said Themesteroth. 'We're supposed to hit that mother right where it lives, no deviation, no error, not one centimeter left or right, full negative blast. So don't start telling *me* that it could be anywhere.'

'Can it, Themesteroth,' said Reblax.

'The hell you say,' Themesteroth retorted.

They searched the gardens again and again; but it had taken them only one search to convince themselves that the shadow-creature had vanished.

Bitterly, Reblax said 'I'll bet you real money that it's back in the waking world, slashing somebody to death.'

'Oh, come on, man,' said Arkestrax. 'Don't let it get to you.'

'And why not, for Christ's sake? Jennifer was my wife. The Pellings were my friends. I loved them all, and I love Lenny, too.'

Arkestrax said nothing, but bowed his head.

Reblax got up and walked across to Oromas I, who was studiously scanning the horizon for any sign of approaching danger.

'Oromas?' he said.

'What is it, Reblax?'

'He's not here, Oromas. You know that as well as I do. We'd be better off back in the waking world.'

Oromas I stood up. 'I guess you're right. I just hope that nobody got hurt.'

Reblax took hold of his hand and squeezed it tight. 'Come on, buddy. Not your fault.'

Oromas I becked to Oromas II. 'Let's do it,' he said. 'Let's get ourselves back. This is like looking for hay in a haystack.'

They gathered together, disappointed, fearful, but ready to leave.

'I'm sorry, people,' said Reblax. 'Maybe we should have hit the big one first and left all those dwarves till later. But they were dangerous, those dwarves – you saw how dangerous – and we couldn't have gone for the big one with those gonzos snapping at our heels. I'm just hoping and praying that nobody got hurt tonight.'

Reblax took a last look around the garden, in the hope that his impressions would register clearly in Dianne Wesley's visual sensors. In particular, he focused his attention on the cracked marble sepulchre, with the letters OM, YE, VA, SH, engraved on it.

He was about to turn around to the rest of the Night Warriors and say, 'Okay, let's get out of here,' when the sun appeared, bright and warm, and the garden faded as if it had been painted in thin colors on theatrical gauze. The Night Warriors looked around to discover that they were standing on a flat, sandy beach.

This beach was less forbidding than the dry

sandy-brown shoreline they had visited yesterday. The sea was clear and sparkling blue, and the sand was powdery white. In the distance, on a long tin spit of land, Reblax could make out coconut palms and yucca.

'Any sign of the shadow-creature?' he demanded.

Oromas I shook his head with frustration, 'I had it there – I *had* it – right on the edge of my screen.'

'And what happened?'

'I don't know. It blipped and vanished, and that was it.'

They walked for a while along the waterline. The sea lapped softly at the ribs of sand. The warm wind blew in their faces. Seven men, enjoying a child's dream, leaving their footprints in the beach of his young imagination.

Reblax turned and gazed out at the distant horizon, and caught sight of a bright blue ball, bobbing in the waves.

Lenny's safe, he thought. *But has anybody else been hurt?*

Chief Molyneux left police headquarters at five after ten. He stood on the steps outside, his crumpled summer coat hung over his arm, his necktie loose, the back of his shirt stained with sweat. It was as hot now as it had been at midday, and the humidity was higher. He hated Philadelphia in the summer. He could never sleep, and the back of his neck always broke out in a rash where his collar had been rubbing.

He walked along the street for a while. Even at the intersections there was no relieving breeze. A thin black man in a sagging straw hat stood on one corner playing the clarinet, an old jazz tune called 'Milneberg Joys.' Chief Molyneux stood close to him for a while, listening.

'Hot night tonight, Chief Molanoo,' the black man

said after he had finished. 'Got me *steam* comin' out of this licorice-stick, 'stead of spit.'

Chief Molyneux grunted. Then he said, 'Franklin, do you believe in the supernatural? Ghosts, and such?'

'Ghosts, Chief?'

'Oh, I don't know. Ghosts or spirits, whatever you like to call them.'

Franklin thoughtfully wiped his clarinet with a large cloth that had once been somebody's best spotted shirt. 'Can't say that I ever thought about it, Chief. But my mammy believed in lepa-cawns.'

'Your mammy believed in leprechauns? Only Irish people believe in leprechauns.'

'That's what I kep' trying to tell her, Chief. But she was my grandma's twelfth child, and the oh-fishul statistics say that every twelfth child born in America is Irish, so she always figured that's what she was.'

Chief Molyneux smacked Franklin on the back, and shook his head. Franklin wheezed with laughter.

'I ought to run you in for telling stories like that,' Chief Molyneux told him.

He crossed the street. As he did so, a Yellow Cab came around the corner, and he hailed it. 'You want to take me to Pattison Avenue?' he asked the cabbie, sliding across the sticky backseat.

The cab pulled away from the curb. But then Chief Molyneux leaned forward and said, 'Listen, I changed my mind. Take me to the Odd Fellows' Orphans Home.'

'That's out at Melrose Park, right?'

'That's the place.'

Chief Molyneux sat back. He didn't quite know why he wanted to check on Lenny Woods. Maybe it was the way that John Woods had spoken so worriedly on the telephone this afternoon, insisting that his son be kept securely locked up. Maybe he found the supernatural

330

aspects of this case too intriguing to ignore. It had been a strain, keeping the commissioner and the press satisfied that his detectives were doing everything they could to track down the 'Philly Slasher,' as the supposed murderer was being referred to. And what had made his job especially difficult was his growing belief that John Woods and Dianne Wesley and the Clay twins were quite right about the murderer being not of this world, but some apparition from the next.

But all the same, Chief Molyneux found this investigation fascinating. How did you go about tracking down a demon? How did you arrest it when you did? Was it a problem for the law, or the church, or your own conscience?

He wasn't at all sure how he was going to deal with it; and that's what he liked. Unpredictability, excitement. He hadn't felt the old adrenaline surging like this for years and years. He reached into his folded coat and took out a small pigskin-covered hip-flask. He swallowed a mouthful of whiskey, and shuddered a little as it went down.

By the time they reached the Orphans Home, thunder was beginning to grumble and collide over the Delaware River. Chief Molyneux paid off the cabbie and shrugged on his coat. He walked through the darkness of the orphanage garden between low, clipped yew hedges until he reached the wing where Lenny was being held. A globe lamp above the door was clustered with moths and flies.

Inside, a cop was sitting on a folding chair, eating a cheese and tomato sandwich and reading *Lord of the Rings*. Chief Molyneux approached him on squeaky shoes, and the cop put down his book and held his sandwich behind his back.

'At ease,' Chief Molyneux told him. 'Even cops are allowed to eat once in a while. How's the prisoner?'

'Not a squeak,' the officer replied. 'I've checked him a couple of times, but he hasn't moved. Guess the poor little bastard's totally bushed.'

Chief Molyneux sniffed. 'Anybody else been in to see him?'

'No, sir. Nobody.'

'Okay,' said Chief Molyneux. 'Why don't you open up for me, so I can take a look for myself?'

'Sure thing.'

The cop lifted down a bunch of keys from a hook on the wall, and opened the plain oak door. 'Goddamned hot in here,' he remarked. 'Godamned air-conditioner's been on the fritz for most of the night. Would've opened a window, but the orders said no.'

'Those were *my* orders,' Chief Molyneux reminded him.

'Yes, sir, Chief,' the cop acknowledged.

He unlocked the second door and opened it. Chief Molyneux stepped into Lenny's bedroom – and was immediately struck by the chill.

'Thought you said it was *hot* in here,' he whispered to the cop. 'This kid's going to die of frostbite before we have the chance to question him.'

'Maybe the air-conditioning's been fixed,' the cop suggested. 'I'll turn the thermostat up.'

'Hey –' said Chief Molyneux, nodding his head across the room. 'The window's open. You said you kept those windows closed.'

The cop was completely perplexed. 'Sir – I promise you – I never even *touched* those windows. Never even *touched* them.'

Chief Molyneux quietly crossed the room, glancing at Lenny lying asleep. He reached out for the open window, and swung it shut. Then, in the darkness, he peered at the lock.

'It's been forced. *Twisted*. Looks like somebody used

332

a chisel on it.'

The cop joined him by the window, and inspected the damaged lock. 'I don't know how the hell that happened, sir. I checked this room less than a half hour ago.'

Chief Molyneux looked back at the bed. Lenny was breathing deeply and regularly, and was obviously sound asleep. Nobody fell deeply asleep like that in a matter of minutes.

'You checked this room a half hour ago and this window was shut – locked shut?'

'I swear it, sir. I made a point of checking the lock.'

Chief Molyneux sniffed. 'Thing is, Patrolman, this lock has been forced from the *inside*. So – either *you* forced it, or the boy forced it, or –'

He stopped in mid-sentence. He swung open the window and stared out at the darkened grounds of the orphanage. There was no wind. The night was as heavy as a damp Turkish towel. No cicadas sang. All he could hear was the burbling of a television from the staff quarters.

'*Pobre mirloj Tú empaste este terreno con algunos bidones de petróleo alque pegaste fuego.*'

'What's wrong, sir?' the cop asked him.

Chief Molyneux reached into his shoulder holster and lifted out his revolver. 'Patrolman – what's your name, Patrolman?'

'Gilman, sir. Eugene Gilman?'

'Well, Gilman, I want you to call in some backup, and then I want you to come straight back here and keep an eye on Lenny Woods for me.'

'Where will you be, sir?'

'I'm going out into the gardens, that's where I'm going.'

'Any … particular reason, sir?'

Chief Molyneux jerked his head around and stared at

333

Officer Gilman as if he were mad. But what was he going to say? That he was going out into the grounds of the orphanage to hunt down a demon?

'We have a fugitive situation here, Gilman. Armed and dangerous.'

'Sir – Chief – there was nobody else in this room, sir, apart from the boy. I checked, sir. I swear to God.'

Chief Molyneux gave him a tight smile, and gripped his arm. 'Yes, Gilman. I know that. Now, do as you're told, will you, and get me that backup?'

'Yes, sir, Chief.'

Chief Molyneux closed the window and wedged the lock so that Lenny would find it impossible to open. Then he told Officer Gilman to lock both doors.

'Don't be too damn long on that telephone,' he said. 'I want you back here guarding this door pronto.'

'Yes, sir, Chief.'

Keeping his revolver raised, Chief Molyneux left the building and went out into the muggy night. He paused for a moment under the moth-infested lamp, listening. Then he skirted the side of the building, and stepped over one of the low hedges onto the lawn. Halfway across the lawn, in the rhomboid of light thrown onto the grass from the open window of the staff quarters, he paused again.

'Damn that goddamned television,' he muttered.

¡Yujuuu¡ ¡same again Esa dido era un fenómeno! Hay que ver cómo se la pegó al rey, je, je, je ...

It was then that he thought he heard a rustling in the tall firs along the back of the gardens. He waited, and listened; then he heard it again, and this time he saw their frondy tops swaying, black against a black sky. There was no wind tonight, so that meant that somebody was moving around in there. Somebody or something.

Cautiously, Chief Molyneux advanced across the

334

Sixteen

John opened his eyes. Dianne was standing beside the bed, shaking his shoulder. He frowned at her, then looked toward the window. It was still dark outside.

'What time is it?' he asked.

'Three-thirty. I saw kind of a flicker, and I guessed you were back.'

John said immediately, 'We messed it up. Total snafu. There were more shadow-creatures – small ones, less developed – and we decided to deal with them first.'

'And?'

'Well – we managed it, we killed them all. But the big one got away. Maybe it got into the real world again, maybe it didn't. We don't know yet.'

Dianne said, 'I have some pictures. The quality isn't too hot, because I don't think you were concentrating. Except toward the end, maybe.'

'Let me take a look,' John said. 'We went into that garden again. You know, the garden with the statues and the tombs and the dried-up weeds?'

'Those are the best pictures of all,' Dianne told him. 'Here – take a look.'

She held up nine or ten blurry computer printouts of the dream in which John had so recently been running. John squinted his eyes, trying to pick out recognizable landmarks – statues that he recognized, pathways that looked familiar.

'Can you have these pictures enhanced?' he asked.

She gave him a grim smile. 'These *are* enhanced.'

'Oh, sorry. It's just that they're so darn foggy.'

'John – this is a *miracle*. We're printing out imaginary images from the human brain. What do you want? Eve Arnold?'

John stared for a very long time at the blurred picture of the sepulchre. He could just make out the letters OM, YE, VA, SH, although he wouldn't have been able to decipher them if he hadn't seen them clear and sharp in Lenny's dream. He made Dianne hold the picture up for so long that her hand began to tremble.

'I don't know …' John told her. 'It looks familiar somehow, but I can't think why.'

'Maybe you ought to show it to Lenny.'

'Yes – maybe you're right. That is, if they'll let me anywhere near him.'

'What are you going to do about the shadow-creature?' asked Dianne. 'You won't be able to go back tonight, will you? You're having your operation today; you'll still be under anesthetic.'

'No, no,' said John. 'I'll have to postpone it. I have to kill that creature if it's the very last thing I do.'

Dianne nodded. 'I understand. Do you want me to talk to Dr. Freytag for you?'

'Don't worry. I'll talk to him myself. Meanwhile – listen, maybe the best thing to do is for you to take these pictures to Lenny yourself. Maybe you can jog his memory.'

With brisk efficiency, Dianne collected her pictures and collated them. 'Later on today, I want you to go through all of these prints and describe them for me. Most of them are pretty dark.'

John said, 'I could use a cup of coffee. You wouldn't call Sister Theresa, would you?'

'Sure thing,' said Dianne, and reached for the telephone. As she did so, however, it rang. 'How about that for coincidence?' she said, and picked it up. She listened for a moment, then said, 'I see. Yes, I see.' She paused. 'Oh God, that's tragic. It really is. When? Okay. Yes. Let me pass you over to John.'

John asked, 'Who is it? What's going on?' But Dianne shook her head, and tucked the receiver firmly between his ear and the pillow.

'Yes?' he said. 'Who is this?'

'John, this is Thaddeus. Listen, John, I have some pretty bad news.'

'Not Lenny?'

'Lenny's okay. It's Bryan Molyneux.'

'Chief Molyneux? What happened? Is he hurt?'

'He's dead, John. It seems he went to visit Lenny at the Odd Fellows' Orphans Home after he left headquarters. He checked Lenny's room and found that the window was open. The patrolman on duty said he went off to check out the gardens, and that was the last he saw of the chief. They found his body ripped open, chest to pelvis. Didn't stand a chance, according to the M.E.'

John swallowed. 'We failed him, didn't we? He had a pretty good idea of what we were trying to do; and we failed him.'

'John –' Thaddeus said, 'Bryan always knew the risks.'

'Did he have family?'

'Wife, three grown-up kids.'

'Oh, shit,' said John in anguish.

Thaddeus paused for a moment. Then he said, 'We're all cut up about it, John, believe me. But you and me and the rest of the Night Warriors, we've got a more immediate problem. And that is, what's going to happen to Lenny? They had to wake the commissioner; and believe me, the commissioner doesn't like being woken up, whatever. And the police department has located a letter that Chief Molyneux left behind, in case anything happened.'

'A letter?' asked John.

'Well, I don't know exactly what it says,' Thaddeus admitted. 'But it seems Chief Molyneux truly believed that Lenny was possessed by some kind of supernatural spirit. Like he was a Sherlock Holmes buff, you know – "Once you have excluded the impossible, whatever remains, however improbable, must be the truth." And Chief Molyneux was definitely coming around to thinking that the shadow-creature was the truth. It was inevitable, I guess. He was a good detective.'

'The commissioner won't go along with that, though, will he?'

'I don't know. He and Bryan went way back together, right back to police academy.'

'Thaddeus, you're trying to tell me something. What else did Chief Molyneux write in this letter of his?'

'Well … I hate to say this, but he suggested that the only option left to the police department might be to knock Lenny off. You know – in the hope that the spirit would be forced to check out at the same time.'

John bit his lip. He was shaking with suppressed anxiety.

Thaddeus said, 'I'm sorry, John; but that's what he wrote. Something like, "How do you get rid of poison? You break the bottle."'

'I knew it,' John told him. 'I damned well knew it. But the commissioner doesn't believe in the supernatural, does he? He's not going to have Lenny killed on the basis of an uncorroborated letter from Chief Molyneux, surely?'

Thaddeus sniffed. 'You don't know the commissioner. The commissioner likes a quiet life. No crime, no problems. He likes clock golf and rice pudding. If he's faced with a choice between Lenny's life and three hundred sixty-five gory and well-publicized homicides per year – then, boy, he's not going to see that he has much in the way of alternative options.'

John took a deep breath. 'Do you have any idea what's going to happen to Lenny now?'

'They've taken him down to police headquarters for questioning. That's all I know.'

'All right, Thaddeus,' John told him. 'Thanks for calling. Let me see if I can get to talk to Lenny … then I'll get straight back to you. Better still – why don't you come around to the hospital? Say, eleven o'clock?'

'We'll be there,' Thaddeus promised.

Dianne lifted the receiver away from John's cheek. John looked at her, and didn't know what to say.

'What are you going to do now?' she asked.

'I'm not entirely sure yet,' John said. 'I'm calling my lawyers and I'm calling the *Philadelphia News*. If anybody so much as lays one finger on Lenny … He wasn't responsible for killing any of those people, you know it and I know it.'

Dianne leaned over the bed and kissed him. 'This is all going to work out,' she reassured him.

John closed his eyes and thought about the collapsing school building, and 'Mr. Isenberg,' and the strange cemetrylike garden to which Lenny's dreams mesmerically returned, time after time. 'If you say so,' he said. 'I'm beginning to think that this shadow-creature is giving us the goddamned runaround.'

Softly but forcefully, Dianne pressed a finger to John's lips. 'Don't lose your cool, okay? Lenny's counting on you. So am I. So are all the rest of the Night Warriors.'

'All right,' John replied, 'all right, all right. I'm sorry. But see if you can get those dream photographs around to Lenny, will you? Even if he doesn't recognize them at all – well, at least we'll know that we're barking up the wrong tree.'

Dianne kissed him again. 'I'll find a way to see Lenny,' she said, 'don't worry. I'll call you as soon as I do.'

John found his mouth tightening; tears squeezed out of the corners of his eyes. 'Tell him I love him,' he told her. 'And tell him he's not to blame.'

She brushed his tears away with soft fingertips. 'You liked him, didn't you? Chief Molyneux?'

341

'Liked him?' John retorted. 'Hell, no. Liked him? No. But at least he believed us.'

Lenny was standing by the window at the far end of the waiting room when Dianne came in to see him. Lieutenant Flexner, Jewish, paunchy, and fortyish, with a heavy black mustache, thrust his thumbs into his belt and said, 'Go ahead. There he is, ma'am. And don't worry, he don't bite.'

Dianne approached Lenny across the room. Lenny didn't even turn his head. He looked pale and tired, and his eyes were fixed dully on the rooftops across the street, where washing hung limply and pigeons strutted in cages and two men sat smoking pipes and talking, all under the heat-haze of midsummer Philadelphia.

Dianne sat on the arm of a sagging sofa, her orange envelope of dreamprints held close to her chest. She smiled at Lenny; and at last he looked around and stared at her.

'Hi, Lenny, how are you?'

He didn't show any sign that he recognized her. 'I'm fine, thanks.'

'Do you remember me?' she asked him. 'Dianne Wesley, from the university?'

He nodded. 'That time the nun got killed.'

She reached out and touched his hand. 'That's right. Sister Perpetua.' She paused for a while, watching him, then said, 'I saw your daddy this morning, at the hospital. He sends his love, "Tell that champ he's the bestest," that's what he said.'

Lenny glanced at her. It was plain from the brightness in his eyes that he believed her.

'And do you know what else he said?' Dianne went on. 'He said, "Ask the champ to take a look at these pictures for me – tell me if there's anything he recognizes."' She held up the envelope. 'Will you do that for me?'

Lenny shuffled his sneakers. 'I guess.'

Over by the door, Lieutenant Flexner snuffled and cleared his throat; and when Dianne turned around, he gave her a flirtatious little finger-wave. She smiled back – a professional, efficient mask.

Dianne and Lenny sat down on the sofa, and Dianne passed him one by one the dream-photographs that she had taken the previous night. Lenny studied them carefully; but it was obvious that he remembered very little of what he had been dreaming about.

'That looks like my schoolyard. But it's kind of different, I don't know. The school isn't as big as that. And that's the hall.'

He peered intently. 'That's my classroom. I *think* that's my classroom. What are all those black shadows sitting at the desks?'

Dianne said gently, 'You *dreamed* this, Lenny, last night. This is a picture of your dream.'

Lenny shook his head. 'I don't remember it at all.'

'Well … that's not surprising. We dream for most of the night, but we don't usually remember what we dreamed about. I'm just trying to find out if any of these pictures jog your memory.'

She watched Lenny as he leafed through picture after picture. At last he stopped, and examined one of them more intently. 'This – I know where this one is.'

Dianne took the picture and held it up. The garden. The sepulchre. Black sky, shriveled grass.

She told Lenny, 'Your daddy told me that he thinks this place is very important, for some reason. He has the feeling that if we can find out where this place is, we might be able to destroy the shadow-thing that keeps coming out of your mind.'

'It's not a real place,' Lenny told her. 'It's in my scripture book.'

'You mean, it's a picture?'

Lenny nodded. 'It's in my scripture book at school.'

Dianne leaned over and gathered up her prints.

343

'Lenny,' she said, 'you're an angel.'

'I used to look at if after Mommy died, and I used to think that she was buried there.'

Dianne said, 'I'll tell you what I'm going to do now, Lenny, I'm going to go to your school and find that book. I think that it can help us a lot. And there's one thing that your daddy and I want *you* to do. It's going to be hard, but we want you to try. We want you to stay awake tonight for as long as you possibly can. Until midnight, at least. In fact, I have some pills here – no, don't let that detective see you. But if you really feel that you can't keep your eyes open any longer, take one of these.'

Lenny took the paper twist with three Benzedrine tablets in it, and tucked it into his jeans pocket.

Poor kid, thought Dianne, *he looks exhausted already. But if he falls asleep too early tonight, and another policeman dies …*

Dianne left police headquarters and drove to the Benjamin Franklin Grade School on Sixteenth Street. She parked in the same parking lot in which the Night Warriors had materialized last night, and walked across the playground. The swingset that had become a nightmare puzzle of twisted metal was crowded with laughing, shouting children, all swinging like monkeys. Dianne went in through the double doors to the hallway, and asked a small, serious-faced girl with pigtails if she could direct her to the principal's office.

At that moment, however, a thin-faced man in a gray summer suit appeared, taking off his gold-rimmed spectacles as he approached her. 'Anthony Isenberg,' he said. 'Is there anything I can do to help?'

Dianne smiled. 'I hope you can. I'm a friend of the Woods family. You know – Lenny Woods?'

'Oh, poor Lenny,' said Mr. Isenberg. 'Believe me, our hearts have really gone out to that young fellow.'

'He's over at police headquarters now,' Dianne told him, 'and I was wondering if it would be possible for

344

him to have his scripture book? He really feels the need for some words of comfort.'

'But, of course,' said Mr. Isenberg. 'I should imagine that all of his books are still in his locker. Why don't you come upstairs and take a look?'

Dianne followed Mr. Isenberg up the wide staircase. At the head of the staircase there was a tall window of yellowish hammered glass, protected by fine steel mesh. It cast a strange light into the building, as if they were walking around inside a sepia photograph of days gone by.

Lenny's locker stood just outside his classroom. Mr. Isenberg opened it, and said, 'Help yourself. And, please – when you take him that book, take him our very best wishes, too, won't you?'

'Believe me, I will,' said Dianne.

Mr. Isenberg left her, and she hurriedly sorted through Lenny's schoolbooks: *Junior Mathematics Part One*, *Grade School English*, *A Shorter History of the United States of America*. Then she found it, a slim, well-worn book with a dark maroon cover: *An Introduction to the Scriptures*.

She opened it and leafed through it. She found the page easily, because Lenny must have turned to it time and time again – seeking some kind of understanding of where his mommy had gone, and why she had left him. The picture was in black and white, a black six-paneled door opening onto a bleak and broken garden. In the center of the garden stood a marble sepulchre, on which was engraved the words YEA THOUGH I WALK THROUGH THE VALLEY OF THE SHADOW OF DEATH. Above those words, in blue ballpoint pen, Lenny had written the word MOM.

In his dreams, the sepulchre had broken open. That was why half of the lettering had been missing. MOM, YEA THOUGH I WALK THROUGH THE VALLEY OF THE SHADOW OF DEATH. The picture was an allegory of the fear of death; and it was more

345

than likely that Lenny's overwhelming fear of death had aroused the embryonic shadow-creature as it nestled in the wall of his house.

There was something else, though. Underneath the picture the full verse was printed. 'Yea though I walk through the Valley of the Shadow of Death, I fear no Evil; for Thou art with me; Thy rod and Thy staff, they comfort me.'

And it was there. Somehow the answer was there. Dianne closed the book and held it in front of her as if it were a holy missal. *Thy rod and Thy staff, they comfort me.*

She closed Lenny's locker and left the school. The day was still unbearably hot. The sky was the color of oxidized bronze, and the heat-haze made everything look blurry, as if the whole world were out of focus. She drove out of the parking lot and headed over to the hospital to tell John what she had found.

Dr. Freytag stood at the end of John's bed and noisily popped his knuckles, one by one. 'Mr Woods – John – there is no reason at all for you to delay this operation. In fact, the sooner you have it, the better. You could suffer permanent impairment if you leave it very much longer. You know what I mean by *impairment*?'

John said, 'You can't change my mind. I'm sorry.'

'You understand that your insurance may not cover the cost of canceled theater time? Especially if there's no good reason for it?'

'Dr. Freytag, I thought that I'd made myself plain. Cost doesn't enter into it. I do not wish to have my operation today, and I may not wish to have my operation tomorrow. It all depends.'

Dr. Freytag blew out his cheeks. 'Are you frightened? Is that it? Maybe you'd like some pre-operative counseling? I mean, that can be arranged. We do have patients who can't stand the thought of being opened up. I mean – not that we're going to be

346

opening you up very *much*. This particular operation is comparatively superficial in terms of how far we're going to go *in*.'

John closed his eyes. 'Dr. Freytag, I respect your professional status; I apologize to you and all of your team for any inconvenience and possible loss of earnings. But I am not going to have my operation today, and that's all there is to it. Period.'

Dr. Freytag went to the window and stared out at the hazy Philadelphia skyline. 'You know something, when I was in med school, they told me that the success of any operation was *cooperation*. That's what they said. The patient and the surgeon, both working together toward the same end.'

He turned back to John. 'For that reason, I have to say okay, let's postpone it. I can't possibly be ready till *you're* ready. But believe me, two dozen people are going to be very pissed about this, including me.'

John said, 'Let me tell you this, Dr. Freytag. When I'm prepared to have this operation, I'll tell you why I'm taking a raincheck. You got me? I'll tell you the whole story.'

'But you can't tell me now?'

John shook his head. 'No, I'm sorry.'

'He's sorry,' said Dr. Freytag to nobody at all.

Just then there was a knock at the door, and Toussaint wheeled himself in. 'Hi, Doctor Fried-egg. Hi, John. Are you coming on out? The Clays are here; so's the whole gang.'

'Sure,' said John. 'Maybe Dr. Freytag can help me into my wheelchair.'

Dr. Freytag said nothing, but assisted John to roll off his bed and into his wheelchair. 'Do you know something?' John said. 'The first time I tried this, I fell flat on the floor.'

Grimacing, tugging his three-piece suit straight, Dr. Freytag said, 'I hope that wasn't too uncomfortable.'

'It's always uncomfortable,' John replied. 'But some times are less uncomfortable than others. You, Dr. Freytag – you were even more gentle with me than Sister Clare.'

'So, what do we do?' Dr. Freytag demanded. 'Postpone this operation *sine die*?'

'I don't have any choice,' John told him. 'I have more important things to take care of.'

'There's something more important than being totally paralyzed?'

John looked him in the eye and said, 'Yes, doctor. There is.'

'This man has hidden depths,' Toussaint put in.

Dr. Freytag turned and stared at Toussaint with bulging eyes. 'I wouldn't mind knowing what the hell is going on around here,' he snapped.

'"There, that is our secret: go to sleep! You will wake, and remember, and understand!"' Toussaint quoted. Then he smiled at Dr. Freytag and said, 'Browning. The poet, not the rifle maker.'

'Toussaint,' said Dr. Freytag, 'you read too much.' He left, closing the door not loudly but with firm disapproval.

Toussaint wheeled himself close to John's bed and sat looking at him for a while, saying nothing.

'We're going out again tonight?' he asked after a while.

'You bet,' John told him.

'And this time, we're going to zap that shadow-creature for good?'

'We have to. Otherwise somebody else is going to die, and maybe Lenny will, too. I can't protect him from the police department, not forever.'

Toussaint reached out and grasped John's shoulder. 'I guess this sounds pretty stupid, pretty sentimental. But I want you to know that being a Night Warrior, that's the very best thing that ever happened to me, ever; and if I never walk again, if I never move from

348

this wheelchair, I'm still going to know that my life was worthwhile, because I walked in dreams and I fought demons in dreams and I was a Night Warrior.'

John nodded. 'You're the best, Toussaint; and nobody can ever take that away from you, ever.'

At that moment, the door opened and Dianne came in, looking flushed and excited and more desirable than ever. She was holding up Lenny's maroon scripture book. 'John – I found it! I found the garden, and what the letters mean! Here, take a look!'

She held the book open for John to look at. When he saw the door and the garden and the sepulchre, he felt a tingling around his shoulders and his mouth went dry. 'That's it, that's exactly it! That's the place in the dream! Toussaint – you recognize that, don't you? You were there!'

Toussaint squinted at it, nodded, and said, 'Sure thing. That's the place. Looks like my uncle's backyard in Camden.'

Dianne said, 'John – you had a feeling, didn't you, that the answer was here? And I agree with you, I think that it is. It all fits into place. The shadow-creature is the fear of death – the actual, physical fear of death – and when Lenny moved into your house on Third Street, his strong feelings of fear woke up that shadow-creature in the wall. The shadow-creature must have felt that it was being *called*, almost – that's how strong Lenny's fear of death was. He was frightened of what had happened to Virginia, and he was frightened that it might unexpectedly happen to you, or to Jennifer, or worst of all, to *him*. A child of that age doesn't watch his mother choke to death and remain unscathed. It isn't possible. It isn't *human*.'

'But how does that help us to exterminate this creature?' John asked her.

'I'm not sure. But delegate Rufus King of Massachusetts knew how to do it, back in 1787; and so did Gouverneur Morris.'

John stared at the picture. He felt that he had discovered at last the shining road that he had been seeking for days, only to find that it amounted to very little more than a dead end.

"'Yea though I walk through the valley of the shadow of death ...'" he whispered. Then he read the verse underneath. "'Thy rod and Thy staff ... Thy staff!'"

'What is it?' asked Dianne. 'What?'

John said, 'Thaddeus and Norman – are they anywhere around?'

'Well, sure they are,' said Toussaint. 'That's what I came in to tell you. They're out in the yard with Che-u and Dean and Billy. They were expecting you to come out and join them.'

'Wheel me out there,' John asked Dianne. 'Quick – wheel me out there!'

'Anything you say, General Patton,' said Dianne. She wheeled him out of the room and along the corridor to the garden. After the sixty-five-degree air-conditioning inside the hospital building, the brick-paved yard was oppressively hot, but John didn't care. Dianne pushed him all the way across to the cedar tree, where Thaddeus and Norman were talking to their fellow Night Warriors.

'Show them the book,' John told Dianne, without any preliminary greeting. Mean Dean took the book, peered at it, and then passed it around.

'Recognize it?' asked John.

They all nodded. 'That weedy old garden, right?' asked Billy. 'The one with the naked statues with no arms and no heads, and that broken-down bandstand.'

'Sepulchre,' John corrected him.

'Bandstand!' Dean teased Billy. 'Frigging A!'

Dianne passed the book to Thaddeus. In silence. Thaddeus studied it. Then he looked up at John and said, 'I'm sorry, but so what? What does this prove?'

'Read what it says underneath.'

350

Thaddeus hesitated, and then he read, "'Yea though I walk through the valley of the shadow of death ... I shall fear no evil; for Thou art with me ...'"

'Go on, go on,' John urged.

Thaddeus frowned. "'Thy rod and Thy staff, they comfort me.'" He closed the book. He looked at John in perplexity.

'Don't you remember all that research you did into Rufus King, and how he went around to Nathan Grant's house and started "a grate commotion"?'

'Sure, yes, but –'

'Don't you remember what you said? "King went round to the Grant house with his staffe."'

'Well, sure, but I kind of assumed that meant the people who worked for him, or maybe the Night Warriors that he managed to rustle up in Massachusetts.'

John said, 'How many staff do you think that a delegate like Rufus King would have taken with him to Philadelphia in 1787? Maybe a manservant to take care of his clothes, a secretary possibly. But no more than that. And I can't imagine that he would have asked either of them to help him exorcise the house of Nathan Grant.'

'Maybe it means the Night Warriors,' put in Che-u.

'Well, that's one explanation,' said John. 'But he wouldn't have taken them *with* him, would he? Night Warriors operate in dreams, invisibly; and nobody would have known that he took them with him. Besides, nobody would have called the Night Warriors "his staffe."'

'But staff doesn't mean anything except stick,' put in Dean. 'Maybe it means that he took his stick. They all used to carry them in those days. I mean, they were historical, right? They were probably afraid of falling over. Or maybe he wanted to hit this guy Nathan Grant over the head.'

'Dean, for Christ's sake,' John protested. 'He took his

staff, His holy staff. The same staff that they talk about in Psalm Twenty-three. And *that's* what can overcome the fear of death.'

There was a very long silence. Then Che-u said, 'John, what you are trying to say – it may mean nothing at all. To be frank, it may all be horseshit. But, on the other hand, it may enable us to conquer the shadow-creature forever.'

'Yes,' said John.

'So where do we find ourselves this holy staff?' Billy wanted to know. 'It's not exactly the kind of item you keep falling over in your average pawnbroker's, right?'

'That's why I wanted to talk to Thaddeus and Norman today,' said John. 'I want them to go back to the library and see if they can dig up anything – anything at all – about Rufus King and a holy staff.'

'You think that's going to be time well spent?' asked Thaddeus.

'Well, do you have any better ideas?' John challenged.

Thaddeus shrugged. 'Guess I don't. Come on, Norman.'

John said, 'Thaddeus, Norman – I'm playing a hunch here. Not much more. But we're running out of time.'

'All right, man.' Thaddeus nodded, not smiling. 'We'll do what we can.'

'There's one more thing,' said John. 'All those years ago, Rufus King went around to Nathan Grant's house in person. He wasn't dressed as a Night Warrior, not as a dream-personality, but in the flesh. I believe that he had *already arranged* for the Night Warriors to chase the shadow-creature out of Nathan Grant's dreams, the idea being that when the shadow-creature manifested itself in the waking world, it could be ambushed and killed.'

'So when it shifts from the dream world to the real world – it could be vulnerable then?' Thaddeus asked.

'I think so. It must suffer some pretty heavy psychic stress. And maybe that's the right moment to hit it.'

Dean snapped his fingers. 'That's great, then. We've cracked it! All we need is a holy staff.'

'Shut up, Dean,' said Thaddeus. 'John, Dianne – you take care. We'll be back from the library just as soon as we can.'

'*Hasta luego*,' said Dean, without any optimism at all.

Just before four o'clock that afternoon, exhausted, John fell asleep. In his room at the Philadelphia police headquarters, Lenny remained doggedly awake, reading heaps of old *National Geographic* magazines and watching television. Outside the window, the day began to darken. Electrical storms were forecast from New York to Charleston. The atmosphere was thick and hot and cheesy, and flies buzzed fitfully against the windows.

In the Pennsylvania University library, Thaddeus and Norman Clay sat at a table in the corner with more than thirty books spread out in front of them, flicking pages, searching for any records of Gouverneur Morris or Rufus King, or the staff that King had taken to Nathan Grant's house the night of the 'grate commotion.'

The Clay twins were beyond exhaustion now. Their closeness kept them going. When one of them stretched or yawned or showed signs of flagging, the other would glance at him sharply and say, 'Come on, man, we have to *find* this thing,' and they would bend their heads to their studies.

Dianne Wesley was sitting in a large basketwork chair in a first-floor apartment on Second Street, holding a huge glass of Cakebread white, her eyes closed, listening to Suzanne Vega on the stereo. She was being watched by a thin dark-haired man with hollow cheeks covered by a day's growth of stubble and eyebrows that knit in the middle. This was Seth

Maxwell, from the biology department of the University of Pennsylvania, who had devoted so much time and so many of the university's specialized research facilities to tracking down the history of the shadow-creature for her.

'You staying tonight?' he asked her. 'You want to have dinner?'

Without opening her eyes, she said, 'I don't think so, Seth. Tonight's the big night.'

'The big night for *what*? You still haven't told me.'

She hesitated for a moment, then opened one eye. 'The big night, that's all.'

Seth got up and walked across and stood over her. His pale green silk shirt was open down to the fourth button, revealing a narrow chest patterned with dark black hairs. 'I thought we had something between us. Maybe I was wrong.'

'I used you, Seth. You know that.'

He grunted in amusement. 'Knowing it doesn't make it any more acceptable. Besides, I still want to take you to dinner.'

'What you really mean is, you want to take me to dinner and then you want to take me to bed. Look at the size of this glass of wine! There are only two reasons for a man giving a woman a glass of wine this big. Either he hates the wine and wants to get rid of it; or else he wants to get the woman drunk and into the sack.'

Seth laughed, but there without much humor. 'I don't know ... In three days you give a woman the whole fruits of your life's work – all that stuff on shadow-creatures, do you realize what a paper that's going to make? And not just a paper, a book. *The Evolution of Psychic DNA in the Quaternary Period of the Cenozic Era*, by Professor Seth Maxwell. That stuff's going to make me famous; and I gave it all to you for nothing.'

Dianne smiled. 'You're a brick, Seth. They don't

make bricks anymore.'

'A brick? Jesus.' He knelt down beside her. 'Don't tell me you're hooked on this quadriplegic friend of yours.'

'He wasn't always quadriplegic.'

'What difference does that make?'

'It doesn't make any difference at all. But I like him. He's suffered a lot, he feels a lot, but he still manages to keep his head together. God knows how. And he loves that son of his, you wouldn't even believe how much he loves that son of his.'

Seth stroked Dianne's hand, then lifted it up and kissed it. 'Change your mind,' he told her. 'Have dinner with me. I've booked a table for two at Bookbinder's.'

'Seth, I can't. Not tonight. Not until everything's settled.'

Seth jerked his hand through his bushy black hair. 'Settled? What's to settle? We've been working together on some creature that dates from twenty-five million years ago, *twenty-five million years*, Dianne – that's more than twelve times longer than man has been walking on this planet – and you can't have dinner *tonight*?'

Dianne reached out and took hold of his wrist, and squeezed it. 'That's right, Seth. I can't have dinner *tonight*.'

Across town, Lenny was finding it hard to focus on a group of dancing Ashanti women in the *National Geographic*. He yawned and shook his head, trying to stay awake. But the room was airless, and the flies buzzed so monotonously, and he was so tired that it was almost impossible for him to keep his eyes open.

In their separate rooms at the hospital, the Night Warriors waited for darkness. Toussaint picked at his acoustic guitar, playing a complicated version of 'When the Levee Breaks.' Che-u was writing in his diary, quick Chinese characters on thin onionskin paper. Billy was drinking Coors Lite out of the can and watching *Falcon Crest*. Mean Dean was out in the yard working with weights to develop his arm muscles, sweating in the humid thunderous heat, his stringy cigarette dangling between his lips.

Somebody else was waiting for this night. By a silvery-gray sea, on a silvery-gray beach, Kasyx sat with his forehead resting on his knees. Since he had discharged all of his energy trying to save an imaginary girl called Katherine, he had spent day after day by this soulless beach, under a soulless sky. Only the nights had come alive, rampant with storms, and volcanoes, and cities that had grown out of nowhere at all. He had set out each night to search for other Night Warriors, through streets busy with giant toy cars, in and out of huge buildings, but so far he had come across nobody real. Only dream people, obliging but insubstantial. He had talked once to Sunny Jim, a living Sunny Jim, complete with monocle and pigtail and bright red cutaway coat; the same night he had come across the crew of the starship *Enterprise*, although he hadn't recognized them at first, because he had never watched *Star Trek* (and after meeting the crew of the *Enterprise*, as dreamed by Lenny, he wasn't going to start watching it, either).

He was a professor of philosophy; and he had reconciled himself to the fact that he probably would never be able to return to the waking world. His real body, which was lying comatose in his beach house in Del Mar, would die of dehydration within a week. Then his soul would remain irrevocably trapped in Lenny's dream-world, until Lenny himself died; and then Kasyx's soul would wink out with it, like an oil-lamp pinched into extinction.

He sat with his forehead resting on his knees, while the silvery-gray sea silently coursed across the beach, and waited for the night to bring him more dreams.

John opened his eyes. Thaddeus and Norman were standing beside his bed. They looked serious, both of them. Almost too serious.

'What's wrong?' he said hoarsely. 'What have you found out?'

Thaddeus said, 'We spent four hours at the university library. We found out more about Rufus King than anybody has a right to know.'

'And?'

'Here, man,' said Thaddeus, and helped John to prop up his head on the pillow.

'I'm fine,' John insisted. 'What did you find out?'

Thaddeus said, 'We found out that Rufus King had a good friend in Salem, Massachusetts, a man called David Barlow who was the owner of a shipping line, spices from the Orient, that kind of trade. And we also found out that David Barlow was the owner of a shepherd's crook that was supposed to have belonged to Moses, and which Moses had used as a walking-stick during the exodus from Egypt.'

'Go on,' John urged him.

Thaddeus said, 'This is all very sketchy. But it seems David Barlow's grandfather Josiah Barlow had bought the stick in Jidda, Saudi Arabia, at the time of the Salem witch trials. His intention was to bring it back to Salem to exorcise the devilry that was going on there. It seems he paid a whole lot of money for it, nearly two thousand dollars' worth of gold. Big deal in those days.'

'And did he get his money's worth?' asked John.

'Well … it seems so. As soon as he brought it back to Salem, the witch trial hysteria collapsed, and the whole business came to an end.'

John said nothing, but waited for Thaddeus to continue.

Thaddeus said, 'That shepherd's crook, that stick, that staff – well, it was kept at the Barlow family home, right up until 1787. Then Rufus King came and took it, and brought it here to Philadelphia. According to the

Barlow family records, nobody knew why. But whatever he brought it here for, it stayed here; and eventually it was given to the American Philosophical Society on Fifth Street, who kept it in their library; and then it was passed to the Conservation Center for Art and Historic Artifacts, whose curators didn't really believe it was authentic, so they stored it in their cellars on Broad Street.'

'What happened to it then?' asked John.

Thaddeus looked glum. 'Two suspended police detectives of mixed racial origin arrived at the Conservation Center and asked to see the said shepherd's crook, stick, or staff; and the gullible curators allowed them to take it away on loan.'

Norman, with a suddenly breaking smile, lifted in his right hand a dark staff of polished wood with a slightly curving top; wood from an olive tree, but centuries old, weathered and battered and polished by the touch of countless human hands.

The shepherd's crook on which an aging Moses was supposed to have leaned as he led the children of Israel out of Egypt into the Promised Land. Thy rod, Thy staff.

John stared at it as Norman brought it closer. He couldn't reach out to touch it, he didn't have the power, but he could feel its magnetism. Tears sprang into his eyes.

'You found it, you bastards. You actually found it.'

'We're detectives,' said Thaddeus smugly.

'Do you think it's going to work?' asked John.

'Who knows? We're not exactly sure what Rufus King did. But your guess was probably right. He used Night Warriors to flush the shadow-creature out of Nathan Grant's dreams; then, when it took on physical form, he used this stick to zap it for good.'

John's eyes ran from one end of the ancient stick to the other. 'God Almighty, I hope it works.'

Seventeen

The Night Warriors assembled late that night at the house on Wissahinnock Avenue, and their mood was unusually grave. Springer was pale and androgynous, neither man nor woman, and dressed in a strange white gauzy suit that was reminiscent of the Arabian Nights.

'We pray that this plan of attack will at last succeed in destroying the shadow-creature,' said Springer. 'Are you all well prepared?'

'Third time lucky,' sniffed Themesteroth.

Ex'ii said, 'We should remember that Reblax has set aside his own interests tonight in order to exterminate the shadow-creature, and all of us should try to equal his devotion.'

'I'll second that,' put in Lyraq.

Arkestrax said, 'Supposing Dianne can't smuggle that staff into police headquarters? What's the plan of action then?'

Oromas I raised his hand reassuringly. 'I arranged with Lieutenant Flexner that she should be allowed unrestricted access to Lenny for the purpose of completing her psychological tests. She carried the staff into the building in the tripod case for her video-recording equipment. The staff will be there when we need it.'

Reblax said, 'This whole thing is going to need nerve

and concentration and perfect timing. We corner the shadow-creature, wherever we locate it. We keep hounding it, until it takes the opportunity to leave the dream and materialize in the real world. We'll know when it's about to do that, because Lenny will be dreaming about the garden in his scripture book. That's the time when Lenny's fear of death is at its strongest – and it's my belief that his fear gives the shadow-creature the extra strength it requires to take on material shape.

'The instant the shadow-creature disappears, Oromas I will take me and Themesteroth back into the waking world. The rest of you will stay in the dream in case the shadow-creature tries to escape back into Lenny's imagination. Don't ask me how we're going to use the staff to destroy the shadow-creature, because I don't know – but from what happened at the Grant house that night in 1787, it seems that it has some powers of its own, if you believe in it enough.'

'Sure,' retorted Themesteroth, 'and maybe it doesn't.'

'Well,' said Reblax, 'tonight we're going to find out for sure.'

They knelt together and spoke the sacred incantation of Ashapola. Tonight, however, Springer spread his arms and asked an additional blessing: that they all return safe from what Edgar Allen Poe had called 'that wild weird clime' of dreams.

He had just finished his prayer when there was a loud pounding at the front door of the house, and a floodlight penetrated the room from the street below.

'What the hell?' Themesteroth demanded, and went to the window.

'Police!' an amplified voice boomed out. 'You're under arrest! Come out of the house with your hands held high!'

Reblax joined Themesteroth at the window. There were four patrol cars parked at all angles in the avenue, with armed police kneeling behind them. Across the street, he could make out two detectives and a man in a green golfing shirt holding a dog on a lead.

'Time to leave, I think,' said Springer. The Night Warriors stood in a circle, closed their eyes, and floated through the molecules of the roof and into the humid night. They circled high above the house, and as they did so they saw the police dodging and darting through the yard.

One of the cops took a sledgehammer to the front door, while three of his colleagues kept him covered Reblax smiled to himself as he turned toward downtown Philadelphia. He saw the patrolmen's flashlights crisscrossing the upstairs room, searching for – what? Anarchists, dope addicts, terrorists, ghosts? All they would find would be dust and dereliction, and the stale odor of a house in which nobody human had lived for thirty years.

The Night Warriors floated darkly through the sky, over the glittering crisscrossed streets of Philadelphia, at last approaching police headquarters like bats, or shadows, or shadows of shadows. They followed Oromas I and Oromas II through the concrete roof and down through floor after floor of darkened offices and corridors, until they arrived at last in the basement security area. In a gray-painted room with no furniture except a bed, a bedside locker, and a folding chair, Lenny lay sleeping. Dianne was there, too, with her video equipment set up, watching him. She was wearing a sand-colored safari suit, and her hair was tied up in a turban. Reblax thought that she looked stunning.

They assembled around her, and although they

were ghostlike and insubstantial, she was aware of their arrival. They appeared to her as distortions in the air, similar to heat ripples rising off a summer sidewalk, and she was conscious of their voices as an almost imperceptible vibration.

Reblax pointed to the staff of Moses, which Dianne had left propped in the corner of the room, beside the bed.

Arkestrax said, 'Dianne knows how dangerous this is? I mean, she's going to be first in line for a slashing, if we don't zap that critter like instantly.'

'She knows,' Reblax told him. 'I tried to talk her out of this, but she wouldn't hear of it.'

'All right, then, let's do it,' said Themesteroth; and Oromas I and Oromas II drew their glowing blue hexagons in the air, their twin gateways to Lenny's dreams.

Reblax nervously cleared his throat. He prayed that Lenny's dream wouldn't be too bizarre, and that the landscape wouldn't prove too difficult for them to track down the shadow-creature quickly.

Oromas I and Oromas II parted the air in front of them, and revealed the huge interior of a brightly lit Byzantine building, tiled in peacock and gold. But as they pulled the hexagons down to the floor and the Night Warriors stepped into Lenny's sleeping imagination, they all realized that this was more than an ordinary dream about a grand, churchlike building. The entire structure was lying on its side, with its elaborately tiled floor rising up to their left, and the Moorish arches of its ceiling rising up to their right. They were actually standing on one of the walls, with a row of decorative windows stretched in front of them and sunlight slanting diagonally *upward* into the building's vast interior.

Above their heads, there were two rows of green

marble pillars, stretching horizontally from one 'side' of the building to the other; higher still, in the 'ceiling', was another row of windows, through which they could see clear violet sky.

Reblax approached the first of the windows in the floor, and cautiously looked down. He could see sky and Eastern-style rooftops and spires. But it was clear at once that not all the buildings were tilted the same way. Some were lying on their sides; others were upside-down, with their roofs against the ground. Reblax felt a deep surge of disorientation and nausea.

'What's going on here?' asked Themesteroth. 'What the hell kind of a dream is this?'

'The whole damned world is lying on its side,' said Arkestrax.

Oromas I was already sweeping the building with his sensors. 'It's close,' he announced almost at once. 'Very close, very strong. I wouldn't be surprised if it's been waiting for us. Intense negative reading close to the building's main door.'

'That's all very well,' Lyraq protested, 'but where *is* the main door?'

Arkestrax lowered his screen in front of his helmet, and scanned a holographic diagram of the building. 'Byzantine church, similar to St. Sophia in Istanbul.' He swiveled the diagram around so that the building appeared to be right way up. 'We're standing close to the ceiling on the south side of the church, about twenty-four meters above the altar. The main door is on the north side of the church, diametrically opposite us.'

They looked up and to the left; and behind the double rows of marble pillars they could make out an archway, its door partially open.

'That's it,' said Oromas I, 'that's where it's coming from. But how the Godfrey Daniels do we get up there?'

Arkestrax punched the buttons of his architectural

theorizer. 'Okay … I can construct a temporary stairway up to the first row of pillars, then a bridge up to the second row of pillars, and finally a platform that will take us to door-level. We're going to need a platform there, because if we step out of that doorway we're simply going to fall straight down, into the sky.'

Themesteroth said, 'Come on, then, let's get going.'

Oromas I adjusted his scanner. 'It's there, the shadow-creature – right by the door – just *above* the door!'

The huge building was shaken by a deep rumbling sound. One window at a time, the rays of the sun died away, and a cold wind began to blow upward, tossing dead leaves into the vaulted interior. Reblax, stepping back to catch his balance, caught a glimpse of something black hanging over the edge of the door. Something black, like funeral robes. Something that stank of death.

Arkestrax checked the atmosphere for mineral content, anything that he could use to construct his stairways and bridges. 'Not enough!' he decided. 'Maybe the shadow-creature's gotten wise!' But he immediately unhooked a hand-held machine that looked like a heavyweight pastry wheel, and knelt down and began to cut slabs of stone out of the church walls. The wheel screeched through the stone at high speed, sending up clouds of gritty dust; but that dust was almost immediately swirled away by the gale-force winds.

Within minutes, Arkestrax had set up the beginnings of a finely balanced stone staircase, only six or seven inches wide, which climbed toward the lower rank of pillars.

He was still ten feet away from reaching the pillars, however, when a small, dark shape detached itself from the doorway on the opposite side of the church, and *ran down the wall*.

'Did you see that?' said Lyraq.

Reblax nodded. 'It's sending something after us. Something that can walk on the floor.'

It was growing darker inside the church. Reblax listened, and thought he heard a sharp scuffling sound, but it was impossible to distinguish anything clearly over the screeching of Arkestrax's stone-cutting and the wind that shrieked in through the open windows. But then he saw a black shape down by the base of one of the pillars – a scrunched-up, scaly thing with claws and spines. It had the same shuddery effect on him as switching on the kitchen light and finding the sink teeming with cockroaches.

'There!' he told Lyraq; and Lyraq swung his music-rifle around, tuned it up to a high-pitched hum, and aimed it close to the creature's hiding place.

Immediately, the creature reappeared, and Lyraq fired. With an ear-splitting chord, the creature burst apart into a shower of black fragments. But the fragments, instead of dropping sideways to the floor or down to the wall or wherever the Night Warriors might have expected them to drop, came hurtling toward *them*, and lashed into them in a stinging shower of broken shell and bits of claw. One of the spines caught Arkestrax across the cheek, and with a wild squeal of metal against marble, he almost lost control of his stone-cutter. Another piece stung Reblax across the shoulder and left a glutinous squiggle of thick yellow liquid across his faceplate.

Now another cockroach-thing appeared at the door and scurried across the floor of the church; then another, and another, until the floor was thick with them.

'How much longer with that damned staircase?' Oromas I shouted. 'All we want is a bridge, not St. Patrick's Cathedral!'

Even before the echoes of his shouting had been blown away by the gusting gale, the air around the Night Warriors was stiff with flying insect-spines, thousands of them. They rattled and cascaded against their armor, stuck into their legs and arms, and bristled out of their helmets. The cockroach-things were lifting their claws and, with a sharp downward sweep, releasing scores of their own black spines.

Ex'ii activated two of his discs, hesitated for a moment while he mentally programmed them, then let them fly. Glowing brightly, they flashed away from his helmet and flew in tight formation up through the gloomy church, weaving in and out between the pillars. The cockroach-things showered the discs with spines, but Ex'ii had anticipated that. The discs oscillated furiously, so that the spines were scattered in all directions.

The discs swooped silently right to the upper quarter of the church, illuminating it for a moment with their rainbow brightness, and then without hesitation they came slashing down the left-hand wall in a perfect series of 6-shaped patterns, one after the other, at exactly the height of the cockroach-things' heads. The church was filled with a hideous screaming sound as hundreds of insect-heads dropped to the opposite wall in an unstoppable torrent, followed by shuddering, headless bodies. Within seconds, almost all of the cockroach-things were heaped up on the wall, their limbs still twitching, their jaws still opening and closing, but undeniably dead.

'Way to go, Ex'ii!' said Lyraq. And now Arkestrax's stone staircase was complete, its last step fitting with a snug grating sound up against the curved side of one of the horizontal pillars.

The storm that was blowing in through the windows beneath their feet grew even fiercer, and it began to

366

rain. The Night Warriors struggled to the foot of Arkestrax's steps, and started to climb – Themesteroth first, with his rockets already activated, followed by Oromas II and Lyraq and Ex'ii.

Oromas I was about to climb up when the building started to vibrate once again, low, thunderous vibration that they could feel right through their teeth. Arkestrax hesitated for a moment, and then he shouted. *'Off the staircase! Off!'*

Without hesitating, the Night Warriors jumped from the staircase down to the floor. Themesteroth landed badly, and lay on his side, winded. Lyraq's music-rifle clattered against the stone, one high-tension string snapping with an off-key *bddoinkk!* The building shook so violently that their vision was blurred, and massive lumps of masonry crashed down through the rows of pillars and bounced against the lower wall. Arkestrax's miraculously constructed staircase toppled, and they were left with nothing but smashed fragments of stone.

Up in the church doorway, Reblax saw the dark flickering shape of the shadow-creature.

'He's getting away!' Oromas I shouted. 'Themesteroth – hit him with a rocket!'

Themesteroth tried to get up; but something must have been broken, because he fell back against the wall, grimacing underneath his faceplate. Oromas II knelt beside him, but there was no chance of him being able to fire a rocket without taking off Themesteroth's backpack and guidance equipment, and by then it would be far too late.

'Oromas I – follow me!' yelled Reblax against the mounting screaming of the storm. He released the steel crescent from the palm of his hand, and whipped the wire out faster and faster and longer and longer, until he was poised on the wall of the church with a whistling wire nearly thirty feet long held high above his head.

Sfffeeeeee, sfffeeeee, sfffeeeee! sang the wire. And then Reblax flicked his wrist, and the wire lashed itself tightly around one of the horizontal pillars above their heads.

Reblax tugged it, to test that it was tight, then braced his feet against the wall, 'Up!' he shouted at Oromas I. 'If we don't get that creature now, it's going to slash Dianne to pieces!'

Oromas I didn't need to be told twice. He grasped the wire in one hand, clicked down two levers on his power-grille, and rose smoothly up the wire until he reached the pillar. Straddling the pillar like a lumberjack straddling a fallen tree, he reached down and hauled Reblax up to join him.

Reblax called down to the rest of the Night Warriors, 'Wait here! If you see the shadow-creature come back – hit it with everything you've got! Negative power, remember!'

Oromas II waved to Reblax to show that he had understood. Then Reblax balanced on the pillar and spun the wire around his head again, and lashed it around one of the second row of pillars, thirty feet above them.

'Hold on to me!' he told Oromas I.

Oromas I stood behind him and gripped him tightly around the waist. 'I hope you know what you're doing,' he breathed, his voice tinny inside his helmet.

'Trying to save some lives,' Reblax replied.

The two of them hesitated for a moment, swaying on the rain-slick marble of the pillar. But then the building shook once again, and some of the pillars started to drop from their pedestals and shatter on the wall beneath them, Lightning flickered in through the windows, and they knew that it was now or never.

'*Ashapola!*' shouted Reblax, and launched himself into the air, with Oromas I still clinging to his back. They swung like a pendulum beneath the pillar; and then, as they swung toward the church's main doors, Reblax released the catch that locked the wire to his wrist. The two of them hurtled through the open doors like tumblers in a circus.

'*Grab something!* Reblax yelled, snatching at the doorhandle. Oromas I reached out for the open door, but missed, and fell down the church's vertically angled steps and the mosaic courtyard in front of it, bouncing off a wall, rolling through an open gateway, and then plunging down a muddy street, trying to dig his fingers into the mud to slow himself down.

Reblax, swinging precariously from the door-handle, glanced upward, and was just in time to see the black figure of the shadow-creature disappearing up an alleyway. But there was nothing he could do without Oromas I – Oromas I was his key to returning to the waking world. He swung twice more, then allowed himself to drop through the courtyard and fall through the gateway into the same muddy street.

He rolled, slithered, bumped, and finished up colliding with a garden wall, where Oromas I had already come to rest. Winded but unhurt, he looked over the edge of the wall, and saw plum trees that grew sideways out of the grass, and birds that flew vertically up and down. But the oddity of the garden was nothing compared with the stark, vertiginous terror of looking down and seeing nothing but empty sky, and the sun burning like the core of a live volcano.

'Are you all right?' Reblax asked Oromas I.

'Bruised, I guess, but otherwise okay.'

Reblax stood up on the wall, keeping one hand pressed against the muddy street to give him support. He hoped that the wall would hold their weight.

'I saw the shadow-creature go thataway,' he said, pointing directly upward.

'So, how are we going to get after him?' Oromas I wanted to know. 'We can't possibly catch him if we have to climb every inch of the way. It's going to be like pushing peanuts up Mount Rushmore with our noses.'

But even as they spoke, the world around them began to change. The sun sank slowly below the horizon, and for a moment they were bathed in shafts of golden light – light that streamed *upward* through the branches of the trees. Then, as the sky darkened and the stars prickled the sky, they felt the world begin to tilt beneath their feet.

Oromas I looked up at the stars. They were wheeling in the sky like the stars in a planetarium. 'We're righting ourselves,' he told Reblax. 'This is a different dream.'

Within a few minutes, Reblax and Oromas I found themselves standing in a small room – a room without windows or furniture. The only light came from the cracks around the door – which, to Reblax's relief, was set in the wall the right way up. He touched the depression on his helmet, and the room was lit up. It was white and completely featureless, except for the door.

The door was black, six-paneled, with a decorative brass handle. The same door that had appeared in Lenny's scripture book.

'The garden!' said Reblax urgently. 'It's gone to the garden!'

He tugged open the door, and there it lay – the darkened garden with its crisscross paths and its broken statues. He and Oromas I stepped out onto the patio and down the steps, anxiously looking around for any sign of the shadow-creature. *God*, thought Reblax, *if it's entered the real world already …*

They hurried along the central pathway between

stalks of bone-white bracken and dried-up heathers. Reblax was sure that the statues changed their positions – that they turned on their pedestals as he and Oromas I went hurrying by. Whichever way he and Oromas I went, they could never see the faces of any of the statues. They were always confronted by broken stone backs.

At last they reached the marble sepulchre. Their feet crunched on the weedy white gravel. 'Any sign of it?' Oromas I panted.

Reblax shook his head. 'God, Ashapola, whatever you are – I'm counting on you now. Keep Dianne safe.'

Oromas I said, 'It's still dark here. Like, there's still a feeling of fear. Can you sense it? Maybe the shadow-creature's still lurking around.'

'Well, let's keep checking,' said Reblax. 'You go round that side of the sepulchre, I'll go round this side. Then we'll meet up again, and try those tombs over there.'

'You got it,' Oromas I agreed.

Oromas I moved off to the left, while Reblax circled the sepulchre to the right. He trod as softly as he could, feeling the sharp gravel beneath his skin-thin shoes. He glanced up one or twice, to make sure that the sky was still inky-black. The first sign of the sun, would mean that the shadow-creature had materialized in the waking world – and Dianne was only two or three feet away from Lenny's bed.

'Where are you, you bastard?' he whispered. 'Where the hell are you?'

Suddenly Oromas I screeched out loud – a screech so agonized that Reblax didn't understand at first that it was him. But the reflexes of Reblax the runner were instantaneous, and even before he fully realized who it was, he was sprinting around the sepulchre to the other side.

When he saw what had happened, he stopped in a slither of gravel. High above him, nearly twenty feet tall, reared the thunderous black shape of the shadow-creature, like the heaped-up black coats of a thousand dead men. Out of the darkness of its body its claws protruded, curving and shiny, and Oromas I was clutched in these claws, his dark-blue armor crushed. His head, already half-severed from his body, dangled down his back like a hood. The shadow-creature was shaking him violently, so that his arms and legs swung in a hideous parody of dancing.

Reblax shrieked, '*Bastard! Let him go!*'

The shadow-creature tossed Oromas I's body away, and breathed a thin, sour stream of freezing breath at Reblax and clashed its claws. Reblax stepped back, and then back again. He didn't even have his wire to protect himself. The shadow-creature shuffled forward once more, hissing, but then Reblax stood his ground.

He had suddenly realized something. The shadow-creature didn't frighten him. *He wasn't afraid to die.*

When he thought of death, all he thought about was relief from his paralysis, relief from pain, and the chance to rejoin Virginia and Jennifer. He would miss Lenny, but Lenny was young, Lenny would be able to make a life for himself. And he would always have his father's spirit watching over him.

The sensation was extraordinary. Reblax felt totally invincible. But he wasn't going to sacrifice his life for nothing at all. He had a duty to stay alive – to protect Dianne and to protect Lenny, and to destroy this shadow-creature forever.

He stood in front of it, waiting, ready to make a run for safety if he had to. He was, after all, the fastest runner imaginable – or even unimaginable.

The shadow-creature remained where it was, the ground trembling beneath it. Perhaps it could sense that Reblax was no longer afraid of it. Perhaps it knew that, if he were to run, not even the wind could catch up with him.

Whatever the reason, the shadow-creature remained where it was, its claws slowly scraping against the marble of Lenny's schoolbook sepulchre, waiting, thinking.

Then, without any warning at all, it seemed to fold up like a huge black umbrella, and vanished.

Reblax almost panicked. If the shadow-creature had vanished, that meant that it had materialized in the waking world. That meant that *now*, at this instant, Dianne was facing the most vicious and soulless beast that had ever stalked the earth.

He stumbled across to Oromas I, hoping that Oromas I might still be alive – alive enough to project him back to reality. But Oromas I's neck was a tangle of slashed gristle, and the shadow-creature's claws had cut through his armor like a chain saw through a tin can.

Reblax tried some of the switches on Oromas I's power-grille. Oromas's psychic energy was fully charged up, but Reblax had no idea how to convert it to his own use. He knelt back on his heels. His only chance of saving Dianne now was to see if he could find the other Night Warriors and get Oromas II to take him back. But by now it was probably too late for that. Too late for anything.

As he knelt by Oromas I's body, the sun began to break through the clouds, and a small brown phoebe settled on the sepulchre and began to sing.

At that moment, a shadow fell across the cracked marble, then another, and a hauntingly familiar voice said, 'John?'

Reblax turned around. Standing a few feet away on the weedy path was Virginia, in a flower pink summer dress. Beside her stood a tall figure in slabby crimson armor, a figure who was unquestionably a Night Warrior – although not a Night Warrior Reblax recognized.

'John, this is Kasyx,' said Virginia. 'I found him on the beach. He said he wanted to meet up with other Night Warriors, so I brought him here to you.'

Reblax stood up shakily, walked over to Virginia, and laid a hand on her shoulder. 'Virginia, you're blessed by God. Kasyx – Springer told me all about you. You're a charge-keeper, aren't you?'

Kasyx shook his hand. 'I was – until I discharged all of my energy trying to blow that shadow-creature away.'

'Well, quick – my own charge-keeper has just been killed. Is there any way that you can use his power? And, please, hurry – the shadow-creature just left the dream-world, and it's in the material world.'

Kasyx knelt down beside Oromas I. He hesitated for just a moment at the sight of Oromas I's ravaged neck, then quickly glanced over his power-grille.

'Almost full,' he remarked. He unhooked an insulated lead from the side of his own armor and connected it quickly to the side of Oromas I's power-grille – the side to which Oromas II used to connect himself, to give the twins double power.

Kasyx threw three levers – *kachunk, kachunk, kachunk* – and then there was an immediate crackling of psychic energy as he drained Oromas I's system and topped up his own. After less then ten seconds, he glanced up at the instruments inside his helmet and said, 'That's it. Full. Let's go.'

He stood up and drew the blue octagon in the air. As he did so, Virginia stepped away and waved, and smiled at Reblax with a regretful smile.

I love you, he mouthed as the octagon descended over him, *and thank you, whatever happens*.

Reblax closed his eyes as Kasyx transported him

through time and space and silent imagination. For one instant he didn't know whether he was alive or dead.

He blinked his eyes open. He was standing in Lenny's room in the police department headquarters, with Kasyx right next to him. The room was almost totally dark, but Reblax could see at once that Lenny was still asleep. He could also see that Dianne was gone, although her video equipment was lying overturned on the floor.

Dianne was gone, and so was the staff of Moses. There was no sign of the shadow-creature.

'Where are we?' Kasyx asked, blundering into Reblax's back.

'Police headquarters. But what's more to the point – where's the goddamned shadow-creature?'

Kasyx said, 'Hold on, and I'll tell you.' He switched on the sensors on his helmet and quickly scanned the building. 'There –' he said. 'Up on the roof, judging from the signals. And a darn sight bigger than it was when *I* went after it.'

'It's stuffed itself on a little more fear and darkness since then,' Reblax told him. 'Come on, let's get after it.'

'If you insist,' said Kasyx without much enthusiasm.

They rose through the building until they reached the roof. The lights of Philadelphia spread out all around them, and the night was heavy and warm. Quickly they looked around – and on the opposite side of the roof, close to the edge, Reblax saw Dianne. She was kneeling, her arms raised.

The night was so dark that he didn't see the shadow-creature at first. It towered over Dianne, its claws hooked back and its teeth bared and its eyes glinting yellow. Reblax had never seen it expose itself so openly before. It was even more grotesque than he had imagined: all the black and twisted ropes of human fear turned into a living being.

'*Dianne!*' he shouted. '*Dianne!*'

Because he was nothing more than a dream-being, Dianne could scarcely hear him. But she turned her head and frowned in his direction.

Reblax ran across the asphalt helicopter-pad. As he came closer, he saw that she was holding up the staff of Moses; and that the staff appeared to be keeping the shadow-creature at bay. She must have snatched it when she first saw the shadow-creature materialize, and run up here.

The shadow-creature roared thunderously as it sensed that Reblax had returned from the world of dreams. It slashed at the air with its claws, ripping up asphalt and striking sparks. But Dianne held her ground – she had to, she was right at the very edge of the roof, with her back against the low parapet.

'Dianne!' Reblax shouted. 'Dianne – give me the staff!'

Kasyx was close behind him. 'You won't be able to hold it, it's a material artifact! You're nothing but a dream! It'll drop straight through your hands!'

The shadow-creature sensed Dianne's heightening fear, and scratched its way closer across the roof.

'Stay back!' she shouted at it, her voice close to hysteria. '*Stay back!*'

She tried to move to the side, to escape from the edge of the building, but the shadow-creature lunged at her, and its claws flew so close to her head that they lifted her hair. She screamed, dodged, then stumbled. The staff fell to the ground and rolled away.

Now the shadow-creature rose up like a mounting thunderstorm. It bellowed in freezing triumph, and advanced on Dianne with its claws sliding along the asphalt. Reblax had never heard a noise like it in his life. It was the sliding sound of imminent death.

He darted forward and snatched for the staff. To his surprise, he could feel it, hold it. It had as much solidity in the world of dreams as it did in reality. He turned to Kasyx, lifted it up, and shook it. Kasyx, baffled, now knowing what it was or what it represented, shouted, 'Go for it!'

Just as the shadow-creature raised its claws for a single murderous slash at Dianne's body, Reblax stepped right in front of it, holding up the staff.

'Yea though I walk through the valley of the shadow of death!' he cried out. *'I shall fear no evil! For Thou art with me! And Thy rod and Thy staff, they comfort me!'*

Even as he uttered these words, the upraised staff burst into dazzling light and became in his hand a rod so brilliant that he couldn't even look at it. White fire streamed out of it in all directions, lighting up the roof, lighting up the clouds, shining over the rooftops of Philadelphia in an incandescent beacon of hope and purity and total fearlessness.

The shadow-creature shrank and writhed, and lashed out at Reblax again and again. But Reblax was unafraid. He walked toward the monster with the blinding white staff upraised; he kept walking deep into the creature's very being. Its flesh spat and crackled; its nerves shriveled up; it collapsed on top of itself, fold after fold of black and thunderous fabric, as if all the tents of all the multitudes of terror were being struck, one after the other.

In a last shuddering effort to escape, the shadow-creature swept its arm at Reblax, and knocked him aside. The dazzling staff fell onto the rooftop, out of his reach. With a rushing, rumbling noise, the shadow-creature fled toward the edge of the roof, like the Phantom of the Opera leaping through the scenery of the Paris Opera House, like Bill Sikes leaping from the rooftops of Victorian London.

It thrust itself into the air and spread billowing black wings. It flapped them once, twice, gaining height. But its whole being had been burned up, its strength was gone, and it began to stagger in the air, and then to fall.

Kasyx hobbled right to the edge of the parapet and pointed his outstretched fingers at the shadow-creature as it lurched and flapped in the air.

'Negative-power!' shouted Reblax. 'Otherwise you'll give it all the energy it needs!'

Kasyx lifted his left hand to acknowledge that he had understood. Then thousands of volts of negative psychic energy spat from his fingertips, and hit the shadow-creature as it tried to fly. This was Oromas I's revenge; his last blow against the fear of death.

There was a sharp implosion, blacker and darker and denser than anything that Reblax had ever seen. The shadow-creature was sucked into it, and compressed into a single black atom.

There was a soft thudding of thunder as it disappeared, as the air rushed in to fill the space that it had left.

Dianne was left on the roof, apparently alone. 'John?' she called. 'John?'

She went across to the fallen staff: dull now, nothing but olive wood. She picked it up and held it in both hands.

'Thank you,' she whispered to the dark night sky. 'Thank you, whoever you are.'

She felt something brush her lips, almost like a kiss. Yet when she put her hand out, there didn't seem to be anybody there.

Eighteen

They were sitting under the cedar tree when John was wheeled out to join them. They greeted him with whistles and loud applause, and Toussaint struck a chord on his guitar. Sister Clare made sure that the plaid blanket was tucked tight around his legs, and then she pushed him close to his friends.

'Don't be overexciting yourself,' she warned him. 'You know what Dr. Freytag said.'

'It's all right, Sister Clare,' John said, smiling. 'I'm hardly likely to excite myself with this gang of paralyzed bores.'

'Now, then,' said Billy, 'Just because you can wave your arms around now, and just because you're going to be able to walk in a year or two, that's no call to get prejudiced. Just remember, you were a cripple once.'

'I'll never forget it, either,' said John. 'And don't you ever call yourself a cripple, not in *my* earshot, anyway.'

'How's Lenny?' asked Che-u.

'You'll be seeing him soon. Dianne's supposed to be bringing him over. But he's fine. Dianne told me that he baked some cookies for you guys, baked them at school.'

'Just hope they're chocolate-chip,' said Mean Dean, his cigarette waggling between his lips. 'I don't eat any other kind but chocolate-chip.'

'Are you going to refuse them if they're not?' Toussaint asked.

'Refuse them? I'm going to grind them underfoot!' He looked down at the neatly folded blanket where his legs were supposed to be, and laughed. 'I'm going to find it hard to forget that I was Themesteroth, believe me.'

John said, 'You're always going to be Themesteroth, as long as you live.' He looked around at all of them, and added, 'You're always going to be Night Warriors. And it doesn't matter who looks down at you – or who ignores you even when you're sitting right in front of them – or who treats you like a child or a moron or an idiot. You're Night Warriors; your legs and your arms are inside your dreams, and nobody can take that away from you.'

Just then Dianne appeared with Lenny. Her hair was brushed and shining, and she was wearing a new white summer dress that John hadn't seen before. Lenny ran over to John and hugged him tight; and then Dianne came over and gave him a kiss that had the rest of the Night Warriors whistling and wolf-howling.

'I talked to Dr. Freytag,' said Dianne. 'He says you're going to make an eighty-five per cent recovery, maybe better. Oh, John, I'm so pleased.'

He stiffly raised one arm and touched her cheek. It was the first time he had been able to touch her since they'd met. She pressed his hand against her cheek, and her eyes filled with sparkling tears.

Dean said to Lenny, 'Hey, champ, how about those cookies?'

'Oh, sure,' said Lenny, and produced a large brown paper sack. 'There are ten cookies each, and each bag has your name on it.'

He delved inside the brown paper sack and took out smaller bags of cookies, which he handed around one by one. On each bag was written in large childish writing 'Thank You From Your Friend Lenny.' Dean carefully opened his bag and peered inside.

Lenny said anxiously. 'They're chocolate-chip. I only know how to make chocolate-chip.'

Dean nodded, and took out one of the cookies, and bit into it. They all waited until he had swallowed his first mouthful.

'You know something?' he said 'This is the best goddamned chocolate-chip cookie I ever tasted in my whole goddamned life.'

Lenny came up to him and grinned, his face bright. 'You mean that?'

'You calling me a liar?' Dean retorted. 'I'll arm-wrestle you for that.'

As they scrapped and wrestled, John turned to Dianne and said, 'I want to thank you, too. We never could have made it without you.'

'Any other psychic researcher would have done the same.'

'I want you to send my thanks to Seth Maxwell, too, and everybody else at the university.'

Dianne smiled. 'I'll tell Seth tonight. He's taking me out to dinner.'

'Oh?' John queried sharply.

She laughed. 'It's not what you think. He's found out some more about Nathan Grant. Some old Osage legend.'

'Really?'

'Don't sound so skeptical. Just because Seth has a thing about my legs.'

'So what's this legend?'

'It's interesting; and from what we already know about Nathan Grant, it seems to fit the historical facts. According to the Osage Indians, they were approached by a white horse-doctor called Grant who was dying of some kind of wasting disease, muscular dystrophy probably. Grant made a deal with an Osage medicine man. In return for being cured, Grant would allow his daughters to be impregnated by an evil spirit, and he would carry these embryonic evil spirits deep into the heart of the white man's government so that white men would always argue with each other, and never be able to form a united nation that would threaten the Indians' heritage.'

'Does the legend say what happened after that?'

Dianne shook her head. 'I don't think the Osages ever found out. But *we* did.'

They talked together for a while, as the sun sank over Philadelphia. At last, when it began to grow cooler, Sister Clare came out and said that John had to return to bed. Tomorrow he was going to begin his therapy sessions.

John kissed Dianne and Lenny good-bye. As they left, however, another familiar figure appeared. Norman Clay, on his own this time, in a shiny gray summer suit and dark glasses. He came across to John and held out his hand.

'I hear you did good,' he said a little hoarsely.

John nodded. 'Yes, thanks, Norman, I did.'

'I'm leaving Philly tomorrow,' said Norman. 'Got myself a job in Seattle, security guard.'

'That's a long way to go.'

'Well, not really. Thaddeus is always going to be there, wherever I go. You know how sensitive I am. I can hear him every night, talking to me just like always, even though his armchair's empty.'

John said, 'I'm sorry, Norman. I'll never forget Thaddeus, never.'

'We lost him in a good cause, John.'

John nodded; he wondered for a moment whether any cause was worth losing a man like Thaddeus.

'Come on, Mr. Woods,' urged Sister Clare. 'We have

to be bathed, and then we have to get some beauty sleep.'

'*Jawohl*, Sister.'

Norman said, 'I had a letter from Henry Watkins this morning – you know, Kasyx. He's some kind of philosophy professor out in California. It was a good letter. He said that without Thaddeus, we never could have done what we did, and that as long as he lives, there's always going to be some little piece of Thaddeus right inside him someplace.'

'I'm glad,' said John gently.

At last they said their good-byes and Sister Clare wheeled John into the hospital. She gave him his usual bed-bath, while he closed his eyes and tried to remember those last desperate moments in the Byzantine church and the world that was tilted sideways, and their fight with the shadow-creature on the roof of the Philadelphia police headquarters.

Those moments had all been a dream; and now, they seemed like nothing more than a dream.

He watched television for a while. Then he reached up and switched off the light, which he still considered a great achievement. He thought of Lenny; and he thought of Dianne; and he thought of the tragedies that had led at last to their security and their freedom.

He was on the edge of falling asleep when he heard the door of his room open, and the rustling sound of somebody coming in. He opened his eyes, and listened. Then, summoning up all the strength and the coordination that he could manage, he raised his head.

Standing at the end of the bed, white-faced, wearing her bloodstained nightdress, was Jennifer.

'*Jennifer?*' he whispered. '*Jennifer?*'